DAVID HARELSON

WHERE IS
JOE MERCHANT?

That's what his sister Trevor Kane, the hemorrhoid ointment heiress, wants to know. For South Seas psychic Desdemona, Merchant is the missing link needed to connect her with other worlds. And the mystery of the presumed dead but oft-sighted rock star's disappearance is pulling renegade sea plane pilot Frank Bama into the perilous path of psychos, wackos, pirates and dictators—on a wild ride from Key West to the Caribbean to a lush tropical paradise where anything can happen . . . and everything does.

"ZAP! BAM! POW! ADVENTURE . . .
A TALE SO TALL EVEN MARK TWAIN HIMSELF
COULDN'T SEE OVER IT . . .
LIGHT-HEARTED, FAST-PACED,
FULL OF WACKY ECCENTRICS,
PACKED WITH ACTION AND
UTTERLY PREPOSTEROUS . . .
KICK BACK IN THE HAMMOCK AND ENJOY."
Long Beach Press-Telegram

JIMMY BUFFETT

WHERE IS
JOE MERCHANT?

AVON BOOKS ▲ NEW YORK

The following songs are quoted and used by permission. All rights reserved. "Lyin' Eyes" by Don Henley and Glenn Frey, copyright © 1975 by Cass County Music/Red Cloud Music. "Carey" by Joni Mitchell, copyright © 1971,1975 by Joni Mitchell Publishing Corp. "You Can't Always Get What You Want" by Mick Jagger and Keith Richards, copyright © 1969 by Abkco Music, Inc. "Happily Ever After, Now and Then" by Jimmy Buffett, copyright © 1992 by Coral Reefer Music, Inc.

Lines from published songs and songs-in-progress by the author appear throughout the book by permission of Coral Reefer Music, Inc. All rights reserved.

Permission was granted by Harcourt Brace Jovanovich, Inc. to print a passage from *Wind, Sand and Stars* by Antoine de Saint-Exupéry, copyright © 1939, translated from the French by Lewis Galantière and copyright renewed in 1967 by Lewis Galantière.

AVON BOOKS
A division of
The Hearst Corporation
1350 Avenue of the Americas
New York, New York 10019

Copyright © 1992 by Jimmy Buffett
Back cover author photo by Ray Stanyard
Published by arrangement with Harcourt Brace Jovanovich Inc.
Library of Congress Catalog Card Number: 92-17136
ISBN: 0-380-72118-X

First Avon Books Printing: August 1993
First Avon Books International Printing: June 1993

AVON TRADEMARK REG. U.S. PAT. OFF. AND IN OTHER COUNTRIES, MARCA REGISTRADA, HECHO EN U.S.A.

Printed in the U.S.A.

RA 10 9 8 7 6 5 4 3 2 1

This book is dedicated to the Buffett girls: Jane, Savannah Jane, and Sarah Delaney, for their patience and love.

Special Thanks

I want to thank the following people for their help and time in assembling the flying information in this book: Dean and Jean Franklin, Bob Hanley, and Mac MacKenzie; the late Maurice Willis and George Faraldo, who taught me to be an older, wiser pilot; Bruce Barth, for his help with the history of the P5M Martins in Vietnam; Orin Seybert, and the staff of Peninsula Airways in Alaska; Kristin Burman; Doug Getting, for showing me life in Talkeetna and on the side of Denali; Ted Spencer, the director of the Alaska Air Museum; Arthur Cambell and Jim Cothran; Jim Powell; Dr. Paul Tobias; Pat Ogden; J. D. Buffett; Admiral Red Best, U.S.N. (retired); Dan "Stinger" Carrol; the pilots of Squadron VF-45 "The Blackbirds" at the Naval Air Station in Key West; the staff of the Naval Aviation Museum, Pensacola, Florida; Pan American Airways; and the Grumman Museum in Bethpage, Long Island.

I would also like to thank Susan Hoban and Loris Magnani for their assistance in Puerto Rico; Coleman Sisson; Beth Slagsvol; Howard Kaufman; Gardner Mckay: the real-life inventor of "codgerisms"; Priscilla Higham; Sunshine Smith for her ever-present help and inspiration; Bonnie Ingber Verburg, the good witch, for helping me to weave the spell; and Philip Burton for teaching me a few old tricks of the masters.

Contents

vii

You Can't Hide Your Mayan Eyes

Anchovies and Antonyms

The Wind Is in from Africa

Tickets to Ride

Livin' on Island Time

Where's the Party?

Rolling with the Punches

Beach Music, Beach Music, Beach Music Just Plays On

Quietly Making Noise

Cabbages and Kings

I remember, for my part, another of those hours in which a pilot finds suddenly that he has slipped beyond the confines of this world. All that night the radio messages sent from the ports in the Sahara concerning our position had been inaccurate, and my radio operator, Néri, and I had been drawn out of our course. . . .

We had no means of angular orientation, were already deafened, and were bit by bit growing blind. The moon like a pallid ember began to go out in the banks of fog. Overhead the sky was filling with clouds, and we flew thenceforth between cloud and fog in a world voided of all substance and all light. The ports that signalled us had given up trying to tell us where we were. 'No bearings, no bearings,' was all their message, for our voice reached them from everywhere and nowhere. With sinking hearts Néri and I leaned out, he on his side and I on mine, to see if anything, anything at all, was distinguishable in this void. Already our tired eyes were seeing things—errant signs, delusive flashes, phantoms.

And suddenly, when already we were in despair, low on the horizon a brilliant point was unveiled on our port bow. A wave of joy went through me. Néri leaned forward, and I could hear him singing. It could not but be the beacon of an airport, for after dark the whole Sahara goes black and forms a great dead expanse. That light twinkled for a space—and then went out! We had been steering for a star which was visible for a few minutes only, just before setting on the horizon between the layer of fog and the clouds.

Then other stars took up the game, and with a sort of dogged hope we set our course for each of them in turn. Each time that a light lingered a while, we performed the same crucial experiment. Néri would send his message to the airport at Cisneros: 'Beacon in view. Put out your light and flash three times.' And Cisneros would put out its beacon and flash three times while the hard light at which we gazed would not, incorruptible star, so much as wink. And despite our dwindling fuel we continued to nibble at the golden bait which each time seemed more surely the true light of a beacon and was each time a promise of a landing and of life—and we had each time to change our star.

And with that we knew ourselves to be lost in interplanetary space among a thousand inaccessible planets, we who sought only the one veritable planet, our own, that planet on which alone we should find our familiar countryside, the houses of our friends, our treasures.

—ANTOINE DE SAINT-EXUPÉRY
Wind, Sand and Stars

This book is a pack of lies.
—COLONEL ADRIAN CAIRO

Introduction

Once upon a time back in the seventies, I worked on my first movie. It was called *Rancho DeLuxe*. Along with my introduction to the real world of business in Hollywood, I was exposed to the real world of filmmaking. I used to watch the setups, poke my head in an available window to watch interior shots, and was fascinated with the whole process. I didn't realize at the time that after that summer I would not be able to look at movies anymore as mere entertainment; I would need more than popcorn, Junior Mints, and a Coke. From that summer on, I would wonder who wrote the script, where the location was, and a lot of other things.

When I began this book two and a half years ago, I found myself in a similar situation. I loved to read and looked forward to browsing through bookstores, looking for topics of interest. As I finish this book, I will never be able to simply browse through a bookstore again without thinking of the author with a hell of a lot more respect, wondering how many lonely hours were spent in front of a typewriter or word processor, or where the story actually came from and how many times he or she thought about quitting and just going to the beach.

For me, my characters were what kept me going. I couldn't leave them at the airport waiting for the next chapter to fill in their blanks. I remember once spending a week locked in a hotel room in Malibu working on a chapter that was set in Havana. I would go out to dinner with friends and not be able to stay with the table conversation—I was in Havana with my pilot.

Frank Bama is now in the charter business, although it took him two and a half years to get there, and the people who inhabit his world are now here to stay. I finally realize there was a purpose to my gypsy-soul-and-wanderlust approach to the years I spent on boats and planes crisscrossing the Caribbean: I didn't have to make a lot of this up.

JIMMY BUFFETT
Stella Maris, Bahamas
April 27, 1992

PROLOGUE: I Fly Boats

My name is Frank Bama, and I fly boats. I can read the heavens and smell the weather, roll with the punches and flow with the tide. I know the channels my life flows through can change course at a moment's notice and send me off again into uncharted waters. It doesn't frighten me; it just keeps me alert; and I know a healthy sense of humor is essential to counter panic and fear.

Airplanes are in my blood. My father, Eddie Bama, flew with Lindbergh when he mapped out the air routes through the Caribbean and South America for Pan Am during the romantic era of seaplanes, splashing down in the backwaters and outposts of the world. When World War II broke out, my father joined the navy and wound up in San Diego, where he met my mom. Her name was Sally, and she hailed from Pensacola. They were married there before he shipped out for the Pacific. I was born during the first year of the war in the naval hospital in San Diego.

My earliest memories are of my mother and the seashore. I was barely able to walk, but I wobbled down the long white

1

beaches of Coronado flapping my tiny, uncoordinated arms, imitating the effortless takeoff runs of the sea gulls that circled above me in the skies. I guess I was a born flier. My father was a combat pilot with VP-33, the Black Cats, a legendary squadron of navy PBYs that operated throughout the islands in the Pacific. The PBYs were painted flat black, equipped with the earliest radar units, and were pioneers in night aircraft attack, chasing Japanese warships making their way down the "Slot" in the Solomon Islands.

Dad's plane was the *No-See-Um.* My favorite photograph is one of him with his copilot, Billy Cruiser, working on planes while native children sit under coconut palms and watch them attach five-hundred-pound bombs to the long dark wings. Throughout my childhood I looked at that picture and wished I had been on that beach with my dad.

The summer of 1945, my father was flying solo and was killed in action. I was almost three and had never laid eyes on him.

We moved back to Pensacola after the war. Lots of young navy widows were there in those days, sharing their grief and trying to return to a normal life. Sally was soon courted by another pilot, who eventually walked on the moon, but her heart belonged to Eddie Bama, who had hung it. I spent a lot of time on the beach, watching the planes going and coming to Saufley Field, hoping that one of them was bringing my father home. It never happened.

The next summer, Billy Cruiser showed up at our front door. I liked him from the start. He was weathered from years of fishing in the sun, and he had an easy way about him, often summing things up in a single phrase—something he called a "codgerism." He had gotten out of the navy and was now on his way back to Miami, where he had a job flying seaplanes to the Bahamas. My mom invited him to stay for supper, and that night Billy told us that before my dad died, he asked Billy to keep an eye on us. It was the first of many visits.

I was just starting to accept the fact that my father wasn't coming back, and I guessed Billy was as close as I would ever come to knowing him. Before Billy left, he pulled a small leather pouch out of his flight jacket and gave it to me. I opened it, and there in my hand lay the most beautiful watch I had ever seen. It was a Longines with a gold bezel and an alligator band. The bezel turned, and Billy told me it was used to take a sun sight. He turned the watch over and read me the words inscribed on the case:

> *To Eddie Bama, a fine navigator*
> *Charles Lindbergh*
> *South America, 1934*

"Some water leaked into it, and your father sent it off to get fixed. That's why he wasn't wearin' it when his plane went down. I know he'd want you to have it."

I slept with my dad's watch under my pillow that night and haven't been without it since. Billy went home to Miami, but he sent me postcards and pictures of the fish he caught, and he called my mom and me every few weeks to see how we were doing. Then, when I was almost seven, Billy told me that my dad had made him promise to take me fishing when I got old enough. Mom said I could go visit in the summer when school let out. By the first of May I was all packed, though school didn't let out until June. Then Mom put me on the train to Miami.

I spent a month with Billy. It was a routine that would continue every year. We fished Raccoon Creek, took canoe trips into the Everglades, and drove down to the Keys in his Packard convertible. I hung around the Chalk's Terminal that summer like a territorial sea gull and helped the line boys wash the salt from the planes. That was where I fell in love with the Grumman Goose.

At the end of each day, after the planes were all washed down and checked, I'd run my hand back and forth over their wings, hoping their magic would rub off on me. I took every opportunity to sit in the cockpits of the planes on the ramp, pretending I was the pilot.

When Billy did run-ups or mechanical checks, he took me along. I sat in the copilot's seat, and he let me fly the plane. Once every visit, we went to Bimini and stayed at the Compleat Angler Hotel, fished for giant tuna or bonefish, and ate lobster-salad sandwiches on Bimini bread.

My mother tried to discourage me from flying, but I took to tradition naturally and clung to it like a life buoy. Twenty years after my father died, I was a navy flier, call sign Brillo. I did my basic training in Pensacola and qualified to fly fighters, but I chose seaplanes instead. I returned to the beaches of my boyhood days to the RAG for training with VP-31 at North Island, and then I went off to war.

• • •

I was flying with VP-40 as part of Operation Market Time, patrolling the coast of Vietnam in a P5A Martin, looking for supplies coming down from the north. We were based out of Sangley Naval Air Station in the Philippines, but we went on station on Cam Ranh Bay every two weeks. I started as a co-pilot but switched to left seat three months after I got there.

We flew eight-hour patrols and were on call for search and rescue. One day we picked up a downed flier out of the South China Sea and made a daring landing to get him back on board his ship. He was from Key West and knew Billy Cruiser. His name was Blanton Meyercord, call sign Ray Ban. He eventually became my best friend.

After the war I wasn't ready to go home. I went to Australia to forget about Vietnam. Australia is a country devoted to beach life, and I wanted to check it out. I got a job flying the shuttle from Sydney Harbor up to Palm Beach in old DeHavilland Beavers, and then I flew ambulance trips to the bush.

In Alice Springs I met an old Kiwi pilot who had been flying back to New Zealand when his Grumman Goose broke down. I helped him fix it, and he told me to look him up if I ever got to Auckland. He ran a little seaplane business for fishermen there. Six months later, I was flying my first Goose, carrying fishermen to the virgin streams of the south island, where the sounds of war hadn't been heard since the days of the Maori.

A year later, my mother died suddenly, and I came back to America. I was going through a box of her things when I found a card she had given me one year for my birthday. It was a painting of the sun peeking out from behind the clouds. The inscription read:

Dear Frank,

Clouds are like erasers. In time they will clear away the pain of not knowing your daddy, but they will always remind you of him. He used to tell me that clouds are the dreams and memories of pilots—that they leave them behind when they come back to earth, but every time they go back into the sky, they can relive them. I know your father is up there watching you like a guardian angel. It is a sad thing for a boy not to have a father. I can't change that. I can only try to be a good mother. I hope that one day you are lucky enough to find someone to love as much as I love you. Happy birthday, son.

Love, Mom

My composure broke like a fever. Fortunately, Billy Cruiser arrived the next day for the funeral, and to my surprise Blanton Meyercord showed up with him. I stayed on in Pensacola for a few days, clearing out my mother's apartment and taking care of her things. Billy and Blanton were good at finding ways to keep me company and make me laugh. We all went to the Naval Air Museum and spent a day looking at the birds we had flown when we were hotshots, and then we drove to Alabama Jack's to toast my mom and dad and tell drunken war stories from two generations.

Billy Cruiser had left Chalk's, and he'd bought an airport called Lone Palm just north of Key West. The heart trouble that had kept him out of Korea had also slowed him down to a more comfortable pace. He was doing repairs, giving a few lessons, and fishing. It sounded like the life. Blanton was now a top flats guide in Key West. He had quit flying. He said the quiet of the flats was every bit as good as the roar of the jets.

"So when are you moving to the Keys, Brillo?" Billy wanted to know.

"Soon as I finish exploring," I said. "I still have a few continents to go."

• • •

Billy Cruiser had a friend in Miami who was in the ferrying business, and for the next five years I drove everything from 707s to Cessna 172s across the Atlantic. If I wasn't going over the big pond, I was headed to South America, and I'm sure I crossed a few old outposts where my dad had gone with Lindbergh. I was trying to save enough money to find the right Goose and make a living flying for myself, maybe even go back to the Keys and hook up with Billy.

One day it all paid off.

I was on a delivery from Miami to Trinidad and had stopped in South Caicos for fuel. When I cleared customs, I saw a group of priests who looked extremely out of place. The leader, Father Ignacio Alvarez, a Jesuit missionary, asked me which way I was going. They had been stranded on the island for three days after their plane had left without them.

In high school the Jesuits had taught me, and I knew the story of Ignatius, the soldier-turned-saint. The priests were on their way to a mission in Venezuela. If all the dogma the Catholic church had drilled into our heads was true, I figured that playing the Good Samaritan would do me good.

On the way down, Father Ignacio sat up on the flight deck with me, and we talked for hours. Somewhere between vocations and the Vietcong, the subject of my dream airplane came up. I described a Grumman Goose in detail: her unique design, the sound of her engines, the floats, how she looked when she splashed down in glassy water. Father Ignacio looked surprised and told me there was a plane just like that on a deserted runway up the Orinoco River in the Guiana highlands near his mission.

I dropped the plane in Port-of-Spain and found us a hop on a freighter heading for Caracas. I was just following a hunch, and as we bounced through the jungles in a VW micro-bus, I had plenty of second thoughts about tagging along with the "black robes." When we finally reached the mission, the plane was right where Father Ignacio had said it would be. God works in mysterious ways.

She was a relic of some long-forgotten revolution, expedition, or pipe dream, and she had a strange totem pole painted on her tail. She sat on hardened, flat tires under the overhanging mahogany trees where monkeys were guarding her from their perches in the branches.

The engines were missing, and all the old Motorola radios and speakers had been removed. The fabric had rotted off the elevator and rudder-trim controls, and a few bullet holes marked the bow locker, but other than that she was remarkably free of corrosion. The good priests at the mission were using her as a toolshed.

The missionaries could neither fly nor wanted to. I worked out a deal with Father Ignacio and traded him two cargo containers for the plane. I used up most of my meager savings to have them towed up the Orinoco River to the mission, and then I sold my soul to a bank in Florida and moved in with the missionaries. I called Billy Cruiser and told him the news.

Within a week, Billy flew to Venezuela to take a look at my dream-come-true, and he declared her fixable. He went back to Florida and found a couple of old, rebuilt Pratt &

Whitney 985 radial engines, some missing parts, tires, and radios, and he shipped them to me. Then he took a commercial flight back down to help me work on the plane. Three months later, I had my own airline. I was broke, with no job and nothing cooking, but I was happier than a pig in shit. I finally had the airplane I had dreamed about, and she was my insurance policy against what I feared most: a boring life.

Billy offered me room in his hangar at the Lone Palm Airport so I could finish her up, and we were ready to make the maiden voyage back to America.

I had seen a lot of the world and was ready to stay in one place for a while. Maybe I would follow Billy's advice and do some fish spotting for the shrimpers and commercial fishing boys. There was plenty of work from the sportfishing charters to the plentiful bonefish flats of the near-at-hand Bahamas. I never intended to get rich. I was just looking for a place to call home.

On a hot day in May, we christened the plane. Indians came from the jungle, and cowboys, called *llaneros,* rode in from the great expansive plain where they spent their lives herding cattle. Word had gone out on the jungle drums that a celebration was in the air. That's what I really liked about the people I met in Venezuela—they were hard-working and God-fearing, but they'd have a festival at the drop of a hat. It usually took some saint's feast day, but the rebirth of an abandoned flying boat was excuse enough.

All day the *llaneros* danced the *joropo* and showed off some footwork that would have made James Brown jealous. The party was a good blend of Catholicism and paganism, and everybody had a great time. It was so much fun I thought twice about leaving, but I knew I had to go. Father Ignacio broke a bottle of wine from the sacristy across the nose of my plane, and we christened her the *Hemisphere Dancer.*

• • •

Father Ignacio walked me to the door of the plane and gave me a big hug. He handed me a small box, blessed it, and told me to open it right before takeoff.

He said, "In this modern world of ours that spins as fast as these propellers do, if a man can cook, or fly, or play the guitar, he will be happy and never go hungry. Two out of three is not bad. I think you have a very attentive angel on your shoulder. Vaya con Dios."

I taxied the *Hemisphere Dancer* to the end of the strip and did my pretakeoff run-up. Billy flew right seat and read me the checklists. I opened the little mahogany box that Father Ignacio had given me, and inside was a St. Christopher medal. It was a shiny pair of wings with St. Christopher, the patron saint of travelers, holding the baby Jesus on his big, broad shoulders. I pinned it to the visor above my head, waved to the crowd on the edge of the runway, advanced the throttles, and initiated a short-field takeoff. When I dropped my feet from the brakes, the *Hemisphere Dancer* lunged forward.

"Bandits at your three o'clock," Billy called out.

The *llaneros* were on their horses, waving their hats in the air, riding down the grass strip on each side of me at full bore, but my horsepower eventually overcame theirs. I pulled back on the yoke, and the houses, horses, people, and coconut trees all got smaller. Strange Bird Airways was off the ground.

•   •   •

It took a few months to get all the control surfaces back in good working order, overhaul the engines, install a stereo, and get a paint job. I ran out of cash halfway through the paint job and had to go to work, but I got used to the "three-tone" look of the original old white paint, new green primer, and new beige wings. The totem pole on the tale just added to the eccentric look of the plane.

I lucked out and got a contract spotting for a fleet of shrimp boats, and that, along with my little bit of charter business, enabled me to get by for a while. It was the seventies, and Key West was cooking. A strange collection of shrimpers, gays, dope dealers, crooked politicians, hippies, and tourists roamed the quaint streets of the little town at the end of the world. I had no trouble adapting to the life-style— fishing guides and pilots were prime candidates for the tourist girls who came to ride the Conch Train and fall in love for the weekend. The real world seemed a million miles away, and that's where I liked it. Then I met Trevor, and I made a big course change. We were lovers for a long time, and then suddenly we had to go our separate ways. She was—and still is—the lady I can't explain.

•   •   •

The years drifted by like turtle grass on the tide. Things seemed to take care of themselves, until all at once the sky started to cave in. The rebuilt Pratt & Whitney engines of the *Hemisphere Dancer* had a little more rot than I had figured, and I had to replace them. Engines aren't cheap. I borrowed money from a hip bank in Miami and found out later that their capital assets were hauled in each day in duffel bags from Colombia. The loan officers were sent to play as a group on the Elgin Prison softball team, and the feds took over the bank. My plane was the collateral on the loan.

Business was worse than lousy, and I could no longer hold the wolves at bay; I'm a good pilot but a bad business-man—an occupational hazard, I guess. Running dope was never an option; I knew a lot of people in the Keys who had tried it, and I didn't like what it did to them. Besides, the *Hemisphere Dancer* was more than an airplane to me.

I had no way of paying my loan, and I wasn't going to let the bank take my plane, so I had decided to make a run for it before they got the *Hemisphere Dancer.*

Alaska was seaplane country, and I'd heard that on Kodiak Island there were more bears than people. An article I'd read said they'd outlawed bear hunting, so now when the bears heard a shotgun, they didn't run away anymore; instead they figured there'd be dead meat waiting, and they'd run toward the gunfire. I figured I could keep my old stainless .357 by my side, and if the repo men dared to set foot on Kodiak, I'd fire a few rounds and the bears would come eat them.

Suddenly I found myself at the end of the eighties, staring the last decade of the twentieth century in the face. The pin-ball game of my world had tilted quite a bit, but the skies hadn't changed much since my days on the beach imitating the gulls.

I guess that's why I will always fly, so I can leave the earth below when things get too complicated. While I'm sitting at the controls of my flying boat high over the ocean, there is no sense of urgency. The tempo allows me to do what needs to be done. But when I'm standing on the earth, I realize how fast things are really moving. All of a sudden another summer is over, and they're playing Christmas music. All of a sudden you get a card in the mail announcing your twenty-fifth high school reunion. All of a sudden Vietnam is another old war fought by the parents of the kids who watch MTV and don't know who Walter Cronkite is. Children you remember as lit-tle babies are getting married. Life is like that. Years pile up like shipwreck debris strewn out across a jagged reef, offer-ing memories of something or someone who came before.

Squalls
Out on the
Gulf Stream

1

When My Ship Comes In, I'll Be at the Airport

I was watching the Cubs game and eating a fried shrimp platter at Bobalou's when Rudy Breno burst through the door like Geraldo Rivera on a drug raid. I had met Rudy at the Chart Room Bar in Key West, and I wasn't a fan. I had no fondness for him or the accusing, fabricated stories he published in his father's paper, a yellow-journalism rag called the *National Lighthouse*.

Rudy Breno was one of those middle-aged men who looked into the mirror and refused to buy the hard truth of the aging process. His squatty frame carried about forty extra pounds above his "fighting weight" in the form of love handles and a pot belly that spilled over the waist of his Sansabelt slacks. He insisted his pants still fit perfectly although the fly would never zip up all the way. Rudy had no ass at all, and from the side it looked as if somebody had flattened his butt with a two by four. Yet when Rudy looked at his physique in the morning, he saw himself as a Tom Selleck look-alike.

He strutted up to me as if he were Marshal Dillon.

"Frank Bama, I need to talk to you in the bathroom, now."

In the fabulous Florida Keys, words like that either announce your sexual preference or your line of work. I waited until Harry Caray finished his unrivaled rendition of "Take Me Out to the Ball Game" before my curiosity got the best of me, and I followed Rudy into the bathroom.

"I need to charter your plane. I've got to get to Havana. Do you know how to get to Cuba?"

"Yeah, take a left at the southernmost point of Florida and keep going till you run into something. That'll be Cuba."

"This is serious business, Bama. I've gotten permission from the Cuban government to make this trip, but I have to let them know the name of the pilot and the serial number of the plane." He leaned over to me and whispered, "Captain Bama, Joe Merchant was spotted yesterday at a baseball game in Havana. There's a man who has pictures. This is the story of the century."

"Right up there with landing on the moon, I'd say."

Rudy wasn't listening. "Joe Merchant not dead at all but alive and well, an expatriate rock star living in a communist country—wow. Well, I need to know—can you take me?"

"Why did we have to come into the bathroom to have this conversation?" I asked.

"It's part of the story. I like the intrigue of taking a seaplane to Cuba and meeting the blond, handsome, maverick pilot—that's you—in a place like this."

"My shrimp's getting cold, Rudy."

"Well, Bama? Are you in?"

"It's two hundred dollars an hour flight time, and forty dollars an hour on the ground."

Rudy nodded his approval.

I took a pen out of my pocket and wrote down my phone number at the hangar. "The serial number is N40SB. I'll call flight service and file a flight plan to Havana. You call me at that number by five and let me know that we do, in fact, have clearance to enter Cuban airspace."

"Right-o, Captain.'

Rudy dropped two quarters in the rubber machine and slipped the aluminum-foil packets into his pocket. "Can't be too careful these days, you know. Say, you went out with Joe Merchant's sister for a while when she lived down here, didn't you?" The words oozed out of Rudy's fat mouth like sludge, and all of a sudden I felt dirty and began to wash my hands.

I yanked on the towel machine. "That's old business, and none of yours. There's weather moving in tomorrow, so I want to leave early and be back as soon as we can. Understood?"

"Aye, aye, Captain."

"And bring cash. Five-hundred-dollar deposit, and I'll expect the rest when we get home."

• • •

Rudy Breno rushed out of the restaurant, leaving a trail of bad will behind him. I finished my shrimp and thought about what had just happened. Rudy was about as pleasant as a root canal, but the job couldn't have come at a better time. I'd been wanting to hightail it out of Key West and escape to a new, debt-free life in the Alaskan wilderness, but I'd been too broke to do it. I figured the trip to Cuba would bring me at least a thousand bucks, and I knew Rudy was good for the money. His old man was loaded and ran the paper as a hobby. His real source of income was hazardous-waste disposal.

I was smiling when I left Bobalou's, and I checked the sky as I headed for my Jeep. A low-pressure trough was moving into the area, and the air was getting thicker as the moisture built up. Squalls out on the Gulf Stream lit the distant horizon, and there wasn't a breath of air stirring.

"We have work!" I shouted to Hoagy, my golden retriever, who sat in the front seat. He sniffed the air and eyed the small brown bag in my hand.

"Oh, it's the noble dog look. What a champion," I said. I opened the bag and tossed a hushpuppy into the air. Hoagy caught it, chewed it once, licked his mouth with his long pink tongue, and waited for the second launch. "It's a high pop-up," I yelled and tossed the second hushpuppy high into the sky. Hoagy bolted from the seat into the parking lot and ran under the hushpuppy, positioning himself for the catch like a confident outfielder. He opened his mouth a split second before the ball of fried cornmeal fell directly down his throat.

"Load up," I called, and Hoagy sprang across the driver's seat to the passenger's side. I tossed him the last hushpuppy and patted his head, and Hoagy barked and gave me a big lick.

I pulled out onto U.S. 1 and drove north, listening to "Time Loves a Hero" by Little Feat. The air was filled with bugs of every description, and they were cannon fodder for the passing cars. I hummed along with Lowell George but made up my own lyrics.

"When my ship comes in," I sang, "I'll be at the airport."

• • •

The next morning, Rudy Breno paraded into the Lone Palm Airport dressed in camouflage fatigues, a green beret, and a bandolier stuffed alternately with Slim Jims and Bic pens. On his wrist he sported a diving watch that looked as if it could tell time in every world time zone, do his banking, and split the atom. A Polaroid camera hung around his stumpy neck, and a wad of Florida lottery tickets protruded from the pocket of his flak jacket.

"What the hell are the lottery tickets for?" I asked.

"Bait," he said proudly.

"Bait?"

"These people have been living in the Stone Age. A little capitalism will go a long way to get the information I need."

Hoagy bounded up the runway with a Frisbee dangling from the side of his mouth, and when he saw Rudy, he dropped it and started barking furiously. I called him to my side and bent down to calm him. That's when I saw the .25-caliber Beretta pistol stuck in Rudy's pants.

"Let's go, Captain. We're hounds on the scent. Joe Merchant is alive and breathing somewhere over there." He pointed at the horizon.

"That's north. Cuba is over there," I said, pointing the opposite direction.

"You're the pilot." Rudy squinted down at his watch and pressed several buttons. "It's exactly 11:30 Zulu. What's our proposed time off and time en route, Captain?"

"I'm not goin' anywhere with you, Clambo. First the gun, and then the money."

"Shit," Rudy muttered as he handed over the gun.

I pulled out the clip and checked the chamber. I felt like Sheriff Andy Taylor taking away Barney Fife's one bullet.

2

See You in C-U-B-A

I'd been to Cuba a number of times with Billy Cruiser during the Mariel boat lift, and just last year I'd flown there and brought Darryl Lemma back to Key West. Darryl was a sleazy charter-boat captain who had been hijacked to Havana, and Rudy Breno had thrown in the Devil's Triangle and made headlines out of it.

Flying to Cuba is always a mystery. Sometimes it's easy, and other times it's a nightmare of paperwork and bullshit. This time we took off into a hefty breeze and bounced along in a steady, moderate chop. I'd expected to spend the trip fighting an onslaught of irritating questions about Joe Merchant and Trevor, but the weather solved that problem. Rudy sat in the copilot's seat as stiff as a mannequin, staring straight ahead and getting paler with each jolt. I hadn't seen Trevor in five years, so I couldn't have told him much anyway, but I still didn't like to talk about her.

Miami Center handed us off to Havana, and all seemed to be going well. If they hadn't been expecting us, they would have let us know right away. The controller cleared me to land at José Martí Airport, and I studied my approach plate since the weather had us landing IFR. We were in the pattern, descending to landing altitude, but when I went to crank down the handle for the landing gear, it came off in my hand.

"Shit," I said, and tossed the gear handle into the bow compartment.

"Do we have parachutes?" Rudy asked in a high-pitched voice. I was enjoying this.

"Don't need 'em. At worst, we might have to get the hell out of Cuban waters. If we run out of fuel, we'll put her down in the Gulf Stream and wait for the Coast Guard."

I reported my problem to Havana control, and they directed me out over the shoreline and told me to hold there. Rudy got busy reciting every childhood prayer he could think of, but I ignored him and reluctantly plotted a course back to Lone Palm. The trip was a bust. Not only would I not get paid, but I would also have to eat the fuel expense. And I did not look forward to explaining the situation to Rudy.

To my astonishment, a controller told me I had been given permission for a water landing in Havana Harbor if I chose to do it, and I was told to continue holding until my escort arrived. I was just below the cloud deck, flying around in circles at about three thousand feet, and I wondered why they were being so cooperative. There probably hadn't been a seaplane landing in Havana Harbor since around the time of the revolution, and it was like trying to figure out if the Big Bad Wolf was honestly being nice or if he really wanted to eat your lunch.

Billy had taught me to be a gas hog when flying over water in the Caribbean. Thunderstorms could materialize out of nowhere, forcing you to fly far off your intended course, but these days I had a cash-flow problem and only had enough fuel for the round-trip and a legal reserve. Any long delays over Havana would be a major problem. I did not share this tidbit with my passenger, who was now vomiting into an Orville Redenbacher popcorn bag.

"We're going in the water," I announced.

Rudy stopped heaving and stared wide-eyed at me. The color of his face matched the milky whites of his eyes, and he screamed, "Holy Mother of God!"

I looked up at the St. Christopher medal and rubbed it for luck.

"Rudy, we're not going to crash. We're going to land in

the water. The gear won't work, but I can fix it when we get down."

"How can we land in the water?"

"Because this is a seaplane, Rudy."

• • •

I could feel the two MiGs before I saw them. They crept up on each side of the *Hemisphere Dancer* like motorcycle cops, and then Havana Center gave me a heading. We all turned together toward the harbor, which was barely visible in the distance. I don't know what got into me, but I decided to fuck with them a little and slowed down to about seventy knots, knowing they would have a hard time staying in the sky at that speed. I guess it was just my way of letting them know I wasn't some yo-yo on a joyride, and I hoped they'd see the humor in it. But humor seemed to be in short supply in Castro's Cuba; Havana Center ordered me to speed up. These guys were armed to the teeth—a 23-mm cannon and a couple of ATOLLs hung under each wing. I shoved the throttles forward.

The MiGs stayed with us not more than twenty feet on each side of the floats. I looked over at one of the pilots just as he snapped a picture of us with his camera. I'm sure he'd never seen a Goose this close before, and I had never been this close to a MiG that wasn't shooting at me.

A little color returned to Rudy's face, and he fumbled with a film cartridge, trying to put it into his camera. He loaded the Polaroid Spectra and fired it as fast as he could. It spit out film like a broken parking-ticket machine. The MiGs escorted us to the harbor entrance and then hit the afterburners and raced ahead, disappearing into the clouds.

I lined up with Morro Castle on the point, and I was told by Havana Center not to fly over the old fort. They directed me to the west side of the harbor, where a patrol boat was waiting for us to land and would direct us to customs. Those little Cuban patrol boats I had seen during the boat lift always made me nervous. They were all manned by teenagers with big automatic weapons, and the teenagers didn't smile.

The entrance to the ancient port opened into a sheltered bay, and the city sprawled out toward the foothills of the southwest. "Looks like the whole place could use a couple of coats of white paint," Rudy said.

I spotted the ship channel and set up my approach between the starboard channel markers and the waterfront. I dropped down until we were barely ten feet above the water and reduced power. The water looked clear of debris, and I kept the patrol boat in sight. I recited my checklist aloud as I always did. It was a good way of not being too casual.

"Fuel tanks to both. Mixtures rich. Horn switch on for water landing. Gear up."

Before the handle had broken off, the gear lever had barely let the tail wheel down. Landing wouldn't be a problem. I scanned the visual inspection ports behind my seat to reconfirm that the gear was up.

"Boost pumps on. Bilge pump on auto. Flaps thirty degrees. Props full."

I dropped below Morro Castle, with its aged towers, modern signal staffs, and black cannons guarding the harbor entrance like a row of teeth. I felt as if I were flying into a time warp. Giant container vessels were lined up at the piers, and tiny wooden fishing boats with patched sails tacked back and forth against the tide and wind. I could see people on the road stopping their cars and running to the rock wall as they waved and pointed in my direction.

I ran the final landing check and told Rudy to fasten his seat belt, then eased the *Hemisphere Dancer* over to the touchdown spot I had picked out. I brought in a little power until I heard the *whsshhhh* sound of the water under the hull and felt her settle on the step. I taxied on the water until we were within a few hundred yards of the patrol boat, and then I cut the power and pulled the steering yoke into my lap. Now we were a boat.

I took off my headset, rubbed my numb ears, and opened the window to let the sea breeze fill the cockpit. It brought in the scent of the sea; the fragrance of the shore; the smell of engine oil; and the universal bouquet of garlic, beans, and rice that surely came from a pot simmering somewhere within the confines of old Havana.

The breeze felt wonderful, and I inhaled heavily. Rudy was busy taking pictures of the teenagers on the gunboat with AK-47s draped across their chests.

"You should have let me keep my gun, Frank," he said bravely. "We might need it." He was panting so hard he was almost hyperventilating. "I'll tell you one goddamn thing. I saw *Salvador* three times, *Die Hard* four times, and *Rambo* ten times, but this is tits above any movie. I think I have a hard-on," he moaned.

"I *know* when I have a hard-on," I said.

"No, this is the real thing," Rudy said.

"You sound like a fucking Coke commercial."

A huge crowd had gathered beyond the fence that surrounded the customs dock, and the dock itself was filled with official-looking Communists.

He lowered his voice. "Hey Frank, don't forget to keep the Joe Merchant thing a secret," he said and winked.

"A secret? What the hell do you mean by that?"

"I told them I was doing a documentary on Hemingway. Didn't I tell you?"

"This is one fuck of a time to be announcing that you're on a secret mission," I hissed. I wanted to throttle him, but this was hardly the time and place. "Stay here until I tell you it's okay to move."

I angrily dropped through the companionway down to the anchor locker, opened the bow hatch, and tossed the dock line to a young soldier who caught it and held it tight. Putting a measured strain on my end, I eased the nose of the plane within inches of the dock.

"Buenos dios, mis amigos Cubano!"

I looked behind me, and Rudy was standing in the hatch opening. He looked like a jack-in-the-box. A cigar was lodged in the corner of his mouth, and he waved the lottery tickets with both hands.

I was still pissed off, but when I took the time to look around I had to smile. If it hadn't been for Rudy Breno and his half-baked idea to come looking for Joe Merchant, I wouldn't have been able to splash down in Havana Harbor—and make the landing of a lifetime.

3

The Blind Leading
the Blind

Although America lay only ninety miles to the north, it might as well have been the moon. A UFO from a distant galaxy couldn't have caused more commotion in Havana Harbor than the *Hemisphere Dancer* did that morning. Rudy looked like a cartoon version of General MacArthur. He handed out lottery tickets to the puzzled gathering until a soldier commanded him to halt.

"Senor Breno, Senor Breno," someone shouted. The sound of his own name ignited Rudy's ego, and he puffed right up.

"Wait here, pilot. I'll return when I have my story," he barked at me.

"Go fuck yourself," I snapped back. Now that I was already involved in the Joe Merchant cover-up, I had no choice but to go along. Rudy had told me he was meeting the man with the photographs at Hemingway's house.

"What if it's all bullshit?" I'd asked.

"Then I'll make the whole thing up. That's the beauty of this kind of work."

• • •

Not too many Americans came to Cuba these days, and even the ugly ones like Rudy were greeted with extreme curiosity. He was talking to the man who had called out his name, a tall Cuban with a pencil-thin mustache who looked like Ricardo Montalban. The crowd on the dock rattled on in machine-gun Spanish and broken English—mindless chatter by government bureaucrats sounds the same regardless of the ideology or tongue. I paid no attention to the hoopla and concerned myself with the plane.

"You are the pilot, senor?" I turned, and the man with the mustache was standing over me.

"Si," I replied.

"You may speak English," he said coolly. "My name is Luis Mercedes, like the car. Your plane will be safe. The launch will take it to the mooring. Now,if you will come with me."

"I'm just the pilot. He's the reporter. I'll stay with my plane, if you don't mind. I have some repairs to make."

"Please, come with us," he said, gesturing toward the waiting van. It was a sugarcoated threat, but I had no choice. I handed the dock line to one of the soldiers.

• • •

I found myself once again in La Bodeguita del Medio in the heart of old Havana. I had been there with Billy Cruiser when we flew Ed Bradley and his cameraman over during the boat lift. We had all spent a couple of days waiting for the last boats to clear out and had downed our share of the bar's famous but deadly *mojitos*. This afternoon, however, I sat alone on a corner stool sipping a Coke. Across the room, a bunch of green plastic palm-tree swizzle sticks were piled up on Rudy's table. Rudy was shitfaced. Luis Mercedes was seeing to that. He was a snake-oil salesman in anybody's language.

Rudy got up to go to the bathroom, and Luis came and stood beside me at the bar. "You are not happy here, Captain Bama. I want you to enjoy our hospitality. Have a drink."

"I'm on duty," I said.

"You are worried about your airplane. She is very beautiful. Let me see if I remember," Luis said. "Grumman Goose JRF-5. I believe 184 of the 345 aircraft produced were built for an all-encompassing 'utility' role for air-sea rescue, combat patrol, photographic work. Powered by two Pratt & Whitney R-985 AN-3 engines capable of producing 450 horsepower each at sea level. She has a gross weight of 9,200 pounds and burns approximately forty gallons of fuel an hour." He smiled smugly, waiting for a comment. I didn't give him one.

"My job today is to stay with you while you are here," Luis finally added. "Think of me as your escort."

"Sort of like I'm a V.I.P. at Disney World, huh?" I ordered another Coke.

"I know all about your wartime flying in Vietnam—Operation Market Time, I think it was called. Also your job in New Zealand. How do you afford to own such a plane? Are you a drug smuggler?" This guy was making Rudy look like Mr. Personality. I started to make a wiseass comment, but I suddenly realized he was fishing for something, and any ill-conceived reaction to his taunts might cost me my plane.

"No. I run a charter service."

"And Mr. Rudy here chartered your airplane to do a story on Papa Hemingway?"

"That's what he told me. Hey, bud, I'm just the pilot. I don't ask questions. It's impolite and bad for business. You know what I mean?"

"You're sure he is not chasing Joe Merchant?" Luis wet his lips. "I read the *National Lighthouse.*"

"Jesus Christ, not you, too. I thought you people didn't like newspapers. Besides, Joe Merchant is dead. He jumped off the back of a cruise ship five years ago."

Luis Mercedes lit a cigarette and ordered another drink. He was right out of "Miami Vice."

"What makes you so sure Joe Merchant is dead?" he asked.

"Even if he were alive—which he isn't—I don't think he would be hanging out around here. Believe me, I know a lot of better places in the Caribbean to hide."

"That kind of remark could get you in big trouble."

I was tired, and I'd had enough. I got up from my stool and looked Luis directly in the eye. "And risk an international incident? Do you have that kind of authority, comrade?"

Luis angrily crushed his cigarette into an ashtray on the bar. "Just remember, Captain, I have lunch on a regular basis with a lot of dead men."

A short, bald man burst through the door of the bar, and when he saw Luis, he ran over and excitedly whispered something to him in Spanish. Luis shook the man's hand and then turned again to me. "You are free to return to your plane now. My men will escort you." He rejoined the *mojito* party at the far table.

On my way out, Rudy finally staggered out of the bathroom and stopped me.

"Nice place, huh?"

"Fucking charming. How long will you be?"

"I still have to go to the Finca, Hemingway's old house." Rudy gave me a drunken, lopsided grin. "I'm on the case," he said and returned to his table.

• • •

I was alone in the van on the way back to the dock. Old Havana must have been a wonder in its day. It reminded me a little of Paris and Madrid. A busload of Russian ballet dancers sat on the curb, fanning themselves under the old Western Union sign. Kids played baseball in the streets. The city was a microcosm of intertwining cultures. What the hell could Rudy Breno know that interested these clowns so much? It was like the blind leading the blind.

The *Hemisphere Dancer* lay just off the customs dock, tied to an orange mooring ball, and the patrol boat took me out to her. A young officer came on board with me and dismissed the two guards who were stationed there. I immediately went about inspecting my plane. In a country under embargo, parts are cherished items, and I wanted to make damn sure that nothing had been lifted in my absence. First I checked the control panel, then the engine compartments. The engines were much too warm. They had been run while I was gone. I looked at the soldier, but he remained stone faced. The fuel gauges read more than when I had left Lone Palm. Now I knew the reason they'd gotten me off the *Dancer.* Somebody had flown my plane.

I walked around the turtle deck and wings to inspect for any damage to the tow. Everything seemed to be in order. Who the hell would fly my airplane? Had they put something in it? These people were so paranoid that they thought a long-dead rock star, a two-bit reporter for a tabloid, and a broke seaplane pilot were somehow involved in a revolutionary plot or something. I couldn't wait to get home. If I'd had any doubts about making my big move to Alaska, they were gone now.

The young officer sat silently in the hot cabin while his starched uniform began to discolor with sweat stains. I stripped down to my khaki shorts, and he watched me change the shear pin and test the gear handle. The steady rolling of the plane on the harbor chop gradually turned him a light shade of green. I asked him in Spanish if he felt okay and gave him a Coke and then a Dramamine from the medicine kit. He asked if the plane would rock as much back at the dock, and I told him no. Then he said something into his radio, and the patrol boat came alongside and towed the *Dancer* back in.

At dark I made myself a peanut-butter-and-jelly sandwich, stretched out on the bench in the back of the plane, and thumbed through my copy of Antoine de Saint Exupéry's *Wind, Sand and Stars*. It wasn't long before I fell asleep.

Around midnight, I heard footsteps. Two soldiers were dragging Rudy down the dock. A wave of anger swept over me at the thought that Luis Mercedes and his goons were so suspicious that they'd interrogated Rudy about Joe Merchant—but then the fumes of the rum hit me, and I realized Rudy was just wasted away again. They laid him in a ball at my feet.

Luis stood over Rudy and lit a cigarette in the darkness. "I wonder why we fear you so when this is what you call a newspaper reporter."

"You're the one who let him in. Can I ask you why the hell you allowed us to land in the first place?"

"Someone wanted to fly your plane."

"Well, he can charter it. You stole my fucking airplane."

"How can we steal your airplane when it sits at the dock? You ask too many questions. I say again, *someone* wanted to fly your plane."

"Fidel?" I asked. "Is that what you're hinting at?"

"Need I say more?"

"You mean Fidel was watching? I'll be damned."

"You want answers to everything. You want them to drop out of the sky like raindrops. You Americans. I will never understand the fascination. You with your rock stars, drug wars, exploitation of the masses, and—"

"Baseball, Luis. Don't forget baseball."

Luis handed me our passports. "You are to be gone tomorrow morning by seven o'clock." He turned and walked back up the dock.

"Tell Fidel thanks for the gas," I called after him.

4

Under the Lone Palm

Billy Cruiser says the best navigators are not always certain where they are, but they are always aware of their uncertainty. Uncertainty was the feeling I had the next morning as I left the birthplace of Ricky Ricardo behind and headed back to the Keys. I was more concerned about the weather than I'd been about crossing Communist airspace.

The Cubans seemed to have lost all interest in us. There had been no crowds and no escorts at first light, just a bleary-eyed customs man who checked our papers.

Now I was in the soup, and I'm not talking chicken broth. This was Brunswick stew. I couldn't see squat out the windshield, so I just listened to Miami Center trying to cope with the situation and get everybody through the muck and back on the ground safely. Cuba seemed to melt away in the blindness of the clouds.

Rudy Breno stirred behind me, and I told him we would be landing soon. He was badly hung over and waved weakly with his left hand. When we left Havana, I had strapped him in and hung a bucket around his neck so he wouldn't barf all over my plane. Now he was slumped in one of the rear seats like a laundry bag full of week-old dirty clothes. He groaned once and then slid back into unconsciousness.

I was looking forward to getting paid, and with Rudy out cold, I'd been thinking about what I'd do with the money. It was clear to me that my time in the tropics had just about run out. I guess I could blame it on the El Niño current or the harmonic convergence or whatever, but my chicken-salad days had turned into chicken shit.

The fish and shrimp had decided to do their thing in other waters, and the boats had followed them down to Central America, so my spotting business dried right up. The cost of insurance to carry passengers in a forty-year-old airplane had gone through the roof. I'd gotten a letter from my loan officer saying the bank would "work with me on the loan," but what that meant was hauling drunks on gambling junkets between Nassau and Key West. I did a couple of runs but got tired of having my plane smell like the men's room in a third-world airport.

Alaska or bust. I had let Billy Cruiser and Blanton Meyercord in on my escape plan; they were the only people I had trusted enough to tell. Now that I would have the travel money, everything was coming together. I figured it would take me the day to tie up loose ends and go over a few last things with Billy before I took off for Kodiak Island. There was no point in putting it off. The longer I waited, the better my chances were of losing my plane. It was time for a change in latitude. We are all born with a little larceny in our hearts, and I was about to become a criminal.

• • •

A shaft of sunlight popped through a hole in the clouds, bringing me back to real time. I pushed the nose over and pulled the power lever back, and the *Hemisphere Dancer* dropped through the opening. I leveled off at about five hundred feet. The hole quickly filled in, and the shark-gray color of the sky was again reflected on the face of the sea.

Having made up my mind that this would be my last day in town, I decided to cancel my flight plan with Key West and got permission to cruise the shore to the east. I now leveled off at a hundred feet. This was the real altitude for a seaplane.

A few crazy windsurfers were taking advantage of the nasty weather, skipping over the waves like flat stones. I rocked my wings back and forth, and the wheel felt alive in my hand. A pelican came into view no more than a hundred feet in front of me, and I released the pressure on the wheel and climbed for a moment. The bird made a graceful dive and disappeared below the surface of the water.

As soon as I saw the ugly condo that marred the shoreline, I had an impulse to do something I'd wanted to do for a long time. I imagined I was in my dad's old PBY, the *No-See-Um,* and had spotted the enemy. I dove at the condo commandos who occupied the giant pillbox on the beach.

The lookouts on the balcony gaped at the *Dancer* with disbelief. I gave the order, and a wingload of invisible bombs rained down on the building, which instantly crumbled from the direct hit.

Big buildings belong in cities, not on the beach. I had come to the Keys because of their isolation, but the tiny string of islands was no longer an outpost. The summer crowds were now as large as the winter ones, and the hurricane that was supposed to clear things out had never materialized.

I pulled up about twenty feet above the roof and banked right. Several residents were running from their tiny aluminum balconies through sliding glass doors.

"Fuck art, fuck nature, build nuclear condos!" I yelled. I would be home before the phones at the Key West tower started to ring off the wall and would be long gone by midnight.

• • •

I came in low over the flats, and a flock of cormorants launched. They looked disoriented on takeoff at having to go west to find the wind; the odd breeze confused everything. Despite the weather, flying along the shoreline was beautiful today, and I would miss it. Down below, sharks and rays on the flats swam helter-skelter, leaving tell-tale trails of mud that were clearly visible even at this altitude. The rays stirred up the food sources on the bottom, and the cormorants bobbed up and down behind them, diving for table scraps. The cormorants always gave away the location of the seafood festival where sometimes a huge mutton snapper or permit was looking for an easy meal. I made a mental note of the spot for Billy Cruiser.

In the distance, I could make out the ancient tree on the beach that had given Billy Cruiser's airport its name. The lone palm stood on a narrow strip of sand surrounded by a

tangle of mangroves. The trunk went up about ten feet and
then made a slow, beautiful curve out over the water and
stretched sixty feet into the sky. It was said by the Arawaks,
who fished these waters long before the Europeans arrived,
that the lone palm had been put here by the gods of the sea
to lead them safely home. It has survived hurricanes, conquis-
tadors, pirates, and condo commandos.

The tire swing had been hung in this century, but nobody
was sure just when. Billy called it "a poor man's way to fly."

I studied the swaying green branches of the ancient tree
and looked at the long, foamy wind lines running toward the
shore for clues about the surface wind. I looked back to
check on Rudy before making the steep bank turn for my approach, but he was still passed out, with his head resting on
the window.

"Lone Palm traffic Grumman 40 Sierra Bravo, we'll be
landing in the water parallel to the runway; got a slight gear
problem," I announced.

Hoagy was leaping in front of the hangar with a deflated
volleyball clenched firmly in his teeth, looking up at the
plane. He would have a swell time in Alaska, chasing mallards and reindeer across the frozen tundra.

"Need any help?" the calm voice of Billy Cruiser asked.

"Negative, Cruise. Sheared a gear handle pin in Havana,
but they let me drop her in the water. I'll tell you about it
when I land."

"You got company," he said. "It ain't who you think it is,"
he added.

As long as it wasn't the bank, I didn't care.

　　• • •

"Final hull check. Clean."

I scanned the landing area for lobster traps, boats, or other
stuff that could spoil my day. I pulled in the reins, and the
Hemisphere Dancer settled into shallow water. Then I opened
the window and let in the fresh air. I dropped the water rudder and steered the plane to the ramp.

Rudy was awake now, but he looked like one of the people
in that old movie *Night of the Living Dead.*

"Where am I? What's going on?" he groaned.

I took off my headset and yelled, "Looks like we defied
death one more time!"

I held my breath as I cranked the gear handle down. The
pin held, and the indicator gave me a green. That's when I

reached up to my St. Christopher medal. I gave it a superstitious rub, as I did after every landing, and a sliver of sunlight popped through an opening in the sky like a flashbulb and bounced off the medal above my head. It blinded me for a moment, and I rubbed my eyes behind my sunglasses.

When I opened them again, I saw her in the tire swing. A shiver ran down my spine. A tension I hadn't felt in a long time returned as I watched the long, slender body of Trevor Kane swing back and forth above the water, her toes skimming the surface.

* * *

I tried to keep my mind on my work, maneuvering the plane up the ramp, taxiing to the hangar, but I kept staring back at Trevor in the swing. I couldn't believe her timing. At this point I didn't need any more problems or excess baggage, and unfortunately Trevor Kane always had plenty of both.

The old Argus radio blasted country music from the corner speaker, and the tones of the pedal steel guitar reverberated off the expansive curved tin roof of the hangar. Country music had played constantly since around 1982 when Billy discovered that it kept the pigeons from roosting in the rafters and shitting on the planes. He had tried classical music and rock 'n' roll, but the birds seemed to enjoy both. There was something about country music that made them stay airborne.

"Been waitin' in that swing 'bout an hour," Billy said as I stepped out of the plane.

Rudy tumbled through the hatch and stabbed into his jacket pocket for his sunglasses. The surprise of seeing Trevor had made me forget about him, but before I could whisper the words "Get him out of here," Billy had pointed Rudy away from the swing.

"Looks like you been shot at and missed, shit at and hit, son. I didn't think those commies had fun anymore in Havana. Not like the old days when I used to go over."

Rudy cut him off. "Could you call me a cab? I don't feel very well."

"Cab, hell. You need a fuckin' ambulance, son. Come on, and I'll take you to town," Billy said and gave me a wink. He had always lived by instinct and could clean up a mess before it happened.

"One last thing, Rudy," I said. "You forgot to pay me."

"Frank, the paper handles expenses," he said with a tired look. "I'm sick as a dog. Give me a call tomorrow."

"Something's come up, and I can't wait around for the fucking paper to pay me when they feel like it."

"Okay, okay. I'll write you a personal check." He took out his checkbook and leaned on Billy Cruiser.

"Cash," I said. "That was the deal. You told me about your secret money belt in Cuba, Rudy. Don't you remember? It was right after your twenty-third *mojito.*"

"Frank, that's not reportable income—that's my stash money," Rudy whined.

"Not anymore," I said. "Fork it over."

"Going somewhere?" Rudy asked, switching to his reporter voice.

"An old friend just showed up, and we might go sightseeing."

Rudy took off his money belt and reluctantly handed me five hundred dollars. His token objection had passed, and his sandpaper charm returned. He had tried to avoid paying me and had failed. He was that kind of guy. "By the way, a little bird tells me some suits have been asking around town about your airplane," he said with sudden energy.

"Where'd you hear this?"

"As a professional journalist, I'm sworn not to reveal my sources of information."

"Rudy, get a life. I'm not the fucking FBI. Now what did you hear and where did you hear it?"

"In the bank two days ago. Lou Anne, that cute little teller with the nice ass, told me. I was describing the daring raid we were going to make on Cuba—"

"Raid?" I said, interrupting him.

"Hey, it sort of was. You still should have let me keep my gun. We were totally defenseless when those MiGs showed up."

"Back to your bank teller."

"Two guys in suits were coming out of the credit department, and they were asking for your address. She said they're going to pay you a visit this week."

My eyes met Billy Cruiser's, and he nodded. I was no longer listening to what Rudy was jabbering about. "Thanks, Rudy," I said.

"Anytime. That's what friends are for."

Billy Cruiser steered him in the direction of the hangar,

and I glanced again at Trevor Kane. I felt like a wild onion trying to stay out of the way of a Weed Eater. Shit was coming at me from every direction, and Alaska was looking better all the time.

I headed for the narrow sand path that cut through the sea oats to the beach. Ten or fifteen clever opening lines sailed through my brain, but the first words I said to the only woman I'd ever loved fumbled off my dry tongue like a miscued pool ball.

"Hello, Ms. Kane. What brings you back to paradise from the Big Easy?"

She said nothing for what seemed like an hour, and then I saw the tears running down her face. Her chin rested on the old rubber tire, and without looking up, she said, "Frank, my mother killed herself."

5

Let's Blame It All on the Weather

Trevor Kane sat in the tire swing, silently looking down at the water. Her blond hair blew in the wind, and behind her, the lumpy gray clouds of a mackerel sky stretched to the horizon. Big drops of rain began to splatter on the runway, and a rumble of thunder unfolded out over the gulf, but Trevor did not move from the swing. She looked like one of her own paintings.

"Come on," I said. "Let's go get a cup of coffee or something."

She swung to the land and slid out of the tire as it passed above the beach.

"Trevor, I'm truly sorry about your mother."

"Thanks." She wiped the tears from her face with the back of her hand. "Oh, what the hell's the use of even talking about it? I need to stop thinking about this stuff for a while."

"You've come to the right place for that."

"Life's a breeze in the Florida Keys," she said. "Put your arms around me, will you?"

She felt wonderful to hold, but it made me very uncomfortable.

34

"This is too easy," I said.

"I know, but let me enjoy it for a minute, will you?"

In our roller-coaster relationship, there had always been an unexplainable ease between Trevor and me, as long as things didn't get too serious or substantive. As soon as that happened, I was gone. I kept my arm around her shoulder, and we walked back to the hangar, where my Jeep was parked.

"I'm starving," she said as we drove along U.S. 1. "I haven't eaten since I left New Orleans. Through all the madness I was dealing with, I kept thinking about the jerk chicken at Bobalou's. Crazy, isn't it?"

The rain had stopped and so had her tears, but I could feel that either might begin again at any moment.

"Thank Billy for keeping that slug Rudy away from me, would you? I'd have gone nuclear if he'd started asking me questions about Joe. So Billy told me you took that pinhead to Havana. What's he up to?" she asked.

I took a deep breath and geared up for her reaction. "He was working on another story about Joe. Rudy said that Joe was sighted at a baseball game in Havana this week."

"Oh Jesus, Frank. How could you?"

"Trevor, give me a fucking break! It's been nearly five years since I've laid eyes on you. I know how much you hate him, but how was I supposed to know that you were going to be sitting in the Lone Palm tire swing when I came back?"

"It's the principle of the thing."

"Principle won't put fuel in my plane. Things are pretty tight around here, and I have to take what I can get these days." I looked over, and Trevor had started crying again. She was as tough as they come, which made her seem even more frail on the rare occasions when I'd seen her cry. "I'm sorry," I told her. "I didn't mean to snap at you. I'm a little on edge, and this weather doesn't help."

"Yeah, well, I've been upset myself."

"I can imagine," I said.

"I don't think so."

I looked at her. She was more than a little on edge. She had that old, familiar time-bomb look. A huge semi roared past us, shaking the Jeep and covering it with a film of water.

"Asshole!" Trevor shouted out the window at the anonymous truck driver. She rubbed Hoagy behind the ears. "Let's blame it all on the weather," she finally added.

"I'm sorry I upset you."

"It's not just you. Everything upsets me right now."

I had no idea what to say next. She was not only my old girlfriend but also a woman whose brother was some ghost of the tabloids and whose mother had just killed herself. I was trying to think of some comforting thing to say when my wipers suddenly stopped working. They just sat there, helplessly stuck to the windshield while the rain came down in buckets. It distracted us, and we occupied ourselves with trying to keep the yellow lines on the highway in sight.

Trevor took the bandanna from her hair and began to wipe the windshield. A few minutes later, I spotted the restaurant sign and turned off the highway, splashing through the puddles to a piece of wet parking lot in front of Bobalou's.

"How's Blanton these days?"

"Crazy as ever."

"He hasn't found Jesus in jail, has he?"

"You'll have to ask him. He got out last week. I'm surprised you even know about it."

"One of those Jet Skiers he beat up was from New Orleans—it was in the papers up there, too," she said, opening the Jeep door.

We ran through the hard rain for the shelter of the porch, shook some of the water off, and walked in. The ceiling fans above the crab-trap tables were trying to stir some coolness up, but there was none to be had. Crosby, Stills, and Nash sang "Suite: Judy Blue Eyes" from the jukebox. On the bar, a bouquet of flowers lay slumped over in an iced-tea pitcher.

"It always amazes me how it can be pouring down rain here and still be ninety degrees," Trevor said.

"Where the hell have you been, young lady, and what are you doing with this bozo? I thought you came to your senses about pilots long ago." It was Curtiss Meyercord, Blanton's older brother. He was sitting at the counter with a plate of cracked conch in front of him.

"I came back to marry you. I'm over pilots. I want a man of the sea," Trevor said as she walked over and kissed him on the cheek. "So how's Blanton these days?"

"He's gettin' by," Curtiss said, a little gruffly. Then he turned to me. "Frank, somebody told me you been to Cuba. That a fact?"

"Yeah."

"What the hell you doin' flyin' Rudy Breno around?"

"I was asking him the same question," Trevor said.

"I'm in the charter business. Rudy's a pain in the ass, but he's also a customer."

"Rudy Breno, the sexual intellectual," Curtiss said in a mocking voice.

"What's a sexual intellectual?" Trevor asked.

"A fucking know-it-all."

Trevor's eyes twinkled.

Curtiss pointed at me with his fork. "If that little shithead shows his face around me, I'm gonna squish him like a shrimp. If you see Blanton today, you tell him to call me. Nice to see ya, Trevor. Let's all go fishin' when this weather breaks."

Curtiss turned his attention back to the plate of cracked conch, and we walked on past the Graceland clock on the wall to the booth by the aquarium. We sat down under the old wooden propeller that Billy Cruiser had given to Bob and Lucy, the owners, at the grand opening.

"He seems angry," Trevor said.

"Rudy Breno has pissed off a lot of people around here. When Blanton went to jail, Rudy's article compared him to Charlie Manson. That didn't sit well with the fishing community or his family. Blood is thicker than water here, and Curtiss Meyercord isn't a man to piss off."

Bob Wingo, the owner and cook, came over to our table. Beads of sweat trickled from his bald spot down to his white headband, and his big forearms were dusted with flour.

"Where you been, sweet thing?" he said to Trevor, leaning over and hugging her.

"I'm back in New Orleans," Trevor told him.

"Well, I hope you didn't bring this nasty-ass weather with you. I'll get you a menu."

"Don't need it," Trevor said. "I've been dreaming about jerk chicken."

"Hey, I just took some off the grill."

"How about bringing me some peas 'n' rice, cole slaw, lima beans, and maybe one of your fried okra appetizers," she said, and Bob looked up from his pad.

"That just for you, Trevor?"

"Sky King here can order for himself. And save me a piece of that peach cobbler."

"I'll have a fried grouper sandwich and a Red Stripe," I said.

"Trevor, how do you keep that girlish figure and eat like that?" Bob Wingo asked.

"It's all in the genes, Bobby," she answered with a smile. It was the first time I'd seen her smile that day, and it send Bob shuffling back to the kitchen whistling. Trevor turned to me and said, ''So what was Cuba like?"

"It wasn't like Trinidad at carnival, that's for damn sure. But I think Fidel Castro flew my plane."

"What do you mean, you think?"

I told Trevor the story of Luis Mercedes and the strange addition of fuel and the warm engines.

"And Rudy?" she asked.

"He got shitfaced at La Bodeguita del Medio, and then he was supposed to go off to Hemingway's house under the guise of doing a film on old Ernesto. That's how he got into Cuba in the first place. But I don't think he ever made it there. He was too drunk. He told me that if he didn't get the photos from the man he was supposed to meet, he'd just make the whole story up anyway."

Trevor shook her head. "It's pathetic. Look what we've stooped to in America, what we consider news. I mean, with all the problems facing the world, you'd think we'd be a little more interested in overpopulation and arms reduction than in who's fucking who in Hollywood and whether Elvis is in Michigan or up on Mars—or if Joe is in Cuba watching a goddamn baseball game."

The waitress brought us a plate of fried okra, and Trevor lunged at it. "People don't want to deal with their own problems," she said as she ate.

The comment made me uneasy, and I shifted in my chair. Trevor continued to talk, but an F-14 taking off from the naval air station nearby deafened the restaurant. When the noise faded away, Trevor was still talking. "The shit Rudy writes about just numbs us and diverts our attention from the things that are bothering us. You never see poor people on soap operas, do you?"

Bob Wingo dropped the big china platters on the table with a thud that startled both of us. "This sandwich was swimming this morning. Still the freshest in town or anywhere around. Bon appétit, y'all."

Trevor splashed an abundant shower of Crystal hot sauce over the food and dug in like a ten-year-old at camp.

Our conversation was put on hold while we attacked our

lunch, listening to Van Morrison's "Tupelo Honey" on the radio. The music set the mood for the stormy afternoon. Outside, the Keys had lost their Caribbean character and looked more like the southeast Irish coast—a place where faint fingers of the Gulf Stream caress the shore with a hint of the tropics, and the evergreens give way to an occasional palm tree. As I ate, I looked out the far window and wondered when Trevor would get around to telling me why she'd come.

"Frank, did you hear that?"

I quit daydreaming and answered with my mouth full. "What?"

Trevor was already up and walking over to the counter. Curtiss Meyercord was now turning the volume up on the old Hallicraft radio.

"I'll be goddamned!" he bellowed in disbelief.

A scratchy nasal voice came out of the radio speaker. "We repeat this special flash bulletin. There has been a serious explosion west of Key West where a Jet Ski commercial was being filmed. It has been confirmed by eyewitnesses that a deranged fishing guide named Blanton Meyercord held a film crew and a cast of actors hostage for thirty minutes and then set off a charge that sent fourteen Jet Skis and an award-winning Hollywood director on an unscheduled lift-off. More on this story as it develops. Now back to the music."

Doin'
the Hemisphere
Dance

6

That's My Story, and I'm Stickin' to It

The spotted gecko moved through the dim light, carefully extending its legs across the rusty metal wall of the old lighthouse. The suction cups on the bottoms of its feet permitted it to cling to the wall and defy gravity.

Blanton Meyercord switched off his hand-held radio and watched the gecko. It stopped for a moment to ponder its next move.

"You look like a living chess piece," Blanton said to the reptile. "Are you a pawn or a rook?" The tiny heart and organs of the creature pulsated through its transparent epidermal layer. "Bishop. No, queen. Access to the whole board. I hereby name you Queenie." Queenie moved a few inches and stopped again.

Blanton's shoulders were knotted and tense. He pressed firmly on his temples and bathed in the temporary relief from the pressure, then stood up from his squatting position and raised his hands high above his head and stretched.

Blanton Meyercord was five feet eight and tan from head to toe. The leathery texture of his skin was a result of endless days under the hot tropical sun. His arms were firm, and his

43

hands were calloused from pushing and poling across the shallow flats of the Florida Keys. While he was in jail, he had kept in shape by lifting weights and jogging, and he had barely lost his color, though his hair had not fared so well. A monk-like bald spot was slowly spreading across the top of his head, and he kept it covered with a baseball cap.

Queenie reappeared from the shadows and slithered closer. Blanton pulled a package of peanut-butter cheese crackers out of his foul-weather jacket and put a crumb on the table beside him. The gecko spotted the food, made a miscalculation, and dropped off the wall.

Blanton scooped her up with a flick of his wrist and gently opened his hand, placing the lizard upright next to the crumb on the table. "Queenie," he said, "looks like we're both working without a net today."

The wind whistled through the winding staircase of Sand Key Lighthouse, making the girders and support cables groan and twang like a gigantic wind chime. Blanton was in the room that housed the batteries for the signal lamp up above. It was familiar territory. He thought of the lighthouse and the tiny spit of land around it as his backyard. As a kid, he had fished and snorkeled nearby, in a place where the greens of the shallow water gave way to the deep blue patterns of the Gulf Stream. In his teenage years, he had learned the secrets of a woman's body on this small island that came and went with the currents of the stream.

Debris of all kinds was scattered across the floor, and a collage of graffiti covered the walls. Blanton walked to the metal hatch on the opposite side of the room and pulled it open.

Outside, big rollers, unfamiliar to these waters, washed across the hazardous coral canyons of the reef, and Blanton looked down at his old flats skiff. After escaping the scene of the explosion, he had sped directly north until he knew he was out of sight of any witness. He had circled west to the Marquesas Keys and then south to Sand Key. He had always been amazed at how well his little skiff functioned in rough weather. The boat was now hidden below, tied to the catwalk with several spring lines.

Blanton had towed one of the Jet Skis with him. It bobbed up and down erratically in the sea like a spoiled brat, and Blanton wondered why fate had cursed him and had hung this high-tech albatross around his neck. Yesterday he had been just another crazy flats guide, but this morning he was a wanted man.

When Jet Skis first showed up in the Keys, all the guides bitched about them. They served no useful purpose and made a hideous noise that sent the fish in a five-mile radius scurrying off the flats into deep water for shelter. They disrupted the nesting of the shore birds in the mangroves, and they were dangerous torpedoes in the hands of the incompetent people who rented them.

Blanton's frustration with the Jet Skis had turned violent one day. He was fishing an older client on the flats just north of Boca Grande, and they were hooked up to a giant tarpon. For nearly two hours, Blanton had coached the inexperienced angler through the fatigue of fighting such a big fish, and finally the client had turned the fish's head toward the boat. This meant the tarpon was tired. About twenty feet from the boat, the big tarpon made a desperate run, which carried him about a hundred feet from the boat. The fisherman was exhausted and fell to the floor of the skiff.

Blanton grabbed the rod just before it flew out of the boat and held on as the fish made a last leap and then rolled over on its side in a silver flash. He held the rod in one hand and splashed water on the angler's face until he opened his eyes.

"He beat me," the man said.

"I'd say it was a tie. You all right?"

"I'm a little woozy. I could use a spot of shade."

"Let me take care of this fish, and then we'll get out of the sun."

Blanton muscled the big fish alongside the boat, grabbed him by the tail, and moved him back and forth to force water through his gills. He felt the tail come alive, and when he released his grip, the fish swam slowly away on the surface. In a few seconds, he would catch his breath and dive for the shelter of the deep water.

From out of nowhere, two hotshots on Jet Skis came roaring across the flats and circled Blanton's skiff. The big tarpon never knew what hit him. The Jet Skis sped off in the direction of the island, and Blanton poled his skiff to the fish, which was now floating on the surface. Its head had been crushed, and the blood had already attracted a school of small bonnet sharks.

In twenty years of guiding, Blanton had never killed a tarpon. Every fish that found its way onto a line from his boat

was revived after the encounter and sent back to the ocean.
Now Blanton pulled the big fish into the boat and headed for
Boca Grande, following the scattered wakes of the two Jet
Skis.

He circled past the point where the Jet Skiers were having
a party, then idled over to a little stretch of beach he called
his "thinking spot." He gave the fisherman a candy bar and
a Coke and told him to rest nearby in the shade of a palmetto.
Then Blanton dug a hole in the sand and buried the tarpon.
He combed the beach for driftwood and debris and erected a
makeshift monument. Using an old piece of charcoal from a
long-extinguished campfire, he wrote an inscription on the
plank:

Here lies a great fish killed by a Jet Ski.

Blanton took the fisherman back to town and then returned
to the island, where the beach party was in full swing. He
sneaked through the mangroves, grabbed the ghetto blaster,
and drop-kicked it into the water. Then he began to beat the
living shit out of the two guys who had killed the tarpon. He
set their Jet Skis on fire and went back to town and turned
himself in to the sheriff.

Blanton was arrested, and charges were pressed. He was
sentenced to six months and was made to pay for the Jet Skis
he had burned. He served his time and had just been released
from jail the week before.

• • •

Queenie continued to eat the cracker crumbs that Blanton
had been feeding her. He turned the radio back on and listened again to the garbled conversations of the boat captains,
relaying accounts of what had happened. He realized things
were already getting blown way out of proportion. He would
have to move soon, but not before he set the record straight.

He walked to the old workbench and pulled a Walkman out
of the yellow waterproof pouch he had brought with him. He
pushed the record button and began to talk.

"This is Blanton Meyercord, and I want to give you my
opinion of what happened at Tell Tale Cut today. I ain't got
much time, so here goes.

"I'll grant you that flats guides are oddballs. I guess you
can't spend half your life bakin' under the sun without it
cookin' some brain cells, but we have a feel for the ocean. It

provides our livin', but we don't own it. We use it. That's what too many people don't realize. If we don't use some common sense, the ocean will all be dirty dishwater before we know it.

"I'm not sayin' it's okay to do what I did—things just got out of hand. But I guess what I'm trying to say is that I feel about the flats the way the Sioux Indians feel about the Black Hills. They're sacred, and when I see them abused, I react. I'm a territorial son of a bitch. I consider Tell Tale Cut *my* flat.

"This trouble I'm havin' started last year when some assholes on Jet Skis murdered a big fish I had on a line. So that you know, I ain't never killed a trophy fish and never will. I don't believe in dead fish hangin' on walls. I went to jail for what I did to the people who killed that fish. I was punished, and so were they. Things even out. But when I was in jail, the thing that got me through was the thought of returnin' to the peace of my spot near Tell Tale Cut.

"I did my time for beatin' up those Jet Skiers and came home a week ago. The first thing I wanted to do was go fishin', but I had people to see, and welcome-home parties, and then the weather went rotten for fishin'. It didn't matter. Catchin' fish is only one reason to go out to the flats. It's the big picture that I love, the beauty of these little shallow flats, smack-dab between two giant oceans. . . . Well, I'm gettin' too sentimental here. I gotta finish this tape before the law shows up.

"Yesterday I decided to go out to Tell Tale Cut and sit on my 'thinkin' spot' even though the weather was bad. I wanted to look around.

"Well, when I get to the channel entrance at Ballast Key, I see this armada parked on *my* spot. The marine patrol, a huge houseboat, six or seven boats full of people, camera gear, makeup, wardrobe, and the frostin' on this mud bath— fifteen Jet Skis tied to the stake where I've fished for tarpon since I was sixteen.

"A marine patrol boat ordered me to leave the area. They said the flats was closed. A very important Hollywood director named Val Vincennes was shootin' a commercial, he said, for Jet Skis. I couldn't believe it. Boy, was I pissed off. But I didn't say a word. I turned my boat around and went on back to Key West to think.

"I gotta be truthful—thinkin' turned to drinkin'. I went

over to the Pirate's Den to try to cool off. I hadn't seen a naked woman in six months, and I thought that might take my mind off my troubles. I had a few shots of tequila and watched the girls dancin' around and humpin' the post behind the bar, but I couldn't keep my mind on the jigglin' tits in front of me. All I could see was Jet Skis, and I couldn't stop 'em from buzzin' around inside my brain. I guess I had a vision.

"I would like to state for the record that neither Frank Bama nor Billy Cruiser had any knowledge that I stole an M-16 and a grenade launcher from their hangar at Lone Palm Airport last night. I did it of my own free will. They are good friends, and I'm sorry if my actions cause them any problems.

"This mornin' I was up with the sun and out near Tell Tale Cut. I studied the scene with my binoculars from a distance. A dozen huge lights was pointin' down on the water, tryin' to make it look like a sunny day. A camera boat was anchored about thirty yards from the houseboat, and a swarm of Jet Skis buzzed around like wasps on speed, churnin' up the shallow water. I figured Val Vincennes was the guy doin' all the hollerin' and lookin' through the camera.

"I idled up to the channel and didn't have to wait long before the same marine patrol boat that stopped me yesterday came up to me again. The guy drivin' the boat signaled for me to turn back, but I acted confused. He came alongside my boat and told me the flats was still closed. It took him a while before he noticed my speargun.

"I was on board his boat and had the point of the power head resting against his neck before he knew it. I took his gun belt and threw it overboard and tied him up and stuck a bandanna in his mouth. I cleated off the bowline of my skiff to the transom and turned to the houseboat.

"Nobody paid much attention to me. They was too busy watching the filmin'. I loaded the grenade launcher and let the patrol boat drift over to where they was shootin', and then I yelled, 'Cut!'

"Val Vincennes spun around so fast he almost fell of the camera boat. He yelled, 'Who the fuck said that? Who the fuck said that?'

"I raised my hand and yelled back, 'It was I, Sir Blanton Meyercord.'

"And then he screamed, 'Keep shootin'!'

" 'Cut!' I yelled again.

"And then he really went off the deep end. 'Somebody get that crazy cocksucker!'

"A skiff started to come at me. I aimed the grenade launcher and fired. The people in the skiff were lookin' at me like I was tryin' to kill them, but I wasn't aimin' at them. I'd targeted a Jet Ski tied to the houseboat right behind them. It blew up good. I shouted out instructions for everybody except Val to clear the area and get back on the houseboat where I could see 'em. I wanted 'em all to get a good view of the new commercial.

"Val hadn't gotten the message. He was raving. 'What new commercial?' he screamed even louder.

" 'The one I'm gonna direct,' I screamed back.

"I fired another grenade and scored a direct hit on another Jet Ski.

"I think Val musta done too much television. I don't think he knew the difference between reality and a stunt. He started talkin' to me like he was Kojak. He started recitin' facts and figures that seemed to matter to him—how many Clios he'd won, all his Japanese connections. I told him to shut up and start rollin'.

"Well, he propped his leg up on the gunwale of the camera boat and started talkin' like Charlton Heston in *Planet of the Apes,* and he says to me, 'Give me the gun. I'm gonna count to three, and then I'm comin' after you.'

"I admit I had the grenade launcher aimed at him, but I never had any intention of shootin'. If the guy was crazy enough to jump me, I was gonna blow up another Jet Ski or two to scare him.

"I felt my boat sway, and some guy in a gray uniform came at me like a blitzin' linebacker. Next thing I knew, I was slammed against the rail of the marine patrol boat. The gun went off in my hands. A huge explosion threw us for a loop. The marine guy went flyin' overboard, and I was knocked against the console.

"The grenade had made a direct hit on the camera boat's fuel tank, and it had blown sky-high. I was real confused after that. I covered the marine in the water until he made it to the houseboat, and then I blew up the patrol boat. I grabbed a Jet Ski, tied it to my skiff, and got the hell out of there.

"Now I'm sittin' here on Sand Key and have had some time to think. I never was a big fan of TV, but that's no excuse for blowin' up a Hollywood director. For that I'm sorry. It was never my intention to harm anybody. I was just after the machines. But I'm not turnin' myself in. I'll take my chances on the run. Some of you may believe me, and some of you may think this is bullshit, but that's my story, and I'm stickin' to it."

Blanton Meyercord pushed the stop button on the tape player and sat in silence for a few minutes. Then he walked to the window. He scanned the horizon with his binoculars and saw nothing. He figured it would be a while before they actually sorted out what had happened and mounted a man-hunt.

A huge gust of wind shook the lighthouse, and the gecko dashed across the wall and disappeared into the dark corner.

"Good-bye, Queenie," Blanton said.

He was about to go down the stairwell, but he stopped and picked up a can of black spray paint. He shook it and added to the graffiti on the wall:

> *The cold war's over.*
> *The Japanese won.*
> *They took all our money*
> *And never used a gun.*

7

Fins to the Left,
Fins to the Right

Billy Cruiser and I sat in the hangar of the Lone Palm Airport. It was a leftover from World War II, when it had housed a squadron of PBY Catalina flying boats that were used to patrol the shipping lanes in the Straits of Florida. The room off to the right of the hangar overlooked the canal and had been my home since I'd brought my plane here from Venezuela. The gray concrete floor smelled of lubricants and machinery, and Billy's Beech 18 and a J3 Cub sat alongside the *Hemisphere Dancer.*

Billy Cruiser wore his familiar blue overalls and long-billed fishing hat, and he rocked back in his chair, chewing on a toothpick.

We had just heard the full recording of a tape that Blanton Meyercord had made and had somehow gotten to a Key West radio station. The DJ was playing it over and over again. It was Blanton, all right. I turned the radio down.

"What do you think?" I asked.

"I think he did the right thing."

"I know that. But I want to know what you think I should do."

"This sure puts a new wrinkle in your plan, son," Billy said.

"What plan is that?" Trevor asked. She'd been resting in my room after lunch, but now she stood next to the Beech 18 in a fresh white shirt and a pair of jeans.

"My escape plan."

"I need to talk to you," she said.

I could tell by the tone of her voice that this was it, the reason she had come back.

"Jesus, look, it's on CNN," Billy said, pointing to the portable TV on the workbench.

The phone started to ring.

"I'm sure that ain't the Avon lady. If it ain't about Blanton yet, it's probably another complaint about some maniac in a seaplane buzzin' a condo this mornin'." Billy raised an eyebrow. "But you wouldn't know anything about that, would you, Frank?" I grinned sheepishly as Billy walked over and unplugged the telephone. "This place is gonna look like Grand Central Station pretty soon. I'm gonna go out and chain the front gate shut." Billy left the hangar and went outside.

"Frank, I have to talk to you," Trevor said again.

"Trev, I can drop you in Miami. I'm leaving before dawn."

"I don't want to go to Miami. I need your help. I have to get to Boomtown."

"Boomtown? Honey, that's a little out of my way."

"What are you running from besides me?"

Silence hung in the air. She had gone for the jugular and had opened a painful old wound.

After Joe Merchant committed suicide by jumping off the back of that cruise ship, Trevor had been derailed, and I hadn't known what to do. The newspapers were filled with headlines and photographs, and every cheap-shot journalist on earth was camped outside the hangar door. They all wanted an exclusive interview with the rock star's sister. I made up a lame excuse to leave immediately and flew off to the islands. When I returned, Trevor had packed her things and had moved back to New Orleans. She had left one sentence on the yellow legal pad by the phone in the hangar: "You never talk to me."

"Now, that's not a fair question," I answered. I could feel my defense mechanisms springing into place like the deflector shields on the *Starship Enterprise*. The only men I'd ever seen who were truly good at talking with women were in the movies, and we all know they use cue cards.

"Listen," I said, "the bank is after my plane. And I'm in hock up to my ass." I tried to control the tone of my voice, but the anger was rising. "My plan was to disappear—to leave quietly in the middle of the night and take off to Alaska until I could get things straightened out. But my plan seems to have hit a snag, hasn't it? My ex-girlfriend shows up out of nowhere—she hasn't so much as phoned me once in five years, but now she's decided I should drop everything and take her to Boomtown, for Christsakes—and my best friend blows up a fucking Hollywood director and announces my name and address on the radio. I don't know who's gonna show up here first, the FBI or the repo men, but I don't plan to stay for the party. I've got better things to do," I said and walked out the door.

8

The Lady I Can't Explain

As I drove down the back road to town, I tried to shake off the anger. I would lay low, take care of a few last errands, and move on from there. I would try not to think too much. For all the time that Trevor and I had been apart, the memories were so fresh I could have seen her yesterday. That's just the kind of woman she was.

One thing was for sure: Trevor Kane still had charisma. It flowed from her clear green eyes, lighting up a face made all the more radiant by the small creases that had begun to develop just above her cheekbones. It was Trevor Kane's charisma that had led her back here, the same stubborn courage that had always made me admire her even when I was angry as hell.

I had fallen in love with her the first time I saw her. She had been sitting in a phone booth around the corner from the Chart Room Bar in Key West, and she'd leaned out and asked to borrow a dime. I didn't have any money, but I showed her how to short the receiver and fuck the phone company. She'd been wearing tight hip huggers and a denim work shirt, unbuttoned and tied in a knot just below her breasts. I asked her to lunch.

The next day we drove up the Keys to the Big Pine Inn for stone crabs. Lunch seemed to last forever. They rolled out the old newspaper and supplied us with hammers, and we banged our way through several dozen claws and a couple of bottles of pouilly-fuissé, telling each other stories of how we'd found ourselves at the end of U.S. 1. We licked the crab juices and mustard sauce from each other's fingers before we ever kissed. When I brushed over my years in Vietnam, she said, "I went to Vietnam, too."

"For what?"

"My father sent me."

I almost choked on a crab claw. "Your father sent you to Vietnam?"

She had gone back to her food and talked without looking up. "He said I was a spoiled navy brat, and I should see the real world. It's a long story."

I refilled her wine glass. "I'm all ears."

She sipped her wine and laughed sarcastically. "I don't really want to talk about it now, but I will say it's the tale of another all-American family. My father was career navy, and my mother was the perfect admiral's wife. She lived for that title. Her father was an immigrant who came to America from Sicily. He was an inventor, and one of his discoveries made him wealthy, but it was terribly embarrassing to my mother."

"What did he invent? Rubbers?"

"Close," she replied. "It was a hemorrhoid ointment. My grandfather was always saying, 'Somebody has to take care of all the assholes.' Boy, that would really get my mother going. She was so ashamed. They used to call her the hemorrhoid heiress. She didn't have a lot of time for us. My brother and I were basically raised by our maid, who came from Martinique."

"What does your brother do?"

"He's Joe Merchant," she said proudly.

"Your brother is Joe Merchant? You're kidding."

"Serious as a heart attack. His real name is Joe Kane, but he changed it when he moved to San Francisco."

"I flew a whole bunch of people up to his show last Saturday. I tried to get a ticket, but it was sold out."

She smiled. "Frank Bama, you should have met me last week."

• • •

We drove back to Key West under a starry sky, and Trevor moved close enough for me to put my arm around her. I drove to the Islander Drive-In, but neither of us was interested in the movie. We were making out in the front of my truck when the credits began to roll.

"*The Green Berets.* Oh, no," she said. We watched the first five minutes, and she added, "That's not the Vietnam I knew."

"Were you really in Vietnam?" I asked.

"Frank Bama, the first thing you better know about me is that I don't lie." She reached into my tub of popcorn, grabbed a handful, and ate while she talked. "When I turned twenty-one, I was supposed to get a big chunk of money from the trust, but my father was the executor, and he told me that first I had to visit the 'hot spots' of the world as a 'character builder.' God, he was full of clichés. But I wanted the money, so I went to Vietnam. I was in my show-business phase then—I thought I wanted to be a singer. When I checked into the Intercontinental Hotel in Saigon, Bob Hope and the Gold Diggers were staying there. I figured what the hell, maybe he could give me a few tips. So I set out to meet him."

"Yeah, right."

"It's the goddamn truth; cross my heart," Trevor said. "But I didn't get to meet him. I ate off his room-service tray one night in the hallway of the hotel, but that was the closest I got to him. Then I went on to Cambodia, where I nearly got killed, and when I got to Bangkok, I took a plane to Paris and used my inheritance to study painting at École des Beaux-Arts. This movie sucks. Is there any place around here to dance?"

• • •

We boogied until dawn at the Boca Chic Bar, and then she said she wanted to see my plane. I took her back to the hangar, and we made love for the first time—in the *Hemisphere Dancer.* In the morning, we kissed for a long time at the hangar door, and then she told me she had a boyfriend who was coming for the weekend from New Orleans.

"Leave him and move in here with me," I said.

"You're crazy."

I didn't deny it. The next week the boyfriend was gone, and I had a girlfriend and a cat named Toulouse.

• • •

From the first day, Trevor and I had a great time together. She flew with me on fish-spotting trips and charters when I had to take the *Hemisphere Dancer* south, and we traveled throughout the exotic islands of the Caribbean. Billy Cruiser let her use part of the hangar as a studio, and she created large oil paintings from the sketches she made when we were traveling. There was a good market for them in New Orleans, and we regularly packed them up and shipped them there. Once in a while her gallery would set up a show in some big city, and we'd fly there together for the opening.

Trevor was a painter, I was a pilot, and we were passionate, crazy, glorious lovers—but we didn't really talk. In all the years we were together, we never once said we loved each other. Years went by, and slowly things began to unravel. Fights became more frequent. So did flights. The honeymoon was over.

It all blew up one night at a party for her "art world" friends. I had invited a few of my fishing buddies, and after a few rum drinks, we slipped the guacamole from the deli tray and replaced it with hot Japanese mustard. We thought it was funny. Trevor didn't.

I got the silent treatment for almost a week, and that's when Trevor's mother called with the news that Joe had committed suicide. Our romance ended as quickly as it had begun. After she moved out, I called her repeatedly in New Orleans, but she never called me back. And then I heard she had a new boyfriend.

A job offer eventually came up in Brazil, and I took the old geographical heartbreak cure. I flew gold prospectors in and out of Sao Paulo and chased every shade of woman around the beaches of Rio, but it had taken years for me to shake Trevor Kane from my thoughts. I wasn't about to get sucked into that again, no matter what she wanted now. I knew I needed to separate my feelings from the facts—but in this case, the facts were as unsettling as the feelings: Trevor Kane was back, and she still had a powerful hold on me.

9

Want What You Have

Trevor was waiting at the hangar when I returned just after sunset.

"I need a drink," she said. She didn't seem angry anymore; she just seemed tired of it all.

I stood in the doorway and looked out at the red sky off toward the Yucatán Peninsula, wondering where the sunrise would find me. Billy had gone to town, and Hoagy was curled up under the wing of the J3 Cub, sound asleep.

Trevor walked up next to me and looked out at the runway. Wind swirled around the point and created tiny waves in the runway puddles, while out on the bay, whitecaps rolled into the mangroves and crashed on top of the ramp where I had landed earlier.

"Can I please tell you why I came down here?"

"Sure," I said. My anger had faded, and I could feel her body next to mine, tugging like a magnet. The familiar scent of coconut oil brought up a surge of old feelings, but I was determined to make them go away. "I could use a drink, too," I said. "Believe it or not, I still have a little DePaz."

I left the doorway and went over to the old Coldspot. I

brought out the rare bottle of rum and sliced a Spanish lime, dropping it into two glasses along with some ice cubes.

"I remember the last time you took me to St. Pierre," Trevor said softly.

We had stayed at the plantation above the hills of St. Pierre where the last of the DePaz family still made rum in the old factory powered by a waterwheel. I hadn't been back since.

When I turned around with the drinks, Trevor was studying the wall near the pay phone. An old Pan Am poster of the *Dixie Clipper* was thumbtacked above the phone, and a chart of the lower Keys was tacked over a collection of Snap-On Tool calendars dating back to 1980. All around the chart, there was a collage of old photographs: pictures of me, my friends, and other aviators who had flown through, and all kinds of planes—fast ones, slow ones, old ones, new ones, and wrecks. Several pictures showed Billy Cruiser when he had hair, and there was a whole collection of photos from the Black Cats' base in the Pacific with the old PBYs sitting on the ramp. The small photos framed a large black-and-white one of Billy and my dad standing in the cockpit of the *No-See-Um*, examining bullet holes in the windshield. Beneath the collage a banner read "Old Pictures of Young Warriors in Far-Off Lands."

Trevor smiled as she focused on the faded shot of a group of sailors gathered on the wing of a camouflaged seaplane. They were mooning the camera. In the corner of the photo someone had scribbled the words "VP-40, Cam Ranh Bay '68: The Wild Bunch."

She pointed to one of the rear ends. "I always liked that pose," she said lightly, and then she came across the tattered old stage pass stuck to the hangar door. It read "Joe Merchant—No Prisoners Tour 1978," and it was from the only time I'd ever seen Joe in real life. He'd been tripping through the entire concert. Trevor moved her finger around the pass in a circular motion and then came back and sat down in one of the vintage ready-room chairs. A set of dominoes was strung out in a long, crooked line on top of the lobster-trap table beside her, and when she gave the first piece a tap, they all collapsed.

I handed Trevor a glass, and she curled up and breathed in the vapors of the punch.

"Have a seat," she said, patting the worn leather of the adjacent chair.

I did. The smell of the leather, rum, and humid air relaxed me, and I lifted my glass. Trevor did the same, and when they touched with a chime, she said, "To answers."

"To answers," I repeated.

We drank from the glasses and waited for the burn to subside in our throats.

"What are the questions?" I asked.

"I'll come right to the point. I think Joe is still alive, and I have to find an old friend of his named Desdemona in Boomtown who can help me find him."

"Trevor, I hate to say it, but this sounds like one of Rudy's stories."

"I know, I know, but I can't help it. My mother jumped out of a boat, Frank. Just like Joe did. Then, out of the blue, I get a letter from this woman about Joe, and . . . I don't know. I think somebody up there is trying to tell me something. I can't explain it, really. But I feel so strongly about it. I know this all sounds crazy, but I've got to follow my instincts and find out."

She gulped down the last of her drink, and I took the glass and refilled it.

"Mother never really accepted the fact that Joe was dead, and now she's gone, too. Drowning seems to run in the family," she said bitterly. "It hurts. It hurts a lot."

"She never said anything to you?" I asked.

"Not a word. I was supposed to have been on the boat, but I canceled at the last minute. If I'd only gone . . ." She bit her lip, and tears welled up in her eyes. She took a couple of deep breaths and held up her hand for me to not move. "It's okay, Frank. This is just part of it."

Trevor took a letter out of her pocket and handed it to me. "This is what came the day they found my mother's boat."

I took the letter and began to read it slowly.

Trevor Kane, I knew your brother long ago and I feel I may see him again. Now there is someone looking for him on the other side. It's a lady, and she hasn't been there long. Could she be your mother? I am in contact with a being from another dimension and your brother's name has come up repeatedly in our sessions. Joe's work on Earth is not finished. Come to Boomtown. I need to

talk with you in person. Ask at the dock for Toosay, and
he will bring you to me.

                                        —Desdemona

"After Joe died, I just tried to forget about him," Trevor
said. "It was too painful, and then the sightings started and
fueled a whole school of weirdos who said they'd seen him
alive. I never took any of them seriously. I thought it was another cult thing like Elvis."

I held the letter in one hand and my glass in the other.
"Trevor, get a grip on yourself."

"Frank, that woman knows my mother is on the 'other
side' and says my brother is still alive. I want you to take me
to Boomtown to see her."

"Based on this?" I asked.

"I have to talk to her."

"What do you know about Boomtown?" I asked.

"Not much. But I do know it's not the kind of place a
woman should go alone—even a woman who went to Vietnam. I remember the stories you told me about the old days,
when it was a wild pirate town."

"It still is. Trevor, maybe Billy Cruiser can find another
bodyguard and another plane for you. I can't go. And I can't
stay here to help you work it out. Believe me, I'm not going
to be any good to anyone if they confiscate the *Dancer.*"

"Do you think it was easy for me to come down here and
see you—especially the way we left things?" she asked. I
didn't answer. "I need your help," she said insistently. *"Your*
help, not Billy's help. We had something—"

I interrupted her. "Trevor, I'm flat broke. I can't go flying
around the Caribbean. Hell, I've been running car gas in the
Dancer for a month. That trip to Havana got me just enough
money to have my plane painted and get a fake registration.
Billy's lending me his credit card for fuel."

"I'll make you a deal. If you take me to Boomtown first,
I'll pay your way to Alaska. And I'll throw in a bonus. In
case you've forgotten, I'm still the heiress of the asshole fortune. I have to go to Miami tomorrow and see Hackney about
Mom's will."

"Who the hell is Hackney?"

"Hackney Primstone III. He's my mother's third cousin—a
real sleazeball lawyer in Miami. He's the executor of Joe's

estate and my mother's estate. I have some money coming from my trust, and I have to talk to him about what to do with my mother's house and a lot of other things. I'm not looking forward to it. He's such a jerk."

She ran her fingers through her curls and took another sip of her drink. "And I'm serious about Joe. I really do think he's alive. Not in Cuba, but somewhere in Africa, maybe. The last few times I heard from him, he was traveling back and forth between London and Nairobi. I couldn't figure out if he'd finally gone over the edge. Joe and I argued a lot then, remember? I never told anybody, but he was keeping company with a band of trained killers."

"Mafia?" I asked.

"No, he'd run into a group of mercenaries in London who were working as bodyguards for a lot of the English rock bands then. That's how Joe got to Africa. After that, he was never the same. In his last letter, he told me he was giving all his money to charity. He'd met a man who had changed his life—a man he called the Colonel. They were setting up a trust fund to endow some African medical college. It sounded like he was trying to buy some peace of mind. I never heard a word from him after that."

"Why didn't you ever tell me any of this?"

"I didn't want to think about Joe any more than I had to at that point. You remember."

"Yeah, he was fucked up," I said softly.

"That's putting it mildly. But I let it all go. I let Joe go. I had to. I didn't give a damn about the money. I didn't even want to speculate. I figured that some deserving people in Africa would at least be helped by Joe's trust fund, and in a way, that helped me. That's where I left it until just the other day, right after my mother's memorial service.

"I knew I had to get away, or I was going to go nuts, so I got a ticket for Bermuda. I wasn't planning to come here. On the way to the airport, I was reading the *Post* and came across this story about a mercenary who had tried to establish his own kingdom on a tiny island off the coast of East Africa. His name was Colonel Cairo. Apparently, he'd disappeared in the process of being deported. The story went on to say that he was tied to every major spy network in the world—the French, the South Africans, the CIA. I had this awful feeling that there was no medical college, but that Joe's Colonel and this Colonel Cairo were one and the same. So I called Hackney and asked him about my brother's trust and if he'd ever heard of Colonel Cairo."

"What did he say?"

"That he couldn't give out that kind of information."

"Nice guy."

"Then I read Desdemona's letter again. That's when I had the feeling that Joe was still alive. I have no idea how to find Colonel Cairo, but I do know how to find Desdemona. I have to put this thing to rest. I changed my flight from Bermuda to Key West and came here. Frank, there were too many co-incidences."

She reached into her pocket again, and this time she pulled out a piece of wadded-up tracing paper and unfolded it. "There's one more thing," she said and handed it to me.

I took the thin piece of paper, but it took a moment before I could read the name that was outlined by smudged pencil marks. It was her father's name, and it must have come from the Vietnam Memorial. I'd been to the Wall and knew that it's a common thing to see people rubbing names from the granite as tears stream down their faces. I have always thought that all those old farts in Washington who so easily make war should be required to walk by that slab of black stone to and from work.

"That came in the mail from my mother the same day as Desdemona's letter. No note, no nothing, just Dad's name. God knows what she was thinking when she sent it."

Trevor took the paper back and walked slowly over to the *Hemisphere Dancer.* She held out her hand and ran her fingers down the skin toward the nose and gently touched the propeller blades that hung below the wing.

"It must be nice to feel your hands on the wheel and know you're in control. I can't seem to accomplish that feat." She looked down at the wrinkled tracing paper in her hand and began to cry. Her words became difficult. "Frank, I had no one else to turn to. I'm starting to feel as if these scraps of paper are the only evidence I have that I ever had a family."

The empty glass slipped from her hand and shattered on the concrete floor. Hoagy barked instinctively.

"Hush," I called to the dog. I scooped Trevor up in my arms and carried her back to the chair where I'd been sitting. I sat down and held her tight while she cried her heart out.

I wanted to help, but I didn't know what to do or say. I had been to war, survived the jungle, had been in the most unimaginable situations flying the bush, and had been able to sort through whatever was thrown my way, but in a situation like this one I was utterly fucking helpless. I stroked Trevor's hair and rocked her, and just let her cry. Her face was buried in my shoulder, and I could feel the moisture of her tears through my T-shirt.

"I think—I understand—a little better now—why you chose the plane over me," she said between sobs. "I can't respond like your plane, can I, Frank?"

I had no answer for that one, not one that I could get out at the time, anyway. "I'll take you to Boomtown," I said.

. . .

Darkness had blanketed the Lone Palm Airport, and Trevor was still nestled in my arms. As I held her, I realized my world was getting more complicated by the minute. I was changing channels. The trip to Cuba now seemed like ancient history, and Alaska had gone from the front burner to the back woodshed of exotic places to be visited someday. Out in the night, strangers were coming for my airplane, I was on my way to the last modern-day pirate stronghold in the Caribbean, and my old girlfriend was now asleep in my arms. I leaned down and rested my chin in her hair. I took a deep breath, and one of Billy's codgerisms popped out of my mouth before I even thought about what I was saying.

"Huh?" Trevor said in a sleepy voice.

"Want what you have," I repeated.

. . .

When Billy Cruiser finally walked back into the hangar he was whistling, but when he saw Trevor still asleep in my arms, he started to tiptoe across the floor. "I don't guess you'll be needin' me to fix that heater now," he whispered.

In a low voice, I told him what had happened. "Since you did such a bang-up job with your life, would you like to run mine for a while?" I asked softly.

Billy patted me on the head and laughed. "It may not seem like it now, but you're doin' the right thing, son. Take the girl to find her brother. Besides, Alaska ain't goin' nowhere fast."

You
Can't Hide
Your Mayan
Eyes

10

Desdemona's Building a Rocket Ship

Desdemona was a woman with a mission. She was up with the sun. There was no lounging in bed or drifting off to catch a few more winks. She was building a rocket ship.

It was not exactly the line of work you would expect a former rock 'n' roll background singer and part-time cookie baker to be tackling. She had made Ds in science back in her school days, but as of late she had become hopelessly entwined in some kind of puzzle that now had her aiming at the stars.

Her launchpad and home lay in a picturesque bay called Frenchman's Lagoon on Little Lorraine Island, one of seven small islands off the windward coast of Hispaniola near the border of Haiti and the Dominican Republic. The seven islands were known as the Sleeping Beauties, and Boomtown was situated on the largest one, not far from Little Lorraine.

It was a sometimes-dangerous place but a tolerable neighborhood, which made her project less suspicious. She was just another wacko who had been out in the sun too long. In the local Boomtown watering hole called the Polar Bar, space travelers occupied the same stools as smugglers, scam artists, runaways, felons, and tourists. A trip to the Pleiades was no more special than the ferryboat ride to Cap Haitien, and the Pleiades were where Desdemona was headed eventually. Boomtown had built its reputation on a solid foundation of lunacy.

The rocket ship hadn't flown yet, and for now it was still a weird houseboat made from an old airplane fuselage. She had named it the *Cosmic Muffin,* and her friend and first mate, Toosay, was helping her work on it. At present, the boat served as Desdemona's home, bake shop, and laboratory.

It was just after dawn now, and the early morning sun spilled through the porthole and lit her cabin. The bizarre dream had come back sometime that night. She reached for her glasses, and once again she read the most recent message she'd recorded in her ship's log:

> *Woman under water*
> *No place to go*
> *Someone tell her daughter*
> *Where is Joe?*

Joe Merchant was a ghost from her past, and he had popped back into her life like a piece of toast. In the dream he was in a bubble, floating above the ocean, and he was trying to get out. He would push and shove, and the bubble would move, but it never broke. She took this as a sign that Joe was trying to contact her, but she didn't understand it. Desdemona wondered what—if anything—this dream had to do with the rocket ship and the messages from the sky.

She splashed her naked body with Skin So Soft to chase away the morning mosquitoes and went up to the dock to do her daily yoga routine. She stretched, breathed, and meditated, then ended her morning ritual with a headstand. Desdemona counted to ten backward and felt a throbbing pressure inside her body as blood from her toes went charging through her circulatory system to her inverted heart and brain. It was always good to feed the old brain cross signals every once in a while.

It had been a week since she had heard anything from the aliens, but the moon was on the wane, and she was about to start her period—which was always a good time for weirdness. The dream had gotten her excited, and in a few minutes Toosay would be there to begin his workday on the launchpad. He was a small Indian with brown leather skin, and was her trusted first mate and the only other person who knew of her intended destination. This morning they were taking the *Cosmic Muffin* to the smallest of the Beauties, Petite Place, where the Healing Hole was located.

Desdemona went below and slipped into her faded blue jumpsuit. It had been a present from the boys in the Boomtown boatyard. "Build Spaceships Now" was written in purple script across the back. Maneuvering through the ship to the galley, she poured herself a glass of fresh passion-fruit juice from the icebox. The bittersweet nectar tasted like the tropics. She hoped they had passion fruit in the Pleiades.

   • • •

Toosay steered the *Cosmic Muffin* up the channel until they reached a small dock on Petite Place where they tied up. He got out his spinning rod and cast at the nervous water on the edge of a small fault. This was a ritual they performed once every week.

"This shouldn't take long, Toosay," Desdemona told him.

"I'll be here," Toosay replied.

Desdemona strolled along the path of crushed oyster shells that led away from the dock to the other side of the island, listening to the calls of nesting birds concealed in the natural canopy of mangrove branches above her head. The ground was cold and hard under her feet. She was glad when it gave way to the warm, soft sand of the old Indian path that crossed the salt pond and led to the Healing Hole.

Legends abounded as to the origin of these warm waters that seemed to have bubbled up since before Columbus's time. Henri Christophe, the Haitian king, had often come to the islands to submerge himself in the magic waters during his short, sad reign. Indians from the village on Little Lorraine Island and occasional visitors from Boomtown walked across the Promenade Flats at low tide to soak away their physical and mental pains.

Small lizards rustled through the leaves on the path before her, running here and there. She thought for a moment that her recent years had been spent just like the lizards'—scurrying around in circles that had brought her to this spot.

Desdemona reached the clearing and sat on the familiar petrified rosewood stump at the water's edge. She thought about the dream, but she couldn't get a grasp on it. Was Joe Merchant a ghost trying to contact her from the other side?

Or was he alive? She had written Joe's sister a letter, hoping Trevor could shed some light on the messages about a brother and a mother and what really happened to Joe. Desdemona had never met any of Joe's family during the years she and Joe had worked together in San Francisco.

She took off her jumpsuit and hung it on the branch of a buttonwood tree and grabbed the black rubber inner tube leaning against the trunk. She eased herself into the water. After hoisting her big ass into the tube, she paddled to the middle of the pond, where she folded her tiny hands across her large stomach and twiddled her thumbs.

This was where the messages came. No telephone, answering machine, or fax. The messages came from another source. Desdemona figured she was a human antenna. The inner tube grounded her. She felt the pull of the Pleiades as she sat there naked, wondering if this whole thing were some kind of bad cosmic joke that the aliens were playing on flawed humans. She floated silently for about five minutes. Then the ringing started in her ears. Another message was coming through. Desdemona was channeling voices she referred to as the Generators.

> *If you figure out that you don't*
> *need to figure it all out, you are*
> *finally getting your shit together.*

Desdemona called this a "floater" message. She had come across them before. In the order of the universe, the Generators had told her, words of perpetual wisdom floated around like soap bubbles and popped into your head unexpectedly. They were like test patterns that came before the real message arrived. She continued to wait, and then a floater "riddle" came through.

> *The ship is here,*
> *You have the paddle.*
> *Find your maiden,*
> *Now skedaddle.*

Desdemona let out a big sigh. The riddles were important, but it often took her weeks to figure them out. Who was the maiden? How would she know? She closed her eyes and got ready for the real message. When it came, it would come heavily and fast. She didn't have to wait long.

Greetings, Earth Mother. It is a time of history repeating itself, and you will be a part of the new history. When your gift comes, use it well. It is a treasure for another time, but beware—the road is not smooth. Because you are human, the big picture remains a mystery. You are trapped by your narrow views. Beldar and the Conehead family know more universal truths than your elected leaders do. Till next time.

Desdemona slapped at the water with her hands and yelled to the sky. "Can't you people be a little more goddamn specific?"

There would be no more messages today; Desdemona could feel it. She toweled off and got dressed, then walked the short distance to the beautiful pink beach on the north end of the island. She was trying to make some sense of it all.

Whatever it was, it was exciting stuff. She saw a little sloop come around the point, and she stared for a moment, watching the boat move effortlessly across the flats toward the lagoon. It was time to go back to the launchpad and get to work. Soon they would fly.

11

Fruitcakes in the Galley, Fruitcakes on the Street

Desdemona walked back to the *Cosmic Muffin*, singing a song she had made up about her life and her boat:

> *Fruitcakes in the galley,*
> *Fruitcakes on the street,*
> *Walkin' naked through the crosswalk*
> *In the middle of the week.*
> *Half-baked cookies in the oven,*
> *Half-baked humans on the bus,*
> *There's a little bit of fruitcake*
> *In every one of us.*

Her thoughts were still on Joe Merchant. It had all started back in the glorious sixties, when countless sons and daughters of well-intentioned parents had forsaken all advice and counsel and had run off to join the circus called rock 'n' roll. Desdemona ran to San Francisco and put her singing voice and baking talents to work. Her band was called Cats in Heat. They played the club scene around the Bay Area to a steady following, and Desdemona subsidized her singing income with her baking talents. Her pot brownies were said to have been the best in Haight-Ashbury at the time.

She had met Joe Merchant in San Anselmo one night at the Lion's Share before he hit the big time. Her boyfriend, Freddy Purvis, was the lead singer of a group called Freddy and the Fishsticks, and they shared the bill that night with Joe.

Joe Merchant was one of the most gifted and demented people she had ever met. He was ruled by the reptilian side of his brain. One minute he was the life of the party, and the next minute he would be trying to rip somebody's head off. Joe was the tower card of the tarot deck personified.

He was the hottest new singer to come out of the Bay Area in years, and when his first album with his band, the Express, came out, it hit the top of the charts. Joe Merchant went from saloon singer to superstar. He was dark-haired, good-looking, wild, and crazy, and he loved Desdemona's brownies.

Desdemona and Freddy tied the knot that summer in a hot tub near Mt. Tamalpais, and Joe Merchant sang at their chaotic wedding. After that, when The Joe Merchant Express played, Cats in Heat always opened. Desdemona became road shrink, healer, and chief brownie maker to the collection of gypsy rockers. She was the perfect band mother—big, jolly, and warmhearted.

Then came the infamous Peace Train Tour. It was the brain-dead child of a slick San Francisco impresario named Bunk Whacker. Young Bunk had always wanted to be a rock star, but he had no talent for writing or playing. Instead, he bought his way into the love generation, running a local head paper called *The Whacker*. He was seen with all the right people and went to all the right parties and finally came upon an idea that would give him the glamour he so desperately sought. The grand adventure was called "Bunk Whacker's Peace Train Tour."

Bunk funded the whole extravaganza. The tour was to circle the world on trains, playing love-ins along the way. Besides the musicians, Bunk had hired animal trainers, clowns, and tattoo artists to amuse the crowds before the shows, and he sent out invitations to a variety of pill pushers, pot dealers, and local chemists. The tour was to be made into a movie—written, produced, and directed by Bunk Whacker.

The train pulled out of Oakland on a rainy June day, and the crowd of press, fans, and curious observers was treated to the delightful sight of Joe Merchant and a groupie fucking on the platform of the last car.

The whole thing fell apart as quickly as it had started. The peace train became a war zone. The tour was subjected to the worst summer weather in years and played to fields of muddy hippies. Bunk Whacker paraded through the train in his director's outfit with a bullhorn, constantly shouting orders which nobody obeyed. He was arrested on the Fourth of July in Boise, Idaho, for soliciting a minor in a Greyhound bus station, and the family lawyers came to bail him out of jail. He had been disinherited by his mother, news he didn't share with the rest of his "brothers and sisters."

In the middle of all the insanity, Desdemona had evolved as one of the few people who could handle the pace, but the psychedelic circus finally even got to her. She and Freddy were divorced in Niagara Falls just before he pulled out of the tour and took off for Australia. Cats in Heat broke up onstage one night when the drummer and guitar player had a knock-down-and-drag-out fight and rolled into the audience—which gave them a standing ovation.

Desdemona stayed on and went to work as a background singer for Joe Merchant. He needed all the help he could get at that point. He had taken up with a gorgeous acid freak and was tripping his brains out twenty-four hours a day. He got busted in the Toronto airport trying to carry a shopping bag full of mushrooms through security, and the tour was canceled. Bunk Whacker ran off to Sweden and tried to have a sex-change operation so he could rename himself Bunny. It didn't work.

Desdemona saw the cards on the table. Her tenure in the music business was over, so she packed her bags and baking pans. Unlike Lot's wife, she never looked back. She bought a dilapidated Kharman Ghia convertible and slowly made her way south from Toronto, living like a gypsy in communes and friends' homes. Eventually she ran out of money and gas in the mountains of West Texas. Then she got a job in a Mexican café near the MacDonald Observatory, a place that drew people who wanted to study the stars. That was where her transformation began.

Desdemona had fluttered on the rim of the cosmic consciousness since the day she bought her first bottle of patchouli oil back in Haight-Ashbury. In Texas she learned to make stone-ground flour tortillas from a cook named Olinda and got hooked on the heavens. She applied for a job at the observatory as a telescope operator and was hired; it required no scientific skills. She was like a chauffeur to the scientists. When they wanted to look at something, she pointed the telescope at their subject. But when she was alone, she gazed for hours into the distant heavens.

Years passed, and Desdemona became infatuated with the Pleiades and Orion and the Gemini twins. She studied the myths and legends of the heavens and spent every spare minute with her eye glued to the mirrors of the telescope. She wondered how she could find a way to reach the stars. She continued to work part-time at the restaurant, and one day when she picked up the newspaper, two stories on the front page rang her bell.

The first was about Bunk Whacker, and it made her laugh. He had opened an amusement park called Cat World across from the Disney complex in Orlando. Disgruntled parents leaving the Magic Kingdom could vent their frustrations by feeding live mice in Mickey Mouse outfits to large, ravenous cats. The Disney Corporation was suing him.

The other story gave her a shock. Joe Merchant had committed suicide. He had left the country for England and then had wound up in Africa, involved with some humanitarian trip. The paper said he had jumped off the back of a cruise ship in the Black Sea. It sounded like a place Joe would pick.

Desdemona spent the night at the telescope, looking out at the stars. Real stars were constant and confident of their place and time—unlike the human variety, who seemed so fragile and in need of help. There was something out there calling to her, but she didn't know what it was.

After so much time in the barren landscape of Texas, a job opened up at the giant radio telescope in Arecibo, Puerto Rico. Desdemona had always dreamed of the tropics, and soon she was on her way to the "island of wayward astronomers." It was in the lush sinkholes and foothills of Puerto Rico that her whole life changed. Raoul was his name, and women were his game. He was the head operator at the observatory and a macho man with all the trimmings—muscles, mustache, tight pants.

More than a year had passed since that incredible night under the giant radio telescope in Puerto Rico. Raoul had taken her down the long, winding path that led to the valley below the thousand-foot dish that probed the universe. He had brought a thermos full of margaritas and told her she had to see the full moon from this viewpoint. While tree frogs and crickets played their symphony, Desdemona and Raoul looked up through the opening in the giant dish, up over the antenna suspended from the three towers eight hundred feet above them.

Desdemona was in a trance. She felt like a small branch of a giant tree—insignificant, but still connected to the massive trunk and roots. Maybe it was the margaritas, or maybe it was the moon; whatever, Desdemona soon found herself horizontal, in a lovelock with Raoul. He thrust away at her, and she was excited and felt as if Raoul were some kind of god.

Then the messages started to arrive.

"Find your ship, find your oar, the Healing Hole will tell you more," Desdemona moaned and wailed in disbelief.

Raoul took her sounds and rantings as evidence that he had overcome yet another woman with his lovemaking. He was glowing with macho self-admiration until the beam of the security guard's flashlight put him in the spotlight. Suddenly he was groveling on his knees, stark naked, pleading with the guard not to report them.

That's how it all started. Desdemona had gone back down under the dish the next night, but there were no voices. She looked up at the fuzzy outline of the Milky Way and wondered about what felt like some mysterious celestial destiny.

• • •

Desdemona was not really upset when she was fired. She didn't know if it had been the sex or the mysterious message, but she was as tranquil now as she had ever been in her life. The change, she knew, had come for a reason.

She decided to use her savings to open a bake shop in the British Virgin Islands. Sitting in the San Juan airport one Sunday waiting for her flight to Tortola, a photo in the *Miami Herald* caught her eye. As soon as she saw the picture, the voices went off again in her head. "Find your ship, find your oar."

The story told the history of an unusual houseboat that had been seized in a drug bust. The boat consisted of an aircraft fuselage sitting on a narrow hull. In the newspaper photo, it was tied up at the Coast Guard dock on Government Cut. It had been seized in a marijuana raid several months before and was due to be auctioned off that afternoon. The story went on to describe the strange craft. The fuselage was from an old Boeing 307 that had been built before World War II as Howard Hughes's private plane.

Hughes had flown the plane only five hundred hours. He had intended to take it around the world, but the war came along, and the plane was retired to a remote tract of the Miami airport known as "corrosion corner." It sat there for fifteen years until it was bought and turned into a private yacht by an eccentric entrepreneur who died before he ever set foot on the bizarre boat, and a series of owners had come and gone after him. The latest master of the vessel was named Richard "Tuna" Robitussun, a convicted smuggler.

Desdemona changed her flight destination from Tortola to Miami and made the auction in time. At the end of the day, her savings were exhausted and she was out of work, but she was the owner of the strangest-looking boat in the Caribbean. She promptly named it the *Cosmic Muffin*. It was all the rocket ship Desdemona could afford at the time, and she wondered how it would ever fly, but she trusted her instincts the same way she trusted the stars.

All her life she had known about boats, having grown up on the Eastern Shore of the Chesapeake Bay where her father had run a ferry that serviced the remote islands. Her baking skills came from her mother, an English war bride who owned a small bakery and tearoom near Cape Charles and created her scones like tiny pieces of art.

Desdemona spent the night on her vessel and thought back to the many trips she had made with her father to the islands. The next morning she bought a logbook and provisions for the trip. She found an old Plath sextant in a marine junk shop on the Miami River and made her way on the *Cosmic Muffin* to Ft. Lauderdale, where she found books on celestial navigation and crystal power. She came across references to crystal engines and chambers that drew upon the proper amounts of yin and yang to transport people to the far reaches of the galaxy. By the end of the week, she was shooting star lines and sun lines, marveling at her results. She was discovering, firsthand, the incredible order of the universe.

Her destination was a mystery, but so was life. She had found her ship, and now—somewhere out in the vast expanse of the Caribbean—there was a mysterious oar. As she passed under the Seventeenth Street Bridge, an old fisherman looked at the strange craft below and turned to his buddy, who was baiting a hook. "Fred," he yelled, "check out that boat. Looks like a goddamn giant dildo."

12

Where Has All the
Time Gone?

Where had all the time gone? It seemed like only yesterday that Desdemona had started her adventurous voyage through the islands, and now she was celebrating her one-year anniversary as a rocket-ship owner. Certainly there were days when she wondered what the hell she was doing, but then again, too much had been happening to discount the possibility of space travel in the *Cosmic Muffin*.

The rain had been coming down for two days, and work on the ship's engine had to take a backseat to plugging leaks in the fuselage. The low pressure didn't help the energy level, either. Desdemona had decided to spend the day in her comfortable bunk with her favorite books and do a little reflecting.

The cabin was cool, and the sound of raindrops landing in the lagoon was perfect background music. The ship's log was propped up in her lap, and she opened it to the first entry, an inscription she'd made the night before she had left Ft. Lauderdale—a year ago to the day.

Most people want to know where they are going.
I think it is a far better idea to always know
where you have been. —Desdemona

She read on:

From the Log of the Cosmic Muffin

DAY ONE

The Maiden voyage—Ft. Lauderdale to Rudderville

The weather today was picture perfect and we (my boat
and me) crossed the the Gulf Stream without a hitch, listening to James Taylor. Waves were in some other part
of the ocean today, and the swells were as smooth as
baby butts and made the boat sway gently. It is a good
thing. I believe in her former life with Mr. Hughes, the
Cosmic Muffin was a very stable airplane. But as a boat,
I am afraid she may be lacking the stability required for
offshore cruising.

I was sure glad to see the shallow green waters of the
Bahama Banks. Heading for Rudderville in the southern
Exumas, take on fuel and if the weather is fair, head out
for Tortola. My plan is to hook up with a UFO somewhere out in the Atlantic. If not, there's always the bake
shop. You always need a plan B.

Desdemona browsed through the pages, stopping at the
passages that set off her memory. This is better than having
a VCR, she thought.

DAY TWO

Altered course from offshore due to the heavy winds and
cruised the Exuma Islands, creeping slowly to the southeast. Anchored last night in Pipe's Creek and practiced
my star sights, hoping to attract a passing UFO overhead. No contact, but some dazzling shooting stars were
enough to keep my confidence up.

DAY FIVE

I have come to the conclusion that the only way the Cosmic Muffin will ever fly is if a giant UFO lifts the ship

on board and takes it somewhere, though I have found a very interesting mention about crystal power in this bizarre book about sailing through the Devil's Triangle. If there are space creatures out there, this sounds like the place to meet them.

DAY TEN

Have kept a constant vigil, but there has been no contact with spaceships and no more messages. Maybe it was just Raoul's fucking. Thought about him a lot last night. Will be in Rudderville tonight. I haven't gotten drunk in a long time, and I think I just might tonight. Island boys love large white women, and that's fine with me.

Landfall in Rudderville: The natives came out in droves to stare at the Cosmic Muffin. Some laughed and carried on, obviously making reference to it looking like a big dick, but others just stared silently with respect like they know something I don't.

Took on fuel and supplies and went to the Dogfish Bar and Supper Club, which is the hot spot in Rudderville. Then danced the night away at a disco called the Sardine Can doing the limbo with some cab drivers.

I made it back to the boat sometime around two and fell fast asleep. It was still dark when I was awakened by splashing sounds around the boat. I was still a little out of focus from my night ashore. I heard someone call my name from the water and looked for a boat, but there was none. That's when I saw the white dolphin. Its body was half out of the water and it swam slowly up to the boat.

"Desdemona," it said, "my name is Albion. How does your rocket ship fly?"

Desdemona put the log down and stretched her shoulders, thinking about the encounter with the dolphin. She went to the galley and pulled a Cadbury bar from the icebox and returned to her reading.

DAY ELEVEN

Still no UFOs, but I have run into a most weird series of

events that makes me think Rod Serling knew more than he was telling us.

I wrote off the dream about the talking fish and managed to work through my hangover with lots of water and chocolate bars. I loaded my supplies, and I was on my way by dark. I was eating a can of tunafish, watching the stars overhead, when I saw a dolphin jump across my bow, not once but several times. Then I heard someone yell, "Hey tuna breath. Don't you know you're killing dolphins when you eat that shit?"

I dropped the can of tuna, brought the boat to a halt, and wallowed in the rollers. I shone by spotlight out, and I couldn't believe it. The same white dolphin I'd seen the night before was there again. I rubbed my eyes, pinched my skin, and shut off the light.

From the darkness, the voice called out, "I really am here."

I know it sounds crazy, but the goddamn dolphin looked familiar. I turned the light back on quickly, and there he was. Then it came to me. "You're the dolphin in that children's book. The one that flies. You're fictitious," I said.

The dolphin swam right up to the boat again. "And you are a Mayan," he told me.

A Mayan—holy shit. This could be it. We drifted and talked together for nearly an hour on the calm seas, and then it dawned on me to get my log book. How often do you get the chance to take notes on your conversation with a dolphin?

Excerpts from Notes on Albion

ALBION: Human beings are a bit off center. You weren't fully developed. What is happening to you has to do with the crystal power, but right now reception is very poor in this part of the universe thanks to your species. The only way your ancestors can contact you is through your dream body. Having any interesting dreams lately?

ME: Am I really awake? Are you real?

ALBION: I am as flawed as you, my dear. I just have a

few different memory chips, that's all. I am a
messenger from the painters of the universe.

ME: Who are they?

ALBION: When they are ready, they will reveal themselves. All I can tell you is they all don't paint
on canvas. Space is their easel. Volcanoes are
their drums. Peals of thunder are their voices.
Stuff like that.

ME: Was it them I heard in Puerto Rico?

ALBION: Let's get one thing straight, sister. It wasn't
the Puerto Rican guy at the observatory who
made you see fireworks. Your planet here is a
far outpost. Your activity as a race makes a lot
of people up there nervous. (Note: Albion
tilted his bottle-shaped nose and gestured up
at the sky.) You guys are in fact pretty primitive. Warlike species don't get too far. Their
energy is all channeled toward the wrong
things. That is why you are only observed and
rarely visited. There is a difference. You look
a little bewildered. Is this too much for you?

ME: It's just a little strange, that's all. A fish is telling
me the secrets of the universe.

ALBION: Dolphin.

ME: Right.

ALBION: I have to go now, but you will be getting
more messages, and you will find someone
who will take you to your true destination.

ME: I am going to Tortola to bake cookies.

ALBION: Not.

Desdemona smiled, flipping forward in the logbook. The
Albion pages were worn from all the times she had thumbed
through them.

DAY FIFTEEN

I am alone again, still trying to convince myself that I
am not going insane. I read a few books about sailors

alone at sea on long voyages. It seems they all found imaginary voices or spirits to talk to, but they didn't have any proof of their conversations. But my notes don't make me feel any better. I guess I'll have to go with the flow. Besides, I have a long trip ahead of me.

Stopped at N. Caicos for fuel and ice. Navigated all the way to northwest coast of Puerto Rico by sextant and was only three minutes off my dead-reckoning arrival time. Daddy would be proud. Somehow I have a feeling that Tortola is not my final destination on this voyage.

DAY SEVENTEEN

All good things must come to an end, and the weather finally tapped me on the shoulder and reminded me to get my head out of the cosmos and my ass back aboard my ship. Approached the north end of the Virgin Islands and identified the silhouette of Jost Van Dyke. Headed for the leeward side of the island. Lined up the lights of the village on shore with the flashing red light that marked the natural breakwater of the reef and slipped into the protected harbor and dropped anchor.

I had been at the wheel for nearly twelve hours and was exhausted. Hit the bunk to catch a few winks and await the light of dawn before making my approach up the Sir Francis Drake Channel. Was awakened by a rumble thirty minutes later and went outside to see what was happening.

At first I thought the aliens had finally come, but then my glee turned to alarm. I saw the hills of the island illuminated by a lightning flash. The lights of the nearby village were shadowed by a storm that came out of nowhere. The terrific force of the winds caused by the downdraft blew the torrential rain in sheets and swung the Cosmic Muffin in a full circle on the anchor line. It reminded me of that childhood game called crack the whip. Then I felt the jerk as the anchor line parted. It threw me to the deck, but I managed to crawl along the rail and slip through the hatch.

My rocket ship was adrift in the lagoon and was at the mercy of the howling wind. I could hear the waves breaking over the coral heads of the reef, but I couldn't see them. Rain pounded the boat, and the giant anvil-shaped cloud of the thunderstorm obscured the moon and stars. I steered by instinct, and I prayed my course would take me through the cut in the reef. I did not want to hear the crunch of wood meeting coral.

I let out a big sigh of relief when the Cosmic Muffin finally started to roll heavily. It meant I was in deep water, and I preferred to take my chances there. The wind began to settle as the thunderstorm let up. A lightning flash lit the sea for an instant, and I got a quick glimpse of what I thought was another boat. I flicked on the spotlight and moved it back and forth, and the beam reached out across the bow into the night.

It was a small sailboat with a broken mast and was barely afloat. It kept disappearing into the troughs of the waves. The spotlight flickered off and on, and I banged the handle. The beam relit, and I found the boat again. This time it was only about twenty feet off the starboard bow. Another lightning flash clearly showed a human figure stretched out in the nearly submerged boat.

I dragged the man from the boat just before it sank, and I carried him below. He had the weatherbeaten look of an old fisherman. There were abysmal scars on the outsides of his index fingers where lines attached to sounding fish had probably cut deep into his flesh. He was waterlogged and very weak but managed to open his clear brown eyes. He whispered, "I have not spoken since da death of my family in da great storm. If I am talking, I must be dead. Are you an angel?"

That made me smile. I told him, "No, I'm just another lost soul like you."

"What is your name?" he asked me.

"Desdemona," I said. "You rest for a while, and we'll talk later. I have some work to do."

Desdemona smiled, remembering her first day with Toosay. After she'd secured the boat, she went back to check on the old man. Somehow he'd gotten the old black-and-white TV to work and was tuned in to the PBS station in San Juan. He was staring, mesmerized, at Big Bird on "Sesame Street" as if he were some kind of deity. Desdemona finally got his attention.

"I have some coffee and chocolate and brandy here. Would you like some?"

"Oh, yes, ma'am. And maybe if you could spare some of doze cookies over dere, I would be most happy."

Desdemona handed him two of the cookies and a large Cadbury fruit-and-nut bar and turned off the television.

"Where does da big bird come from?" he asked.

"New York. It's a nice place to visit, but you wouldn't want to live there. So where do you come from?"

That was all the old man needed. He chomped on the candy bar, then went for one whole cookie and stuffed it into his mouth like a chipmunk. He chewed for about a minute, then took a big breath. "Truly delicious, truly delicious, praise da Lord. I am called Toosay, and I come from Little Lorraine Island. It is a small island near Boomtown. I am a Carib Indian and a fisherman. Do you know of my ancestors? Dey were da fiercest people on earth."

"Yes, I'm sure they ate a couple of my ancestors," Desdemona said. She poured him a cup of coffee and placed the brandy bottle next to him.

"But dat's all past now. Anyway, it was said by da old people dat da flesh of da whites had no taste." He laughed and took a sip of the warm coffee.

"That's comforting."

"I come to Little Lorraine Island from Dominica to fish wid my fadder a long time ago. We lived in a small village on da Frenchman's Lagoon. Pretty water and lots of fish. I am a boat engine man, too. Work on da motors for people in Boomtown." His old face turned into a sad mask, and he went silent for a moment.

"Da big storm took it all away. I be a widow man now. Hurricane took my family, took da village, lots of people drownded. Island was a sea bottom. Two days I sat in da top of a tree till some army men come and pull me down. I was plenty scared in da storm, and when I find my family is all gone, I plenty sad, too. Too sad to say anyting, too sad to answer stupid questions. I just fish and work on da motors, waiting to die so I can see my family.

"One night on da full moon, a voice wake me up in da middle of da night. I tought it was a dream. It say to go and find da storm. I tought it was da voice of God sending me out to sea to be eat up by anodder storm so I can find my family on da udder side. I was tree days to sea when I get too weak to look for storms anymore. I fell asleep, and den I wake up on dis boat. It is a strange boat."

"A strange boat indeed, Toosay. You rest now."

"But ma'am, I don't want to die no mo', I want to go home. I don't want to be no mo' bodder. I feel much better with cookies and chocolate and liquor in me. I will be on my way if you could give me a hand to my boat."

Desdemona bent down and took Toosay's small hand.

"It sank in the storm, Toosay, but I'll take you home."

Toosay covered his eyes and then just nodded his head up and down. "Tank you, ma'am. You may not tink you are an angel, but you are."

•   •   •

Desdemona pulled out the big chart of the Lesser Antilles and asked Toosay to show her his island. It was the first chart Toosay had ever seen, and he stared in wonder at all the islands laid out before him.

"We are here," Desdemona said and pointed to Jost Van Dyke.

Toosay went silent and studied the chart for a long time. "I don't reads too well, ma'am, but I be lookin' for da shape of da island."

"What does it look like?"

"It is in da shape of a long oar."

Desdemona looked down at the chart, and goose pimples chilled her spine. Toosay had a difficult time finding his home, but finally he jabbed his bent finger down and smiled. "I found da oar."

Desdemona looked back at the chart and smiled. "Me too." Then she turned Big Bird back on, and Toosay fell asleep.

DAY TWENTY

Made a damage assessment before crossing the Anegada Passage. I must have brushed the reef in the storm and separated a seam, for I was taking in a good bit of water. Toosay checked the engine and told me there was a boatyard in Boomtown where we could haul out and check the damage.

Listened to weather radio from San Juan and all indications were for a good stretch of weather. Crossed the passage in fourteen hours, and Toosay jabbered on. He rigged a hand line off the stern of the Cosmic Muffin and caught a huge dorado which he filleted and cooked when we anchored up near Dog Island. I made an impromptu dessert cobbler out of canned peaches and Bisquick, and we shared a bottle of red wine.

Toosay told all the stories he knew, and then he started to repeat them. I told him about the talking dolphin and the voice I had heard, and I told him the part about finding the boat and now the oar. All that was left for me to find was the Healing Hole. Two days later he led me into Frenchman's Lagoon. The Cosmic Muffin had made it, leaks and all, across the Caribbean Sea. Next time I can make it alone with all the local information I now have in my head. I learned the names of his dead family, the names of the surviving villagers, the history of Boomtown, the name of each flat and channel that surrounds the island, and now he knows every character on Sesame Street.

It was still dark when we docked at a small island Toosay called Petite Place. He took me by the hand and led me along an oyster-shell path through the little Indian village and then into the jungle. "Where are we going?" I asked. Toosay went mute again. We went down a sandy path that cut across a salt pond, and he led me through the trees.

"You have to close your eyes now," Toosay said, "and promise not to peek. I have a surprise for you, missus." I stumbled behind him till he told me to stop. I opened my eyes. "I tink you are looking for dis, no?"

We were in a clearing. I looked down into the aquamarine depths of a clear freshwater spring and saw my reflection. "It's da Healing Hole," Toosay said. "Go ahead, jump in."

My ears started to ring like they had under the giant dish in Puerto Rico, and the voices were laughing. Then they said, "Welcome to the launchpad."

"Can I ask someting of you, missus?" Toosay said. I was still reveling in the discovery of the Healing Hole and splashing around in the warm water. I didn't hear Toosay's question until he shyly asked again.

"I'm sorry, Toosay. What did you say?"

He pointed his finger straight above his head where

the Pleiades still twinkled in the distance. "I want to go, too."

Desdemona's eyelids were heavy and closed involuntarily. The ship's log fell across her chest, and she pulled the cotton quilt up over her shoulders. It had been a hell of a year.

Anchovies
and Antonyms

13

I'll Be Your Pizza Tonight

Rudy Breno smelled like tomato sauce and was ten seconds from coming when the phone rang. "Oh no, not now," he moaned.

"Don't stop, baby . . . Don't stop, baby," Lou Anne gasped.

She lay flat on her back with her legs locked around Rudy's neck, and her inch-long acrylic fingernails were firmly dug into the cheeks of his ass. Sometime during the lust wrestling, Lou Anne had skewered one of the empty Domino's pizza boxes with one of the red spiked heels of what she called her "fuck me pumps," and it twirled like a giant tassel as she responded to Rudy's lunges. If he tried to make a move for the phone, Lou Anne would claw cartoon-sized scratch marks in his butt, and he could possibly bleed to death and become one of his own headlines.

He kept thrusting away at the gasping Lou Anne and nimbly pulled the phone cord over toward him. He couldn't decide which he liked better, talking on the phone or fucking, so like any selfish red-blooded American stud, he would try to do both.

Lou Anne climaxed in a series of whimpers and rolls of

93

her tongue and repeatedly whispered "Oh baby, oh baby" for a good thirty seconds.

"Rudy, is that you?"

"Dad."

"Rudy, you're on top of this Jet Ski thing aren't you?"

"Yeah, Dad, right."

Rudy climbed off Lou Anne and walked slowly to the bathroom and closed the door.

"This Jet Ski Killer thing is going to be big, and you're my Johnny-on-the-spot."

Rudy didn't have a clue as to what his old man was talking about. The headache he'd brought back from Cuba had been so bad he'd emptied half a bottle of Tylenol P.M. during the last nine hours and had called Lou Anne to nurse him back to health.

They had smoked the big joint she brought over and then ordered pizzas. Lou Anne had mentioned the news of the Jet Ski Killer to Rudy, knowing his lust for that kind of story, but at the time he hadn't been in his work mode. He was more interested in making Lou Anne into a pizza and had stuck slices of pepperoni and pieces of olives and mushrooms from her neck to her crotch and had eaten them all off.

"Rudy, this Jet Ski Killer story is the hottest thing going, and we have our hands right on it." Rudy stopped scratching himself and wondered what he was missing. "Son, are you there?"

"Yeah, Dad, I'm here."

"You know the people down there. With this storm, nobody can get to Key West. I want this Jet Ski Killer thing to be big. It's hot, it's fresh, and looking for a dead rock star is not. I want you off that Joe Merchant shit and onto this Jet Ski Killer thing. Do a good job. Be creative, bring me something imaginative. Give me a reason to give you that promotion. This is your big break, son. Don't fuck it up."

Rudy showered quickly, dropped Lou Anne off in front of her houseboat, and went to his tiny office above Fast Buck Freddy's on Duval Street. He called the *Key West Citizen* and got the basics on the Jet Ski Killer story and then sat in front of his word processor for two hours thinking about his father's instructions. Suddenly it hit him. He ran across the street to the radio station, bribed the nighttime DJ, and got a copy of Blanton Meyercord's tape.

Rudy Breno went back to his apartment and wrote his best

piece ever. He took yellow journalism to its brightest color and compared Blanton to every killer back to Cain and Abel, although he got the brothers mixed up as far as who killed whom. He faxed the story and his idea off to his father, and his father called him back immediately to congratulate him on his incredible plan. He said it was something he himself should have thought of.

When his father finally got off the phone, Rudy read the story into his Mr. Microphone and then played it back, lip-synching to the tape while he studied himself in the mirror.

"I belong on television," he said.

Rudy picked up the yellow pages and turned to the listing for charter boats. "An admiral needs a flagship," he said as he thumbed through the listings.

14

You've Got the Wrong Man

I expected to be running from the authorities at some point, but if you'd told me last week that Trevor Kane would be back in town and that I would be taking her to Boomtown instead of escaping to the wild beauty of Alaska, I would have told you that you had the wrong man.

Billy Cruiser and I rolled the *Hemisphere Dancer* out onto the wet asphalt, and it was time to go. I went to wake up Trevor. I'd carried her to my room last night and had fallen asleep curled around her in the old bamboo bed. We'd always done our best communicating without words.

"There's a fresh pot of coffee on," Billy called to Trevor as she sleepily made her way across the hangar. "You just take your time wakin' up. I'll put your things on the plane."

"That's the first decent sleep I've had in a while," she said as she poured herself a cup of coffee.

"It's that tropical air," Billy said. "Works on the blood flow."

I took a walk down to the lone palm with Hoagy to get a last look at the backcountry. The tire swing hung in the morning dew, and the branches of the old palm tree started to sway ever so slightly in the early morning breeze. I filed the tranquil scene away. I had no idea when I would see it again.

• • •

I was glad to be going back up in the air, regardless of where I might land, and Billy Cruiser gave us a send-off salute as we sped down the runway. I climbed to five hundred feet, turned to the north, and then plotted my course. The weather was improving. Trevor tapped me on the shoulder, and I lifted the right ear of my headset. She pointed to Hoagy, who sat on the rear bench watching me with a keen eye. "He looks like he's ready to take the controls," she said.

"This is no dog to be humiliated by stupid pet tricks on 'David Letterman.' "

"Wake me when we get there, would you?" she said as she laid her head against the window and closed her eyes.

I surveyed the sky ahead. The dismal remnants of the tropical depression had moved off to Mexico, and flight conditions were severely clear with ten knots on the tail. I was on my way to a very remote field on the edge of the Everglades where an old scammer named Ace Parsley ran a repair/paint shop that catered to people in a hurry.

I needed a new set of numbers on the plane to cover our escape, and I'd already set up the appointment when I'd made my Alaska plans. I'd called Ace earlier and had told him I had a passenger who needed to be taken to Miami, and he said he would have his son drive her there. I would meet up with Trevor tomorrow in Rudderville, a small town in the Bahamas, after she had seen her cousin in Miami. We'd go on to Boomtown from there. I was anxious and wanted to put some miles between the *Dancer* and the bank.

It took me a while to find the small grass strip in the ground fog. I finally spotted a red truck parked next to the line shack as I overflew the field.

When I turned a short final, I shook Trevor awake. "We're here," I said.

She rubbed her eyes and looked down at the deserted blanket of sawgrass that stretched to the horizon.

"Where's here?" she asked.

"The Everglades. There's the airport," I said and pointed straight ahead. "Here we go."

I set up for landing and cocked the nose of the plane into the slight crosswind, and the *Hemisphere Dancer* settled onto the soft grass. Ace was standing by the taxiway and directed us to the hangar. I pulled the *Dancer* inside and shut down the engines. Before the propeller blades had stopped spinning, two men were already grinding the totem pole and the numbers off the plane. I crossed my fingers and promised the spirits I would paint the pole back on as soon as I could.

"Morning, Frank. Long time no see. Got any special requests?"

"What?"

"Any numbers in particular you want? Birthday, anniversary, lucky numbers?"

"Just something Canadian," I said.

Trevor came to the door and climbed out of the plane with her duffel bag.

"This here is Ace Jr. He's a very safe driver, and he'll take you to Miami, ma'am," Ace said. "I hate to be pushy, but we're in a hurry today, if you don't mind."

Trevor gave me a worried look as she got into the truck. "You *are* going to Rudderville, aren't you, Frank?" she asked.

"I'll meet you there tomorrow," I said.

"Don't be late."

"Me?" I waved to her as Ace Jr. floored the accelerator and sped off to Alligator Alley.

I was painted and fueled in less than an hour. Old Ace kept on working and never hinted at being interested in why I was changing numbers or where I was going. His work was expensive and cleaned out most of my cash, but he'd never say a word to anybody.

• • •

I took off and flew fifty feet above the ground over the Everglades in the direction of Key Largo and away from the crowded skies around Miami. The sun was now high enough to give color back to the gray water. Pockets of deep blue cut through the shallow flats like lifelines on a weathered hand. I felt as if I were reading some giant palm that held the history of my past.

I gazed at the small channels that branched out south of the bridge and emptied into the blue Atlantic. One of them was Raccoon Creek, the fishing spot where Billy Cruiser had taken me my first summer in the Keys. Over the years, he had told me a lot of nice things about my dad, and as I flew, the song Billy had taught me that summer came to mind. He said that my dad and all the other pilots had sung it in the officer's club after every mission, and they'd toasted the miss-

ing in action with a beer. We had done the same for my dad
that day on Raccoon Creek. Now I sang it to Hoagy:

They'll tear down the officers' clubs
And write off the overdue subs,
So let's drink to our memories,
Our heroes, and our pals, to those crazy navy fliers,
To those swell Hawaiian gals.
The sailors will dance in the street,
Then they'll mothball the whole damn fleet—
We'll only have our memories
Of land and sea and foam
'Cause they're sending the old man home.

I adjusted the RPMs on the propeller and listened to the
sound that meant they were in sync and did a quick calcula-
tion of my groundspeed. I was on my way to an outpost
called Pass Her By Cay. It wasn't a necessary stop, but I was
already going in that direction, and it was the kind of place
where I could fuel and clear customs without all the bullshit
in Rudderville. There was a great restaurant on Pass Her By,
and for years I used to stop there just to eat their conch bur-
gers and do some fishing. I would still catch up with Trevor
in Rudderville by early morning with no problem. Then we
would fly on to Boomtown together.

I tuned in a Miami station on the ADF looking for some
music, but like a ghost, the voice of Blanton Meyercord came
across the airways. It scared the hell out of me to think what
Rudy Breno would write about the Jet Ski Killer.

The upper Keys had disappeared behind me, and I saw
only water when I looked around. No one has ever seen the
whole ocean. I thought there was ample room for Blanton
Meyercord to get lost in.

15

Shelter in the Storm

Blanton heard the eerie hoot of an owl and scanned the overhanging tangle of leaves and branches until he spotted a pair of eyes. He let out a sigh, lifted the bill of his baseball cap, and ran his fingers through his thinning strands of hair. "Got any ideas?" he asked the owl.

A piece of fly line hung from the sunglasses around his neck, and Blanton chewed on it as he thought about his options. In the distance he heard the high-pitched whine of an outboard engine, and he quickly began to climb to the high branches of the tree. The owl remained motionless but kept his eyes fixed on the two-legged creature now perched on a nearby limb.

Down below were the endless string of mango thickets that fishing guides called "the backcountry." Blanton had taken temporary refuge in a well-hidden spot east of the Barracuda Keys. He scanned the mangrove patches, which appeared to float on the surface like giant toadstools of Wonderland. Somewhere in Hollywood, Blanton thought, his name would bring up cries of "Off with his head."

The director was not dead, but the explosions had made the

production exceed its budget, which was a more serious crime in Hollywood than murder itself—or so the local DJ had said. Blanton smiled in the darkness but then got serious when he saw a boat pitching and tossing among the endless procession of curling whitecaps. Slowly he descended the tree.

· · ·

Billy Cruiser hadn't realized how much worse the weather had gotten until he stuck his nose into the ship channel. He'd been monitoring the Coast Guard frequency and heard the operator talking to one of the cutters that was looking for a missing fishing boat. It had capsized near the Dry Tortugas. The skies had changed dramatically over the past three hours. Only a crazy man would be out on a day like this, he said to himself.

He wiped the stinging salt spray from his eyes for the thousandth time and held on tightly to the wheel. He had been wallowing in the troughs of the jumbo waves for the last hour as he inched his way to the Barracudas. The shallow-water waves felt different from their deep-water cousins, and Billy could suddenly feel the bottom. It was the only way he had to find the entrance.

He moved cautiously through the shallow water, maneuvering the overloaded skiff, and then he spotted the slick water that told him the location of the channel. Billy felt the tension leave his back as the waves melted to a light chop.

He was startled by the appearance of a pattern of perfectly symmetrical black triangles that stretched out below the hull of the boat. He thought his aging eyes were playing tricks on him again until he realized that it was a huge school of spotted leopard rays. They were swimming in formation toward the gulf on the outgoing tide. He cut the engine and picked up his push pole, nudging the skiff the last hundred yards to the edge of the mangrove stand.

Long strands of turtle grass uprooted by the storm lay tangled in the miniature forest of tiny sprigs, old lobster traps, multicolored Styrofoam floats, and pieces of line that littered the shallow water. Billy kept an eye on the narrow channel that snaked ahead of him through the flats. It shrank until it was barely as wide as the beam of his skiff, then disappeared into the mangroves.

Billy Cruiser put the pole back in the chocks and moved forward. Grabbing the limbs of a poisonwood tree, he pulled his way through. Several cormorants skimmed the surface of the water and fled to the shelter of the island, and a rat snake fell onto the poling platform of the boat and slithered overboard. He had turned back to look at the snake and hadn't seen the spiderweb in front of him. The sticky strands enveloped his face and head, and he spit and flailed with his hands, hoping the spider wouldn't fall down the open collar of his shirt.

The dense underbrush formed a small canopy, and Billy stooped down to prod the skiff along with the push pole. Tiny snapper and permit filled the tidal creek; they knew a good hiding place when they saw one. Spotting an opening in the distance, he gave the boat a final shove and glided to the middle of the hidden cove.

That was when he saw Blanton. He was seated on the bow of his boat, making slow roll casts with a small fly rod. An owl stood on the poling platform surveying the situation, and it let out a hoot. Blanton reeled in his line, looked up, and waved to Billy.

"I guess I fucked up, huh?"

    • • •

There were only about fifteen minutes until the outgoing tide would make it impossible for them to get back out the channel, so they moved quickly to tie up the boats and transfer the supplies.

"What's goin' on?" Blanton asked.

"Well, the hornets are buzzin', son. The FBI, the marine patrol, and God knows who else have been to the hangar since they played that tape of yours on the radio yesterday. The advertising agency in New York has offered a reward for your capture."

"That means every fuckin' yahoo between here and Orlando will be trompin' through the mangroves as soon as the weather breaks."

"That's the good news," Billy said.

"And the bad?"

Billy handed Blanton a copy of the morning edition of the *National Lighthouse.* "Rudy Breno has announced an expedition to track down the Jet Ski Killer."

"Who's that?"

"You."

"I didn't kill nobody," Blanton said.

"It doesn't matter to him. You know how he writes. That's what they're calling you, sport."

Blanton unfolded the paper. There, in a box in the middle of the front page, was a picture of Rudy. He was standing in front of a barge piled high with the twisted remains of the Jet Skis that Blanton had blown up. He read the copy that surrounded the picture.

You just don't think it's going to happen in your own backyard. Dogs don't mess where they sleep, but mass murderers are not dogs. They're worse. This one blew up his own backyard, a maniac lashing out at progress and man's march to the future. This is not Dodge City. The days of horses and cowboys are history. Faster toys are what made us what we are today. This fishing guide who decided to take the law into his own hands has gone too far. The ocean belongs to all of us to do with as we please. It's not some pet-shop aquarium. These varmint guides have a long history of recklessness and usually die off from skin cancer, dope, or booze, but when they assault one of the most successful television commercial directors in America, I say that is enough.

Val Vincennes should not have been treated this way. His commercials pump much-needed money into this town. Give us more men like Val Vincennes and fewer like Blanton Meyercord, a deranged Rambo with a fishing pole. He claimed he was sorry. He said it was an accident. Ha! Accidents don't just happen, and Blanton Meyercord is no Rambo. Let's call him what he is: a maniac. He is now at large, free to strike again whenever and wherever he chooses. The time has come to make a stand, and the *National Lighthouse* will lead the way to apprehend this lunatic. I have been authorized to lead an expedition to track down this Jet Ski Killer and bring him to justice. I will be reporting my progress, and as you read this article, I have already begun my pursuit. Justice shall be served.

Blanton decided not to read the other two articles Rudy had written about him. Instead, he wadded up the paper and stuffed it in his pocket. He looked out at the gray sky. "Well, I better get movin'."

"I don't suppose it ever crossed your mind to turn yourself in and explain your side of the story," Billy said gently.

"Not really." Blanton shrugged and pulled on the bill of his baseball cap. "Fishin' ain't been the same in the Keys since George Bush caught a bonefish and stuffed its eye sockets with presidential-seal eyeballs. Every goddamn greedy Republican wants to catch a bonefish now and put it on his office wall, and the fuckin' politicians still don't understand that you can't put twenty pounds of shit into a five-pound bag. Nobody can stop 'em from turnin' the whole string of islands into a fuckin' RV parkin' lot."

"Well, at least the helicopters haven't been able to get down here from Miami. I would consider that a big head start, but the weather service says the depression is moving off to the west, and things should begin to clear up in a few hours."

"I need you to do me one more favor if you would, Billy." Blanton climbed to the back of the boat and untied the line leading to the Jet Ski. "If you could drop this off in a pretty visible spot somewhere up 'round Cape Sable, it might send 'em off into the Everglades and buy me some time."

"Hell, I'm already halfway there," Billy said, taking the line from Blanton. "I guess you're headin' in the opposite direction."

"I thought about Australia, but I had a friend who ran away there once from a pot rap. He was livin' on the ocean, thinkin' he'd beaten the rap, and they nabbed him while he was surfin'. Narcs on long-boards chased him to the beach. They sent him back to South Carolina, and he's still in jail. Hey, murderers walk the streets, but James Brown gets two years for runnin' a stop sign. I don't like the way justice is handed out by these Reaganite bastards."

"Yeah, but you're a war hero. That surely had to count for something."

Blanton stowed the meatloaf sandwiches in his cooler, looked at Billy, and shook his head. "Wrong war."

Billy Cruiser tied the Jet Ski to his boat, and they started back through the mangroves in single file. "It's still pretty easy to get lost in South America," Billy said. "I got a couple of old pirate buddies dug in down there who might be able to help you along."

Blanton straddled the bow of his skiff and pushed a small wooden paddle back and forth. "I hear there are still Nazi war criminals livin' happily ever after in South America who gassed hundreds of thousands of Jews. All I did was blow up a bunch of Jet Skis."

They stopped at the edge of the island, and Blanton climbed a gumbo-limbo tree and surveyed the area. "No planes, no boats," he called down to Billy.

They broke out into the open. The carpet of grass on the flats lay exposed by the tide, and the air was filled with the hazy salt residue that came along with the storm.

Blanton paused for a second, shook his head, and then rubbed his hand across his mouth. He looked at his watch and then at the sky. "Just like me to be lookin' for shelter in the belly of the storm. Say good-bye to everyone for me, Billy, and tell Brillo I'll send him the money I owe him when I get settled. When's he headin' for Alaska?"

"He ain't goin'. Trevor showed up yesterday, and they took off early this mornin'. He's takin' her to Boomtown."

Blanton whistled and laughed. "And I thought I had problems. Looks like these days, everybody's on the run."

Billy lowered his engine and fired up. He eased the boat next to Blanton's and leaned over the rail and gave him a bear hug. "Take care of yourself, son," Billy said, and he moved on ahead of Blanton, towing the Jet Ski.

Blanton waited until Billy cleared the channel, and then he turned southeast. He sat with his chin on the steering console of the skiff and pressed his lips tightly together. He was no painter, but he tried to capture the panorama of the flats to take with him wherever it was he was going. He was no poet, so he borrowed lines that fit what he saw. " 'Don't try to describe the ocean if you've never seen it.' "

Blanton started his engine and saluted the owl. The bird spread its small wings and lifted off the poling platform. "Pray for me, Pablo Neruda," Blanton said and headed southeast into the large ocean.

The Wind
Is in from Africa

16

Beyond the Low-Water Mark

Charleston slept under a fluffy vaporous ground fog that covered the streets like a faded old quilt. It was Saturday, a day off for most people, but Charlie Fabian had been working hard all night.

He was not a twentieth-century man; he'd been born two hundred years too late. Charlie would have been much more at home when the country was new and piracy was in its heyday. He peered through the window on the far side of the spacious old room at the dying reflection of the moon and slipped through the French doors onto the balcony.

To the east, the waters of the Ashley River entered the harbor and lapped against the stoic seawall where spiked cannons were still positioned at fifty-yard intervals. A gazebo stood in the center of the Battery, poking up above the fog, and footpaths ran in all directions like spokes on a wheel.

During the night, a late cold front had bucked its way through the first hints of the scalding summer to come. Now the inevitable heat would be slightly delayed. The Charlestonians would have plenty to be thankful for when they rose this Sunday.

Charlie Fabian was also a thankful man. He stood in the cool breeze and thought how glad he was to be out of Africa, though the spirit of the dark continent was hard to dislodge from his mind. He was working for the infamous mercenary leader Colonel Adrian Cairo, the "White Terror of Africa." The Colonel had been forced from his island sanctuary off the Ivory Coast. His attempt to establish a kingdom on the island of Wulanda had not gone unnoticed by the major powers of the world, who thought it unwise for a man to own a country. Now the Colonel was on the run.

For the last month, Charlie had been holed up in Cacheau, a small town in the West African state of Guinea-Bissau, waiting for further word from Colonel Cairo. Whatever the Colonel was up to, Charlie was in. Colonel Cairo had saved his life.

The month of waiting had been painfully long, but one day a dusty Bushman had ambled through the door of the Equator Bar in Cacheau with a large manila envelope addressed to Charlie Fabian. He had his traveling orders. He had been sent to Charleston to find a treasure diver named Little Elmo. It didn't take him long. Like most smugglers, Little Elmo suffered from a bad case of grandiosity and took every opportunity to let the rest of the world know how clever he was. Tonight Little Elmo would be holding court in the lobby bar of the Palmetto Hotel.

• • •

When Charlie Fabian entered the bar, all eyes looked his way. He was long and lean, stood six feet two, and weighed 190 pounds. He wore a black silk shirt unbuttoned to the waist and a pair of tight jeans stuffed into black leather boots with silver-pointed toes. His eyes were concealed behind a pair of reflector sunglasses that he wore both day and night. A mop of thick blond hair was pulled back and fastened into a ponytail, and a sack of gris-gris charms hung from his neck. He carried a brown leather bag and looked like a shrimper who had just hit town on Saturday night after a month at sea.

Little Elmo was perched on a stool, drinking oyster shooters. Seated next to him was a very large man with stringy brown hair who glared coldly at Charlie. Elmo was talking fast and sweated a lot as he poured Tabasco sauce into the oyster-and-vodka mixture in front of him. The bartender politely asked Charlie for his drink order.

"That's on me, Avery," Little Elmo grandly blurted out.

"The gentleman from the Keys is buying tonight," the bartender said dryly, placing a beer before Charlie.

"Thank you," Charlie said as he took a long, hard pull on the cold bottle. He scanned the man next to Elmo and saw the impression of a pistol under his coat.

"Where you from, cowboy?" Elmo asked.

"Just got back from Provo."

"Provo? Jesus, that place is a pit. I spent a lifetime there one summer, but never again. No more check's-in-the-mail bullshit for this boy. I didn't get your name, Cap. I'm Elmo, and this here is my sidekick, Sledge. He works for me."

"The name is Wood, Danny Wood," Charlie told him.

"Well, Danny, it is surely a pleasure to meet another man of the world."

Little Elmo slid off his stool and extended his hand, and Charlie shook it. Sledge continued to sit at the bar, blowing Camel smoke at the ceiling.

"Why don't you two boys get a little better acquainted while I drain the old lizard and make a phone call for some party favors and pussy. God bless America." Little Elmo hopscotched to the bathroom.

Charlie nursed his beer and listened to Al Green's "Love and Happiness' flow out of the speakers behind the bar while Sledge polished off a shot of tequila and burped.

Two girls walked in and spoke to the bartender. "Hi Avery, honey," drawled the tall blond.

The lady with her was shorter and slimmer, with curly red hair. They both wore tank tops that compressed their breasts into perfect melon shapes, skintight stretch pants, thick socks, and white Reeboks. They passed inches from Charlie, moving like inquisitive cats, stretching and purring their way to a table in the corner.

A short, stocky man stood to greet them. When he flicked his head, every hair shook for a second and then settled back on his scalp in exactly the same place. His compact jeans emphasized the bulge in his pants.

He took the blond by the hand and gave her a long, hard kiss on the mouth. While they were in the lip lock, the redhead sneaked a quick glance at the two desperadoes at the bar, but she turned her head away the moment she was detected by Charlie Fabian. Charlie pivoted on the stool and followed the girl with his eyes, and Sledge scanned from the opposite direction. They bumped heads like Curly and Moe.

"They ain't got on no underwear," Sledge sighed. His voice had a nasal tone. They looked at each other, and both men laughed.

"Only women can do that," Charlie said. "They're smarter than us, and they never play fair."

"You're bein' a bit cynical for a hard dick just off a boat," Sledge said. "They look pretty as peaches to me."

• • •

"Hey, Avery, who's the chick with Ken and Barbie?" Sledge asked.

"Works next door in the health club. The guy is a narc," the bartender answered nonchalantly.

"Figures," Charlie mumbled.

"Cops," Sledge snarled.

The narc paid the bill, and the three got up to leave. When they passed Charlie and Sledge, the testosterone level of the cop went through the roof. He flexed the tendons in his neck like a rooster in a barnyard and herded his little hens to the door. Charlie and Sledge just smiled and nodded.

"You know, cops have a certain smell. Like rotten shrimp," Charlie said.

Sledge took a deep breath and inhaled the lingering scent of hair spray and department-store perfume that trailed the girls as they disappeared into the lobby.

"I can tell somebody's done time. It shows. The joint puts an invisible warnin' tag on you, and it don't never come off. Am I right?"

Charlie nodded and laughed. Sledge began to frown and gave Charlie a wicked glance. "What's so fuckin' funny there, shrimper Dan?"

"You've got a gift, Sledge. Is it okay if I call you Sledge?"

"That's the name, Budro."

"I wasn't laughin' at you. That narc reminds me of a joke I heard in jail. See, this little accountant gets locked up for not paying his taxes, and they throw him in a cell with this bad-ass three-hundred-pounder. Well, the accountant sits there for about a week, and the big guy doesn't say shit. Finally one day he yells across the cell to the kid, 'Hey you, since we gonna be in here for a while together, one of us is gonna have to be da husband, and one of us is gonna have to be da wife. Which one you wanna be?' Well, it doesn't take long for the little guy to answer. 'I'll be the husband,' he squeals. So the big guy sits there for about two more days sayin' nothing, and then one morning, he yells across the room, 'Hey, honey, why don't you come on over here and suck your wife's dick.' "

When Sledge quit laughing, he slapped Charlie on the back, and Charlie punched him lightly on the arm. Charlie picked a toothpick out of a shot glass on the bar and stuck it in the side of his mouth with a sucking sound. "So," he said, "what's the story on Little Elmo?"

"Nothin' special," Sledge told him. "Just one of those little guys who has to be stronger, tougher, and smarter than anybody in the world. I used to be his dealer back when I was druggin', but I got popped, and they sent me to the federal pen in Tallahassee for a while. Elmo's come into some money and hit Key West about a week ago. Treasure business off No Man's Cay—but now there's lawsuits between Elmo and his partners.

"How could anybody not get along with that charming personality?" Charlie said, finishing his beer.

"Treasure-huntin' scams make dope deals look like wise investments," Sledge continued. "You ever been to the Bahamas?"

"Can't say I have."

"Beautiful water, but no puss. Bring your own woman if you go. Anyway, I've been bouncin' at a titty bar in Key West called the Pirate's Den. I ain't been off that goddamn island for two years, and I just got done with my probation. It was a first-class ticket to somewhere."

Little Elmo bounded back into the bar looking like a drunk Cabbage Patch doll. He climbed up on the stool next to Charlie and hooked the heels of his cowboy boots around the legs. He pulled a package out of his pocket and slipped it to Charlie Fabian under the bar while Sledge looked on.

"It ain't often that a dirt-poor low-county shrimper gets an opportunity like this to make an investment. Last wreck I did paid two thousand for every dollar. You will thank the good Lord for the day that Elmo entered into your life."

Charlie unfolded the Burger King napkin carefully and glanced down at the heavy coin in his hand. It looked exactly like the drawing the Colonel had sent him.

"Interested?" Elmo asked.

"Very," Charlie replied. "How many of these do you have so far?"

"More than you can afford, sport." Elmo snickered and

slurped down another shooter. "But we've done enough business for a while. Me and Sledge here are only in town for one more day, but we'd be quite pleased if you joined our little party here—that is, if you think he's safe, Big Mover." He elbowed Sledge.

"He's one of us, Elmo."

"Men of the sea and all." Elmo laughed. "I remember when this used to be a pretty wild-ass town, but now it looks like a fucking boutique. Oh, I think we might be able to have us a killer party tonight."

Charlie laughed, knowing Little Elmo had no idea how true his statement was.

Little Elmo leaned over to Charlie and whispered, "Pick up any of them square groupers on the way back from Provo?"

"Just a simple fisherman," Charlie said.

"Ain't we all, ain't we all."

Elmo ordered two more oyster shooters and gulped the first one down. "One for me, and one for Mr. Happy," he said and giggled as he grabbed his crotch and finished off the second shooter. "There's a party in these pants tonight. Let's rock."

They set off for a bar called Hot Wind, where Little Elmo had arranged for party favors. Charlie was still not used to seeing so many white people on the streets, and he took in the sights and sounds as they made their way down Meeting Street to the bar. A crowd of young black kids cruised by them, whistling and jiving at Charlie's outfit. "Purple Rain" by Prince blared out of the giant ghetto blaster one of the boys carried like a suitcase, and one of them yelled out, "Watch out tonight, boogie man's out." Charlie caught himself about to answer in Swahili, but then the words "Right on, bro" effortlessly rolled off his tongue. It was strange for him to hear black people speaking English.

It was Saturday night, and the joint was jumping. A blues band called Missing Milk Carton Children was cranking out a succession of shuffles. It only took a few minutes for Little Elmo to get the party started. Three girls sat down with Charlie and Sledge while Little Elmo and his friend Evan went for a walk. Soon they returned, sniffing and swallowing, and a procession to the bathroom began. Half an hour later Little Elmo was fully recharged and speaking his own language, which Sledge called "Elmoese." The girls forgave his rude jokes and ill manners as long as the cocaine kept flowing. He spilled drinks, dropped money, and sang "Oh darlin', Oh darlin' " in a flat, high-pitched screech to every tune the Missing Milk Carton Children put out.

Charlie Fabian nursed his second beer of the evening and remained silent as he tapped his foot to the infectious music. It was the same beat he knew so well from Africa, but this was a far cry from the Equator Bar. He hadn't said a word since they had been seated, and the girls at the table grew more and more curious. Finally one of them teasingly asked, "What goes on behind those shades?" She reached for Charlie's sunglasses, and he sharply raised a warning finger. She yanked her hand away. "Weirdo fucking shrimper," she grumbled and went back to checking out the boys in the band.

Charlie watched the room like a customs agent, making sure the narc from the hotel bar hadn't slipped in on them. These people were much too loose with their crime. He was still used to African ways where AK-47s and Uzis were more efficient than an arrest and a reading of your rights. America was going to hell, no doubt about it.

Sledge was much more interested in the coke whores than his client, and Charlie finally cut Little Elmo out of the bathroom conga line and reminded him about the coins. Fortunately, the waitress had given last call, and the party was moving to Evan's house.

"Sledge, take these ladies over to Evan's, and me and Dan here will catch up with you after we tend to bidness. I don't need no protection from him. He couldn't' harm a flea. He's my asshole buddy." Little Elmo squeezed himself between two of the girls like peanut butter between two cheese crackers and lay his short arms on their shoulders. "I just want you girls to know that this dummy dust don't leave me mean, sexy, and harmless like normal men. Mr. Happy here is a sixty-minute man."

The girls looked down. He did have a hard-on.

"Sledge, get some champagne to go, and we'll see you in a bit." Elmo kissed the girls good-bye as if he would never see them again, and he and Charlie jumped into a cab for the short ride to the hotel.

Storm clouds had moved in suddenly over the city, and the sky opened up. They strolled past the inattentive desk clerk, who was posting room-service receipts. Little Elmo let out a yell that echoed through the marble foyer, but the clerk paid him no mind.

"Hey, are you the motherfucker in charge? I want to buy

this hotel. How much you want for it?" Elmo hollered at the man.

The desk clerk peered up over his glasses, gave Elmo a once-over, and said, "More than you would ever imagine. Now I would suggest you quiet down, or I'll call the police."

"Listen, you wienie muncher," Elmo began, but before he could finish, Charlie Fabian pushed him aside and dropped a hundred-dollar bill on the counter.

"I hope this will compensate for my friend's rudeness, and I don't think you have to worry about calling the police. I'll have him quieted down in no time. You know how it is."

The desk clerk raised his eyebrows and said in a congenial tone, "Thank you, sir. Just see that he doesn't disturb any of our other guests."

Charlie steered Little Elmo into the waiting elevator, and Elmo walked straight into the rear wall. He hit his head squarely, and the thud echoed through the lobby.

"Come on Einstein. We got some business to attend to."

Little Elmo lunged for the buttons and pressed them all. "Going up," he said, laughing.

"That's right," Charlie added with a smile.

17

Housekeeping

The Waterford crystal chandelier above Charlie's head shook, and the pendants began to swing. A trace of heat lightning spilled across the eastern sky, and Little Elmo lit up like a disco ball. He dangled from a heavy piece of Dacron dock line that was snugged tightly beneath his armpits. He was spinning slowly clockwise, and his eyes bulged out to the rims of his sockets in an expression of pure terror.

Little Elmo had gotten out of control in the elevator, and Charlie had wrestled him to the room. In the struggle, Elmo had knocked Charlie's sunglasses off and had seen his other eyes. For Charlie Fabian had two pairs: the piercing green ones God had given him and the ghastly ones tattooed onto his eyelids.

Charlie had seen the tattoos on the eyes of an old witch doctor in Uganda. The extra pair of eyes, he was told, kept a lookout while you slept for potential enemies and snakes falling from trees. They seemed to have worked so far. He was still alive, and no snakes had fallen on him. His eyes were his identity, his radar, and his secret. Elmo would have to die, but first Charlie needed the information he'd come for.

He had worked fast. It hadn't taken long to get the location of the wreck out of Elmo after Charlie crammed a bandanna soaked with lighter fluid down Elmo's throat. The bandanna jutted out of Little Elmo's mouth like the wick of a candle, and when Charlie lit a match, Elmo told him everything he needed to know—the location of the wreck, the story of the treasure, and a list of the few things they had found so far. Little Elmo was getting ready to fire two of the divers because something was already missing—a crystal-and-ruby wand—and Little Elmo suspected that one of them had stolen it and sold it behind his back.

On a piece of hotel stationery Charlie wrote down the directions to the wreck. Then he stuffed the bandanna back into Elmo's mouth and inspected the weapons that were spread across one of the double beds in Little Elmo's suite. Apparently Elmo had made a big buy at a local antique-weapon store, for there were two Colts, a dagger, a Henry rifle, and a cutlass.

"You're just a regular one-man army, Elmo." Charlie Fabian picked up the cutlass and held it up in the moonlight. Elmo's eyes bugged out with fear.

> *"Pray then, ye learned ghost, do show,*
> *Where can this fearsome brute now go,*
> *Whose life is one continuous evil,*
> *Striving to cheat God, Man, and Devil?*

"The last words of Steed Bonnet, the gentleman pirate," Charlie said, pointing out the window with the blade of the sword. "He was hanged right over there in the Battery and was buried beyond the low-water mark."

The moonlight reflected off the long curved blade. "Some people say the fog is the spirit of Steed Bonnet, let loose by the low tide. Do you think so, Elmo?" Charlie Fabian turned and lunged.

The cutlass skewered Little Elmo. He wiggled like a catfish on a cane pole, then twitched for a few seconds until his body went limp. He looked like an hors d'oeuvre.

Charlie gathered the bed linens and bath towels and piled them under Little Elmo. A steady stream of blood quickly turned the linens crimson. He went into the bathroom, stripped his clothes, tore off his blond wig, and pulled a smartly tailored uniform out of his leather bag. A moment later he was smiling in the mirror at his transformation into a dark-haired U.S. Navy lieutenant commander, but he was startled when the phone rang.

"Elmo, that you?" a slurred voice asked.

"Sledge, this is Danny," Charlie said calmly. He could tell Sledge was drunk. "I don't think Elmo will make the party. He passed out."

"That figures. Well, I was wonderin' if maybe you could keep an eye on him for me. This hot tub party looks like it's gonna go on into today, and I'm feelin' sexy tonight."

"You mean sexy, mean, and harmless, right?" Charlie heard a big laugh and lots of splashing through the receiver.

"I feel like I'm in a big root-beer float here, Danny. I'd sure like to stay and enjoy this Carolina hospitality a little longer."

"You go ahead and have a blast. Elmo's not gonna bother anybody for a while."

"Okay, buddy. If there's anything I can do for you, you leave a message in Key West at Sloppy Joe's."

"Take care," Charlie said and hung up.

He stuffed all of Little Elmo's coins into his bag, straightened his tie, checked the angle of his hat, and donned his sunglasses. He had what he had come for.

Charlie hung a Do Not Disturb sign on the handle of the cutlass and laughed at the thought of the effect the discovery of Little Elmo would have on the maids when they banged on the door too early the next morning yelling "Housekeeping!" at the tops of their lungs.

• • •

Out on King Street the wet pavement was beginning to steam as the earth heated up. The upstanding citizens of Charleston were on their way to Sunday morning services as Charlie walked into the vestibule of the old Episcopal church and dropped two of the gold pieces into the poor box. He tipped his hat to two old matrons and left them sighing. "Such an officer and a gentleman," one said to the other.

When Charlie reached the Battery, he climbed the steps of the old gazebo. He took a worn photograph out of his wallet and looked at the woman in the picture for a moment. He was many years and many lives away from her now. He walked past the monuments on either side of the brick path and somehow knew this would be the last time he would ever see Charleston—like so many things for him now, it was another place and another time.

18

I'm Clean

Trevor Kane read Rudy Breno's editorial on the front page of the special edition of the *National Lighthouse*. What the hell was she doing in a place like downtown Miami at noon on a Friday?

The ride down Alligator Alley had taken her from the most remote wilderness of the Everglades to the sprawl of the city in less than an hour, and Ace Jr. had seemed a little shocked when she'd slipped out of her jeans and donned a skirt while she talked to him about flying.

Now Trevor sat on a stool at La Taza de Oro, a bustling eatery tucked in behind the storefronts near the intersection of First Street and First Avenue where stereos, sunglasses, Mario Brothers video games, calculators, video cameras, knives, luggage, platinum wigs, and lots of gold chains were all available at bargain prices. Ace Jr. had dropped her off at the intersection, where she was supposed to meet Hackney Primstone III to discuss her estate. Her shady lawyer cousin was late—as usual.

Trevor tapped her nails on the shiny plastic placemat to a song by Tito Puente and finished reading Rudy's article. At the end of the counter, a man in a sleeveless undershirt sang along, word for word, with Tito.

When she finished the article, Trevor wadded up the paper and hurled it in the direction of the blue-and-white trash basket.

"That is bad writing at its best," she muttered aloud. "They all come down here thinking they're Hemingway. That's what's wrong with the fucking world these days. Nobody wants to put in the time it takes to be legendary. Mythology is not fast food."

She hadn't eaten that morning back at Lone Palm, and she felt a rumble in her stomach. On the well-used Wolf stove behind the counter, she could see large aluminum pots of soup, black beans, and *boliche,* and she caught a whiff of grilled onions.

It was going to be one of those scorching afternoons. It was already summer weather in South Florida, and most people up north still hadn't dug out of the winter snow. Ceiling fans twirled as quickly as the radio DJ talked, and the wind scattered hot dog wrappers down First Avenue faster than the traffic was moving. Horns blared from a tangle of automobiles, mopeds, and buses that looked like a bumper-car ride at the fair, and accents from Brooklyn to Bogotá could be heard from the passersby.

Trevor ordered a *coco frio* from the stocky waitress who yelled to the tenor sitting on the last stool. He kept singing along with the radio while he dismounted and went behind the counter. He pulled out a large machete and plucked a big green coconut from the Styrofoam ice chest, lopped the top off, popped a straw in the hole, and handed it to Trevor. She sipped the cool liquid and walked out to the pay phone in the alley to call Hackney again.

The coconut water tasted like the tropics and settled her nerves somewhat. Her cousin was now twenty minutes late for their lunch date, and she didn't feel like talking to his answering machine again. Her life seemed to be a series of messages these days. Real people had a habit of disappearing.

A gust of wind lifted her skirt above her knees and revealed her pink cotton panties to the delight of several men standing in line to pay for lottery tickets. A black man was screaming into the pay phone in French. Trevor kept her distance from him and the thongs of workers on their lunch hour who crowded the sidewalk. Why had she dressed up in the first place? She hadn't worn a skirt in a year. She went back into the restaurant, paid the waitress, and walked out to the bus bench and scanned the traffic.

Trevor wondered if she was doing the right thing, going after Desdemona on such flimsy evidence that Joe might still be alive. The day after her mother's death, she had decided she should make plans to check herself into a clinic in New Mexico to try to deal with the scar tissue left by her family. She was all set to go until the woman at the clinic told her that part of the program included a "family week." The woman on the phone had described it as a week where your whole family comes to air out the dirty laundry, loves and hates, good times and bad times, so you could get on with your life. But Trevor had no family. Instead of sending in her deposit, she had hung up the phone.

• • •

"Hey, pretty cousin, hop in," a voice called from the black Mercedes convertible that had just cut off the city bus. The bus driver leaned on the horn and cursed in Spanish, but Hackney Primstone III smiled and waved as if he were the pope. Trevor glanced at the black license plate in the chrome frame, which read "I'm Clean."

Hackney Primstone III sat behind the wheel in a custom-tailored khaki suit and a pair of Persol water-buffalo-frame sunglasses. In one hand he gripped the steering wheel and a Monte Cristo cigar, and his other hand was outstretched to help Trevor into the car.

Hackney was the Napoleonic complex personified. He stood five feet barefoot, which was hardly ever, for he was permanently attached to several hundred pairs of elevator shoes. He even had a pair of custom-made elevator flip-flops for his beach outfits. He charged exorbitant fees and concentrated on estates, with an occasional ambulance chaser thrown in. Recently, Hackney had been under investigation in connection with a black-market organ-donor scam, but he'd been cleared of any wrongdoing. He was additional testimony to the lunacy that seemed to fester on both sides of Trevor's family.

Trevor despised Hackney and had only agreed to go to lunch with him because she refused to set foot in his penthouse office at the top of the CenTrust building where he displayed the prizes of his big-game-hunting passion. She'd been there once with her mother and had gotten ill looking at the countless heads of animals and pictures of Hackney with political figures and sports stars that covered every square foot of wall space. But it was the gorilla-hand ashtray that had unleashed her anger and had sent her for the door.

Hackney Primstone III leaned over to kiss her on the cheek, and Trevor cringed. He smelled like cigar smoke and English Leather, and the thought came to Trevor that only highly paid women would ever get into bed with this slimeball.

"Sorry I'm late. I know you must be beside yourself about your dear mother, precious. I never knew she was in such pain. I know how you feel. How does Joe's sound for lunch?" he asked.

"Fine."

Hackney was still stopping the flow of traffic, and horns and angry voices echoed behind the Mercedes. In downtown Miami, stopping traffic is justification for being shot. He reached across Trevor and pulled her door shut, brushing his arm across her breasts. The seat belt automatically shot forward from some hidden compartment, and Trevor fastened it around herself.

"I certainly enjoy hearing from you, even if it's only when monetary concerns seem to be the business of the day. I hope I can be of some comfort in your hour of need."

Trevor frowned out the window at a patch of ocean-blue sky that had squeezed its way through the concrete angles of the tall buildings along the street.

"Let's cut the bullshit, Hackney. I need some money, and I need it quick. I have a plane to catch this afternoon."

Hackney Primstone III smiled. "Not a problem, precious. We can work it out."

He turned onto Biscayne Boulevard and floored the gas pedal of the Mercedes and blew his horn. The traffic cop at the intersection nodded to the oncoming car and signaled for the cross-traffic to stop.

Hackney roared through the intersection at ninety and blew his horn again; the cop waved and smiled. He sucked on the big cigar until the end glowed red, and he blew out a cloud of blue smoke. He laughed and turned to Trevor.

"I just love Miami,' he said.

"You would."

19

Colonel Cairo

Colonel Adrian Cairo listed into the wind and leaned against the rail with his one good hand. He looked like an aging patriarch as he peered out over his temporary domain with the cold eye of a man who knew authority.

The old house he had been using as his hideout in Bimini rose above the long, flat island like the superstructure of an ocean liner. Down below, at the foot of the walkway, a faded sign with the words *Casa Grande* hung from a rusty chain, and a partially submerged dredge lay in the mudflat nearby. Hurricane shutters in various states of disrepair offered little protection to the once-grand fishing palace that was now gradually deteriorating—just another folly of man in the slow process of being reclaimed by nature.

The Colonel had been furious after his deportation. Wulanda had been the perfect setup for his plans, but then the superpowers who had paid him to do their dirty work and run illegal guns to the third-world nations of Africa had pulled the plug. Capitalism, communism—there wasn't much difference to Colonel Cairo. Both systems stank. Dictatorship was the only way to get something done.

Now Colonel Cairo was posing as a movie producer looking at locations for a slasher film and was renting Casa
Grande until his boat arrived from the Azores. The political
turmoil in Africa was not a popular subject in the island bars,
and the Colonel's disappearance from the African continent
did not seem to matter to the locals of Bimini; they had a
long tradition of minding their own business and cashing in
when the opportunity presented itself. They had lived through
blockade running in the Civil War, prohibition in the thirties,
and cocaine cowboys in the eighties. Baseball and fishing
were the primary topics of conversation these days.

The house had been built in the forties by an underwear
and girdle tycoon. It had been the ultimate sport-fishing re-
treat back in the days following World War II. The estate had
been sold to a retired baseball star and his famous movie-star
wife in the early fifties, and a skating rink had been constructed on the second story. Schools of giant tuna and blue
marlin cruised the eastern edge of the Gulf Stream where the
water depth went from sixty to one thousand feet over what
the locals called "the edge." But as time wore on, the grand
estate had proved too extravagant for a changing economy
worried about income taxes, the value of the dollar, and the
rising cost of fossil fuels.

Casa Grande had been abandoned in the sixties and put up
for sale at too high a price. The furnishings followed the sons
and daughters of the original owner back to Maine and Palm
Beach, and in the early eighties, the property was sold to a
group of developers who envisioned a time-share on what
some people believed to be the ancient shores of Atlantis.
The company was called American Atlantis, and it took them
only two years to go bankrupt. The storm shutters went back
up to stay.

American Atlantis had been thrilled when the Colonel
asked about the property as the site of his slasher movie. Finally, they had a sucker they could unload on. For the time
being, any income would be better than what they had now,
but they didn't know the Colonel. He was not staying long.
He had no intention of paying anybody. He was on a hunt.

The heat lightning above the jagged horizon flashed on and
off like a distant strobe light. Colonel Cairo inhaled deeply. "I
am running out of world," he bellowed. "Banished from the
continent I gave my life to. Was it asking too much to have
a small kingdom where I could do my work? That half-crazed

sand nigger who called himself a king forgot that it was I who put him in power. He was going to deport me, so I deported him. To hell."

Colonel Cairo started to roll. He was wearing a pair of black-and-yellow roller skates, and he started to move in circles on the skating rink that surrounded his living quarters on the second story of the old house. The wind whipped about his head, and he moved in his own small elliptical orbit around the rink. The world flashed by as a pastel swirl.

A portable stereo propped up on a folding metal chair blared out the music of Burundi drummers beating hypnotic war chants on drums made of antelope hides. The Colonel skated feverishly, and the music filled the empty night. He scratched at his left arm to brush away the mosquitoes but once again realized it was just a phantom itch on the arm that was no longer there. The years had neither erased nor softened the memory of the moment he had lost his arm near Timbuktu.

The orange glow of Miami appeared where the sun had been. This was as close as he had ever come to America or ever wanted to come. "Liberty and justice for all" was not his style. He started to snicker.

Down below, a school of tarpon rolled happily in the calm water with no sense of the evil that skated so gracefully above them on the balcony. The Colonel continued to circle the building. He leaned into the turn, careful not to shift his body weight too far. His left arm had been severed at the shoulder, so his center of gravity was off.

The skates had been a present from Rolf, his attaché, who had bought them in Miami. He figured it would give the old man something to do while they waited for the boat to arrive. Cairo had gone nuts for the skates and spent countless hours spinning around in circles.

The ever-present breeze from the ocean cooled the inflexible side of his head. It had been charred by a napalm fire, which had melted his pores, singed the nerve endings, and left him completely bald. The entire right side of his face never moved. He carried scars and shrapnel wounds from many battles, and when he walked, it was with a limp from his nagging bout with phlebitis. Life as a soldier had taken its toll on Adrian Cairo, but he did not mind. His duty was not to any country. His duty had always been to himself and to his survival. He had never really gotten rich, and his body

had been a Spartan shield that had always protected the work-
ings of his razor-sharp mind. His armor was now bent and
weak, but he was on the verge of changing all that.

"The world is changing!" he shouted above the music.
"People are more concerned about the slaughter of animals
than the slaughter of armies. They should have let me keep
my kingdom, for there I might have been content to spend
immortality in a different light." He laughed aloud. "Hah, I
was beginning to mellow, to feel human. The smell of blood
and powder had grown faint in my nostrils. The hate of old
was becoming a distant wind. Who would have thought that
those ungrateful bureaucrats would make that rat into a mar-
tyr? Bananas and beer were all they cared about, not who
provided it. But I did misjudge them slightly. I thought shooting a few of them and hanging them in the streets would
quell their loyalty to their dead king. Then those swine from
America and France told me I had to leave or they would
force me out. No thanks for all the cheating, lying, and stealing I had done for them over the years because they were too
spineless to do the dirty work themselves. Their policies created the likes of me. All I wanted was a place for a soldier
to spend his final days in pursuit of a dream. Is that too much
to ask of a greedy, unfair world? I think not."

The wheels of his skates rolled over the limestone rink and
made a humming sound. It was the hum of motion. Motion
was the glue of the universe. Colonel Cairo had been in motion all his life. If he stopped, he would die.

"My revenge will be sweet as jasmine in the night air in
these torrid latitudes. I will have my riches. And I will have
my retribution in due time." He heard the rusty door of the
parlor creak open, and Rolf stepped out onto the balcony.
Colonel Cairo glided slowly to the stereo and pushed the stop
button; the sounds of the night returned.

"Charlie Fabian has just arrived, Colonel," the tall blond
man announced.

"Show him to the gazebo, and I will meet him there for
dinner."

Rolf snapped off a salute and went back inside.

Colonel Cairo gazed out at the lights of a freighter moving
north astride the current of the Gulf Stream. "I am not a man
to be humiliated. I will seek out my enemies, and I will crush
them like a snake's head under my boot heel. I will have my
fortune, and I will have my wish."

He raised his arm above his head to signal the conclusion of his speech and waited for the rabid response to his words, but there was only the sound of fat doves cooing as they left the ground below the tamarind tree for the protection of the limbs above. Tree frogs grunted in primal tones along the crumbling seawall, and wary shore birds shrieked loudly overhead, sounding an alert to the presence of evil in the air, but their warning fell on deaf ears.

20

Who's Eating Who?

Colonel Cairo was glad he had dressed for the occasion. The night breeze held, and he had ordered a table for two set in the gazebo. The dinner was fresh lobster and salad. He wore a white dinner jacket, black tuxedo pants, a silk shirt, a cummerbund, and a bow tie, and he still had his skates on. Little Elmo's gold coins sat on the table.

Colonel Cairo was finishing the turtle soup appetizer. "Charlie, you're not eating your soup. Please, it's delicious."

Charlie stirred the soup as if it were a cup of coffee. He was nervous. He was a cold-blooded killer who could run someone like Little Elmo through with a cutlass, but he still feared the Colonel. Charlie had been uneasy at the thought of just the two of them having dinner; he was sitting on a secret, and the Colonel had a way of making you say things you did not want to say.

Charlie Fabian sat across from the Colonel and waited to be asked about the events in Charleston. He had ditched his navy outfit at a surf store where he'd bought a new disguise. Dressing up was one of the more entertaining parts of his job. It fascinated him to see how easily Americans were fooled by outward appearances. Change your clothes, change your slang, and the whole world changes with you. Now he wore a pair of Guatemalan drawstring pants and a purple sweatshirt that said "Hobie" in rainbow colors across the chest. He was dressed to surf.

The Colonel picked up one of the coins and examined it. "Quite an artifact, wouldn't you say? There aren't too many like this. I have to hand it to Elmo. He did have a streak of luck."

"What's the deal with the coins?" Charlie asked.

Colonel Cairo let the silence of authority linger and then said, "The gold is just a key that will lead me to the real treasure."

•   •   •

It had taken Charlie three vodkas before dinner and a couple of Calvados after to feel more at ease in the Colonel's presence, and now the liquor loosened his tongue.

"But, but—" Charlie took another swig of the Calvados. "Just for once I thought it would be nice to know what's going on. I mean, things haven't been quite the same since we were run out of Africa. You promised me we were going to go to Thailand and live like kings. I'd like to know when that's going to happen."

Colonel Cairo knew Charlie Fabian was a loose cannon. Charlie was not ambitious like that bastard Monty Potter. He merely followed orders with no questions asked. That was Charlie's function. The Colonel had plans for Charlie, but right now he did not need him upsetting the apple cart. Colonel Cairo lifted one of the shiny gold pieces and flipped it with his thumb at Charlie, who caught it. "Charlie, is there something you aren't telling me?"

"No, not at all. Colonel, I'm more loyal to you than any of that bunch up there in that house." From the gazebo he pointed up to the dark house on the hill where Rolf stood watching them from the balcony. "I never deserted you like Monty Potter did. I've always been there when you needed me. But I've been wondering—what's in this for me? I mean, you have your dreams—"

"Charlie, I apologize for not being attentive to your needs. What would you like?"

"Maybe a little bar on the beach in Thailand."

"And I bet there are girls in this dream world," the Colonel added.

"Yeah," Charlie said. "Lots of 'em."

The Colonel rose from the table and rolled to the end of the gazebo. He stared up at the clear night. "It's all written in the stars." The Colonel sighed. "It's where life comes from, Charlie."

Colonel Cairo loved an audience, even if it was only his hit man. "The Pleiades, the seven beautiful sisters, once attracted the attention of the handsome giant Orion, but although six of them had passionate affairs with various gods, they all rejected Orion's advances and fled. Orion and his trusted dog, Sirius, followed the sisters and pestered them for five years without managing to conquer any of them. At last they grew so weary of his pursuit that they begged the great god Zeus to hide them. Zeus responded with the ironic trick of changing the sisters into stars; he also placed Orion and Sirius in the heavens. The Pleiades, Orion, and Sirius are now fixed in eternal pursuit."

The Colonel turned back to Charlie and spoke softly. "You will have your dancing girls in Thailand, my boy. In time, in time." Then he lifted his hand and bellowed, "All skate!"

21

Skating with the Devil

Charlie Fabian had followed the Colonel back to the house, and they had been skating for about thirty minutes. It felt like an eternity to Charlie. The Colonel had removed his dinner jacket and was circling the track with the loose left sleeve of his silk shirt waving in the breeze like a battle flag.

This skating is ridiculous, Charlie thought. The old man's losing it. His new Hobie shirt was soaked with sweat, and he wobbled along on his skates, feeling blisters rise on the tops of his toes, trying not to throw up.

"That Orion story is a pretty far-out tale, Colonel, but what does it have to do with making us rich so I can retire in Thailand with a flock of little Bangkok biscuits?"

"Charles, I would appreciate it if you would refrain from vulgarity," the Colonel said.

"Oh, sorry, Colonel."

Colonel Cairo put on the brakes, and Charlie gratefully did the same. Toweling the scorched side of his head, the Colonel gulped the large glass of water that Rolf had placed on the bench.

"Charlie, there are so many unexplained mysteries on this

earth that one only has to conclude that we humans are mis-informed. Come, I have something to show you."

They moved to the front room, which had been turned into a makeshift study. A desk lamp sat on a wooden table piled high with books, charts, and yellow legal pads filled with notes. Colonel Cairo rolled to the window and stared out over the dark ocean, then glided across the floor and sat in the metal chair behind the desk. Behind him, in a large glass cage, Afro, the Colonel's green mamba, licked the air with a forked tongue. The Colonel smiled at the snake and drew a cigar from the tin on his desk and lit it.

"How long have we known each other, Charlie?"

"Going on six years, sir." Charlie still stood at attention out of habit. "A lot of water under the bridge."

"At ease, at ease," the Colonel ordered. Charlie relaxed his tense body and wiggled his feet in the tight skates, trying to ease the pain in his throbbing toes. "Did you ever hear how I lost my arm?" the Colonel asked.

"Well, I heard some stories about a battle in the bush, and—"

The Colonel interrupted him. "Not just some battle, not just some bush, not just some flesh wound. *This.*" In a savage stroke, the Colonel ripped open his shirt, and it fell to his waist to reveal the damaged shoulder. His eyes sank back into his head, and he hunched over. He hissed more than he spoke. "Come here, Charlie. Feel it. Feel what it's like not to be whole."

"Naw, Colonel, that's okay."

"Feel it! That's an order!" he shouted.

Charlie walked over to where the Colonel was standing. He looked for a wound, a nasty nub of an arm, a mangled, with-ered piece of bone, but there was none. It was as if the Colonel had been born with only one arm. Charlie tentatively reached out for the shoulder, and the Colonel grasped his hand and placed it firmly on the wound. It felt as smooth as baby skin.

"A block of marble looks like a block of marble to the nor-mal person, Charlie, but to the sculptor, it is always a statue. The work of the sculptor is to chip away the pieces that are hiding the statue, so he creates what he has seen within the stone. I have seen my statue, Charlie, but it has taken a long time to chip it out of the cold stone that is life. You would think this was the work of a highly skilled surgeon to save my life and make such a flawless repair, wouldn't you?"

"It's nice work for sure, Colonel," Charlie said nervously.

"Witch doctors," Cairo replied. "A witch doctor did this—a witch doctor with a magic wand."

"What magic wand?" Charlie asked.

The Colonel took another puff on his cigar and opened the desk. He pulled out a weathered book bound in leather and opened it to a drawing.

"This wand," he said, thrusting the book at Charlie. The scepter in the drawing had a crystal in the shape of a naked woman on one end and a triangular piece of stone on the other. "This is what you are looking for."

Colonel Cairo rebuttoned his shirt and slid a chart of the Bahamas out from under the pile of papers on his desk. "Now show me where this boat is working."

Charlie Fabian took the piece of hotel stationery from his pocket and traced the lines of latitude and longitude, then pressed his finger on the map in the middle of the Exuma Islands. "Here," he said.

The Colonel reached out and clutched Charlie's arm. "Find it. Find the scepter, and bring it to me."

"I'm going to have to have a boat, and some supplies in case I encounter any resistance," Charlie said.

"See Rolf for what you need. We will be leaving Bimini and will be arriving in Rudderville in four days. Meet us there. And Charlie? Save your surfer disguise for Halloween. That will be all."

"Yes, sir."

• • •

Colonel Cairo stood on the balcony, watching Charlie amble up the road to town. Then he returned to the rink. He skated alone and reviewed his plan with himself.

"Charlie Fabian seems happy to be a pawn on the prowl, but pawns are not privileged to know the whole story. They are always sacrificed for the good of the king. I did not become an old soldier by being stupid."

He gazed out over the water to the east. Once again he instinctively slapped at an insect on his left arm but realized it was only a phantom when he felt his open hand slap his rib cage.

"I want my arm back. I want to be whole again. I am a

flawed human, and I deserve better than that. I want my arm back!"

The Colonel slammed his fist against the thick concrete wall of the house. He was startled by Rolf's voice.

"Sir, we have just made contact with your boat. The *Nomad* will be here within the hour."

• • •

Charlie needed a drink. He walked down the dirt road toward Adamstown, thinking how much the little Bimini village reminded him of Africa. He had heard stories of how the Colonel has lost his arm, how he and Monty Potter had together been the most feared mercenaries in all of Africa, but he had never heard why they became mortal enemies. He wondered if it had something to do with the witch doctors and the Colonel's arm. He had lied about the scepter, but he wasn't sure why. He just liked having at least one trump card when dealing with the old man.

The Colonel was cracking up. "And I thought I was the crazy one," he said aloud. He was thinking that it might be time to consider his options, but first he would check out the treasure ship.

Charlie Fabian could hear music in the distance, and he followed it down the road to the Compleat Angler Hotel. He sat alone at a table in the corner and listened to a junkanoo band until the early hours of the morning, then walked over to the Chalk's terminal and sat on the seawall, waiting for the early plane to Miami.

22

It's Better in the Bahamas

Charlie Fabian arrived in Miami a few minutes before nine o'clock. He checked into a sleazy motel on Biscayne Boulevard, bought a *Herald*, and ran quickly through the listings until he found what he was looking for.

He met the potential seller an hour later at the address on the Intracoastal Waterway. There was a For Sale sign in front of the house, on each of the two Mercedes 450SLs in the driveway, and on the boat at the dock. It looked like somebody was leaving town in a hurry or going to jail.

The owner was a small, nervous Colombian who chainsmoked Virginia Slims and spoke bad English, repeating "Fasty boat, fasty very" every time Charlie asked a question. The boat was a 1980 Scarab II powered by twin T-330 Mercury engines, and it was built to go fast in heavy water. The hull was solid black, and an orange-and-green stripe ran along it. The words *Wet Dream* were painted in giant Day-Glo orange letters across the stern. Charlie spent twenty minutes checking the boat, and when he was satisfied, he made the man a cash offer, which was happily accepted.

• • •

Charlie picked up some more clothes at the surf shop. The hell with the Colonel, he thought. The loose T-shirt and jams gave him room to breathe. The freedom of movement triggered thoughts of total release from the Colonel's web of secrets and plots. Charlie laughed. He too would have a boat. He was cooking up a way out in his twisted brain.

He topped off his fuel tanks at Pier 66, and two hours later, Charlie was in possession of more information about seamanship than most boat owners in South Florida acquire in a lifetime. He had paid an electronics salesman at a local shop two hundred dollars to show him how to run the Loran unit, and he'd bought a cruising guide to the Bahamas.

The prerecorded weather information on the VHF radio called for southeast winds of ten to fifteen knots, with a possibility of an increase by evening. There was a tropical depression advisory about a storm down south of Cuba, but the skies above Miami were sunny and bright.

Charlie cleared the ship channel and punched in the coordinates on the Loran. He calculated the drift of the Gulf Stream and plotted his course on the chart. He moved the throttles to full forward and put the *Wet Dream* up on a plane. He felt like a pirate.

An hour later he sighted the radio tower on Gun Cay and entered the channel. He cleared customs in Cat Cay using his false Canadian passport and took on fuel. He then rendezvoused with Rolf near Bird Cay in the Berry Islands and loaded his diving gear and weapons.

Charlie entered Nassau Harbor from the east, sped past Paradise Island Light, and stayed to the left side of the channel, watching the tugs assist a giant cruise ship in the turning basin. He fueled at Hurricane Hole and then headed east through Montagu Bay and entered his coordinates for Beacon Cay.

Maneuvering his way through the coral heads, he crossed the Yellow Bank and picked up the range poles of the small channel that led to No Man's Cay, the place Sledge had mentioned in Charleston. He eased the *Wet Dream* up to the only wooden dock under a sign that read Driftwood Marina. There was no one on the dock.

Sunset in the islands meant cocktail hour, and Charlie followed the sound of a bass-and-drum reggae groove to a yellow-framed bar called the Culture Club and ordered a beer. A group of tourists sat at a table reliving their day underwa-

ter, and in the center of the room, four black men were totally
wrapped up in a domino game. The aroma of home-cooked
fried food filled the air, and a menu was written on a black-
board behind the bar, where a tall, thin black man moved to
the music. Charlie took a seat at the bar.

"How it goes, Captain mon?" the bartender asked with a
smile. He wore a pair of cutoffs and a Bob Marley T-shirt.'

Charlie focused on the gold *R* and *B* that glistened on the
man's two front teeth. "What do the initials stand for?"

"Root Boy."

"That your Christian name?"

"Dat be my name," Root Boy answered. "What can I be
gettin' fo you?"

Root Boy had watched the man in the mirrored sunglasses
dock his flashy boat. It was the same old story. Big boat, one
guy asking too many questions. No doubt about what he was
doing in these parts. He was either a cop or a scammer.

"How about a beer?"

"Beck's or Kalik?"

"Beck's, Charlie replied.

"You be needin' a room?" Root Boy asked.

"No, I'm lookin' for some friends."

Charlie grabbed the beer and walked to a corner table and
watched the domino game in progress. A sunburned couple
yelled out from the end of the bar, "Hey Roof Boy, got any
of that conch salad?"

Root Boy shook his head and laughed. "Da name be *Root*
Boy like deez initials on my teef, and da meal be cracked
conch like *honk,* not *conch* like *haunch.* You know, I saw dis
movie once wif Humphrey Bogart where dere be a boat captain from Key West, and he tell da policeman his boat be
called da Queen Conch, but he say it wrong. Din' sound too
believable to me."

"If you want da knowledge, you come to Domino College!" one of the black men yelled from the table. He
slammed the last domino so hard it lifted all the rest off the
table.

Charlie Fabian ordered dinner and gulped down the
cracked conch and several more beers. He played a few
rounds of dominoes and actually won—to the surprise of the
men at the table. Charlie had spent his share of time in third-
world bars.

He bought the table several rounds and struck up a conversation with the tourists at the bar. Root Boy dropped in on the conversation and heard the stranger tell the couple that he was a photographer for a travel agency that booked diving trips. He was here on No Man's Cay to shoot pictures for a story on the romantic life of treasure divers.

Whatever this guy was, he was no photographer. He was chumming for information.

"I'm supposed to hook up with a couple of guys named Pete and RePete. They're on a dive boat out of Key West named the *Bottoms Up,*" Charlie said casually. The woman shoveled a large forkful of conch salad into her mouth and talked as she chewed.

"Oh, they were in here yesterday," she said. "They looked like real pirates. It was quite exciting. We bought these coins from them. Show the man, Morris." Her husband pulled a gold chain out from under his shirt and dangled the coin for Charlie to see. It was the same coin as the ones he had taken from Little Elmo.

"Nice," he said with a friendly smile.

"I just love the thought of sunken treasure," the lady added.

"Me, too."

• • •

The squall line moved like an advancing army across the Bahama Banks. A symphony of thunderclaps rumbled in the distance. Pelicans, snail kites, and kingfishers flew in various formations away from the approaching cumulonimbus clouds. Only the turkey buzzards remained. They circled above the tiny sand spit waiting for something to happen. They never missed a meal.

Wind gusts swept the palms back and forth; they swayed like the baton of a conductor, and then rain slashed across the sky in sheets. Invisible ions and electrons filled the air, and lightning surged from the base of the clouds to the surface of the sea.

Charlie Fabian's sunglasses sat on the dashboard of the boat, and he made slow circles on his temples with ice cubes. His eyes ached from the trip across the shallow Exuma Banks, dodging coral heads and searching the shoreline of the low barren cays for his prey. The pain in his head came from the music he had been forced to listen to for the past hour.

He had spotted the salvage tug just before dawn. It had been lit up like a Christmas tree and was anchored off a place called Horseshoe Cove. A long speedboat was rafted up next to the tug.

Charlie couldn't tell from the screaming whether a party or an interrogation was taking place. The music of Joe Merchant had once again come back to haunt him. Above the steady clatter of human voices, the all-too-familiar sound of Joe's classic hit "Little Boy Gone" came from a tape player somewhere on the salvage boat.

He added it to his target list.

23

The Day Cain Slew Abel

Thorn Marshall was partied out. Three naked hookers were huddled together in the small bunk like sleeping puppies, and Thorn lay like a spent salmon on the floor of the seedy little cabin.

Thorn was employed by Monty Potter, and at the current time he was bag man. He and Potter had worked out a scam to pay off the divers on Little Elmo's boat to send Potter samples of what was coming off the bottom. They were searching for the lost treasure of Henri Christophe, and all the evidence so far indicated they were on the right track. Once the divers found the motherlode, Potter planned to move in and take the treasure for himself while Little Elmo was on the mainland entertaining coke whores.

Word had not yet reached them of Little Elmo's death. Thorn's two informants had told him that the salvage tug was about to move south, and they were now alone on the boat. It was the perfect time for Thorn to visit his two snitches.

The run from Santo Domingo to the southern Bahamas was a breeze in a fast boat. He had been holed up in Puerto Plata with a few "working girls" until he could make telephone contact with the divers. The girls took the edge off the boredom of waiting by the pay phone at the marina every afternoon. They'd been very impressed with his speedboat and his story of sunken treasure, but it was the blow job that had gotten them aboard. There, in the throes of passion, Thorn had agreed to smuggle them into America.

Pete Moss and RePete Preacher had been left to stand watch while the rest of the crew had gone to Nassau for the weekend. They couldn't believe their luck when Thorn had pulled alongside the treasure boat, and three bare-breasted beauties had jumped out.

Pete and RePete were typical modern-day salvage divers—nineteen, blond, and looking for adventure. They were the latest victims of the lure of gold bars; in the clear shallow waters, money glistened, waiting to be found and spent. But treasure hunting is a hit-and-miss business, with more misses than hits—especially if you were working for Little Elmo. The chance to make some cash on the side and the possibility of hooking up with a real pirate like Monty Potter thrilled them to no end.

It had been a wild night. Thorn felt his dick start to get hard, and he gazed at the pile of girls and thought about a quickie. He realized his head hurt too much, and anyway, he needed to figure out what to do with the girls. He had fucked up and stayed too late at the ball. One thing was for certain: he had no intention of taking the girls to America. He needed coffee.

He quietly rose from the deck and slipped into his jeans. He dug the 9-mm pistol out from under the bunk and tucked it into the back of his waistband.

Thorn walked outside to an eerie morning. Thunder rumbled off on the horizon, and squall lines were visible. The threatening skies gave a strange cast to the morning. It looked as if the clouds were about to explode again, yet the water was flat calm, and there were no birds in the sky. Music was blaring from the galley, and he headed toward the smell of coffee.

• • •

"What the fuck are we guarding against? Aliens? A nuclear attack?" Pete asked Thorn. "I want to know where all this fucking treasure is supposed to be. So far we've brought up sixteen goddamn coins, ten cannonballs, and some kind of fucking magic wand. I'd have a better chance of winning the goddamn lottery."

The screeching guitar of Joe Merchant rattled the rivets in the steel hull of the *Bottoms Up.* "Turn that shit down, will ya? It's a little early in the morning for that crap, and I gotta think."

"Hey, man, Joe Merchant is God. He knew how to live and when to check out. Besides, it's like our alarm clock, man," Pete said.

"Yeah, and I'm the fucking tooth fairy. I gotta figure out what to do with the girls," Thorn told him.

"Leave 'em with us. Tell 'em this is the *Love Boat.* They could teach us Spanish," RePete said as he came through the galley door.

"Potter would kick my ass if he knew I'd stopped in Puerto Plata in the first place," Thorn said.

"And I bet you promised them all you'd take 'em to Graceland, right?" RePete sneered.

"It's easy," Pete said. "Drop 'em on the south end of Andros with some food and water. Tell 'em it's Key Largo, and get the fuck out of there. Coast Guard'll find 'em in a couple of days, or they'll walk to Congo Town, and the Bahamians'll send 'em home."

Thorn smiled and held up the palm of his hand. Pete slapped it.

"That's why I get paid the big bucks," Pete said. "Now that I've solved your problem, you have to help me with the anchor."

• • •

The girls were up and had put their skimpy clothes back on. They chattered excitedly to one another in Spanish as they sat in Thorn's boat, waiting to be taken to Key Largo.

"Uno momento," Thorn called to them as the *Bottoms Up* swung on the rusty anchor chain.

The wind shifted to the southwest under a two-tone sky, and low clouds to the south were growing darker. Rain showers could again be seen in the distance.

Thorn stood with his boot on the foot switch of the electric windlass, and Pete straddled the bowsprit. He kept an eye on the wet, rusty chain that banged loudly against the deck and disappeared into the chain locker. Thorn watched the black clouds building on the horizon and mumbled to himself. One of the girls waved at him from his boat.

"Uno momento," he shouted again.

"Whad'dya say?" Pete yelled, but Thorn couldn't hear him.

Pete looked down over the bow. The normally clear water was now blurred with sand and debris that the anchor had dislodged from the bottom. Sea fans, turtle grass, and tiny pieces of flotsam and jetsam swirled around in the discolored water. The tip of the anchor emerged from the mud cloud.

"Anchor's aweigh!" Pete yelled to RePete, who was standing by at the wheel.

"Oh, shit, looks like we picked up a garbage bag on the hook. Keep her coming, Thorn. I'll knock it off."

Pete grabbed the gin pole. He thrust it down at the black object hanging on the anchor, trying to dislodge it. He held the pole tightly and jabbed hard.

Before Pete knew what happened, the pole jerked back violently, and he somersaulted over the bowsprit and fell headfirst into the water.

Thorn lifted his foot off the windlass switch, and the anchor hung a foot from the end of the bowsprit. The girls were laughing at Pete like Hekyll and Jekyll, and Thorn joined them.

"April fool," Charlie Fabian said.

Thorn's mouth froze in silence, and the girls began to scream when they saw the man in the wet suit straddling the anchor with a speargun in his hand.

"It's the day Cain slew Abel, sailor. Not a very good day to start a voyage."

Thorn reached for the gun on his hip, but the blast of Charlie's power head lifted his body off the deck and catapulted it into the ocean.

Pete screamed from the water nearby. "Hey, man, what the fuck is happening here? Who the fuck are you?"

Charlie Fabian leaned over the rail and grinned. "Jealous, dude? You'll get yours soon enough." He pulled a shotgun out of his waterproof pouch and pumped three rounds into the wheelhouse, where RePete stood in shock.

The first shot scored a direct hit on the radio antenna, and the next one shattered the windscreen. The third exploded the boom box, and that was the end of Joe Merchant's guitar solo. RePete scurried for cover on the aft deck, leaving the boat out of control and drifting in the current toward the reef.

Charlie got out of his scuba rig and moved carefully in the direction of the wheelhouse. Rain fell out of the dark cloud that had overtaken the foundering salvage tug, and the gusting wind sent salt spray across the decks. The girls in the speedboat ducked down in fear.

Still clutching the gin pole, Pete fought through the waves and swam over to Thorn. He grabbed Thorn's arm and turned him over to get his head out of the water, but Thorn had no head. Blood poured from the severed jugular veins that dangled out of his neck, turning the seawater crimson.

It didn't take long for the sharks to appear. In minutes, they were lunging and thrashing at Thorn's body, holding onto the corpse with their razor-sharp teeth. They shook him like a rag doll till the flesh separated from the bone.

Using the pole, Pete flailed in a hysterical attempt to drive away the darting predators. The girls were now shrieking in panic.

"Oh God, I don't want to die. Oh God," Pete cried from the bloody water.

Shots came from the stern of the salvage tug, and Charlie dove for cover behind the crane. When the firing stopped, he cautiously peeked and saw RePete moving aft. He leveled his shotgun and fired. RePete let out a yell as blood began gushing down his leg.

Charlie Fabian then extracted a grenade from the waterproof pouch that hung across his shoulder.

"Totally rad, man. Bet you dudes weren't expectin' me. I think we can keep things from gettin' too gnarly here for your bro. I need a little info, and then I'll help him back up," Charlie said. "I'm lookin' for a scepter. You seen it?"

"Fuck you, Sledge, and fuck Little Elmo. You bunch of lame motherfuckers. Monty Potter will skewer your ass when he finds out about this. You want me? Come and get me, cocksucker," yelled RePete. A hail of bullets came from the stern and ricocheted around the wheelhouse.

"Monty Potter," Charlie said with a laugh. So Potter was involved somehow. This was interesting news.

"Say, dude, I got a little present for you." Charlie was in the process of hurling the grenade at the sound of RePete's voice when the bow of the *Bottoms Up* slammed into the coral reef. Charlie was hurled onto the open deck. The grenade fell from his hand and rolled back and forth on the deck only a few feet from his head.

More shots struck all around him, and Charlie felt a thud

in his upper arm. He scrambled like mad and managed to roll off the deck just as the grenade exploded amidships.

Charlie Fabian found himself sprawled on top of the hookers. He had landed in the open speedboat, and he was a sitting duck. He grabbed his last grenade and waited for RePete to appear above him. It was his only hope.

Suddenly he heard the sound of an outboard motor and caught a glimpse of RePete in a dinghy, roaring across the tops of the waves like a bronc rider, past the stern of the *Bottoms Up*. RePete disappeared into the dim confines of the storm.

Charlie relaxed and untangled himself from the pile of terrified women and pushed them to the side of the boat. He unzipped his wet suit and pulled down the sleeves. The bullet had grazed his left deltoid, and he took the bandanna from his neck and tied it around the wound. He motioned to one of the women and spoke to her in Spanish. The girl told him she and her friends wanted to go to America.

Charlie untied the speedboat and started the engines. He placed one girl's hand on the wheel and showed her how to operate the throttles. He checked the compass, then pointed northeast with his good arm. "America está allá. Comprende?" he asked.

"Sí, sí," the girl replied. "America." The women all started repeating "America."

Charlie nudged the boat into gear and pointed them at the land of the free, and then he slipped over the side and disappeared beneath the waves.

• • •

Pete had managed to escape the sharks. He wasn't far from shallow water and safety. His ears and nose were bleeding, and his head rang like a fire alarm from the concussion of the grenade explosion, but he was alive. He let the waves carry him as he slowly lost consciousness.

When he finally came to, he had no idea how long he had been passed out on the beach. The first thing he saw was the turkey buzzards circling overhead, and then he heard the muffled rumble of engines. Someone was singing. His hands were cold and numb, and when he tried to move them he realized they were tied together. Pete raised his head and screamed.

The *Wet Dream* idled in the cut between the reefs, and Pete could see that the line attached to his wrists was also attached to the boat. Charlie Fabian was standing at the controls, singing.

> *"Away to the fleeting world go you,*
> *Where pirates all are well-to-do.*
> *But I'll be true to the song I sing*
> *And live and die a pirate king."*

The boat idled slowly forward until the slack was out of the line. In a flash, Pete was sliding across the sand, kicking and screeching.

"Let's go waterskiing," Charlie yelled and advanced the throttle to full speed.

• • •

From about a quarter of a mile down the beach, Root Boy had watched the whole attack take place. He had been gathering lobsters, working the long, narrow sandbar that jutted out from Horseshoe Cove. When the storm came up, he had taken temporary shelter in a lean-to on the beach.

The salvo of cloudbursts had now moved across the water, and the sun glinted out from behind the clouds. He saw the big black boat run close to the exposed portions of the reef, and he watched as the man behind the boat bounced off the razor-sharp coral and iron rock.

White men killing white men was of no concern to him. He had seen it before and knew not to get involved. It would only bring him trouble.

24

Suntans and Percodans

The morning's business had gone splendidly, and Charlie felt like a soldier again. He stood behind the wheel of the big Scarab, naked to the waist.

The sun felt good on his salt-covered body, but his arm ached. The pain had been made tolerable by the bottle of Percodan he'd found in the first aid kit behind the head. He had eaten half the pills as if they were M&M's, and now he floundered in the euphoria between comfort and discomfort.

The waterskiing run along the reef had finally convinced Pete to tell Charlie what he needed to know. In pirate fashion, Charlie had hung what was left of the driver on a stake near the channel, like a giant piece of beef jerky. The turkey buzzards were only too happy to make a meal out of the remaining strips of flesh.

When he was far enough away from the scene of the crime, Charlie stopped and took care of the hole in his arm. He scrubbed it with saltwater, coated it with aloe, and ripped his shirt into bandages to reduce the chance of infection until he got to the Colonel's boat. Though he had been wounded, he had hoped for a little more resistance from the salvage divers.

He felt good about liberating the women, but he had really wanted the whole crew on board the boat. It would have made for a more exciting battle. He hadn't gotten to use all the weapons he'd brought along for the kill.

The flat light of the evening sun made for poor visibility in the shallow water, but Charlie was not thinking about seamanship. His orders were to rendezvous with the Colonel in Rudderville at noon, and he was already late. The Colonel would be pissed off, but that didn't scare him now as much as it used to.

What would he tell Cairo? There had been a time when Charlie and the Colonel complemented each other perfectly. One conceived the plan, and the other carried it out. The Colonel was the charmer, and Charlie was the cobra—slithering through the killing fields of backwater countries as if they were his personal playgrounds.

Charlie Fabian loved the way he traveled. The sphere of time held no boundaries for him. He made up his own dimensions, and his tattooed eyes kept him alert to danger. He held on to the wheel of the boat and felt the power of the engines vibrating his hands. His tattooed eyes now told him that the danger ahead was the Colonel himself. He would have to be careful. He would have to be patient and pick his time to make a break. He decided not to tell the Colonel about Monty Potter, knowing the Colonel would head directly to Boomtown to take his revenge on the man who had betrayed him. And he thought it wise to keep the location of the scepter to himself, knowing that this was what the Colonel was really after. He smiled. His plan was becoming clear.

Charlie's Percodan daydream came to a sudden halt with the alarming *scrunch* of a high-speed impact.

"Goddamn it, fucking coral head." He went to the stern and sat on the diving platform, staring at the twisted pieces of metal that moments before had been propelling him at sixty-five miles an hour across the water. One lower unit had been completely sheared away, and the other had been twisted 180 degrees.

Charlie Fabian was dead in the water, but things like this happened. He was a soldier and knew the first rule was to stay calm and work out an alternative. He tossed out the anchor to keep from drifting to the islands and started to think. He couldn't radio for help and risk being seen in the area. He checked his Bahamas guide and then got a fix from the Loran unit. He estimated his present location to be about seven miles east of Pass Her By Cay. He verified his position when he picked up the unusual shape of a car on stilts that the cruising guide had pointed out. He wrestled the small rubber dinghy out of the storage locker, banging his wounded arm against the bulkhead.

"Motherfucker!" he cried and shook his arm. He popped another Percodan, then began the tedious job of inflating the dinghy with the awkward foot pump. As he listened to the sound of air rushing into the limp rubber boat, he decided what he would do. He would sink the *Wet Dream* and row to the fishing village on Pass Her By Cay, lay low until after dark, and steal a boat.

He was dripping wet and out of breath when he pushed against the side of the dinghy. The pontoons were firm, and he dropped it over the side and tied it off to a cleat on the transom, then loaded the RPG-2 rocket launcher. He climbed up on the dashboard and took aim at the deck. He would blow the bottom out of the boat, and it would disappear below the surface in a matter of minutes.

As he was about to squeeze the trigger, he heard the droning of airplane engines coming his way. He jumped down out of sight, grabbed his binoculars, and searched the evening sky for the plane. He scrambled to the forward cabin and found more rockets for the launcher. He was ready in case it was the cops.

The plane appeared in the viewing circle of the binoculars. Charlie followed the old Grumman Goose across the sky. It didn't look threatening, and it had no military markings, which made him happy. The seaplane descended and turned into the wind. The pitch of the engine noise faded as the plane gradually landed on the surface of the water near the cut in the reef.

Charlie rowed the rubber boat a hundred yards from the stern of the *Wet Dream* and fired the rocket launcher. It let out a roar and blew a hole the size of a garbage-can lid in the side of the Scarab. The boat lifted momentarily out of the water, then settled to one side, and the bow began to rise slowly. By the time Charlie Fabian had rowed another hundred yards toward Pass Her By Cay, the *Wet Dream* was at the bottom of Exuma Sound.

Tickets
to Ride

25

Stand by Your Passenger

I planned to stay on Pass Her By Cay just long enough to refuel, take a piss, grab a conch burger, and let Hoagy stretch his legs. But the closer I got to the island, the more I realized I needed a break from all the shit that had blown my direction. Pass Her By Cay had some of the best bonefishing in the Bahamas, and I figured it would be better for me to hide out in the boondocks than to be sneaking around Rudderville.

There was a reason Pass Her By Cay had such a strange name. The island lay hidden away in the southern Bahamas and had been pretty much overlooked by the world since Columbus ran aground near the one small harbor on the south end of the island. It was the attack of the mosquitoes, not the Indians, that caused him to mention the place at all in his log. When the tide released the hull of the *Santa Maria* from the grip of the coral reef, Columbus gave the island a wide berth and sailed south to name island after island. The place had been passed by ever since, and the name stuck.

Pass Her By Cay was a barren, windswept fragment of dead coral speckled with a few stunted shrubs and bushes. The rest of the shoreline was fringed with reef. For generations, fishermen had flung their nets into the ocean for fish and had gathered sponges and lobsters from the bountiful reefs. The years just passed by. The young grew old, and the old died. Each generation mirrored the previous one. Well, if you wait long enough, something will happen, and Pass Her By Cay just lay baking in the sun for several centuries like an incubating egg.

Then it happened. The big metal birds with shiny wings and loud engines swooped down from the skies and hatched the island into the twentieth century.

Contact with the outside world was established in the fifties when a Grumman Mallard brought Isaac Spiegel, chairman of the board of the Spiegel Sponge Company, to the island. He made a speech to the crowd of locals who had gathered more to admire the beautiful plane than to listen to the fat white man in the suit. Isaac spoke of the history of the sponge back to the time one soaked with vinegar had been mockingly presented to Christ on the cross. He spoke of the new era of the sponge. It was no longer just a bathroom item. It was now an industrial commodity used by potters, bricklayers, lithographers, jewelers, and silversmiths. When he was through, Isaac basked in the applause given to him by his board of directors, and then they all jumped back on the plane and took off.

The town dock was soon abuzz with the sponge trade. Orange, violet, green, and rich brown sheep's wool and velvet sponges dried in the sun and were taken to market in Nassau. A ramp was built for the company plane, and the island enjoyed additional prosperity by selling mosquito nets and citronella candles to the Spiegel bosses for protection against the persistent mosquitoes. Several local fishermen were shocked when the Americans actually paid them money to catch the bonefish that spread across the flats by the thousands.

The economic boom hit its peak in the late fifties when the Cadillac arrived. At this point, Isaac Spiegel weighed in at about three hundred pounds and had a bad case of gout. On one of his visits, he had been wheeled about the island in a rusty grocery cart. That did not suit a captain of industry. Consequently, he had a special runway constructed on the island and had a black Cadillac convertible flown in directly from Detroit for his use when he visited the offices.

Isaac Spiegel never saw the car. He choked to death on a

chunk of rib eye at the 21 Club in New York. The sponge market bottomed out with the advent of synthetic sponges, and the company closed its sponging operations shortly after Isaac's death and diversified into trashbag futures. The ponds were left to the mosquitoes and bonefish, and the airport was inherited by the pelicans and flamingos that hatched their young there and slowly circled the thermals above the soft asphalt runway.

The Cadillac was donated to the Mt. Zion Fundamentalist African Reform Church and put under the care and protection of the Reverend Hampton Johnston. He used it well for funerals and visits to the other side of the island until the suspension system caved in and the engine fell out. The Cadillac was painted pink, hoisted up on stilts above the bar owned by the Reverend Johnston's brother Maurice, and lined up with a palm tree on the beach to make range markers to steer boats through the cut in the reef. From the front seat, the locals could sip a beer and look a little farther over the horizon and dream about what was really out there in America.

On the first day of the second-to-last decade of the century, the islanders woke up to no noise. The birds had deserted the runway and had vanished overnight. That evening, the Americans came again, but they were not interested in the sponges. They carried big guns and lots of cash. Money changed hands, deals were cut, and Maurice Johnston supervised the planting of four giant fuel-storage tanks in the sand.

Soon dope planes arrived nightly. The bar was filled with young pirates throwing their money around as if they were playing Monopoly. Locals began sporting gold Rolexes, and a satellite dish was planted in every yard. The Cadillac was painted red and green, and the name of the bar was changed to the Afterburner Lounge. Nobody asked any questions. The people of Pass Her By Cay were just trying to make a buck. It was the first lesson they had been taught by the original Americans—who had long ago dried up and vanished like the sponges that had brought them.

It all ended one day as quickly as it began with a full-scale attack by the Bahamian Defense Force and the DEA. Two planes were shot out of the sky, and several Colombians were killed. Maurice escaped with a few other men and disappeared into the mountains on the north coast of Haiti.

Reporters came with video cameras, and the Cadillac made the "NBC Nightly News." Then, once again, the invaders flew away as quickly as they had come, and Pass Her By Cay went back to its legacy of abandonment. The Cadillac was repainted pink, and the bar went back to its original name.

I had visited Pass Her By Cay often when I'd run bonefishing charters but steered clear when the dopers took over. I had asked Maurice once if it bothered him to be in cahoots with those guys. He told me, "In deez parts when da good times come, dey gallop in like wild horses. You try and ride 'em for as long as you can, and when dey trow you off, you just wait in da shade til dey come by again."

I lined up the palm tree on the beach with the pink Cadillac on the hill and steered a compass heading of eighty-nine degrees. I hadn't been to Pass Her By Cay in about two years, and I felt my way through the break in the reef, making sure the channel had not meandered in my absence.

In the air, the Goose is a wonderful flying machine, but once you hit water, you are basically in a boat with a forty-nine-foot beam, not much steerage, and a tendency to cock into the wind. I picked up the cut between the dark grass to the south and a sandbar to the north and eased off the power when I saw green water out the window. Thank God for Polaroid sunglasses.

The old engines chugged away and pushed the *Hemisphere Dancer* through the clear water. They had run smooth as silk on the crossing, and I had come nearly all the way from Florida five feet above the waves. That's not much altitude if you have a problem, but I had no choice if I didn't want to show up as a blip on the radar screen attached to the high-altitude balloon called "Fat Albert," a Big-Brother device that loomed thirty thousand feet above the Keys like a prison guard in a watchtower.

I slid the window open, and over the low idle of the engines, I could just make out the sound of music coming from the Friday night service at the little church at the far end of the village. The steady backbeat of a heavy-footed bass drummer carried the chords of the guitar and organ out the window where they floated above the waves and mixed with the call of the birds perched on the dock.

A couple of kids had come down to the beach, and they waved to me. Hoagy saw them and started barking. I used a little differential power and moved the starboard throttle forward slightly to compensate for a gust of wind that whipped a patch of cattails across the shallow water in front of the ramp. When the wheels touched, I gave her the juice, and the *Dancer* waddled forward and up the incline as the kids took off running up the dirt road. I spun her around so her nose faced the water in case I had to leave in a hurry.

I shut the engines down, and Hoagy bounded for the cargo door with a demanding bark. I swung the hatch open, and he sprang for the ground, circling the plane several times before heading for the rusty ruins of a pickup truck, where he cocked his leg and took a long, satisfying piss.

Friday evening was a good time for an arrival, because chances were the place would be deserted. I could make out a wisp of black smoke to the north on the edge of the vacant Caribbean Sea, and I wondered if a ship of some kind was under it. There wasn't anyone to ask, and there didn't seem to be anybody around the faded red roof of the customshouse next to the ramp. That was lucky, because I was having a hard time remembering my new tail number. I glanced down at my clipboard and studied the new numbers on the forged cruising permits I had bought from Ace. I dropped one in the box in front of the customshouse, then grabbed my fly rod and tackle bag and walked to the airport building.

The old rusty rental bikes were still there. I dropped a dollar in the box and pedaled through town to the big flat on the other end of the island. Hoagy ran along beside me, pausing from time to time to investigate the long grasses on each side of the road. There was an incoming tide, and if I was lucky, I would get in an hour or so of fishing before sunset. I needed it. After what had happened in the last twenty-four hours, the healthiest thing I could do was stop thinking. I wanted to think of nothing but a big forked tail flashing in front of me.

I pedaled past a large stagnant pond where the mosquitoes were cooling off, but as sunset approached, you were fair game. They never bit the locals. These mosquitoes seemed to enjoy holding out and tormenting the fresh meat of the occasional visitor. I always had a feeling that the Nazi SS were reincarnated as mosquitoes and horseflies.

I fished until dark, and despite the wind, I caught two eight-pound bonefish. Then I called Hoagy out of the nearby pond where he was bobbing for minnows and rode my bike up the old, familiar road to get a conch burger and a couple of beers.

I climbed into the pink Cadillac and ate my dinner, dropping conch fritters to Hoagy on the ground, who kept a targeted eye on the falling food. Then I pedaled back to the plane and set up my hammock under the wing, covered myself with Skin So Soft, and hid beneath my mosquito net. Once again, I was lulled to sleep by the whisper of the trade winds through the palms.

Hoagy and I were up with the sun the next morning. Hoagy took off down the beach, and I went for a swim. While I was drying off and packing up, a skinny black man shuffled over to the plane from under the porch of the small wooden fuel shack. He was wearing a pair of cutoff sweatpants and a white T-shirt decorated with a giant mosquito dripping red blood. "I Gave Blood on Pass Her By Cay" was stenciled below the insect. Dreadlocks streamed out from under the man's baseball hat and dangled to his waist.

This was B.M. Johnston, and B.M. stood for Bob Marley. He was Maurice's son, and he had changed his name the day Bob Marley passed away in a New York hospital from brain cancer. Bob Marley was the St. Jude of the third world. I had first seen B.M. when he was a little boy. B.M. was an okay kid, but a hustler.

Well, everything had a price on Pass Her By Cay—fuel, ice, beer, information, lack of information. He obviously didn't recognize me and started his usual speech: "B.M. Johnston be my name, and petrol be my game—" He stopped in midsentence when a hint of recognition filtered through his ganja-soaked brain. "Dat be you dere, Captain Bama? Ain't seen you 'round deez parts in a while. Dis here a different plane you had since last time, ain't it?"

"I'm delivering it down to Haiti. It belongs to a timber baron up in Alaska," I said.

A look of cold hate sprang from his eyes at the mention of Haiti. "Doz are evil people on dat island. Cursed by da devil. Baby Doc kill my daddy. One day, I gonna kill his ass dead, too. You betta watch you ass in Haiti, mon."

"I'll do that."

After the warning, B.M. switched back to his jovial mode. Like the lizards on these barren islands, the natives knew adaptability was essential to survival. There was money to be made.

"Fill 'er up t'day, boss?"

"What you be askin' for dat one-hundred-octane stuff deez days, mon?" I asked in my best Bahamian accent. Fuel prices were calculated according to the size of your plane, the look of your clothes, and your sense of urgency.

B.M. scratched his head and pulled a small notepad and a calculator from his pocket. I braced myself for the figure. I had burned a lot more fuel by wave-hopping than I would have at a higher altitude. My gauges had shown only about fourteen gallons remaining in the tanks when I had shut down. That was cutting it closer than I liked.

"You in luck, mon, I got a special Goombay price today. Two-fifty a gallon."

I didn't flinch, though it was twice what the same fuel cost in Key West. I had only two hundred dollars left after paying for the paint job and forged documents yesterday. It was just one-hundred-seventy miles from Pass Her By to Rudderville, but I needed to hold on to a little "gettin' around money."

I quickly figured the fuel burn for the trip, calculating how much reserve I could spare and still get a few beers, a room, and a grouper fingers lunch when I got to town later. I was never very good at bargaining, but I was rapidly approaching the point of being as broke as I had ever been in my life.

"B.M., I could sure live a little better at, say, two twenty-five."

B.M. said nothing. He buried his face again in the small calculator. You would have thought he was trying to figure out the theory of relativity. I waited for the decision like it was the end of a heavyweight fight.

"I can live wif dat," B.M. said and walked off to get the fueling hose.

I heard Hoagy barking and saw him with two kids by the salt pond. One of the boys heaved a stick into the pond, and Hoagy did a Hollywood stunt-dog leap over the water, but when he came down, all four of his paws sank into the soft mud, and he was stuck for a moment with a puzzled look on his big face. It took him a while to figure out his predicament, but he freed himself and went off in search of the stick.

I paid B.M. for the "cut-rate" fuel. "I got something for you," I said and walked to the door of the plane.

Though Pass Her By Cay was no longer a pit stop for DC-3s filled with marching powder, it was still steeped in the tradition of "no questions asked." If someone did pick up my trail and came here looking for clues, they would get no answers from the Pass Her Bys, but it would cost me. I pulled my Sony multiband digital shortwave out from under my bunk. It had been given to me by Billy Cruiser for my thirty-fifth birthday and had been my contact with the outside world when I was flying the bush.

"This is for you."

Bob Marley Johnston whistled and reached out for the radio. He cradled it in his arms as if it were a newborn baby.

"Anybody comes asking around here about an old seaplane, you ain't seen nothin'," I said.

He looked at me, stared out over the ramp, and then turned in a slow circle. "What plane? I don't see no seaplane. I don't even know what one looks like."

• • •

Quick bursts of music, news, and static filled the air as Bob Marley Johnston went back to the shade and began rapidly turning the dial. I would miss the Sony, but I still had my old VHF. Right now I needed anonymity more than I needed information. I called Hoagy away from the pond; it was time to move on.

The *Hemisphere Dancer* sat patiently on the ramp, but for a moment I didn't recognize her without the totem pole on the tail. I had taken some Polaroids along the way, and I pulled them out of my shirt pocket and looked at them. One was a view of the new paint job and numbers, and the other was a "before" shot of the *Dancer*. I was still very troubled that I'd had to paint over the totem pole. I take my good-luck charms seriously; St. Christopher has been pinned above my head ever since I left Venezuela. I had no idea what the totem pole meant, but I hoped the spirits that had ridden with me since I'd come out of the bush would understand that the paint job had been necessary. If I ever did make it to Alaska, the first thing I would do would be to repaint the exact totem pole back on the tail.

I closed my eyes and saw the last week of my life speed by without a sound. When I opened them, I saw a large flock of flamingos on approach for a landing in the salt ponds, and I saw Hoagy make one last attempt to catch a bonefish near the edge of the pond. But I never saw the man slide out of the empty cistern and climb onto the plane. I never would have guessed that Bob Marley Johnston had booked me a standby passenger.

26

What Has Four Eyes and Two Barrels?

The old girl seemed a little nose-heavy when I took off. I made a mental note to check the bow compartment and see if anything had shifted. I hoped that was all it was. A break-down out here would make me a very unhappy camper. I adjusted the elevator trim, then switched on the autopilot and let her do the flying.

I hadn't made a trip down-island in a while and had forgotten how special the flying was. I had always thought that when it was all over and done, one of these little cays would be the right place to grow old.

I followed a familiar route down the small land masses that lay on a southeasterly course toward Rudderville and looked out the window at the beautiful Caribbean morning. The ocean below was devoid of whitecaps, which meant light surface winds and balmy temperatures. Ahead of me, several small islands protruded from the emerald water between the breaks in the clouds, and on the distant horizon, the buildups above the mountains of Hispaniola were just becoming visible. Most people think of the Caribbean as Nassau or Freeport, when in fact there are more than three thousand islands that span the Caribbean Sea from the east coast of Florida down to the northern edge of South America.

I had forgotten how much I loved island time. You are your own boss, and you feel the romance of the early fliers who pioneered over-water flight when there were still missions and adventures—not just routine milkruns. In the Caribbean it never pays to be in a hurry, and surprise is a constant copilot, which keeps you on your toes. Each stop has its own history and its own set of characters. There is more to Caribbean life than the view from a hotel window or cruise-ship porthole, but most of the time people are more tourists than travelers. That was another reason why I was out of business. I couldn't think of flying as routine.

I checked my watch and figured I had another thirty minutes before I would have to descend back to wave-hopping altitude as I got near enough to the Turks and Caicos to be picked up on someone's radar relay to Miami Center. I planned to land midday about ten miles north of Rudderville at a little bonefishing camp I knew about and then get a water taxi to town. As Trevor would say, I didn't want to kick open any anthills if I could avoid it.

Hoagy was exhausted from his early morning romp around the pond and lay curled in a tight ball under my bunk in the cabin. I adjusted the pitch of the propellers, listening for the sound that told me they were synced up, and the old radial engines purred along in a mesmerizing hum that had been the background music to most of my life. I looked down at the vast blue emptiness below. The sea was bewildering. City life makes the earth seem like an overstuffed suitcase, but from twelve hundred feet, it's a deserted playground. I thought about Blanton and wondered where he was hiding. When I got to Rudderville, I would try to call Billy Cruiser from a pay phone to find out what was going on.

"Nice view, huh?" The words jolted me out of the seat. The strap across my shoulder was the only thing that kept me from hitting the control panel above my head. I spun around, and the last thing I saw was four eyes and two barrels.

27

The Ferry of the Dead

"**B**oat drinks; boys in the bar ordered boat drinks. Visitors scored on the home rinks; everything seems to be wrong."

I regained slight consciousness with singing in my ears and the unmistakable taste of blood in my throat. My lips were sealed together, and when I tried to shout, I only made a muffled sound.

I knew I wasn't dead. I hurt too much to be dead, and I didn't think I had been bad enough to have to spend eternity with an off-key singer. I managed to inhale fully through my clogged nasal passages and felt my chest rise. The whole right side of my head throbbed with pain. A warm, steady flow of blood was dripping from my brow. It dribbled into the crow's feet around my right eye, then spread across my cheek and down my neck, where it soaked the collar of my T-shirt.

I blinked, and the pain intensified. I should never have painted over the totem pole. I had offended some ancient god, and this was my payback. Signals finally started to make it from my brain down to my fingers, and I instinctively tried to grab for the wheel of the plane. I couldn't move. I looked down at what resembled the body of a mummy, but it was mine. I was wound in silver gaffer's tape tighter than a roll of toilet paper, and I was stuck to my seat. I could barely move my shoulders. My mouth was taped tightly shut, but somehow the blood had managed to find its way down my throat.

"This morning I shot six holes in my freezer. I think I got cabin fever. Somebody sound the alarm."

The song was coming from a fuzzy figure sitting in the co-pilot's seat. Someone else was flying my airplane.

"Hang on there, cowboy. Everything's under control."

I knew I was on my way to jail. My airplane would be scrapped for parts or bought by some war-bird collector, or she would be put into service by the government.

"Ever been to Africa?" the stranger asked. "Great place. These islands sort of remind me of the coast of Kenya. You're not my first hijacking, you know. No, I grabbed an old DC-3 once that flew the milkrun from Nairobi to Lamu. Hit every fuckin' pothole in the sky. The passengers were all vomiting chunks about ten minutes out of Nairobi. The pilot said I was pretty good. I always wanted to take flying lessons but never quite got around to it."

I managed to squint with my good left eye and tried to focus on the altimeter, but I could only make out blurry numbers that tumbled and spun on a blue-green backdrop like the balls after a break on a pool table. The singing torture continued.

"I know I should be leaving this climate. I got a verse but can't rhyme it. I gotta go where it's warm."

The altimeter finally came into focus. It was steady at five hundred feet, and the vertical speed indicator sat right on zero. The altitude indicator showed straight and level, and the autopilot switch was disengaged. The directional gyro appeared to be showing a course of 120 degrees. If this were the repo man, we would have been aimed in the opposite direction, on our way to Nassau or Ft. Lauderdale.

The singer wore mirrored sunglasses and a short black wet suit with purple and green stripes, which he had stripped down to his waist. A tattered bandage was wrapped around his left arm, and a faint blood stain ran up one side. He had found my Cubs hat in the back of the plane, and he'd stuffed his hair up into it. It was hard to get a handle on what he really looked like, now that he had the sunglasses on. I remembered the tattooed eyes I'd seen right before I'd blacked out—it wasn't something you could put out of your mind. Now he had the Goose flight manual spread open on his lap, and he was reading intently.

It is an utterly helpless feeling to have your mind spinning at top speed and have no motor functions. The singer thumbed through the flight manual, and I said my act of contrition. I didn't have a chance. If he wasn't Cuban or working for the feds, then he had to be a drug dealer. Whoever the hell he was, I was not in his future plans.

"That's a mighty mean-lookin' gun you carry behind that seat of yours. Is that for protection against hijackers?" He laughed. "You a dope dealer, maybe? Well, whoever the fuck you are, I threw a big monkey wrench into your day, didn't I? You would just love to get at me with your big gun, shoot me into little pieces, and use me for chum. Well, that's not the way the cards fell, is it, Captain? You just ran out of luck today, didn't you? Came falling out of the sky like that Greek faggot with the wax wings. What was his name?"

It was Icarus. Icarus who had flown too close to the sun, just as Frank Bama had flown too close to the edge.

The man laughed again loudly. "I am the guy flying the plane, and you're the schmuck taped to the seat."

How could I have been so fucking stupid? B.M. had set me up to have this guy just waltz aboard the plane. And I gave him my goddamn radio. If I ever got out of this jam, I would go straight back and strangle that cocksucker. But who was I kidding? It was my own damn fault. Good-bye, Trevor; good-bye, Alaska.

Hoagy was up. I could hear him rustling around in the cabin. He padded slowly to the flight deck and surveyed the situation, then nudged the hijacker's hand to pet him.

"Great watchdog."

No Lassie or Rin Tin Tin rescue for me. No trusty canine to attack the hijacker, tear the tape from my body, and save the day. Instead the son of a bitch rested his head in the hijacker's lap. God. What had I done to deserve this?

"Time to check in," the hijacker said as he scratched Hoagy behind the ear. He reached for the microphone and pushed the talk switch.

"Charlie Fabian to Steed Bonnet, Charlie Fabian to Steed Bonnet. Come in. Come in." He waited for a reply, then looked at me. "Somewhere out there are all of our past lives. My best was a pirate, and I do miss it so."

This guy was not running on all his cylinders. I glanced at the fuel gauges above my head. Whatever was going to happen, I figured I had about thirty minutes to live before we ran out of fuel. I wondered what kind of horseshit article Rudy Breno would write about my mysterious disappearance in the Devil's Triangle. Maybe all that shit about the Devil's Triangle was true. Maybe this lunatic flying my airplane was the devil himself dressed up as a skin diver. Who the hell knew?

Charlie Fabian spotted a small island on the horizon and banked the plane steeply, then rolled out when it was at twelve o'clock. He didn't fly too badly, but I couldn't conceive of his landing the *Dancer*. She wasn't some Cessna 172 that you could just drop out of the sky. Water landings required the right nose-high altitude or you would plow her right into the waves. On a runway, the narrow wheelbase of the gear made her squirrelly in a crosswind, and if you didn't lock the tail wheel, you would have a hell of a time keeping her from ground-looping.

My tongue was raw from trying to work through the tape across my mouth. It was the only thing I could do. This was not how I had envisioned my last day on earth. I was supposed to grow old and rock away on the breezeway of an old plantation house in Martinique, telling stories of my adventures to my grandchildren who would tell me that I didn't look bad for being ninety.

The hijacker checked his watch and then glanced at the manual. He pulled the throttles back and lowered the flaps sixty degrees. We would be close to stall speed any minute. What the fuck was he doing?

"Well, I've got to be going now," Charlie said. He pulled the throttles back, engaged the autopilot, unbuckled his seat belt, and crawled out of the copilot's seat. He leaned down and put the shotgun to the side of my head.

I could smell the stale beer on his breath and could feel the cold blue barrel against my temple. My face, distorted, looked back at me from his reflector sunglasses. My ears started ringing, and suddenly I saw myself as a toddler on the beach in Coronado, running to my mother. He brought his face even closer to mine, and I was more angry than scared. If I was to die, I at least wanted a crack at this bastard. Suddenly I managed to get a piece of the tape clenched in my teeth and tore a hole to the outside world. I spit into his face.

It jolted the hijacker out of his trance, and he wiped the spit from his cheek with the bandage on his arm. "You're in luck today, mate. If you don't believe me, ask the boys I killed yesterday. They shouldn't be too far ahead of you on the road to eternity. They shot at me, and they paid the price. But I like your display of courage. Courage is what separates the men from the boys, the brave from the timid. In the old days, I would have just put you ashore, naked on some desert island, but alas, these modern times require modern solutions. I am going to let you see your death. You'll climb on up till you run out of fuel or air, and then you'll go tumbling, tumbling, tumbling out of the sky. Sort of like a mercy killing, wouldn't you say?"

He reached for the rudder control handwheel on the side of my seat, and cranked it to the "up" position. Then he jammed the throttles to full. Instantly the *Hemisphere Dancer* lunged, and then I felt her start to climb. He located the main fuel-supply valves above my head and closed them off tight.

"Bon voyage, mate," he said, grabbing a leather bag. "And so long, dog," he called to Hoagy, who didn't know what to make of this but watched him go to the rear of the plane. "Twenty degrees, and a hockey game's on. Nobody cares, they're way too far gone."

I turned my head and saw him at the door, zipping up his wet suit. A Cheshire-cat grin spread across his face, and he yelled, "See you in hell!" Then he jumped out the door.

• • •

The propellers bit at the humid tropical air, and the vertical speed indicator told me the rate. I flashed to a line on the men's room wall in Captain Tony's Saloon in Key West:

> *It's not that I am afraid to die,*
> *I just don't want to be there*
> *when it happens.*

I was fighting with all my strength to free myself, but I couldn't get unstuck. Behind me, the old VHF was picking up a weak, scratchy signal coming from Nassau. An organ solo was playing, and in deep, comforting tones, a radio preacher was reading the obituaries and epitaphs of the day.

I stopped moving and listened for a moment, wondering if the epitaph applied to me:

His lifetime is used up.
He goes to heaven in his own boat,
having no need for the ferry of the dead.

Livin' on
Island Time

28

Friday Was the Coolest

Charlie Fabian had not been the only stowaway. Back on Pass Her By Cay, Root Boy had sneaked aboard the *Hemisphere Dancer* while Frank Bama was asleep in his hammock under the wing.

Root Boy had been the only witness to the murders on the treasure boat, but he had no intention of volunteering any information. He had a habit of steering clear of the law, and pretty soon the small cluster of islands would be crawling with cops. He'd been diving for lobster in the shallow waters off Pass Her By when he'd seen the *Dancer*. He had climbed up on the nose and had hidden in the forward baggage compartment, and he'd been lulled to sleep by the hypnotic hum of the radial engines. He had no idea that Charlie Fabian lay coiled in the rear of the plane.

Silence was what woke him. The absence of engine noise and the whistling of the wind delivered a primitive warning to Root Boy that he was about to fall out of the sky.

It had all happened so fast—climbing up onto the flight deck to see the bloody pilot taped to his seat; the disorienting spin; cutting away the tape from the pilot's hands with his knife. He'd followed the pilot's instructions carefully and had helped restart the engines. The plane had pulled out the spin, and they had made a feather-soft landing in the lee of a nearby island. They taxied up the narrow channel and jockeyed the plane into the shallow mangroves until the left float was grounded. Then Root Boy pulled the power. The pilot introduced himself and then fainted.

Root Boy had dragged Frank out of the plane and into the shade of a royal palm. At first he was worried that Frank's dog might bite him, but the retriever happily took off down the beach as if life were one long vacation. Root Boy had located the first aid kit under the rear seat and had cleaned up the cuts and scrapes on Frank's face before he carefully stitched the nasty gash above his eye with dental floss and a sail needle. He'd covered the wound with a cotton gauze pad that he first soaked in aloe.

Root Boy had rummaged through the foliage for familiar herbs and brewed up some bush tea, adding a little rum from the bottle on the plane. He dove up half a dozen slipper lobsters from the channel and made a fire from coconuts and palm fronds, on which he roasted the lobsters till the shells were pink.

• • •

Frank lay in his hammock, exhausted but grateful, while Root Boy poked at the fire. The cut above his eye was throbbing, and he was still feeling very weak. Hoagy was now curled up beside the hammock.

"So what do you know about this guy?" Frank asked.

"Dat mon be trouble from da moment I see him come into da bar."

"I thought the guy was a repo man coming after my plane until he jumped out," Frank said. "I don't get it. Who would want to jump out of a perfectly good, running airplane, even if he were hijacking it?"

"A fuckin' crazy mon," Root Boy replied.

"It never entered my mind that he wanted to kill me," Frank said.

"You be da lucky one, Cap'n," Root Boy told him. "Should see dat po' fella from dee dive boot. Four Eyes gotta nose fa blood—like a shark. Shark don' hold no grudges. We jus' food to him. Same wif Mr. Four Eyes. He a dangerous person, Cap'n, make no mistake. Could be he's dat Jet Ski Killer I been readin' 'bout."

Frank laughed. "That four-eyed son of a bitch who tried to kill me is not the Jet Ski Killer. The weirdo's name is Charlie Fabian."

"How you know dat?" Root Boy asked.

"He called himself Charlie Fabian when he was talking into the microphone. Besides, the Jet Ski Killer is a friend of mine."

"Shhhhh," Root Boy said, shaking his head. "Hawd to figga out how you folks managed to rule da wuld. God a'mighty." Root Boy sat down beside the fire. "Come on now, legs stop all dis wigglin'. I'm shakin' like a hound dog shittin' peach seeds," he said.

"Were they shakin' when you cut me loose from that seat?"

"No."

"It's just the adrenaline, then. It'll stop soon."

• • •

Root Boy spent the night sitting atop a large coconut tree, guarding the hammock where Frank Bama slept with his dog beside him. Root Boy felt a little bit like Friday in the movie *Robinson Crusoe*. Friday was the coolest.

He'd been watching the injured man closely and wondered what thoughts occupied the brain that operated him.

Frank was not a big man; he was maybe six feet. He was clearly not a tourist. His tan branded him as an island resident, probably the Keys. His hands bore the scars of labor. He was no weekend flier or scammer, and his plane was more than just a vehicle. Root Boy had seen gray strands in Frank's blond hair when he washed the scalp wound. He was not at all like the killer who had come through the bar. This man had a positive energy, and after what Root Boy had seen him do in a pinch, he was impressed.

Root Boy scanned the horizon for any signs of trouble and watched the dark moon fade like a song into the light of the morning sky. Frank's shotgun lay across Root Boy's lap, but there had been no sign of the four-eyed man. Still, his legs continued to tremble.

29

No Plane on Sunday

Trevor imagined the new day before she ever saw it. She could hear waves breaking on the distant shore and felt the warm morning sun on her skin. She remained motionless in bed as the cool breeze stirred the air around her.

The lunch with Hackney two days earlier had revealed nothing but a legal tangle of wills, estates, living trusts, and unanswered questions. Hackney had seemed even more nervous and fidgety than normal and dropped a crab claw in his lap when she wanted to talk about the colonel she had read about in the news. It all made her very uneasy.

Trevor shifted from the lingering white-space limbo between dreams and consciousness and sat up in bed to find herself under a cocoon of mosquito net. She stared at the slowly moving blades of the ceiling fan above her head, not fully aware yet of where she was. She was stuck in the tropics.

Trevor was still in Rudderville, waiting for Frank to show up. She had waited all day yesterday, and thoughts of romance had filled her head as she'd sat on the beach sketching: a quiet dinner by the sea, a few glasses of wine, who knew? All the grieving had made her incredibly horny. By the end of the day, though, her mood had gone sour when no planes came or went from the small airport near her hotel.

She had called Billy Cruiser at the Lone Palm Airport, and he had told her that he hadn't heard a word from Frank and had assumed he was with Trevor. He'd said he would check with Ace and see how things had gone there. Now even the phone lines were dead. It seemed that a tourist on an out-of-control moped had taken out a pole that supported the new telephone cable, and they were waiting for a new one to arrive from Miami.

Late last night, after a few drinks, she had made up her mind to go find an apartment in Paris, buy a Persian cat, and live alone for a while. But this morning she found she had some doubts about her plan. She didn't know what to do next, but she wasn't going to wait for Frank to get here in his own sweet time. She was as mad at herself as she was at him. How foolish, she thought, to hold out hope that Frank Bama could ever change.

Trevor was also beginning to have even more doubts about Desdemona and the notion that her brother might still be alive. She suspected that the whole idea, in some twisted way, had been spawned out of an unconscious longing for Frank to show that he cared more for her than he did about his seaplane and his gypsy existence. Let's face it—she had been lying to herself.

Trevor had checked the airline schedule and would catch the morning plane back to Miami. She would cut a deal of some kind with Hackney Primstone III and get what she could of her inheritance. She had packed the night before and now looked over at the open duffel bag beneath the window. She slowly eased herself out of the old mahogany bed and went into the small bathroom where she splashed water in her face and brushed her teeth. She tried to phone Hackney again, but the lines were still dead, so she gathered her things and went to the lobby to catch a cab to the airport.

• • •

There were only two other people waiting for the morning plane to Miami at the brand-new Rudderville customs office and terminal that smelled of freshly poured concrete. The building still held a bit of the nighttime coolness, but it was quickly being overcome by the early morning heat. Church services blared out from the radio on the desk where a young customs man was talking on an intercom phone in a hushed voice, paying no attention to Trevor and the other two passengers.

The official finally hung up the phone and took the immigration card Trevor handed him. Fifteen minutes later he had finally found the receipt book and had written one out. Trevor walked into the empty passenger terminal where a sign on the desk told the story. It read "No Plane on Sunday. Maybe One Come Monday."

"Asshole," Trevor hissed under her breath, but there was no point in going back and yelling at the customs official; there was nothing she could do about the situation. Instead she woke the cab driver on the bench and directed him back to the hotel.

"Just couldn't tear yo'self way from dis beautiful island, now could you?" Percy, the small gay desk clerk, bubbled.

"I have no place else to go," Trevor said with a sigh.

30

Paradise Lost

Desdemona did not visit Boomtown often. Her work on the rocket ship kept her close to home, and besides, there was too much about Boomtown that reminded her of a paradise lost. But Monty Potter was willing to pay a lot of money for some insight, and Desdemona needed money for the rocket ship.

Toosay held on to the weather-worn mahogany tiller. He steered the little sloop on a broad reach toward the gaslights that marked the spot where Rue Christophe met the Boomtown quay. He tightened his mainsheet and headed up a few degrees to pass on the upwind side of the *La Brisa,* a seedy cruise ship that was anchored in the harbor. It swung slowly on its mooring as if trying to avoid the direct light of the sun, which would expose the sad condition of the vessel and its crew. He passed the metal hull close enough to hear the clanking generators and smell the strong cigarette smoke from the fantail, where a collection of third-world deckhands were watching the sun come up.

Desdemona leaned against the mast and stared at the streams of rust that ran from the scuppers over the nameplate on the bow to the waterline of the iron ship. The boat belonged to Monty Potter, and she was a bit apprehensive about meeting him. The workmen at the local boatyard where she had hauled out the *Cosmic Muffin* last year were full of rumors about Potter and his activities—how he had been involved in the death of old Gaston La Rue, the former boss of the waterfront, and how after Gaston's death, Monty Potter had conveniently become the owner of the Polar Bar. Potter was just the most recent addition to a long line of pirates, rogues, and reprobates who inhabited the remote islands of the Caribbean and took advantage of their unique adaptation of laissez-faire economics.

Crime had been a way of life in Boomtown since the time of the colonization of the Indies. The Indians had been too savage for most God-fearing settlers, who did not want to wind up as a plat du jour, and the land was too hard and hostile for planting sugarcane. So the islands were bypassed for the fertile hills and valleys of Hispaniola. The seven islands called the Sleeping Beauties had existed in limbo while the Spanish, English, and French monarchs played murderous chess with their colonial pawns. Eventually the Beauties wound up as a French possession.

When a slave revolt resulted in the birth of the black republic of Haiti, the islands became part of Henri Christophe's kingdom. The black king saw the advantage of having a no-man's-land far outside commerce and protection, so he looked the other way as runaway slaves and pirate bands merged their common interests, and a Creole culture sprang up. Bon Temps became Boomtown.

Henri Christophe went insane in his mountain fortress, and the castles and châteaus that dotted the hillsides were reclaimed by the jungle. Boomtown had gone its own way and had survived into the twentieth century as the last pirate town in the Caribbean. Like Hong Kong, Casablanca, Beirut, and Mombasa, Boomtown had secured its place in a modern world by relying on peoples' time-old desire to have "something for nothing." The means of survival had always been contraband, and even to this day, you could get anything you wanted in Boomtown.

Toosay dropped the red mutton sail, and the little boat glided to the concrete steps at the far end of the quay. Desdemona leaped down from the bow at Toosay's command and ascended the steps to Rue Christophe. She sniffed the air and recognized the smell of hot toasted bread, sausages, and strong coffee, and she decided to go to the Café Creola. However, her willpower prevailed over the temptation to indulge in a big breakfast, and she ordered only a cup of espresso with an ice cube and swallowed it in one quick gulp.

• • •

Monty Potter's request for a tarot reading had come to Desdemona through Fernando Orlando, a local musician. Fernando and the Cane Thrashers were the house band at Boomtown's Polar Bar. Fernando was also a frequent visitor to the Healing Hole, where he would play his conga drum and sing "Babalu" as if it were a religious experience. Fernando believed he was the reincarnation of Ricky Ricardo. Desdemona had tried to explain to him that Ricky was not a real person, just a character played by Desi Arnaz, but Fernando would not accept the hard reality. To him, time was just a magazine.

It was market day in Boomtown, and Desdemona had a little time before she was due to meet Monty Potter. She decided to take advantage of this infrequent visit to town to stock up on supplies. She let her nose do the work and inhaled the alkaline odor of the dirt that still clung to the roots of scallions and citronella as she worked her way through the vendor stalls. The caffeine ignited her turbobabble, and she jabbered away with the old women and picked through the bananas and oranges, sugarcane stalks, tomatoes, and goat peppers. She bought a large stick of pure chocolate and nibbled on it while the rest of her food was boxed up.

She balanced the load gracefully on the top of her head and headed for her favorite stop: Mango Man's. She spoke to the old man in French while he fished through the icy slosh of his cooler for a perfect mango. Wielding a machete like a scalpel, he promptly sculpted the mango into a cascade of bite-sized chunks that could be plucked from the stem with a nibble. Desdemona paid for her mango lollipop and headed for the fisherman's pier with the box of veggies still on her head.

A knot of traditional wooden boats in all shapes, sizes, and colors were tied up to a long rickety pier where flies swarmed in small clouds above fresh carcasses, conch shells, and sponges. A squadron of sea gulls stood lookout above the fish market from atop a broken street lamp. A thin black man in a dirty foul-weather suit was at work spreading and sorting his catch according to size and species. Small barracudas, grunts, parrot fish, and snappers covered the table. The birds eyed him eagerly as he whittled away with his knife. When he discarded the remains of his cleaning operation into the harbor, the sea gulls dove for the water. Less daring birds glided lazily above umbrellas that lined the walkway, squawking and jabbering like the men below them.

A young boy Desdemona recognized was talking with a group of tourists who were admiring his conch shells. He had lined up the shells in perfect rows so the morning sun illuminated their pink insides and made them the most colorful things on the dock. He held one of the shells as he talked. "Conchs spend most of der lifes face down, creepin' 'cross da ocean floor, and only in death is dere beauty revealed up above da surface of da warm Caribbean waters."

Desdemona spotted Toosay's boat near the end of the dock, and before she could look for him, he was right beside her. "You be cookin' tonight, missus?" he asked.

"It looks that way, Toosay." She lowered the box into his steady hands. "This shouldn't take too long, so I guess I'll meet you back here in an hour."

"I be right here."

Toosay went back to the fishermen gathered in a small group around a long bench where the domino games were already in progress. He would spend the next hour talking to the other fishermen, who would be full of questions about the crazy woman and the rocket ship, and he would happily answer them all.

Out on Rue Christophe, taxicabs were lined up at the stand waiting for the cruise-ship passengers to arrive. Shop owners brought out their gold trinkets, and pickpockets talked openly about the prospects of the day. Dogs meandered along the street, careful not to catch a broom blast from one of the women minding the vegetables.

Desdemona strolled across the street, and Fernando met her at the doorway of the Polar Bar.

"Bonjour, Fernando. Comment vas-tu?"

"Muy bien, senora. I'll tell the boss you're here."

Desdemona took a seat at one of the sidewalk tables and popped open her fan and began to cool her face with a steady motion. She waved to people who recognized her as they passed in their cars, but her mind was occupied with wondering what Monty Porter really wanted. She was sure it had something to do with her rocket ship, and she was scared.

The horn blast from a passing garbage truck startled her. The truck pulled up in front of the Polar Bar, and two men jumped off and quickly removed plastic bags of garbage from the street in front of her. The music of Kassav blasted from the cab of the truck, and the men sang along. The truck sped off, swerving to miss an oncoming Deux Chevaux, and disappeared around the corner.

From the balcony over her head, Desdemona heard a voice shouting above the din of the marketplace.

"What a wonderful sight," Monty Potter called out. "Boomtown is truly unparalleled. We have fostered the best qualities of the French: culture, food, love, and profit—but in our own island style. Only in Boomtown is a trip to the dump by the garbage truck called a *voyage.*"

Desdemona looked up at Monty Potter. He reminded her of Mussolini, in those old photos where he was addressing the crowds in the heyday of Fascism. Then she flashed to a grisly shot of the dead Italian dictator hanging upside down, being beaten and kicked by an angry mob.

"Fernando," Monty Potter ordered, "show the lady up."

31

Tell It Like It Is

Fernando led Desdemona through the Polar Bar. It looked odd in its empty state, but remnants of the night before lingered in the stale air.

A solitary black man mopped the floor back by the bandstand, and the smell of pine oil and old beer filled the room. They climbed the stairs to Monty Potter's apartment, and Desdemona detected the slightest trace of opium in the air when Fernando opened the door.

"That will be all, Fernando," Monty Potter said from the balcony where he stood leaning against a brass spyglass.

"Good luck," Fernando whispered to Desdemona.

Desdemona walked into the room, and Fernando closed the door behind her.

"Please make yourself at home."

"Before we get started, could I possibly use your bathroom?" Desdemona asked.

"There's one right behind you in the hallway."

"Thank you." Desdemona locked the bathroom door behind her and fumbled through her bag for the tarot-card book. She skimmed over the procedures for the reading and the

184

brief description of the cards and what they all meant, then straightened her tie-dyed muumuu and flushed the toilet.

When she came out of the bathroom, the room was dark, but she could see that Monty Potter was now seated at the table. He was a very large man.

"I took the liberty to draw the curtains," he said, not unkindly.

"Thank you."

"No last name?" Monty Potter asked.

"Just plain Desdemona."

"Are you hiding something, Miss Desdemona?"

"We all have our skeletons, don't we, Mr. Potter?"

"Fernando tells me that you have amazing powers. Here you have only been in my presence for a minute or so, and you are already reading my mind."

Desdemona tried to look like the cat that ate the canary, but she didn't have a clue about the meaning behind Monty Potter's statement.

She took a seat and pulled the tarot cards from her bag and placed them on the table.

"Mr. Potter, uh, if it's okay with you, it might be better if you put out the cigar. It could block the messages, you know."

Monty Potter rose and walked to the balcony. He tossed the cigar down onto the street and returned to the table.

Desdemona shuffled and cut the cards several times, and then she placed them on the table. "Are you comfortable?" she asked.

"Of course. I'm in my own house."

"For the first ten minutes of this reading, I ask that you refrain from offering any information unless you do not understand what I am saying. This will keep your mind clear and intuitive."

Monty Potter let out a deep breath and wiped his forehead with a handkerchief. She instructed him to cut the cards and lay them in three piles on the table, and then she proceeded with the reading, trying to turn images into ideas. Finally she told Potter to write a question down on a piece of paper.

Desdemona placed the paper under the significator card in the middle of the Celtic cross. "This will focus the energy of the reading on your question."

It all came back to her pretty quickly, even though she hadn't done a professional reading since she'd worked at the observatory in Puerto Rico. She spoke of inner and outer experiences, and Monty Potter was totally immersed in her dialog.

"Now, this reveals your hopes and fears," she said, turning over the ten of swords.

The card hit a nerve. On it, a man lay prone atop a slab, and ten swords were embedded in his back along the spine. His right arm was covered by a crystal-like design.

Monty Potter tried to act indifferent, but Desdemona picked up the vibe and a strange vision: a man was dangling from a rope with a sword in his back. She described it to Potter and then added, "It's not you, but it is someone you know."

Potter smiled, and the word "Cairo" passed across his lips.

When the session was finished, Monty Potter lit a cigar and walked to the window, throwing back the thick drapes. "Thank you. That was very enlightening. We'll have to do it again sometime." The look in his eye seemed a little too friendly to Desdemona, but she smiled. "I think this will cover the session, and here's a little something extra." He pulled a box from his desk drawer. "This may help you in your travels."

Desdemona took the box and opened it. Inside lay a remarkable wand. On one end was a crystal in the shape of a naked woman with large breasts. Her nipples were rubies.

"Pick it up," Potter said firmly.

Desdemona slowly lifted the scepter out of the box. The shaft was a glass rod encrusted with various stones. On the opposite end, a triangular piece of malachite was soldered to the rod. Desdemona was astonished.

"This is not from this world," she said in a low voice. She did not mention the fact that the Generators had told her to be expecting a gift with some special significance.

"Just a trinket from my treasure chest. Perhaps it will help you see the future more clearly. Perhaps it will make your ship fly." Monty Potter gave a deep laugh.

Desdemona clutched the wand tightly and smiled. "Perhaps."

32

I'm a Mayan

"So what was the message from the Generators today?" Fernando asked, looking up into the night sky.

"Something to do with the Mayans. I have a feeling I'm being prepared so I can better handle my task."

"And what task is that?" Fernando wanted to know.

"That's when the voices get too cosmic for me. They say I'll know it when I find it."

"The Mayans. Very, very powerful people. Built civilizations, and then—" Fernando clicked the castanet he was holding "—like that, they disappeared into the jungle."

"They did not."

"You know the mystery of the Mayans?" Fernando asked.

"I'm learning."

"I wish I had someone like that to tell me how to waltz through time," Fernando said. "I've been trying every day since the death of Ricky Ricardo to contact him. I need lessons."

"Fernando! You can't channel to Ricky Ricardo. I keep telling you he wasn't a real person. He was a television character."

"Not true," Fernando retorted. "He's as real as your Generators. I don't understand you, Desdemona. On the one hand, you say the space people talk to you, but on the other hand, you don't know how to make a rocket ship work." Fernando shook his head.

"I know what I need to know, Fernando, but now I'm expanding my horizons. There's more to life in this century than television. I want to seek out new civilizations, to go where no man has gone before." Desdemona did her impersonation of Captain Kirk at the bridge of the *Enterprise*. "Mr. Scott, warp power."

"Huht Captain, we'll melt the bloody dilithium crystals," Fernando answered obediently. They both giggled.

"And you think I'm crazy for coming out here trying to contact Ricky Ricardo. Look at you and your Mayan voices. How do you know all that shit, man?" Fernando asked.

Desdemona smiled and kept looking up at the stars. "I think I might be one," she said nonchalantly.

Desdemona and Fernando sat on the deck of the *Cosmic Muffin* in Frenchman's Lagoon watching a meteor shower coming at the earth from the region of the Scorpion. She held the crystal wand in her hand and waved it across the sky.

"Where do you think it came from?" Fernando asked, his eyes following the wand.

"Up there, of course," Desdemona said. "But why did he give it to me? I barely know him, and he gives me the creeps."

"He's obviously after your body. He's sweet on you," Fernando teased.

"Cut it out," Desdemona snapped.

"I'm serious. Look at that thing. That's not a housewarming gift. That's something very powerful."

"And how do you suppose Monty Potter got his hands on something like this?" Desdemona wondered.

"Monty Potter has a whole room filled with artifacts and things. He was a soldier once, you know, so he has lots of souvenirs from his battles."

"Really?"

"Maybe it came from the wreck. He's involved with some big treasure ship up in the Bahamas. Monty's counting on this being the lost treasure of Henri Christophe."

Desdemona rotated the scepter in her hand, and the light of the moon reflected off the figurine and onto the water. She did not see the water turn to steam. "Crystals," she said solemnly, "are the medicine of the earth. They were planted here eons ago by the Mayans, who are now trying to contact their people. The crystals are the keys that will eventually unlock all the mysteries, Fernando."

The Generators had told her there were relics of this kind on old ships scattered all over the earth. They called them cosmic fender benders. These special crystals, she thought, would be the propulsion source for her rocket ship. She had collected quite a variety of them in the past year for the secret engine she and Toosay were building.

"You say that ship he's working on belonged to Henri Christophe?" she asked.

"I hear that Monty is planning to screw Little Elmo out of the treasure. They were partners once, but I haven't known many thieves who lasted too long as partners. It's all blood money anyway. That's what the reading's all about. He wants to make sure the treasure isn't cursed."

"What's the real story on him? Somehow I feel strings are attached to this crystal."

"You can be sure of that," Fernando said.

"Did he kill Gaston La Rue?"

"Where did you hear that?"

"I have my sources."

"It all does go back to Gaston La Rue," Fernando said and sighed.

Another meteor streaked at them from the Gemini constellation and disintegrated directly above their heads.

"He owned the Polar Bar before Potter, right?"

"That and just about everything else in town. He was a customs inspector from French Guiana but wound up on the wrong end of a coup d'état and fled to Boomtown back in the twenties. Old Gaston ruled this place from Prohibition through the war. He made a fortune selling diesel fuel to German U-boats that were prowling the Caribbean, and he was king of these parts right up until the day he died. He brought us here in the first place. Heard me and the band in San Juan one night and hired us on the spot to come and play his bar. Gaston loved the mambo."

"So when did Monty Potter come into the picture?"

"He washed up on the beach one night, claiming his boat had sunk along with all his missionary supplies."

"Missionary? That guy?"

"Whatever. It didn't take him long to sidle up to Gaston. Next thing we knew, he was a partner in the bar, and then came the accident."

"What accident?"

"Monty convinced Gaston to expand his activities into smuggling aliens. There is a lot of money in that racket. They dump them in Puerto Rico, and from Puerto Rico they can easily slip into Miami—everybody in the Caribbean has a cousin in Miami. Gaston and Monty Potter were very successful. Next thing we knew, Monty bought Gaston a brand-new, forty-foot ocean racer; very loud and very fast. One night, Gaston and a friend were practicing their turns, and the boat went out of control. They say both men were vaporized in the Anegada Passage when three thousand gallons of nitro-glycerin in the fuel tanks ignited. There was a day of mourning on the island. They closed the bakery and cremated Gaston in the oven. The next morning, Monty Potter moved into his apartment."

"So why do you still work for him?" Desdemona asked.

"Why do you accept his presents? He's got charm. Besides, it's the only show in town, and I don't ever want to think about having to get a real job."

"Well, you're not the only one with all the inside news. I hear you may be leaving soon," Desdemona said.

"I have my irons in the fire."

"Monty Potter didn't like what he saw in the ten of swords. He's very afraid of someone named Cairo."

"How do you know?" Fernando asked.

"He whispered the name when I told him that he wasn't the dead man on the card. You ever heard of someone named Cairo?"

"No," Fernando replied. "But Monty Potter wants to see your rocket ship."

"I can't let him do that," Desdemona said.

"He'll see it whether you want him to or not. I guarantee you that."

"Are you a spy, Fernando?"

"I'm a survivor. I play the gig until my big break comes along. I take his shit because I know that one day I won't have to take it anymore. I do all that, but no—I do not rat on my friends. And you are my friend."

33

Raw, Naked Fear

Rudy Breno was as excited as a child at Christmas when he presented his "wish list" to his father for the expedition. Rudy had asked for a flagship—an air-conditioned, deep-V power boat with state-of-the-art electronics—which he would use to track down the Jet Ski Killer. He had located such a boat in Ft. Lauderdale, and Rudy saw it as the water chariot he would ride to his rightful position as editor-in-chief of the *National Lighthouse.*

When he told his father the cost of the vessel, Rudolph Sr. went into sticker shock. "Request denied. I am not King Ferdinand, and besides, the New World has been discovered. Get a cheaper boat, or stay home and make up the story, Rudy!" he roared over the phone.

Bad timing was the menu from which Rudy Breno always seemed to order. He walked the town docks and scoured the marina for a boat, but every piece of floatable fiberglass in the Keys was involved in the massive manhunt taking place near Cape Florida in the Everglades, where one of the Jet Skis had been found.

Rudy had been extremely disappointed when they found

the Jet Ski near Cape Florida, because he could not go to the Everglades. He was extremely allergic to mosquitoes, and if he were bitten repeatedly, he would swell up like a blowfish. Things were about down to rock bottom when Rudy finally got a break.

Sledge Sawyer had just returned to Key West. He had been held in custody as the investigation began of the brutal murder of Little Elmo Robinson, a local yahoo diver/coke dealer who had been run through with a sword up in Charleston. Sledge had been working for Little Elmo and had been a prime suspect in the murder until some women in Charleston had supported his alibi, and he had been released.

Sledge had previously worked for Blanton Meyercord during stone crab season. Rudy had found him hunkered down in a corner booth of the Full Moon Saloon sipping peach schnapps and eating a fish sandwich. Rudy had wanted to talk. Sledge had burped in his face. It only wound Rudy up like an overly excited Yorkshire terrier.

Rudy pursued the matter until Sledge came unglued and grabbed him by the throat, stretching his neck like a Slinky.

"Listen, you fuckwad, if you want to know what happened, go ask the cops."

Rudy hit the floor gagging and crawled to the door. He loved this part of being an investigative reporter. The only thing more exciting was Lou Anne's new trick of whipping him with car radio antennas.

Sledge's refusal only egged Rudy on. Finally, for the right amount of money, Sledge agreed to talk. They settled on two hundred dollars, and for that, Rudy turned on his tape recorder and heard the story of the long-haired shrimper named Danny Wood who, Sledge said, killed Little Elmo and stole the gold. What bullshit, Rudy thought. Obviously Sledge was covering up for Blanton Meyercord.

A few hours later, Rudy heard a story on the radio about three divers missing in a storm in the Bahamas. Their boat had disappeared. Rudy was trying to figure out some kind of connection to Blanton Meyercord when his phone rang.

"I read your article in that scandal sheet about the Jet Ski Killer. I know where that bastard is headed, but it'll cost you. Call this number tonight at six o'clock if you're interested, and we'll talk money."

Rudy scribbled the number down on a Kleenex box with his shaking hands, but before he could utter a word, the line went dead. Jesus Christ, he really was on the trail of the killer. He read the number over and over.

Rudy Breno went to the video store and rented several Alfred Hitchcock movies and copied down the good lines in preparation for his return call. He went to the Full Moon and had two double 151 Cuba Libres and then called the number.

"This is Rudy Breno. I'm listening. What's on your mind?"

"I will be in Nassau tomorrow. If you want to know where the Jet Ski Killer is going, I suggest you come with a thousand dollars cash to the pay phone at the old Chalk's Terminal, and I will contact you," the voice said.

"I need some proof, pal," Rudy said confidently.

There was dead silence on the line. "Hey, asshole, cut the bullshit. We got a deal or not?" the voice on the phone snarled.

Rudy thought about the movie lines, but nothing came to him. He stuttered. "I . . . I . . . need more proof, pal."

"Fuck you," the voice said.

"No, hang on, hang on. Sorry. Listen, I need something more to go on. I'm on my own nickel here." There was a pause on the line. "Oh, don't hang up, Mystery Man. Please don't hang up," Rudy pleaded.

"Does the name Little Elmo mean anything to you?" the voice asked.

"Yes. Oh, yes," Rudy answered.

"A thousand cash. Go to the pay phone at Chalk's Terminal in Nassau tomorrow, and I'll tell you the rest."

The phone went dead.

Rudy had to find a boat no matter what it cost. He would even use some of his own money. His relentless search for Joe Merchant would have to be put on hold for a while. This was a hot story, and he had something to prove to his old man. Let all those deep-throat anchormen with network hair stumble through the swamps. He was headed for Nassau, and he knew where to find a flagship.

• • •

Darryl Lemma had a fast boat, but that was the only qualification he had to be called a captain. He was what the locals called a "smoke-stack captain," which meant that if he lost sight of the smokestacks of the city electric plant, he couldn't navigate his way home. Darryl had been a carpet salesman from Tulsa before he ran away to Key West with his son's babysitter—who, in turn, ran off with a cocaine dealer. Darryl had been a big fan of "Crunch 'n' Des" back in Tulsa and decided that he had what it took to be a charter captain. His boat was a Cigarette named the *Party Animal,* and he had bought it at a government auction of seized vessels.

Darryl had recently been in the news when he had been hijacked to Cuba by a ventriloquist and a dummy. The ventriloquist turned out to be the illegitimate son of the Reverend Jimmy Linseed, a very famous TV evangelist. Rudy Breno had broken the story and had interviewed Darryl Lemma on his return.

Darryl had been too busy enjoying himself at the bar to go running off like everyone else had, looking for Blanton Meyercord in the Everglades. Rudy built up his plans and poured lots of rum. Darryl warmed to the idea of an expedition in the Bahamas, and after a bit of haggling, he agreed to take Rudy to Nassau. Darryl Lemma could give a rat's ass about the Jet Ski Killer. Hell, he liked Blanton Meyercord. Darryl was more tuned in to any excuse to sin—he was focused on whores, liquor, and gambling. They were all waiting for him on Paradise Island, and Rudy Breno was footing the bill.

The Jet Ski Killer Expedition left the dock at dawn the next day and set off down Hawk Channel for the Devil's Triangle. Of course, Darryl had no idea how many miles Nassau was from Key West. And Rudy had been too busy getting "Jet Ski Killer Expedition" T-shirts printed up to ask about a schedule. When they rounded the southern tip of Florida and stuck their noses into the Gulf Stream, it was not long before they both were wishing for dry land and a warm place to shit. The late-moving cold front surprised everyone and had turned the dark blue water of the Gulf Stream into mountains.

In the middle of the storm, Rudy had looked out over the stern of the *Party Animal* and had had a vision. He was sick as a dog and had followed Captain Lemma's orders. He had lashed himself to the fighting chair with a bottle of Chivas Regal in one hand, a waterproof flashlight in the other, and an orange life preserver around his neck. He had looked up through the stinging rain into the dark haze above him, and a giant letter *U* had filled the sky. He was about to be swallowed up by the mysterious forces of the Devil's Triangle. He blinked his eyes and then saw more letters and realized that the letters put together spelled G-U-L-F, which was the first word of *Gulf Advancer*. That was the name painted on the bow of the ship that was about to cut the *Party Animal* in two.

Rudy had screamed a warning to Darryl, who spun the wheel violently to the right and surfed clear of the ship on the bow wave. Though they had nearly been killed, Rudy had discovered a cure for his motion-sickness problem. It was called raw, naked fear.

The storm spared them, and they were headed into the Bahamas when Captain Lemma informed Rudy that he had somehow gotten confused as to where Nassau was. He had mixed up Nassau with Bimini, which meant they had an additional 120 miles to travel.

After the near collision, Captain Darryl had no real idea of where he was, and he missed his first landfall at Bimini completely. He fell asleep at the wheel and ran aground on Mama Rhoda Rock near the harbor entrance at Chub Cay, only sixty miles south of where he thought he was. He declined any assistance from the nearby marina and simply backed the steel hull off the reef with a horrendous noise and continued on.

Nassau harbor was much bigger than the other island harbors, so it was a lot easier to see. Darryl finally steered his way up the channel and into the calm waters of Hurricane Hole. He tied up the *Party Animal* in a slip within crawling distance of the casinos and then announced to Rudy that they would have to take a couple of days to check for damages.

Rudy wired Key West for more money and had a beer at the Beachcomber before walking over to the old Chalk's Terminal. He was standing in the urine-saturated phone booth wondering whether Kevin Costner was the right actor to play him in the movie version of his story when the phone rang.

34

Bless Me, Father

Rudy Breno's sweat-soaked shirt stuck like glue to the rear seat of the dilapidated white Cadillac taxi that had picked him up at Chalk's Terminal. Traffic packed the narrow bridge that connected the casinos and hotels to the main island—an urban nightmare never described or photographed in Nassau travel brochures. Steam escaped from under the long hood of the Cadillac with an angry hiss that was barely audible above the rantings of a fundamentalist preacher on the radio.

Rudy slouched and tried to lower the electric window, but the Cadillac was without power. He opened the door to get some air but was overcome with engine-exhaust fumes and a hodgepodge of waterfront smells. They had mixed with the stifling heat into some kind of evil potion that hung over downtown Nassau and had the islanders in a very bad mood. He fanned himself rapidly with his reporter's notepad—the one he'd used when the mystery man had called him at the Chalk's pay phone an hour earlier. He'd made a tape of the conversation and had jotted down the directions to the rendezvous spot.

A loud bang unglued Rudy from the Naugahyde seat cover.

The driver cranked and cranked at the ignition until the grinding noise of the starter was replaced by the clicking sound of the exhausted solenoid.

"Dis a worthless pile a Detroit shit," the driver snarled.

"Praise Jesus and all His glory," the radio preacher wailed as a woman began speaking in tongues.

"What seems to be the problem, sir?" Rudy asked.

The cab driver did not respond. His eyes were fixed on the rearview mirror. A cacophony of horn blasts and curses rose from the line of cars that was now backed up beyond the tollbooth. A couple in matching blue-and-orange polyester shirts shouted insults from their rented compact directly behind the wheezing Cadillac, accenting their outbursts with long blares of their high-pitched horn.

"Hey, lardass, move that hunk of junk," the man said. "Our ship leaves in thirty minutes."

The large black taxi driver pulled out the key, got out of the Cadillac, and walked back to the rental car. He wore his contempt like an airport identity card.

The terrified tourist started yelling for the police and tried to roll up the window of his car, but not in time. The cab driver reached in and plucked the man from behind the wheel like a grape, walked him to the railing, and dropped him kicking and screaming off the side of the bridge into the harbor below.

"Dis be a shortcut to da boat, azzhole," the driver yelled down to the man who had begun swimming furiously for a blue Bahamian smack boat working its way to the bridge against the tide.

A duo of policemen had arrived from the station next to the tollbooth and reluctantly became involved in the scene, trying to keep the frantic wife and the cab driver apart.

Normally, Rudy would have feasted on such a spectacle. It was the perfect kind of story he could blow out of proportion, but today he let the mayhem on the bridge alone. He had more serious things on his mind.

He tossed a ten-dollar bill onto the front seat, got out of the cab, and walked to the other side of the bridge. He was wringing wet with perspiration when he finally got to Queen Street and stopped at a snack shack on Potter's Key and bought a Coke.

The thousand-dollar payoff for the mystery man was stuffed in his underwear, and he readjusted the bulge in his pants, drawing cackles from a crowd of old women gathered around a fruit stand. He had tucked his pistol in the left side of his pants like Al Pacino had in the movie *Serpico,* but the snub-nosed barrel of the .38 now chafed away at his love handle. Still, he didn't dare mess with the gun. Suppose it dropped down the leg of his pants and shot his dick off or caused him to be jailed for concealing a deadly weapon?

Rudy checked the map and made his way through the maze of traffic. He did not want to be late for his meeting.

• • •

The church had been the mystery man's idea. Rudy trotted up the steps of St. Francis Xavier Cathedral and entered the quiet vestibule.

The air was damp but cool, and he stopped to catch his breath. Out of habit, Rudy dipped his hand into the holy-water font, made the sign of the cross, and pushed the old oak doors apart. Cavernous limestone walls made his footsteps echo as he crept over to the confessional booth on the right.

The unmistakable scent of candle wax brought back memories of Rudy's altar-boy days before he had been thrown out of Catholic school for jacking off in the wine cellar and sent away to boarding school. He tiptoed under the cold gazes of the statues above and entered the confessional. He knelt down, trying to adjust his eyes to the darkness, and rubbed himself where the gun had been chafing his skin.

The small sliding door between the sinner and the confessor opened quickly and startled Rudy for a moment. He could barely make out a figure on the other side of the thin screen. His heart was pounding in his ears, and it was hard to contain himself. Now this was exactly like an Alfred Hitchcock movie. He fumbled with the gun and checked the roll of bills in his underwear, then pushed the record button on his tape recorder.

"Go ahead, my son." The words came from the silhouette beyond the screen.

"Very clever," Rudy snapped. He liked his opening line and the confidence he'd felt when he'd delivered it. He was into his role. Rudy leaned toward the screen until his lips were almost touching it. "Now let's cut the pious priest shit and get to business. I've got a killer to catch."

"If you wish to make a confession, my son, then do so, but do not blaspheme within these holy walls."

Rudy went limp. He focused on the silhouette and then saw the distinct patch of white collar at the throat of the priest.

"Let's start again, my son."

A tidal wave of Catholic guilt rolled over Rudy and lit his old buttons like a Roman candle. He was no longer the cocky tabloid reporter; he was an embarrassed sinner. Automatically he began his confession.

"Bah-bah-bless me, Father, for I have sinned. It has been—ahh, let's see—twenty-one years since my last confession, and these are my sins."

• • •

Rudy finally exited the booth and faced the now-long line of sinners, who gave him degrading looks. He was sweating and shaking, and was still astonished at how much penance he'd been given by the priest. For a moment he had no idea what he was doing in the cathedral. He was walking in a zombie-like trance to the sacristy when he saw a hand signal him from the other confessional on the far side of the cathedral. He looked back to see if the people in the line were watching him, then ducked into the other booth.

The man inside spoke in a hoarse whisper. "I said *left* side, asshole. Did you bring the money?"

"Yes, I have the money. Here it is."

Rudy reached inside his pants and pulled out the wadded hundred-dollar bills and held them up to the window. He gasped and lurched back when the long, shiny blade of a diving knife split the screen, and a large hairy hand with a tattoo of a fighter plane sprang out of the darkness like a moray eel. It snatched the money and disappeared again to the other side of the screen.

"Good. Very good. Now I'm gonna to tell you a little story." Rudy fumbled with his tape recorder and managed to get the pause button turned off.

"This killer you're after? He's hidin' in an ancient palace in the mountains of northern Haiti called the Citadel."

"Holy shit. Haiti. I'll bet the Jet Ski Killer is working for the Tontons Macoutes, probably the CIA, and the Medellin cartel. Wow. And all this time I thought he was just one of those deranged Vietnam nuts. This guy is a voodoo killer. What a story. Where did you say he was hiding again? I forgot to write it down—"

The mystery man interrupted Rudy. "You want the rest of

the information, or you just want to listen to your head rattle?"

Rudy clammed up.

"When you get to Cap Haitien, go to the Brise de Mer restaurant and ask for Fast Eddie. He'll tell you what to do next."

"Do you need a passport to get into Haiti?" Rudy asked.

"Do I look like a fuckin' travel agent?"

"I don't know. I can't see you. Anyway, how do I know that you're telling me the truth and not sending me on some wild-goose chase?"

"That's the chance you take, chief. Now stay put here for five minutes, and then leave out the front of the church. And don't try any tricks. You got it?"

"Yes, Father," Rudy answered.

"And don't forget to do your penance."

• • •

Rudy checked his watch, and when the five minutes were up, he eased out of the church and headed for the boat. His bravado returned in the hot streets of Nassau. He stopped in the marine supply store and asked for a chart that had Haiti on it. The salesman looked at him warily as he paid for the chart.

"Dat Haiti be a bad place, mistah. What you gwan der fa?"

"It's my job," Rudy said and puffed out his chest.

This was real adventure. He would send in his latest article to the paper, find that rum-head captain of his, and get his expedition on its way to the Citadel. He repeated the man's name over and over again so he wouldn't forget: "Fast Eddie, Fast Eddie."

Where's
the Party?

35

It's Time

Charlie Fabian peered into the shattered mirror, and for the first time ever, he felt old.

He had decided the attack on the salvage boat was his last job for the Colonel. He'd thought about skipping out while he was in Africa, but he hadn't had the courage then to make the move. It was easier for him to skewer somebody than to deal with the cunning, baffling mind of Colonel Cairo. He always felt intimidated, but now he had finally made his decision to go. But where? He'd been toying with the idea of going to Bali; maybe he could open a bar there, or even write a book about his adventures.

Charlie Fabian was locked in the men's room of the ferry-boat with his pants down. He dipped his hand into the small glass jar of Tiger Balm and spread it down the side of his left leg. He paid particular attention to the hip joint where he'd taken the full impact of the water when he'd jumped out of the plane. He had barely missed the coral heads, and his leather bag had gone flying. Yet he had somehow managed to keep a visual reference on the bright orange emergency life raft he had thrown out of the plane shortly before he had bailed out.

It had worked like a charm; Charlie simply inflated the raft, climbed in, and paddled to a nearby hunk of coral where he ditched the raft.

A clerk in a rundown diving resort called Blackbeard's Bungalow listened sympathetically to Charlie's story of wiping out on a huge wave and smashing his board to smithereens. He gave him a bottle of Mandrax and some fresh surfer duds. The clerk helped him cleanse and bandage the gunshot wound; Charlie had passed it off as the work of a broken bottle. Humpty Dumpty had been put back together again.

Charlie had lifted an Out of Order sign off the telephone and boarded the *Jason Mason,* the island ferry, where he hung the sign on the bathroom door. He was still safely locked inside when the muffled loudspeaker announced Rudderville. Charlie peeked out the porthole and saw the glistening black hull of the Colonel's new boat, which was sitting at the dock.

• • •

Colonel Cairo held the small urn that contained the ashes of his arm and dreamed of what it would feel like to be whole again. He sat in the aft lounge on the second level of the boat. He was beside himself with pride, for he had finally figured out a very important piece of the puzzle that would get his arm back.

It was one of those things you search for on the horizon when, in fact, it is right under your nose. He scanned the world map that lay across his desk and retraced his discovery.

He followed the line of latitude from X, which marked the site of the African cave where he'd been saved by the old witch doctor after the ambush, across the South Atlantic and into the Caribbean Sea. It was all beginning to make sense now. The location of the black king, Haiti, and the small group of islands offshore were on the same latitude—the same trajectory for an object falling to earth.

He thumbed through the world atlas to get a closer look. He turned to the page that showed the northern coast of Hispaniola and drew a circle around the same cluster of islands. The degrees of latitude that traveled through the *X* in Africa also dissected the heart of the Sleeping Beauties near Boomtown. By now he was certain the other power the old witch doctor had described meant another crystal—*a crystal with the same healing power as the first.*

The black kingdom in the west had been a mystery to him until he stumbled across an old book called *Black Majesty* in a shop in Léopoldville. It told the story of Henri Christophe, and Colonel Cairo had gotten his hands on all the information he could about this strange, forgotten piece of history. He had tracked down a historical expert, Vincent Vickman, who lived in Paris.

Vickman was a retired planter who had spent most of his life in the village of Kenscoff in the cool green hills above Port-au-Prince, the Haitian capital. He had been fascinated by the very thought of a black monarchy thriving in the steamy jungles of one of the poorest countries in the world. Vickman had recovered artifacts from Sans Souci, the king's palace, and the Citadel, the monstrous fort built in the mountains that Henri Christophe had called La Ferrière. Vickman had pieced together a theory that a treasure ship had contained the secret artifacts of King Henri Christophe, but it had been stolen by a nephew after the king committed suicide.

The treasure ship had disappeared in a storm in the southern Bahamas and had never been found. Vickman's search had turned up a few old French coins, but nothing more. He had abandoned the project.

The Colonel had recently offered to buy Vickman's maps, notes, and memoirs, but the old man told him he had already sold them to another gentleman, an American. Vickman could not remember the man's name offhand but found a receipt in his bureau. The man who had bought the items was Elmo Robinson.

• • •

Colonel Cairo had docked in Rudderville earlier that morning, making the trip from Bimini in amazing time. A crowd had gathered at the dock upon their arrival to admire the big boat. The Colonel had never been a man of the sea, but he had always been a man with contingency plans. The boat, named the *Nomad*, had been accepted as payment on a bad debt from Ahmad Kontu, a world-renowned arms trader who was now doing time in a French prison. *Nomad* was a fitting name for the craft, and the Colonel had issued orders to the crew and his guards that while he was on the boat, he was to be addressed as Admiral.

The Colonel had welcomed the customs and immigration officials aboard for breakfast and a discussion of the "film" he was making, which Rolf had handled flawlessly. The mere mention of a movie—and the possibility that the officials might have bit parts—transformed the bureaucrats into obliging, obedient children. Once he had the money, maybe he *would* make a movie, a pirate film based on his own life. The Caribbean had such a colorful history of cutthroats, contraband, drug smuggling, and corrupt government officials that the Colonel was most pleased his destiny had brought him here in search of the crystal that would give him back his arm.

He had paid off the local police chief and escorted the officials to the gangway. Then he went to the bridge. He sat in the helmsman's chair and moved his hand along the chrome wheel; he loved the idea of a command ship.

"Admiral," a voice called out over the intercom, "Charlie Fabian is here."

• • •

"Sorry, Admiral," Charlie said, biting his lip to keep from laughing. Colonel Cairo stared down at the white spot of seagull shit that landed squarely in the middle of his shoe. "Chicken Little was right?"

Charlie Fabian knew his boss was not in a good mood. Nobody shit on Colonel Cairo and got away with it. If they hadn't been in port, the Colonel would have drawn his pistol and blown the birds out of the sky. Charlie hoped his news would cheer the Colonel up.

"You're late," the Colonel barked. "So?"

Charlie Fabian took the bag of gold coins from his jacket and handed them to the Colonel, who opened the bag and examined the coins. He held the coins close and squinted. "Twenty-franc gold pieces, circa 1806."

"Same as the ones Little Elmo had," Charlie said nervously.

The Colonel stared at the wreath-adorned head of Napoleon Bonaparte. "I like the idea of men of power putting their images on coins. I will have to keep that in mind when I have my kingdom. So you found the wreck."

"I have the boat."

"So tell me of the scepter, Charles." The Colonel rolled the coins in his hand like dice.

"I didn't find the scepter, but I do know where Monty Potter is."

Colonel Cairo became as rigid as a statue. He did an about-face and walked back to the bridge and sat down again in the helmsman's chair. Charlie followed and now stood at attention beside him.

"Potter is in Boomtown. He's the king of the waterfront there. The divers were working for him behind the scenes."

Charlie looked at the Colonel, but the Colonel was four thousand miles away, back in the jungle heat with his throat filled with black cotton soil, hiding from the men who had come to kill him—men under the command of Monty Potter. The Colonel's gaze moved back to Charlie, and a smile crossed his lips.

"So Monty Potter is in Boomtown. How fitting, how truly fitting. I can have my cake and eat it, too."

"Sir?"

The Colonel didn't answer. He was staring eye-to-eye at the green mamba in the cage beside the chair. "I think we might have to drop in on him. Right, Afro?"

The Colonel stood and patted Charlie on his shoulder. He flinched in pain.

"You're wounded?"

"I ran into some trouble I wasn't expecting. They were armed to the teeth, and I wasn't able to eliminate all of them."

The Colonel's mood changed faster than the weather in the Anegada Passage. *"What?"*

"The dive boat ran up on a reef and started taking on water, fast. One of them got away in a dinghy."

"You didn't chase him down?"

"I had to plug the hole in my arm, and by that time I thought it best—"

"Don't think. You are not paid to think. I am the thinker. You are the help. Understand this: Without me, you would be rotting in that jail in Africa with the rest of your friends." The Colonel turned the gold coins over in his hand. "The flamboyance associated with men of our profession should be left to the book writers and movie makers, Charlie. Your mission was to find the scepter, not to go on a fucking safari."

"Yes, sir."

The Colonel reached into the snake cage beside the chair and grasped the deadly mamba at the base of the skull. The snake wrapped around his one arm. Charlie Fabian blinked his eyes. The Colonel was pointing the snake at him.

"Soon I will be whole again, and that is all that matters in the world to me. The time is approaching." He dropped the snake back into the cage and wiped his forehead with a linen handkerchief. "I want everything to be perfect when the time comes. You will meet me when I arrive in Boomtown on Tuesday. Rolf can arrange a flight. That will be all."

"How long will we be in Boomtown?" Charlie asked.

A wave of white anger passed over the Colonel's face, but his voice remained level and calm. "I am the thinker, Charles. Don't forget it."

• • •

Charlie Fabian left the cabin, but he stopped outside the door when he heard the phone ring. He put his ear to the bulkhead.

"Any news of the girl?" the Colonel asked. Then silence. "I will be in Boomtown as planned. No, he's going there, too. History is such a strange top. It could spin here, it could spin there. I will deal with Charlie. You find the girl. It's time."

36

We Do Have a History

Root Boy's bush tea and a handful of French aspirin had sent me to sleep with thoughts of cold Alaskan mountain streams where giant steelhead lay hidden beneath the overhanging banks.

I woke feeling remarkably well for a man who had faced death the day before. It was funny—the whole time that maniac had the gun pointed at me and was flying my plane, I had no real thought of dying. I was just pissed off at myself for getting into trouble in the first place. I had felt the weight when I took off but had just dismissed it. Never again.

I spent the morning checking out the plane to make sure there were no bombs planted or hydraulic hoses slashed. Root Boy got a quick lesson on how a Goose is put together and watched carefully as I pulled the floorboards and inspected all the watertight compartments. I put my sawed-off shotgun back in its hiding place behind my seat where it had done me absolutely no goddamn good.

Root Boy had seen enough of the guts of the Goose and went out to catch a fish for lunch. My fearless watchdog followed him down the beach as if they'd been friends forever.

They returned in about an hour with a nice pink grouper. Root Boy quickly filleted it, wrapped it in palm leaves, and baked it on the fire.

We drank the last two root beers in the ice chest and split a Snickers, and then he told me about the old days when he had been a human cannonball in a traveling circus. I told him what I could about Trevor and me, Joe Merchant, and how I had gotten into this mess in the first place. Now I was a day late, and I could already see myself being punished like a fourth grader having to write "I am personally responsible for the unhappiness of Trevor Kane" two thousand times.

After hearing the story he looked at me and simply said, "You still in love wif dis girl."

"No kidding."

• • •

We waited for the tide to flood the creek and float the *Hemisphere Dancer* enough to get her turned around and aimed out to sea. I primed the number two engine with the wobble pump and hit the starter only to hear the telltale clicking that meant we weren't going anywhere yet. Root Boy sat in the copilot's seat and looked worried.

"No problem," I said. "I need a hand, and we'll get her started in a jiffy."

I looped a half-inch line around a prop blade of the number one engine, then tied a rubber snatch block to a cleat above the cockpit. I instructed Root Boy to wrap the line tightly around the spinner hub of the number two propeller like a yo-yo. I shut the fuel off to the good engine and gave the wobble pump behind me another few strokes to get the fuel pressure up on number two, and then I cranked number one. The line tightened around the prop and got the number two prop turning.

There was a loud pop and a gasp of gray smoke, and then the old radial sputtered to life. I climbed out of the cockpit and unwound the rope while Root Boy stayed in the plane and stared out at me in disbelief.

When I climbed back in, Root Boy was still gawking. "I don't believe what I be seein'. I ain't never heard dat a fuckin' airplane be started like it be a goddamn mower. How you learn dat, mon?"

"You're not the only circus performer on this flight."

Root Boy laughed. "You do dee normal kinda flyin' ever?

Da kinda flyin' where you ain't jump startin' engines, dodgin' bullets, or gettin' hijacked by da sickos?"

"Not lately."

I advanced the throttles all the way and worked the rudder pedals, and the *Hemisphere Dancer* made her way off the sandbar and out into the channel. Hoagy barked as if to signal our departure, and I taxied out of the lagoon, did my pretakeoff check, and put the *Dancer* on the step. Water take-offs are the best part of flying a boat. You're idling along, feeling the plane try to keep her balance in a rolling sea, and then you give her the juice. The engine noise screams with power. Twenty seconds of salt spray, bounces, and lunges later, the boat is a bird, and you feel the hull slip away. Suddenly your vocabulary changes from depth to altitude.

The afternoon sky was beginning to fill with clouds, and we would be able to slip into Rudderville without arousing much attention. I would worry about fuel later. Right now, I was finally in a good mood.

"Root Boy, you look like a natural flier to me. Grab hold of that wheel."

Root Boy calmly placed his hands on the worn wheel.

"Flying is all touch. An airplane is never in the same place at the same time. The trick is to anticipate what she wants to do and where she wants to go, and then gently persuade her to go where you want to go and do what you want to do. A good pilot anticipates; a bad pilot reacts."

Root Boy was listening very carefully to my instructions, and it didn't take him long to get the feel of the *Dancer*.

"It ain't dee same as bein' shot out of a fuckin' cannon, dat's fo sure."

He kept scanning the instruments on my side of the cockpit to be certain he was on course, and then he looked out the windshield at the gray clouds forming in the distance.

"We gonna run into doze clouds up dere?"

"Not if you fly level. Remember, the earth is a big round ball. Things are farther away than they seem. You're doing great." The plane swayed slightly, but Root Boy recognized the altitude change and compensated.

"You think yo' boy be in Rudderville?"

"I don't think he's working alone, and Rudderville would be the nearest place to catch a fast plane or boat."

"Mr. Four Eyes don' give a shit 'bout anyting. Dat's what make him so dangerous. If he's dere, we find out. Nobody fart in Rudderville widout da whole place knowin' what dey ate fo dinner."

"If Trevor's still waiting there, by now she'll be pissed as hell."

Root Boy put the microphone closer to his mouth. "Don' it amaze ya how women and men see da same ting from two diff'rent point a view? It's dat baby ting, you know. Dey ain't gonna let up on our asses till some scientist invent a way for da men to get fucked and have babies and go tru all dat pain. Until den, shit—we be jus' buckin' da tide and ain't ever gonna win. I learned dat in my circus days. Got more pussy dan I ever dreamed of, and I tought it was all because a me, you know, Mandingo wid a big dick, only black man any da girls ever seen 'cept in da movies. But den I saw it be nottin' to do wid me. Da girls it was who knew what was happenin'. Dey din even have to tink 'bout a second date or takin' me home to meet Daddy."

"Oh yeah," I said.

"Can you jus' see 'em bringin' me home fo dinner to meet Lester and Polly Esther, and after dinner da ol' mon say to me, 'and Jammal, what is it dat you do fo a livin'?' and der leetle princess answer, 'Oh Daddy, why Jammal ees in da show bidness. He a human cannonball.' "

We were both laughing now, and I had to stop because it hurt my head.

"It's da 'can't live wid 'em, can't live widout 'em' school of tought. So you and Trevor been doin' dis boomerang love ting for a while, huh?" Root Boy asked.

I nodded. "Yeah. We do have a history."

• • •

Time passed, and we were both silent, watching the clouds out the window. I guess it shocked Root Boy when I dropped my hat over my swollen, tender eye, gave him the heading for Rudderville, and told him to fly straight and level.

"Hey, what the hell you tink you doin'?"

"Little combat nap. You're goin' great. Just watch out for flying saucers. You fly a lot better than the four-eyed bastard. Wake me up when we get close to those clouds up there."

• • •

I didn't know how long I'd been asleep when I felt the tap on my shoulder and sprang awake. For a second I had a flash of the hijacker and then realized it was Root Boy.

"Clouds ahead, Frank. Wake up. Wake up."

I looked at my watch and saw that I had indeed gotten a fifteen-minute nap. I checked the heading and altitude. Root Boy was right on the money.

"I've done enough flyin' fo today," he told me.

"You don't want to follow me through the landing?"

"Dat's okay, mon."

I eased the power back and leveled off just below the clouds. I made a straight approach from the sea and pulled the power almost back to idle so I could keep our engine noise to a minimum.

A dark cloud lay above the long, thin island, and sheets of gray rain stretched over the hills to the north, where we were going. It was merely an afternoon shower and was actually perfect cover for our arrival. The rain began to pelt the plane, and we were engulfed in a milky mist.

"Why we flyin' into da storm?" Root Boy asked.

"This isn't a storm—it's a flying car wash. As long as you can see the horizon through the clouds, it's not going to hurt you."

Root Boy looked straight ahead and relaxed when he saw the precise line in the distance behind the scattered rain clouds. I made my approach to Milkman Bay and flew low over the old bonefishing camp tucked back in the eastern corner, just a few miles outside Rudderville. It looked abandoned, frozen in time like so many things in the Caribbean.

I flew downwind above the channel where the rusted, broken hulls of several fishing boats lay along the clearly visible flat. Root Boy read off the items on my water-landing checklist with the efficiency of a three-thousand-hour pilot. I turned on the wipers, lined up on the color change, and pulled the throttles.

The rain appeared to be a welcome caller to the parched brown hills that surrounded the cove. It had been a long, dry winter in the Caribbean, and everywhere people were predicting a bad hurricane season ahead. The smell of grass filled the cockpit with a slight fragrance of wild onion that made my stomach growl.

I skimmed along the surface of the bay and touched down next to an old shrimp boat. The gulls and frigate birds that had laid claim to this prize made no motion to become airborne but simply watched us pass with contentious faces and stared at me from the top of the faded nameboard, which read *Good Luck.*

"Guess da name don' work, do it?" Root Boy said.

The rain clouds dissipated above the low hills, and the sun reappeared as a sliver above the horizon and reflected off something on the dock of the bonefishing camp. I idled the plane toward the camp.

"We got company, boss," Root Boy said, and I eased the shotgun from behind my seat and handed it to him.

37

I Must Confess, I Could Use Some Rest

Trevor Kane had spent the day on the beach in a string bikini with her sketch pad in her lap. She was no longer holding out any hope that Frank would show up, but it was too pretty a day to be miserable. When she returned from the Rudderville airport that morning, she had dropped her duffel bag in the room, changed quickly, tossed her sketch pads and paint box into her knapsack, and had gone down to the beach. She lost herself in her work and spent several hours sketching. First she drew a seaplane on fire, plummeting to the earth, and then she made a cubist collage of ornate question marks.

Suddenly a dog was standing at her feet. It was a red chow, and he had a deflated football hanging from the side of his mouth. He looked at Trevor, defying her to try to grab the ball.

In a flash, Trevor lunged for the ball and jerked it from the bewildered dog's mouth. "It's an old trick, Cheer Up," she said, laughing. The dog looked at her oddly, and then she caught herself.

Cheer Up was the name of the dog she'd had when she

was a kid. "Sorry, pup. You favor a dog I once knew," she said, scratching the chow behind his ear. The dog moved on down the beach.

Cheer Up had been the center of her life when she was growing up. He was a birthday present from her mother the summer they had rented a small cabin on the Eastern Shore near Salisbury. The dog was a diver. He'd walk along in the shallow water with his head submerged, looking for blue crabs. Invariably he'd pop out of the water with a crab firmly clamped to his nose, sending Trevor and Joe to the ground with laughter. Cheer Up had also been her first and most painted subject. She must have painted a thousand portraits of her dog. He would sit quietly while she sketched him from every angle she could dream up.

When Trevor was eleven, her father came home from the Pentagon one day and ordered his family to pack. He had been promoted, and they were on their way to Japan. The following week, according to the Captain's orders, all unnecessary items were peddled at a garage sale.

Cheer Up was sold along with bicycles, clothes, and household items. Trevor had wailed, and her father had slapped her. It was the only time he had ever physically harmed her, and she'd rarely spoken to him after that. The silence didn't seem to bother her father; in fact, he seemed to prefer it. Years later, she recreated the experience in a complicated painting she called *Excess Baggage*.

As always, the sketching helped Trevor take her mind off of her problems. She realized she hadn't been thinking enough about her work lately, and she missed it. Maybe if the phones were back in order later, she'd call her gallery in New Orleans and see if anything was happening.

She was not aware of the time until three small black girls came over to her and broke her concentration. They were dressed in their Sunday best, and they surrounded her, watching motionlessly while she added a sail to the boat she was drawing.

The smallest of the girls broke the silence. "Dat boat ain't out dere. How come you put it dere?"

"Don't you know nuttin', fool?" her sister said. "Dis lady be an arteest. God dun give her da touch, and she can do whatever she dun want. She can paint da sky green or da ocean red or put a boat where dere ain't one. She can even draw you wif a nose da sizza Pinocchio. Ain't dat right, ma'am?"

Trevor stopped sketching and turned to the little girl with the pink-and-white ribbon on her head. Her innocent face was filled with questions.

"It's all make-believe. You see what you want to see, not what's really there."

The little girl looked puzzled. Suddenly a beat-up van roared down the main street of town, did a 360-degree turn around the rotary, and came to a halt where the shell road met the crumbling town dock. The van was filled with children who were laughing and singing as a large woman in a purple dress banged her tambourine. The trio rushed off, leaving Trevor alone on the beach as the van disappeared in a cloud of dust and song.

In an instant it was quiet again, and Trevor watched the first stars of the night appear in the sky. She put down her pencil and gazed across the water at the white beaches where a flock of gulls gathered, settling in for the night. A whiff of garlic from some kitchen had made its way out over the water, and Trevor realized she was hungry. This was the first sane moment she'd had since she'd arrived in Rudderville.

She picked up her knapsack and decided to walk to the end of the town dock and catch the sunset. A small fleet of sailboats lay at anchor, and the words of a song floated across the harbor. "I must confess, I could use some rest. I can't run at this pace very long."

Trevor hummed the tune and walked down the dock. Halfway to the end she heard laughing and splashing below her feet and leaned over to see what was happening. A group of young boys with masks, snorkels, and underwater lights probed the rocks in the shallow water for crayfish. She flashed back to a similar scene—long ago where boys in wet suits and diving gear were playing like seals beneath Cap Canaille on the Mediterranean coast.

Her mother had arrived unannounced in Paris, where Trevor was enrolled at École des Beaux-Arts. It was the dead of winter, but she was consumed by an obsession to go see Joe; he had rented a house on the water and was staying there with one of his groupie girlfriends in a state of narcotic obliteration. Trevor knew that Joe was beyond help at this point, and she tried to talk her troubled mother out of the trip, but it was no use.

They had rented a Mercedes and had driven south in the freezing rain to Aix-en-Provence. It was a tense trip, and her mother spoke little on the drive. The only relief Trevor had was watching a street circus outside a small café in Cassis.

She smiled, remembering the ringmaster, a toothless old man wearing a beret and a tattered army jacket with insignia and mementos of the French campaign in Dien Bien Phu stitched to the sleeves. The circus was composed of four alley cats, an old goat, and the spectacular Mademoiselle Pompinette, a white Persian with long, delicate legs. The alley cats crawled through tubes, jumped in and out of hoops held by the old man, and balanced on a tightwire that stretched a death-defying three feet above the street.

The finale featured Mademoiselle Pompinette, who rode bareback on the goat in continuing circles while the neighborhood dogs looked on. The whole show was done to a scratchy Debussy record that wobbled as it spun around on an ancient record player. Trevor had gulped down her lunch and worked on her sketch pad. A year later, the huge oil painting that followed was entitled *Mademoiselle Pompinette* and was the centerpiece of her first solo show in Paris.

After the circus, she and her mother had driven southwest of Cassis to the house that Joe was renting. He not only refused to see his mother but threw a broom and two bricks out the window at her in a drunken rage. Afterward, Trevor had driven her inconsolable mother to Cap Canaille, hoping to cheer her up with a breathtaking view. She realized her mistake when she learned that it had been a favorite jumping spot for the desperate for centuries. The ageless boulders and cliffs were frozen in time, and the view had not changed since the Romans had named the land Gaul. Her mother sobbed uncontrollably for a long time, and Trevor watched carefully to make sure her mother didn't leap.

Finally they walked to the edge and tossed down a handful of coins, which fell among a group of boys who were playing on the rocks below.

Trevor sighed, remembering that day. It was all in the past now. It was time to move forward, or she would end up feeling that it was her destiny to paint only her family until they faded away. She watched the sun go down and turned to walk back to the hotel. When she passed the divers, she tossed a pocketful of change into the water and heard the gurgling and splashing sounds as the boys dove to the bottom, searching for the coins.

38

Do Not Pass Go, Do Not Collect Two Hundred Dollars

Law enforcement in the third world gets a lot of its inspiration from police shows on American television, so when I heard a deep voice yell "Freeze, pal," I knew what the metal flash I'd seen in the mangroves outside Rudderville meant: guns.

Freeze, hell. Just try stopping the inertia of an eight-thousand-pound airplane being pushed along by two six-hundred-horsepower engines.

My initial instinct was to jam the throttles full forward and run for it, knowing most of these clowns had never fired at a moving target before. But one look at my escape route was enough.

I was too close to the dock to get the plane up on a step before we could run into the rocky hills and be turned into Spam. Night was coming fast, and a 180 back down the channel strewn with hurricane debris might turn the *Dancer* into another perch for the pelicans. Even if we did get off, we only had enough fuel to make it to Georgetown, where there would be plenty more cops around and DEA Black Hawk helicopters waiting to shoot us out of the sky.

I told Root Boy to throw out the shotgun. Maybe that would keep them from ventilating my airplane and our bodies. Cops were everywhere, and they ran around like chickens in a barnyard. Some scurried to the dock with their guns pointed at us, and others jumped in the water to flank our approach. The whistles and shouting sounded like a bad rap record.

A black Mako skiff came up at my three o'clock position, and the two young soldiers with machine guns looked very menacing—that was, until the driver hit a sandbar and launched the soldiers thirty feet ahead of the boat. One actually landed headfirst in the mud. The other gunman pulled on the guy's legs until he popped out like a cork.

Once they were out of the mud, they aimed their guns at us until the plane nudged the dock, and we were ordered out with our hands in the air by a large sergeant waving a baton. Sweat poured from the brim of his starched white hat, and he jerked constantly at the high collar of his blue wool tunic. He did not look happy, but I was hopeful I still might be able to bullshit my way out of the situation. I knew I had been mistaken for a dope smuggler.

It had happened several times before, and my plan was ready. I would courteously inform the man in charge that I had been to the camp before and was scouting fishing locations for George Bush and Dan Quayle, and I was sorry for the inconvenience. Of course I had no problem with paying an overtime charge.

The look on Root Boy's face disturbed me. He was listening intently to one of the junior officers rattling on in patois to the big sergeant in the blue coat. It was too fast for me to keep up with.

"Shit," Root Boy said.

"What is it?"

"Dey sayin' you be da Jet Ski Killer."

• • •

I guess it's the heat, but nothing—I mean nothing—in the tropics can keep any intensity for a long period of time. It took a good hour for the soldiers to search the plane, and they were very upset at not finding six tons of cocaine on board. The sergeant lightened up as the evening breeze cooled off the harbor. He introduced himself as Sergeant King and said we were in a lot of trouble.

If it hadn't been for the goddamn Jet Ski Killer accusation,

I could have been on my way in an hour. The sergeant had loosened his collar and was asking lots of questions about the plane. I happily answered him. I wanted to show I wasn't some wired-up punk hot-rodding around the skies for cash. I was trying to convey a bit of professionalism.

Somehow I talked the sergeant into letting me fly the plane back to town, where he could then confiscate it. I wanted to avoid the awful alternative of having the bozo who'd run around in the Mako tow the *Hemisphere Dancer* the fifteen miles to Rudderville over open water. Sergeant King was very keen on the idea of flying and loaded himself and seven soldiers on board. Hoagy greeted them like new friends and wagged his tail as they settled in. I knew the sergeant was lusting over my plane, and the *Hemisphere Dancer* would never make it off the island if he had anything to do with it. He would take ownership and put it into service.

I was getting used to flying at gunpoint and made a very long, graceful takeoff from the harbor and flew the short distance to town. I landed not far from Crooked Point Marina and taxied to the ramp by the town dock. As we left, I patted the *Dancer* affectionately on the nose. I didn't know if I would ever again have my hands on the throttles. The plane was locked and put under guard, and we were hustled off to jail. The last I saw of Hoagy, he was sitting outside the door, watching us as if this were all some kind of game.

39

I'd Rather Watch Paint Dry

When Trevor came back from the beach, a piece of pink notepaper hung from the clothespin nailed to her bungalow door. It was from Percy, the desk clerk. He was in the bar and had good news.

The children at the beach had given her spirits a lift, and Trevor had decided to put all her troubles aside for the night and have a good time. She stepped out of her bikini and rummaged through the duffel bag for her black off-the-shoulder minidress and her black heels. She lay the dress on the bed, smoothed the wrinkles out, and then grabbed a towel and went to the enclosed patio to take a cold shower.

She loved taking a shower outdoors. Her skin had been tanned by the sun all day, and the cool water was exhilarating. Crickets in the overhanging ficus trees rubbed their legs in time to the refrains of "Feeling Hot Hot Hot" that drifted in from the bar on the beach.

Trevor dried off, took a quick look in the mirror, and decided to wear her hair down. She ran her Mason Pearson brush through her blond curls, anointed herself with coconut-scented aloe lotion, and did several pirouettes beneath the ceiling fan. Then she slipped into her evening dress. She had bought it in Miami, thinking she might have a romantic moment with Frank—ha! She checked her reflection in the mirror, and after giving herself an approving look, she said, "Your loss, buddy."

• • •

Large flambeaux scented with citronella oil lit the path down to the beach, and Trevor strolled along to the steady thump of a bass guitar.

The Dogfish Bar and Supper Club was no more than a driftwood beach shack with a purple tin roof on a small isthmus that jutted out into the channel. The entrance was decorated with fishnets, glass trap balls, and blowfish lamps that hung from a gumbo-limbo tree. Tarpon-scale wind chimes twisted in the breeze, but their soothing sound was drowned out by the music. Trevor parted the dangling bamboo curtains and walked in.

Inside, the temperature was twenty degrees warmer, and she waved her hands in front of her face to clear a path through the fog of cigarette smoke in the front bar. Every eye in the place was on her. She scanned the bar quickly, looking for Percy, and she hoped her gaze would not fall on Frank Bama. Instead, her eyes met those of a tall blond stranger in a beige linen suit who lifted his sunglasses above his eyebrows and raised his glass to her. He grinned widely, revealing a too-perfect set of sparkling white teeth.

Trevor turned away immediately and then saw someone signaling from a table at the far end of the restaurant. She stared in disbelief at the black woman with platinum blond hair who was wearing a strapless white crepe dress.

"Mizz Kane, Mizz Kane, back here."

Trevor's mouth dropped open when she realized it was Percy, in drag. She made her way to the table, and Percy rose and pulled her chair out. "It's my Marilyn look. I bring dis out only fo special occasions."

"Hot, hot, hot," Trevor said.

"I bought it in Hollywood on my trip, but 'nuff a me and my weirdness. Check you out. Gawd a'mighty. You be lookin' man killa tonight, girl."

"I guess that's a compliment," Trevor said. The man in the beige suit was still staring at her.

"You sho' got da 'tenchun a dem land sharks at da bar. Dey be doze movie people I be tellin' you 'bout. Dey got da biggest yacht in da marina—dey take up da whole damn dock." Trevor did not look back. She could feel their lustful glances over her shoulder. "Dey be hittin' on you fo da night is tru. Be careful."

"They get enough rum in them, and they'll be after *you*," Trevor said.

"Dem macho white men ain't my type. I be havin' my eye on a cute little cook dat come off dat big boat. Very exotic."

The waiter emerged out of the crowd of tourists and locals who were jammed around a backgammon table where a heavy game was in progress. Trevor ordered a double rum and tonic, and Percy asked for a Goombay Smash.

"I got news 'bout da plane from Port-au-Prince. Dat plane be at da airport now, and it be leavin' at seven in da mawnin'. You got a confirmed seat."

"That's great news, Percy. Thank you."

"I hate to see you go, Mizz Kane. We wuz jus' startin' to have a good time. Pace of life get pretty routine down here."

"Why don't you go back to the States?"

"It's nice place to visit, but it ain't no place to live."

The drinks came, and Trevor held hers up. "Here's to our short but good time, Percy. And the name is Trevor. Miss Kane is—was—my mother. I forgot."

She gulped half the rum down and sat back in her chair with a big sigh. She closed her eyes. "Layla" cut through the night, and she threw her head back. "Goddamn now, that is a rock 'n' roll song." She played a few bars of air guitar and finished her drink.

"I met Clapton once in Key West, Percy. He knew my brother real well. I was walking down Duval Street past Sloppy Joe's, and I saw my friend Blanton's Jeep. They're calling Blanton the Jet Ski Killer now, but you'd like him."

Percy almost choked on his drink. "Jeez, you know da Jet Ski Killa? I been readin' all 'bout him in da *Lighthouse*."

"I do know him, and I also know the jerk who wrote those dumbass articles. Blanton's crazy, but he's not a killer. The guy who wrote that is just plain stupid, and he's blown the whole thing out of proportion. It's a career move. He wants to be like Geraldo."

"You know he be on dis expedition to track down da Jet Ski Killa. Say he's comin' dis way. I got da latest paper at da desk if you wanna read it."

"Have they caught him yet?"

"No, but dey be lookin'. Cops is all over dis island waitin' for him to show." Percy picked the maraschino cherry out of his drink and dropped it on his tongue. "Anyway, finish yo' story 'bout Clapton."

"Well, Frank was gone to Belize on a job, and I saw Blanton in his Jeep on Caroline Street, and I walked up to talk to him. He introduced me to this guy, but I didn't pay much attention to him. He was cute but quiet, and I figured he was just one of Blanton's fishing customers. We went into Sloppy Joe's and had a few beers and listened to a blues band. We were talking fishing and stuff, and then Blanton mentioned my brother. Eric said he knew him, and I figured, sure—I stopped mentioning that my brother was a big rock star even before he died because most people would say they knew him and then start in on some lame story about how they'd met Joe in a bar somewhere."

"Joe who?" Percy asked.

"Joe Merchant."

"Joe Merchant was your brother?"

"Yeah. It's a long story, Percy, and not a very pretty one."

"So you was in Sloppy Joe's—"

"Yes, and I still didn't get the picture. Well, Eric gets up and goes to the bandstand and picks up a guitar. It finally hit me like a ton of bricks, and I felt like a huge dumbass. He played till four in the morning, and then we went to Shorty's and had breakfast before we went fishing. He was really nice—"

A loud crash interrupted her, and the crowd of people by the backgammon table began shouting. A large man in a black suit with a clean-shaven head jumped up and jabbed his finger at a small plump woman seated across from him.

"That fuckin' bird of yours stole the dice! He's a trained saboteur."

"You dick. I'm surprised you can count how many there are," the woman hissed.

"Dat pearlhead betta not fuck wif her," Percy said. "Dat's East Side Louise. She be meaner dan a mongoose in a snake pit. Uh-oh."

The big man flipped Louise the bird and turned to whisper something to one of his friends. When he did, she leaped up onto the backgammon table and creased his shiny skull with a beer bottle. The big man collapsed like a wet noodle and crashed into a waiter; orange slices and tiny umbrellas flew everywhere. Trevor and Percy burst out laughing at the up-roar.

"She is something," Trevor said, watching the scuffle.

Bouncers were quickly at the scene, and the man in the beige linen suit was suddenly between the combatants and spoke in German to several other men, who then carried the bleeding man away. The music kept playing, and the broken glass and tiny umbrellas were swept into the sea by the bus-boy. Calm was restored.

"Must be a dark moon or sometin'," Percy said. At that moment, a blue macaw landed on Trevor's side of the table. In its beak it held one of the dice.

The man in the beige suit walked over to the table, and the bird flew to the rafters. The man had taken his sunglasses off, and his eyes were riveted to Trevor's breasts.

"Hope this disturbance didn't inconvenience you, ladies," he said in a continental voice. The man's smile was blinding.

"Haven't I seen you on TV in a toothpaste ad?" Percy asked. The man gave him an icy look.

"No, you must be with the movie crew," Trevor said.

"Word gets around fast on this island, doesn't it? I'm Rolf, the location director for a major motion picture company, and we're scouting locations and holding auditions this week. Would you be interested in auditioning?" He laid his business card on the table beside Trevor's drink.

"I'd rather watch paint dry."

Percy spit out a mouthful of Goombay Smash, and a pink mist covered the man's jacket.

Rolf wiped at the stain with his hand.

"Sorry 'bout dat," Percy said.

Rolf stared straight at Trevor. "I see. Well, this could have been your lucky day." He turned and walked out of the Dog-fish, followed by several members of his crew.

"To quote dat honest man President Cahtah, I tink he be lustin' in his heart fo you."

"Heart-on is more like it. Those movie pukes are all alike." Trevor looked at the card he had given her. The number rang a bell, but she couldn't place it.

She was too hungry to dwell on it. She dropped the card onto the table, then signaled for a waiter to take her order. They ate fried grouper, homemade potato salad, and garlic cheese bread. After dinner, they had several Grand Marniers. The crowd at the Dogfish eventually thinned out, and

Trevor and Percy walked down the road to a late-night disco called the Sardine Can where they drank double shots of tequila and wedged themselves onto the tiny dance floor with a horde of sweaty bodies. They danced until well after midnight, when they were soaked. Trevor had hooked up with a couple of young research students and was singing along at the top of her voice with Mick Jagger to the chorus of "Emotional Rescue" when the number clicked.

"I'm clean, I'm clean." She squeezed herself free from the dance floor and found Percy at the bar talking to the cook. "I gotta make a call; I'll be right back."

She hurried up the hill to her room and dialed the number on the card. The phone was finally working. After several rings, a machine answered: "You have reached the offices of Hackney Primstone III . . ."

She waited for the beep. "You're fired, you slimy son of a bitch. This is Trevor, and I just ran into your movie-producer-slash-private-eye in Rudderville. Movie producer my butt—you had me followed. I'm flying home tomorrow, and your ass is grass." She slammed down the phone so hard the bell rang.

Trevor walked down to the beach and let the sea breeze cool her off. The night air helped shake the alcohol from her brain. Who was this asshole Rolf? The idea that Hackney was having her followed infuriated her, and she decided to find out about it.

Trevor bypassed the nightclub on her way to the Crooked Point Marina. She could make out the big yacht lying at the end of the main dock. It sat in the darkness with only an anchor light glowing, but someone was watching her from the massive bridge.

"Hey Mr. Hollywood, I got some questions for you," Trevor yelled as she got closer to the boat. She was weaving slightly as she walked down the dock, and one of her spiked heels jammed between two planks of wood. She stumbled out of the shoe, lost her balance, and tumbled over the side of the dock into the water.

Trevor swam to the surface and saw a rubber dinghy lying next to a ladder that hung on the starboard side of the boat. She climbed into the dinghy and sat for a minute to catch her breath. Her black dress was up around her waist, and there was a stinging pain across the right cheek of her butt where she had rubbed across some barnacles on a piling. Her stubbed toe was bleeding, and she examined her wounds.

"God is punishing me for not wearing underwear," she said aloud and climbed gingerly up the unsteady ladder that banged against the hull of the ship.

"Rolf, I'm here for my audition, you prick."

It was very dark, and she was still feeling the effects of the tequilla and Grand Marnier, but she pulled her skirt back down over her bare ass and scanned the deck in both directions, looking for obstacles. She felt something sticky on her hands and held them up to the moonlight. "Just great." Her palms were covered with white paint from the ladder. She held the pose for a minute.

Her outstretched hands had formed a frame around the silhouette of what could only be the *Hemisphere Dancer,* which was sitting on the ramp. There were two soldiers smoking cigarettes beneath the wing. "Frank?" she called.

Before she knew it, Trevor had been jerked by the hair and felt herself wedged tightly against a hard, muscular chest behind her. The smell of cigarette smoke and whiskey surrounded her as she was forced to move sideways. Her skull ached where her hair had been yanked, and a large calloused hand covered her mouth. She tried to bite it, but when she opened her mouth, her adversary tugged at her hair again, and her scream came out as an inaudible whimper.

A light flickered from a cigarette lighter in front of her, and she made out the face of Rolf. He grabbed her left hand and twisted it.

"I should apologize. It seems the paint isn't quite dry, but do come aboard. Someone is dying to meet you."

40

No Bird Flies by My Window

There's something unsettling about a jail cell, especially a third-world jail cell. Root Boy was sawing logs on the iron bunk above me, and I was amazed that he could sleep in such a predicament. I guess years of being shot out of a cannon make most other life-threatening situations seem mild.

I had tried to lie down and go to sleep and forget what was happening, but I couldn't. Instead I wound up reading the graffiti scribbled in several languages on the walls—desperate thoughts written by despairing men. The natural slapback echo of the long sullen corridor carried the sound of canned laughter, applause, and the unmistakable voice of Pat Sajak orchestrating another episode of "Wheel of Fortune." The jailers were hooting and hollering obscenities at Vanna White and yelling encouragement to the contestants.

If I had to be in jail, I wanted to hear Mose Allison or Muddy Waters. God, how I hated what satellite dishes had done to the culture of the Caribbean. Soon there would be more satellite dishes than palm trees.

A faint scent of grilled onions came through the window and mixed with the musty air of the dungeon. We had been fed a plate of rice and beans shortly after our arrival, but we hadn't laid eyes on our captors since they had taken our passports and personal effects and had marched us off to this cell. Not a word, of course, about phone calls or rights to an attorney.

We were somewhere in the bowels of the old British fortress outside Rudderville that was now called Government House. It was no jail; it was a real dungeon. Shackles and chains still hung from the walls, and kerosene torches lit the corridor where shadows danced like tortured ghosts, laughing at my predicament, waiting for me to rot away and join them.

I thought about the movie *Papillon* with Steve McQueen. That didn't help much. It gave me no clue about how I should handle this situation and only increased my anxiety. I knew that in time I could straighten out this Jet Ski Killer accusation so at least I wouldn't be tried as a murderer, but whichever way you sliced the pie, I was still in hot water. I hadn't forgotten about the false registration numbers on my airplane, the default on my loan, and the fact that the real Jet Ski Killer was my best friend and we had coincidentally skipped town about the same time.

I was not in the best shape and had been doing way too much thinking. I stood on a leaky sink, peering out through a six-inch slit of window that provided a very limited ground-level view of the town dock. No bird flew by this window.

I studied the few stars that were in my frame of reference, trying to get my mind off the terrible reality of my situation. I could see a big yacht slipping quietly away from the dock in the early morning darkness. I wondered why he didn't display his running lights. The yacht moved on out to the middle of the channel without incident, and I could make out the silhouette of the *Hemisphere Dancer* sitting alone at the end of the ramp by the gas pump. Hoagy was nowhere to be seen. How in the hell had I gotten myself into this mess?

I knew Trevor's crazy-ass brother was long dead, but I'd thought that if I could help her find Desdemona, somewhere along the way things would come back into play for us. There weren't too many women around like Trevor Kane, and I wanted her back in my life. I was tired of trying to converse with twenty-year-old college girls on vacation in Key West. I would rather cook myself dinner in the hangar and sit with Hoagy in my lap, reading a good book. The thought made me even more depressed.

Well, as Billy Cruiser used to say, if a frog had wings, his ass wouldn't hit the ground. I could fly a plane, navigate by the stars, throw a baseball ninety miles an hour, cook a piece of fish better than most restaurants, but I couldn't figure out how to handle my finances or my feelings—both of which had all of a sudden painted me into the corner of this dark and lonely jail cell. By now I was a day and a half late, and Trevor had no doubt given up on me and was long gone.

I climbed down from the sink and pitched into the metal bunk beneath Root Boy, who was still snoring away. I felt as if I were back at summer camp the time my mother had come down to visit me. I had been so homesick I begged her to take me back to Pensacola, but she made me stay. I had gone to my bunk and cried my eyes out until the fellow next to me offered me some chocolate chip cookies.

That was camp.

This was jail.

A well of old feelings came gushing to the surface. I hadn't felt like this since Billy Cruiser had told me about my father and had given me his watch. I had let Trevor down, and I had lost my dog, who was probably wandering around outside, wondering where I was. Either that or he was looking for his next meal and a new owner. Most likely I would lose my plane, too. I missed my hangar and Billy's wit. I was no doubt destined to spend a long time in jail.

Through the tiny window, I saw a shooting star with a tail as long as South America streak across the sky. I made a wish. I wished I were somewhere other than here.

I don't know how long I was out when I was awakened by the sound of my name. "Root?" I said, but I only heard snoring from above.

"Frank," the voice called out again. It came from beyond the window. At first I thought I was dreaming, but when I hit my head on the bunk, I knew I was awake. It was still dark.

"Yeah?" I whispered. I eased myself up onto the sink beneath the window. Suddenly a face popped into view.

"What the fuck's happening, Brillo?" The adrenaline launch had my heart pounding in my chest. I couldn't believe it. My face was inches away from the unmistakable wild eyes of Blanton Meyercord.

"You look awful. What are you mopin' about, Brillo? Ray Ban's here to get you out of this shithole."

Rolling
with the Punches

41

Somebody Else's Troubles

On the anniversary of the independence of Rudderville and the Bentwood Islands from Great Britain, the newly elected prime minister, Willy Gambas, gave his country a birthday present. It was not a memorial to the history of colonial rule and isolation. Willy Gambas perceived himself as a man of the future, and he wanted a modern monument erected that people would remember him by long after he was gone. It had come in two cargo containers with easy-to-assemble directions and had been erected overnight and placed on a giant pedestal behind Government House outside Rudderville.

Willy Gambas's present to the island was unveiled on a bright Sunday morning before a huge crowd that covered the hill behind Government House like ants. It was the largest satellite antenna in the Caribbean. One of his campaign promises had been to link his country to the world. Financing for the project had come from the ganja growers in the hills of Jamaica, with whom Willy Gambas did an incredible amount of business.

The people of the Bentwood Islands were jubilant. It did

not matter to them that Willy Gambas was stealing signals by means of a descrambler. They were overwhelmed with the quantity of programming that had never before been available. This was progress.

The dish was controlled by a remote box in the office of Willy Gambas, so the country watched whatever Willy wanted to watch. They watched at home, in the bars, in the streets, and at work. He beamed in the Movie Channel, HBO, Cinemax, the Cubs, the Mets, the Braves, the shopping channels, the superchannels, and God in three languages and living color; at night, after the kids were all tucked in, the porno channels ran until dawn when the islanders woke to Gene Scott and his cigar.

• • •

The country was soon addicted to television. The station ran twenty-four hours a day, seven days a week, and everybody watched. Willy Gambas went away on business to Jamaica for a month, and he returned to an island of video zombies. Nobody wanted to load the shrimpboats from Florida with the ganja from Jamaica. They slept all day and watched TV all night. From Ted Koppel to Hugh Hefner, they stayed tuned in. The whole dope economy was in danger of collapsing, so Willy took action. Programming was put on a schedule from eight in the morning until midnight, and the zombies soon began to revert back to island time.

Willy Gambas was indicted two years into his first term, brought down by the technology that he loved so much. He had been videotaped in a Coconut Grove hotel room taking a hundred-thousand-dollar cash bribe from a DEA informant to add three hundred pounds of sugar to the fuel trucks that supplied the DEA Black Hawk helicopters stationed at the U.S. Army base in Georgetown. Willy left his island home and his satellite dish in the middle of the night on a chartered Lear 35. He was welcomed to Panama by General Manuel Noriega and bought a giant mansion overlooking the Pacific Ocean from which he ran his business in exile.

Back home in Rudderville, Sergeant Augustus Caesar King, the chief of police, took over the prime minister responsibilities and control of the dish, which he promptly renamed in his honor. Sergeant King had ratted on Willy in the sugar scandal. He knew that television was the way to power. He had carefully watched the way the Americans had been sold a B-rated Hollywood actor and TV star as their president. He never could understand the Americans. If they wanted an actor for president, why didn't they choose a good one?

But if they could do it in America, Augustus Caesar King could do it in the Bentwood Islands. He had come up with the idea of writing, producing, and directing his own television show called "Coffee with the King," on which he read the news, funeral announcements, and want ads from a small studio he had built in the basement of Government House. Sergeant Augustus Caesar King loved the dish even more than Willy Gambas had.

• • •

Sergeant King had made the satellite dish an important part of the security setup at the Rudderville jail. He had put video cameras in the cells so the prisoners could be watched from the control room, and he had been given a giant-screen Advent projector by the TV-actor president of the United States—which more than made up for the loss of King's small cut in the Jamaican ganja operation. The satellite dish still sucked microwaves from the sky, but the studio in the police station was the only place where programs still ran twenty-four hours a day. The television there was a matter of national security and was never turned off. Sergeant King had implemented an emergency generator for the frequent power outages, so the juice kicked in automatically and kept the signal alive.

With the "eye on crime" camera system watching over the prisoners, there was usually only one guard on duty at night. But due to the importance of the recent captives, Sergeant King had ordered four men on the night shift. They worked out a rotation to check on the prisoners, which left plenty of time for TV.

This night, the dish was aimed at the Spacenet 1. Three of the on-duty soldiers lay asleep, sprawled out on an old Castro convertible couch covered with popcorn, candy-bar wrappers, and empty Goombay Punch cans. The remnants of a card game lay on the table. The young corporal who had the watch was not at his post in the hallway. He was in a trance, watching a film about sorority girls and their pet dogs called *Hoochie Poochie*.

Six seconds before three naked women were to step into a kiddie pool filled with Jell-O and large snakes, the picture went out. The guard was pissed. The screen had turned from flesh tones to a snowy pattern, and a loud hissing sound came from the speakers. He mashed the "mute" button, and the set went silent. He then mashed the "on" button repeatedly and aimed it at the big screen. The set came on, but the picture did not reappear.

This could be a potential national emergency, and the young guard thought what a good impression he could make on the sergeant if he fixed the problem all by himself. He put down the popcorn bowl and pried himself up off the couch. He yawned, scratched at his crotch, and strapped on his gun.

The soldier glanced at the black-and-white monitor under the cardboard sign that read "Cell 1" and saw the two prisoners asleep. All the other cells were vacant. He exited through the back door and walked out into the night. Taking a big drag on his unfiltered Camel, he began to climb the hill. He moved the flashlight along the path, and when it illuminated a pair of tattered Top-Siders, the facts didn't quite register until it was too late.

When the thick piece of waterlogged driftwood made contact with his skull, it produced a ringing sound like a basketball being bounced on a hardwood floor.

• • •

"Hello, boys. Today we are going to do something very exciting. Can you boys say 'jailbreak'?"

Blanton had a bandanna over his mouth and a pair of sunglasses on, and he was jingling the keys to the cell door. Root Boy finally woke up and just laughed.

"What da fuck you doin' here, Mr. Rogers, mon?"

"No time to explain right now. We need to be runnin' before the sun catches up," Blanton said.

"Root Boy, meet the real Jet Ski Killer."

Blanton opened the door, and we hugged. "It ain't as flashy as an open-sea rescue, but it's all I could think of with such short notice."

"It be a pleasure to meet you, Mr. Killer, mon," Root Boy said.

We wrapped the three sleeping guards tightly with duct tape and handcuffed them in a circle around the bunk in the cell at the end of the hall. I took the poker winnings from their pockets to supplement my cash flow since I figured Trevor had probably given up on me and left.

Blanton wheeled a small portable TV into the cell. He turned it on, raised the volume, and switched to "Headline

News." "What's happening tonight ain't no television show, boys. This here is real life. Just think—after tonight, you boys might be on this show. Better work on your proper English." He turned to me and flashed that wild-eyed grin. "Frank, let's blow this pop stand."

• • •

We made our way through the back streets of Rudderville, down to the ramp where the *Hemisphere Dancer* sat. I tried not to think about the fact that I had just broken out of jail and could be shot dead at any moment, winding up on the front page of the *National Lighthouse* with a Rudy Breno headline. God, what an epitaph.

I knew the armed guards surrounding the *Hemisphere Dancer* were not going to simply move out of the way and wave us bon voyage. Two of them sat in worn beach chairs beneath the port wing, studying a set of dominoes under a dim light. The third guard slowly circled the plane with his rifle slung over his shoulder.

"If you can take care of the sentry, we can secure the boys over there, but we gotta move quick," Blanton said to me.

"Why do I have to go after the guy with the gun?"

"You're the only one here with experience, and besides, it's your plane." Blanton handed me the .45-caliber pistol he'd swiped from one of the guards and a roll of duct tape.

"The burden of command, huh?"

"Yeah, somethin' like that."

"You been in hand-to-hand combat?" Root Boy asked.

"Ol' Frank here got a medal for that. Took out a team of VC frogmen. Underwater," Blanton said.

"Tell me 'bout dat."

"They were trying to blow up my fucking plane. I didn't think it was such a good idea. Jesus, I thought we were in such a goddamn hurry."

I circled around the tail of the plane and pulled the pistol from my belt, then jumped down off the dock and made my way along the sliver of beach that ran out to the jetty. I signaled to Root Boy and Blanton. They were crouched behind a long row of crawfish traps on the far side of the dock.

Quietly I slapped my thigh to try to stop my right leg from shaking and breathed deeply, hoping if I filled my lungs with air, I would be lighter on my feet and not make as much noise. I slipped my tennis shoes off, tied the shoestrings together, and slung them around my neck. As the soldier circled the plane, I waited until his boots were even with my eyes, then sprang up behind him. I walked a few steps in his shadow and then let him have it over the head with the butt of the pistol.

He fell backward into my arms, and I dragged him to the beach and taped him tight. I slung the rifle on my shoulder and quickly put my shoes back on, then took up his route around the front of the plane.

Root Boy and Blanton slipped into position behind the tail. I tried to mimic the guards' speech pattern with my best patois, but it wasn't necessary. These guys were so into the game I had to stop and speak plain English to get their attention.

"Hey, Hulksters, who's winning?" I asked.

By the time they looked up, they each had a gun at their head. Root Boy tied them and tucked them deep in the row of traps and went after the guy on the beach. I dragged the long fueling hose from the pump on the end of the dock and jimmied the padlock of the pump handle.

"That ain't avgas, Brillo," Blanton said.

"Hell, I ain't run hardly anything but car gas in this baby for the past year and a half. That's all I can afford."

There was still about half an hour until daybreak, and I climbed up on the wing and watched uneasily while the tanks slowly filled. Headlights began to pass intermittently along the road, and we ducked into the traps each time a car passed. It took what seemed to be an eternity, but I finally topped off all the tanks.

"We're ready," I said and opened the cabin door. I was home again. I breathed in the smell of my plane, the oil, the salt, the smell of fuel.

"Somebody be comin'," Root Boy called out.

"Jesus fucking Christ, what the hell is that?" Blanton said.

From the pilot's seat, I couldn't see what he was talking about. I grabbed the pistol, slipped down into the bow compartment, and eased open the hatch. I prayed to God I wouldn't die in a Bonnie-and-Clyde shoot-out. If it was the cops, we were dead in the water.

"Frank Bama, wait, wait."

"Freeze, sister," I said.

Blanton burst out laughing in the rear of the plane where he had the woman in the sights of his M-16. She wore a tight white dress and a blond wig, and something dangled from her index finger.

"Freeze? Come on, Frank, be original, for Christsakes."

"Not another step, and drop the gun."

"Gun? I ain't carryin' no gun. Dis be a shoe. I need to talk to Frank Bama. It's 'bout Trevor Kane," the woman half whispered in a husky male voice.

Jet Ski Killers, jailbreaks, and now transvestites. What next? I jumped out of the hatch. "Talk, but make it fast," I said.

"I'm Percy. I work at da hotel where Mizz Kane was stayin'. She been waitin' fo you fo a while, chile, and she is mad. Anyway, we went out on da town and was drinkin' and dancin' and partyin', but she left real quick-like and went to make a call. She never came back. I was worried 'bout her, and when I went lookin' fo her, I foun' her shoe down by da dock where da big boat wif da movie people was. 'Cept dat boat weren't dere no mo'. I tink she be in trouble on dat boat. Den I hear you was in da jail, and I went dere right 'bout da time you was breakin' out. So I followed you here."

"That's fast?" Blanton grumbled.

"Can I put my hands down? I got her purse here," Percy said.

I felt a rush of anger. I didn't believe for a minute that Trevor was in trouble. I had been hijacked, left for dead, and had now broken out of jail to try to catch up with her—and she had left town on a fucking party boat full of movie people.

I grabbed the purse from Percy and tossed it in the baggage compartment and made my way back to the flight deck.

"Would you like da shoe? Maybe it give you a clue to where she's gone," Percy said.

"What is this—*Cinderella?*" I snapped.

"Everybody wants to be Travis McGee," Blanton added.

Percy dropped the shoe in my lap, leaned in the window, and kissed me on the cheek.

"Don' worry, Captain. Yo' secret be safe wif me."

I wiped my face in disgust and hurled Trevor's shoe out the window as hard as I could. Blanton strapped himself into the copilot's seat and scanned the street for signs of our captors, but Rudderville was quiet.

I was still thinking about Trevor. I imagined her dancing

on the stern of some big, tacky boat with a man who'd been in a tanning salon too long.

"Hey, Captain, let's try to stay out of condition white, huh? Now do you think you can jump this bird off in the dark, or are we gonna wait here for the sergeant to come for tea?"

Blanton was right. My mind was certainly not focused on my plane. I shook off my thoughts about Trevor. "Condition red," I said, flicking on the battery switch. I began to work the wobble pump. "Let's go, Root."

Root Boy was standing near the dock, still covering my six o'clock position. He walked to the window with a slight smile on his lips "I be stayin', boss."

"What the hell are you talking about?"

"Dis enough adventure to last me a while. I lef home to get away from da Mad Hatter ball, and you boys be on yo' way to da party. Besides, you two don' need no mo' help."

"Are you crazy? If you stay here, they're gonna throw your ass under the jail."

"No way." He looked over at a small sailboat at the end of a rickety dock. "You know how it goes down here, mon. Sergeant King ain't gonna mount no posse and come gallopin' after you. Anodder island, anodder country, anodder bureaucratic ball a snakes. Once you fly 'way from Rudderville, you be somebody else's troubles. Just try and not get caught, and watch out fo dat four-eyed bastard. He still out dere."

I knew what Root Boy said was true, and I couldn't really blame him for not wanting to go on with us. In a way, I wished I could go with him. "What are you gonna do?"

"Dey'll tink I fly off wid you, but in a couple a minutes I be makin' my way back to No Mon's Cay." He extended his hand through the window, and I reached out and hugged him. "Stay in touch. You know where I be."

"I'm glad somebody does."

Root Boy laughed and then looked me straight in the eye. "Don' be mad at Trevor no mo'. Go see Desdemona. I tink dis be some kinda quiz show dat da boys upstairs be givin' you. She jus' might have da answers."

"Brillo, we gotta go," Blanton said.

"Nice to make yo' 'quaintance, Mr. Killer, mon," Root Boy said.

Blanton reached across me and grabbed Root Boy's hand. "Same here, Cannonball."

"Clear one," I said instinctively, and Root Boy walked backward toward the little boat.

"Tanks fo da flyin' lesson."

I closed the window, released the parking brake, and nudged the throttles slightly forward; the *Dancer* moved down the inclined ramp. Blanton put on his headset and looked behind us to see if any soldiers had shown up yet, then started to read the checklist.

"Holy shit," I said. I slammed on the brakes just at the water's edge. "I forgot about Hoagy." I didn't know what to do. Our escape couldn't wait, but what about my dog? Fortunately I didn't have to choose. When I looked back, I spotted Hoagy running for the plane at full speed. He raced down the dock, and Trevor's shoe was hanging from the side of his mouth. "I'll be goddamned," I said.

Blanton had already unstrapped himself and had taken off his headset. Now he was on his way to the rear door. Before the door swung fully open, Hoagy had timed his leap and came bounding through the hatch. He raced up to me and decided to shake the water out of his coat. He dropped the shoe between the seats, and then he picked it up again.

"Can he fly, too?" Blanton asked.

I rubbed Hoagy's head and sent him to the rear of the plane where he lay down with the shoe. I advanced the throttles, and we slid into the water.

By the time I looked back at the dock, I saw that Root Boy had commandeered the little boat and had already hoisted the sail. It was gliding across the harbor on a northerly course. He was on his way to the place where he had come from. He was lucky. He waved slowly, and I waved back.

Once airborne, I pulled on the yoke to get her above the scattered layer of early morning clouds. They would help to shield our departure from anybody looking for us. I pointed the *Dancer* in the direction of the barely visible rim of the sun. My world may have been coming apart like a frog in a blender, but at least I was back in the sky. Blanton turned to me with that grin and spoke into his headset. "Now, Mr. Bama, let's put a little distance between causes and effects."

42

Where Is Joe Merchant?

Colonel Cairo held the binoculars and took in the Haitian coastline. It was early morning, and a thin layer of perspiration already covered his whole face. His starched khaki shirt was limp. A sheen of condensation began to form on the small lenses, and he called from the turtle deck to one of the soldiers, who climbed quickly through the wheelhouse door with a chamois cloth, dried the binoculars, and handed them back to the Colonel.

Colonel Cairo looked out at the town of Cap Haitien. It had been born in the era of pirates and had evolved into the capital of the richest colony in the West Indies. The city had been through the slave revolts and the defeat and exodus of the French. It had fostered the home of the first black republic in the Western Hemisphere, ruled by Henri Christophe. That was long ago. Cap Haitien was now a town made languid by the sun. It sat on the shore of the tropic sea like a tired old woman trying to catch her breath in the heat of the eternal summer.

Colonel Cairo scanned the faded red-roofed colonial buildings and Victorian gingerbread houses that stretched from

Mont Joli on the north end of town past the old city gates to the south. Beyond the town, a desolate warm wilderness of untamed mangroves, bougainvillea, and bananas formed a dwarf scrub forest that lay nestled between two distant mountain ranges where the coffee trees grew.

The Colonel heard the sound of steps, and Rolf came up out of the gangway in his beige linen suit.

"Breakfast will be ready in fifteen minutes, Admiral."

The Colonel continued to survey the shore. "And our guest?"

Rolf let out a grunt. "She should be interesting company."

The morning sun had risen above the mountains, and a land breeze cleared away the smoky haze that forever enveloped the town.

"There it is." The Colonel sighed. "The Citadel, Henri Christophe's monument to himself."

The giant fortress squared off the peak of a mountain perch that rose above the thick jungle and loomed like a ghostly ship in the sky. On this day, the morning mists rising up from the sea seemed to break against the prow, and the silent fortress appeared to be riding the wind.

"There is an energy in these latitudes, Rolf. Do you feel it?"

"What do you mean, sir, and who is Henri Christophe?"

"Henri Christophe was a man like me. He could not exist in the idiotic world of politics. After the Haitian revolution, he proclaimed himself king of the North and built the Citadel both as a monument to himself and a place from which to defend his kingdom. It took him thirteen years and two hundred thousand workers. The walls of the Citadel are fifteen feet thick, and all 365 cannons in the fort had to be carried up that mountain. He carved his kingdom out of the colonial malaise and was determined to defend it to the death, but the French never came. There was never a shot fired. I need my kingdom, Rolf."

The fortress disappeared behind the low morning clouds. "This is the land of conquerors," Colonel Cairo continued and looked to the south. "Somewhere over there, Columbus built the first fort in the New World from the splintered timbers of his beloved *Santa Maria*. It inspires me, Rolf. Boomtown will be my kingdom."

"Potter isn't going to like that, and what are you going to do with Charlie Fabian?"

The Colonel dropped the binoculars, and they slapped against his thick chest. "I have plans for Mr. Potter, and we have discussed what to do about Charlie Fabian."

A soldier carrying an AK-47 stepped from the wheelhouse. "Breakfast is served."

* * *

Trevor Kane had been escorted to the dining salon by two soldiers who carried serious-looking weapons and didn't speak. She was still in her party dress, and the barnacle scrape on her butt throbbed with pain. The interior of the boat smelled of teak oil, and the aroma of coffee made her light-headed with hunger and thirst.

The elegant dining salon was empty except for the guards, who stood on each side of her chair and said nothing. Out the window, she could barely make out the jagged shapes of a mountain range. They could only be the high mountains of Hispaniola or Puerto Rico. She figured they had been traveling a little more than five hours now since her capture, and she put their location somewhere between the Caicos Islands and the west coast of Haiti, whatever good that would do her.

She was ravenous, and it appeared she was at least not going to be starved to death by her captors. She knew Hackney Primstone III was somehow involved with all this. It must have something to do with her trust fund. Her head began to pound again. It was bad enough to be kidnapped, but she was also nursing a throbbing hangover from the night of partying with Percy. Her scalp still hurt from having her hair yanked so hard by Rolf.

She had been dragged, kicking and biting, below decks and handcuffed to a bed in a small cabin. She'd been alert enough to realize there'd been only an occasional splash of saltwater against the porthole, and the yawing motion of the ship indicated that they were going somewhere in a hurry.

Trevor had never been seasick, but when Rolf came in to check on her, she asked him for some Dramamine. That on top of the alcohol put her into a half-conscious state until well after sunrise. When the guards shook her awake, she had been dreaming of her mother and brother. They were waving to her from Frank's plane. It was floating down Park Avenue and had stopped at a traffic light. The streets of New York were canals crowded with floating taxis and Jet Skis. She kept yelling out to them, "What are you doing in New York? Don't you know you're dead?" She had tried frantically to reach the plane and ask them what was going on, but the light turned green, and they flew off to the Pan American building.

   • • •

She was startled when the ship's clock sounded seven bells, and the door that led to the aft deck opened. A hideously scarred man in a khaki uniform limped through the corridor and took a seat at the head of the table. The empty left sleeve of his jacket was pinned neatly behind his back, and dark spots of sweat stained the breast of his shirt. It wasn't hard for her to figure out that the man before her was Colonel Cairo. She felt a flood of anger.

Rolf followed him and sat to his right. The guards snapped to attention, and Trevor took a long look at the one-armed man. "Has anybody ever told you that you look like Klaus von Bulow?" she asked.

The Colonel laughed. "I'm glad to see you still have a sense of humor, Miss Kane, but I don't know whether you're being affectionate or nasty, my dear."

Trevor was studying this strange man and didn't see Rolf come up behind her. He had hold of her hands before she knew it. He unlocked the metal bracelets and slipped them into his jacket pocket and started to rub her wrists.

"This will help the circulation return."

"Don't you touch me, you slime." Trevor jerked away with a poisonous look.

"Now try to be a little more pleasant, will you, Miss Kane?" the Colonel said.

"How do you know my name? And why are you treating me like some kind of hostage? You people aren't in the movie business. What kind of scam have you got going with that bottom-feeding cousin of mine?"

"We should eat before we talk."

The Colonel pressed a button on the table, and a waiter in a starched white jacket vaulted into the room through the swinging door of the galley. He poured the coffee, then carried in a large platter and presented it to the Colonel for inspection. The Colonel helped himself to a large portion of eggs and meat, and then the server presented the platter to Rolf. Another servant appeared and quickly set about cutting the meat on the Colonel's plate.'

"Manatee steak. Care for some?"

"Manatee? That's an endangered species."

He jabbed a loaded fork into his mouth and spoke as he chewed. "Aren't we all."

• • •

Trevor sat through breakfast listening to her stomach growl, thinking of the baby manatee she had once helped Frank rescue from a sandbar near Cabbage Key. Her hands were trembling too hard to lift her coffee cup, so she simply sat in silence.

The Colonel and Rolf had finished their meal and were now having more coffee. Colonel Cairo let out a loud belch, and Trevor felt as if she were going to vomit. So this was Colonel Cairo, the man she had read about in the paper. The man who had made such an impression on Joe. He did not look like a humanitarian. Trevor's anger and questions twisted her insides into knots, and she tried to find an explanation for what was happening. The Colonel stood up and limped to the bar. With one-armed dexterity he carefully poured a shot of rum into his coffee.

"You have questions written all over your face. Where would you like me to start?"

"Why have you kidnapped me?"

The Colonel sipped his rum and coffee. He smiled. "You are not being kidnapped, my dear."

The frustration inside her made something snap, and Trevor began to cry. "Then what the fuck am I doing on this goddamn boat?"

"My name is Colonel Cairo," he began.

"I know that, you asshole. This has something to do with my brother, doesn't it? Holy shit—Desdemona was right."

Trevor jumped up out of her chair but was immediately forced back down and held tight by Rolf.

"My, my. Such a filthy mouth this morning. You are an excitable girl, Miss Kane. Trevor Kane, daughter of Remington and Rebecca Kane, and sister of Joe Merchant Kane, correct?"

She could feel the fear start to take hold of her, and she fought it.

"Where is my brother?" she asked.

The Colonel lit a cigar and blew the smoke across the table. "I'd rather talk about what made you decide not to go sailing with Mummy that day."

Trevor heard the mocking tone in Colonel Cairo's voice

and felt her knees start to shake. She closed her eyes, and her blood pounded. "What do you mean?" she heard herself ask.

"I had hoped to do away with both of you at once. That would put me in direct line to inherit your brother's estate. It is amazing, isn't it, how many more records these rock stars sell dead than when they're alive? I had no idea." Colonel Cairo rose from his chair and began to circle the room. "It was your cousin Hackney who concocted this scheme, of course cutting himself in for a nice percentage. My funds were running low, and Africa is changing. The carefree days of overthrowing countries for a living are gone.

"Hackney came up with a rather clever way to attach me to the trust fund in Africa while still making him sole surviving relative of your family trust. All we had to do was get rid of you and Mummy dear."

Trevor gripped the edge of the table so hard her fingernails dug into the varnish.

The Colonel chuckled. "Did you have a premonition, or were you just being conveniently unavailable the day your lunatic mother asked you to go sailing with her? You ruined my plan and slipped out of sight. Then, out of the blue, you marched into Hackney's office, but then you disappeared again. And last night, you simply walked up onto my boat. I would call that poetic justice, wouldn't you?"

Trevor could say nothing and kept her eyes closed. She shuddered, thinking about her mother.

"I had hoped to let the interest build a while longer on the estates, but there was a scandal brewing at the bank in London, so you and Mummy became top priority. It's nothing personal, you see. Just a cash-flow problem."

The Colonel took another sip of his rum and coffee, and suddenly Trevor sprang like a cat across the table. She was on top of him, clawing his face. "You son of a bitch, you animal! You killed my mother! Where is my brother?"

Rolf pried her off the Colonel and refastened the handcuffs behind her back while the guards manhandled her into the chair. The Colonel straightened his jacket, wiped the scratch mark on his cheek, and walked around the table.

"That is a waste of very expensive rum, Miss Kane." He slapped her across the face. "You are in my way, and nobody stands in my way. Get her ready, Rolf."

• • •

Trevor thought about the scene in *Peter Pan* in which Captain Hook made Wendy walk the plank. This couldn't really be happening. This was the twentieth century. People were shot to death in fast-food stores by crack freaks for spare change, but nobody was made to walk the plank.

Rolf had taken Trevor below, and at gunpoint he'd ordered her to put on a pair of roller skates. The whole time she was lacing them up, he'd looked a her as if he'd never seen a woman before in his life. "Such a waste, such a waste," he'd repeated.

Now she stood in the port passageway in the grip of the guards who kept her from teetering over when the ship rolled. She looked out at the ocean, and her teeth chattered from fear. While they were having breakfast, the clouds had rolled in. A sudden squall had shattered the tranquility of the morning, and at this moment the big ship was lumbering up and over the whitecaps. The Colonel and Rolf had put on yellow foul-weather slickers and stood on one side of the rail. "You're crazy!" she yelled at Cairo. "You know you can't get away with this!"

"I'm sure I will. Drowning seems to be a family tradition with the Kanes."

The Colonel pulled a book out from under his slicker and began to read aloud. "The Mono Passage is one of the deepest and most threatening bodies of water on earth. It has the highest recorded concentration of hammerhead sharks—" He stopped and put the book back in his pocket. "Wherever your remains might wash up, you'll merely be remembered as that silly white girl in the skimpy dress who was last seen drunk in a bar in Rudderville.

"Engines to idle."

The boat pitched violently back and forth as it wallowed in the trough of a huge wave.

"If I were a writer, I couldn't think of a more clever demise for you—sort of following in your brother's footsteps, leaping from a ship into the sea."

Trevor looked from the Colonel up to the sky and asked God what she had done to deserve this. Her family was cursed. "Can't we talk about this? You can have the goddamn money," she yelled, but the Colonel wasn't listening.

"I remember when I first met your brother in Lamu. He was a burned-out beanpole looking for cheap thrills. He had met a couple of my soldiers on holiday at the Peponi Hotel.

They had thrown a hell of a party that night and ended up firing machine guns in the square and shooting the loudspeaker off the tip of the mosque. Joe spent a week with the troops in jail and found his new calling. His days as a rock star were over. He was going to be a soldier. Isn't life grand?"

"Goddamn you, Joe," Trevor cursed under her breath.

"I bailed your brother out of jail. He asked to go to the Congo with us, but I wouldn't give him the time of day. Then Joe offered me twenty-five thousand dollars cash to train him to be a mercenary. I know a bargain when I see one, so I turned Joe over to Rolf here for training. Within two weeks he had put on some muscle and was in half-decent shape. The last I heard, he was spotted in Cuba. Yes, we faked his suicide, my dear."

"You did *what?*" Trevor screamed.

"That's right, Miss Kane. I hate to disappoint you, but when you get to the other side, don't waste your time looking for Joe Merchant. He isn't there yet, but he'll be joining you soon enough." The Colonel raised his arm to the soldier. "Now for some morning exercise. Nothing like a swim after a good breakfast, is there, Miss Kane?" And as the boat rolled down into the trough again, they released Trevor. She rolled off and disappeared into the stormy morning, her screams muted by the wind and the sound of the engines revving up.

43

The Price of Tea in China

The weight of the roller skates was draining Trevor's strength. She did not want to end her life as a meal for some prehistoric fish with a brain the size of her fist. *Survive* was the only word that occupied her thoughts. She was devoid of anything else. No thoughts of Frank, her mother, her brother, why she was where she was, the price of tea in China.

Trevor Kane left her body and watched her own struggle to survive from a distance. She was a little girl watching her grown-up self as if she were in an aquarium. She looked like one of the mermaids at the underwater ballet in Weeki Wachee, Florida, one of the few pleasant memories from her childhood. She saw herself struggling with the heavy roller skates, sinking below the surface, reaching for the tangled laces. She shouted directions to herself. Tiny bubbles escaped from her tightly pursed lips and floated to the surface. Finally, the skates were off and spiraling down into the abyss, leaving a phosphorescent trail.

Trevor broke to the surface like an exhausted tarpon, and her mind joined her waterlogged body. A sharp pain shot through her chest as she gulped for air.

How long could she bob around on these huge swells on the surface of the Caribbean like a crouton in a bowl of fish soup? Trevor beat at the water in her frustration and exhaustion. Her breath became sounds, and the sounds were without syllables. She cried like a dolphin trapped in a drift net.

Her cries skipped like renegade radio waves across the African rollers as they plodded along to distant and unknown shores. A million images flashed by. Images of her drunken father in his navy whites with piss stains on the trousers where he had forgotten to shake his dick before leaving the bathroom at the officer's club Christmas party, loud sounds of her brother's Stratocaster guitar crying out for help, the face of Desdemona as puffy as a cloud, calling to her from the sky.

Trevor was now inhaling as much water as air, panting, choking, and crying. Her limbs were numb, and she felt her will to survive being beaten down by the power of the sea. If this was death, she was not going quietly.

"Why?" she screamed. She tried to raise her arms, but they fell limply out of the air. Her left arm came to rest on a soft, floating object. Trevor threw himself at it.

Her eyes stung from the saltwater, but she immediately knew what it was. This is too much, she thought. Two months ago she had been organizing an anti-ocean-pollution group and had done a series of murals and collages to help benefit beach cleanup. This was not a whale or a magic dolphin that had come to save her from the ocean. She was hanging onto an enormous black plastic garbage bag, one of millions that had been thrown from the transoms of ships under the cover of darkness. All over the globe they aimlessly floated on the face of the ocean like pimples, spewing the pus of human refuse. But for once she was grateful for pollution.

The huge plastic garbage bag was half-filled with air. She relaxed her grip on the bag slightly, not wanting to tear it with her fingernails, and she tried to catch her breath. She was floating now, and for the first time since she had been rolled off the stern of Colonel Cairo's boat, she stopped moving. Still, her muscles fluttered and pulsated. She was not going to drown. At least not this very moment. She stared up at the dark clouds and envisioned the whole sky as a painting. The clouds began to change positions, and she lay back and let the sea take her where it intended.

44

Old Habits Die Hard

As we were flying from Rudderville toward Boomtown, I'd been telling Blanton all about Ace in the Everglades, Pass Her By Cay, and my hijacking. In telling the story, I couldn't believe it had happened.

"That sounds like somethin' out of a book," he said.

Now the old engines droned away, and I looked at my contorted reflection in the hub of the spinning prop. The gash above my eye was still throbbing. My body was healing, but my mind was an open sore.

I corrected my course with a little left rudder and put my headset back on.

"You've been driftin' around the sky like a tourist lost in downtown Miami. What's eatin' you?" Blanton asked. He was sitting in the copilot's seat munching cheese crackers and drinking a Goombay Punch while Hoagy watched him intently.

"What's wrong with me? I'm pissed off. If Trevor hadn't made me come down here, I'd probably be with my dog somewhere off the coast past Juneau watching herds of sea lions on my way to Kodiak Island. But no, here I am on some wild-goose chase that's brought me to the brink of death and turned me into a fugitive. I can't believe it. I did all this for her, and she's run off with a bunch of fuckin' Hollywood actors."

"Producers. Hollywood producers," Blanton said. "There's a difference, Frank, but our boys on that boat ain't neither."

"What do you mean?"

"I mean they ain't who they say they are."

"Well who the hell are they?"

"The guy who owns the boat is really an old war-horse mercenary guy named Adrian Cairo."

"Wait a minute. This is the guy Trevor told me about in Key West."

"Did she know him?"

"No, she'd read about him in the paper, and she put two and two together. It has something to do with her brother. She's determined to find out what happened to Joe."

"Well, this guy ain't no Aristotle Onassis. He was deported from Africa and then disappeared. Seems he's come out of nowhere all of a sudden with a big boat and his little band of cutthroats. No way they're makin' movies."

"How do you know all this shit?" I asked.

"Frank, you're not the only honky who can maneuver through these islands."

I had to laugh.

"This Colonel Cairo ain't no fake wrestler. He's the real thing."

"You think she was kidnapped?"

"Makes more sense, and besides, you got a glass slipper," Blanton said. "This fugitive-on-the-run shit gives you an entirely different perspective on life."

"How the hell did you find us in Rudderville?" I asked.

"I skidded across the Gulf Stream to Cay Sal in my skiff and snuck across to Staniel Cay and stashed my boat with Jermain Jarvis."

"I thought he was in jail," I said.

"He was tied up in that Willy Gambas thing in Rudderville, but he only did a year, and they never got his money. I helped him out with some charters in Georgetown one time, and he sort of owed me a favor, and I needed a place to hide my boat. I told him what happened. He'd read about me, and he'd seen the story on CNN on the dish. He said some divers who worked for a guy named Little Elmo were killed the other day near No Man's Cay, and they were blamin' it on the Jet Ski Killer. I told him I didn't do it, and then he showed me Rudy's article in the *Lighthouse.* Seems like everywhere I go, somebody's shovin' that article in my face."

"The one announcing the expedition?" I asked.

"Yeah. I gotta admit that I was flattered by all the attention, but I knew I needed to get Rudy off my tail. So I called him."

"You talked to him? Where?"

"In Nassau. I was his unnamed source."

"What do you mean?"

"Hell, it made perfect sense. When I was in Andros I called him up in Key West and started him on this crazy-ass chase, tellin' him I had information about the whereabouts of the Jet Ski Killer. He swallowed it hook, line, and sinker. Next, I set up a meetin' in Nassau in a confessional in the cathedral, and I told him the Jet Ski Killer was hidin' out in the Citadel on Haiti. For that he gave me a big wad of cash. God knows I needed it. Then I called an old friend in Cap Haitien and told him to be on the lookout and to take Rudy on a ride he'd never forget. I had wonderful dreams about leading Rudy into a pit full of zombie vipers on his way to find the Jet Ski Killer. I stole a dinghy from Paradise and worked my way down the Exumas. With Rudy's money I figured I could get a plane south out of Rudderville with no questions asked—that was before you guys showed up and brought out the troops. Well, I haven't seen any more stories in the *Lighthouse,* so I guess Rudy's on his expedition." Blanton laughed.

"You're too much."

"And exactly what were you two doin' down here, anyway?" Blanton asked.

"I was on my way to Alaska, and Trevor showed up and told me her mother'd killed herself. She wanted me to take her to Boomtown to find some woman named Desdemona who used to sing with her brother—she's a voodoo woman or something and sent Trevor messages that her brother's still alive."

"Frank, these guys on the boat are dangerous. Trevor ain't at no cocktail party. Jermain told me that a big boat had just passed through claimin' they were some movie people on location, but he said they looked more like dopers. He showed me some Polaroids of a party that were on the bulletin board at the yacht club, and I saw the one-armed man again, and it came to me. I'd seen him in *Soldier of Fortune* when I was in jail.

"Well, anyway, when I'm in Nassau, I pick up a local paper one morning lookin' for news, and I see this picture of some tourist officials and a movie producer workin' in the islands. It was our boy. I had a hunch Cairo was involved with those treasure-diver murders that were blamed on me. This guy ain't on a fuckin' vacation cruise here. Somethin's goin' on, and Trevor's involved in it, buddy."

"Well, it's either go after the boat or find this Desdemona character," I said, hoping for advice.

"You're the captain. I'm just your average Jet Ski Killer," Blanton said with a smile.

"I'm going after my girl."

"Old habits die hard."

"Very funny."

I grabbed the sectional chart from between the seats and unfolded it across my lap. I quickly plotted out a rescue grid that would cover the area between Rudderville and Boomtown—I was guessing that was where the Colonel was headed.

"I figure we can zigzag along his probable course and pick him up pretty easily. Question is, what do we do then?"

• • •

I reduced my throttles and fuel flow and started making the old familiar zigzag maneuvers, focusing my eyes on any speck of debris on the surface of the ocean. At one thousand feet, we started our search.

I was looking for the telltale signs of the ship's wake, which would lag behind the hull for a good distance. Blanton spotted the first one through the binoculars, and I climbed into the clouds to conceal our position and flew over the ship. It was not the Colonel's boat but a big cruise ship lumbering south to San Juan.

We repeated this pattern several times. I knew we'd also need a place to hide the plane if we didn't have any luck, so I pulled the chart back out and quickly found what I was looking for.

"Sleeping Beauties. Perfect," I said.

"What are they?"

"A string of little islands. Boomtown's on one of them.

There's a lagoon on the south shore of one of the smaller ones where we can hide the plane if we need to."

I was measuring the distance on the chart with my fingers when I saw a small reflection on the water out of the corner of my eye. I turned my head and scanned the spot instinctively. I saw it again. The sun was reflecting off something in the water.

"You see that?" I asked Blanton.

"See what?"

"I had a flash of something at eleven o'clock. Might be a piece of driftwood, but I want to check it out."

I banked the plane to the left and pulled the throttles back and put the *Hemisphere Dancer* into a slow descent. I saw the flash again. Blanton had the big binoculars to his eyes.

"Frank," he said, "that piece of driftwood is waving."

45

The Things We Do for Love

We had made two passes over the person in the water, and although I couldn't believe it, there was no doubting what I saw. Down below me, hanging onto a black garbage bag in the middle of the Atlantic Ocean was my girlfriend. Even from our altitude, I could tell she was pale and weak. She looked as if she'd been in the water a long time. There was not a boat in sight, but this was not the time to wonder how she'd gotten there or to worry about what was going to happen. I had to stuff my emotions and concentrate on flying.

"Have you ever done this before?" Blanton asked.

"Not in this plane, but I've heard stories about old Bob Hanley doing it at Catalina."

"This is what you're a hero for, Brillo. Just tell me what I need to do."

"We'll make a timing run for the swells and then land. The trick is this: once we're on the water, we have to ride the swell and get as close to her as we can. We don't want to turn around in this shit, or we'll all be tits up. Once I get down, I want you up in the nose. Don't open the bow hatch until I tell you to. There's a half-inch line with a grappling hook. We'll try to snag the bag first and bring her in.

"I'll swing the plane around so she'll come alongside behind the props at the rear door. I can't leave the controls. You'll have to haul ass back there to get her in. I have blankets under the seat. Get her strapped in, then secure the grappling hook, and stay with her. We won't have much time to enjoy the view."

"Got it," Blanton said in a matter-of-fact voice.

"If you can't get the hook on the bag, pop the life raft and get her in it. Make sure it's tied to the plane."

"Hey, you talk like you know what you're doing."

"Getting her on board is going to be easy compared to what happens after that."

There was no time for a practice run. It was now or never. I set up an imaginary runway in the middle of the ocean with the bag as my touchdown point. Blanton kept an eye on Trevor. Meanwhile I scanned the ocean surface from horizon to horizon to get a picture of the movement of the swells; the small whitecaps told me the wind was blowing a steady ten to fifteen knots.

Instructions for a crosswind landing on ten-foot swells were not in the flight manual, but I had no time to think about the consequences. People who think too much before they act don't act too much.

"The things we do for love," Blanton said into his mike. "Hey, don't look now, but we've got company."

I looked across the windshield and saw a column of prancing waterspouts hanging like tentacles from the bottom of a dark cloud ahead. I was too busy to count them or estimate how far away they were, but I wanted no part of that airspace today.

"If this thing turns to shit, I'll call Mayday, and you go for the life raft."

"Roger."

I rubbed my St. Christopher medal and patted the wheel with a word of encouragement to the *Hemisphere Dancer*. The trick to an open-sea landing is to touch down along the swell and not slip into the trough. The engines were purring. They had to. Any engine trouble in these conditions would be curtains, and we would wind up as another mystery in the Bermuda Triangle.

I kept an eye on the waterspouts, set the flaps, shoved the

prop levers all the way forward, and concentrated on the throttles. Power was the key to this landing. Not too little, not too much. I crabbed slightly into the wind and got myself parallel to the swells. I eased the power back and checked the altimeter.

"Two hundred feet," I called out.

Trevor disappeared behind a huge swell but then reappeared. I glanced quickly at the compass and got my bearings.

"Here we go," I called to Blanton and eased the throttles slightly. I heard the sound of water on the hull. We were down and surfing like teenagers at Malibu.

I advanced the left throttle when I felt myself slipping downward into the trough. Shit was flying everywhere in the back of the plane. We were at a twenty-degree incline, and I had my foot pressed hard on the right rudder pedal. The *Hemisphere Dancer* fought the motion of the ocean, climbed the crest, and came off the step.

When spray cleared the windshield, Trevor was waving weakly, fifty feet away at twelve o'clock.

"Go!"

Blanton disappeared through the opening.

"Wait for my command to open the hatch. We don't want to sink after I made such a perfect goddamn landing."

I checked the advancing swells to my right, working the rudder pedals as I moved forward. We had about thirty seconds before we would slide into the trough and I would have to power up. The sounds of the waterspouts were now audible like the distant roar of a waterfall. They were coming right at us.

"Now!"

The plane was rocking and rolling with the motion of the swells. The bow hatch popped open. Blanton braced himself in the hatch with the grappling hook in his hand. He calmly measured the distance to the bag and made his throw.

If it were the Olympics, he would have won a gold medal. The hook sailed through the air, over the bag. With only two pulls back, the hook was snugged against the bag, and the line cleated off. Blanton's footsteps sounded on the turtle deck above me. He dodged the swirling propellers and was at the cargo door, hauling Trevor in. I fought the desire to turn around and see what was happening—my job now was to keep the *Dancer* pointed in the right direction for takeoff.

I heard three bangs on the hull and increased the power on the left engine. The bag swung in behind the props, and I heard a welcoming thud as it hit the fuselage.

"Ten seconds and I got to move!" I yelled.

"She's in," Blanton called back.

In a split second, Blanton was on the bow, winding in the rope. "Hatch secured," he called out and then crawled past me.

"Stay with her and get her warm. Strap yourself in. We're out of here."

I started my downwind takeoff at a three-quarter angle into the swell, and as soon as the *Dancer* got up on the step, I turned her down the swell and surfed the giant wave.

The windshield was filled with spray, and I could see the tightly wound tail of a waterspout directly ahead. I felt the old girl sinking and braced myself.

At that moment, the wave seemed to stretch upward, and a whitecap tumbled down on my left float. The entire plane shuddered, and I pushed the left rudder pedal hard into the wave to break the wing free, then pulled hard on the yoke. The stall warnings screamed.

The first bounce was light. The second bounce shook the fillings in my teeth, and I heard Trevor cry out. I prayed to St. Christopher that there would not be a third.

My view through the windshield was spray and dark blue mountains of water until I finally saw a patch of sky above the wave directly in front of me. After what seemed like an eternity, the vertical speed indicator needle started to point to the sky, and the *Hemisphere Dancer* lifted her nose and climbed above the oncoming wall of water. The windshield filled with pale blue Caribbean sky.

I breathed a big sigh of relief and relaxed my grip on the wheel. My legs were shaking, and I planted my heels on the floorboard to try to stop them. I pushed my headphones back and turned around to see how Trevor was doing. Blanton had wrapped her in a green wool army blanket and was feeding her cheese crackers.

Blanton gave me a thumbs up and a slight smile, and I nodded. Then my eyes caught Trevor's.

"Where the hell have you been?" she asked slowly.

"Better late than never," I said.

Beach Music,
Beach Music,
Beach Music
Just Plays On

46

The Skeleton in the Closet

Monty Potter believed in opportunity. Like many before him, he had used the geography and isolation of the Antilles to his advantage. Opportunities had taken him from Port Moresby to Tasmania to Africa to London to Belfast to Boomtown, which he now called home.

He gazed into the large mirror and finished trimming his beard, an extension of his fiery red curls. He admired his physique in the mirror for a moment. He liked being big. If felt comfortable for him to carry 220 pounds on his broad frame. He splashed several drops of bay rum into the palms of his hands and slapped his cheeks, then went to his cedar-lined closet and picked out one of the forty white linen suits hanging there.

After dressing, he donned his black cap and opened the French doors to the balcony above the Polar Bar. Monty Potter took in the morning.

The sun climbed over Lookout Hill and chased the shadows into the sea. In the early morning light, the old-world charm of the unmistakable French architecture painted an impressionistic mural of a quiet little Caribbean fishing village.

Square stone buildings, shuttered windows, and overhanging balconies lined the natural horseshoe-shaped harbor.

Mourning doves circled the weathered statue of Saint Christopher perched on the steps of the old stone church. It had been carved from a giant lignum vitae tree and had been transported from the rain forests above Cap Haitien by the soldiers of Henri Christophe as a present to the islands. The patron saint of travelers cast his protective gaze across the fleet of yachts and fishing boats that lay at anchor in the calm waters of the harbor.

It was all a masquerade. Boomtown was a pirate town. He looked out over the harbor and exhaled with a nod. "Monty Potter's town," he said proudly.

Monty Potter had changed his name so many times since leaving his home in Port Moresby thirty years earlier that he had a hard time remembering who he was. In these times and in this part of the world, he was known as Monty Potter.

He walked to the large brass spyglass that stood on a tripod at the far end of the balcony. "Fernando!" he shouted.

Fernando Orlando appeared on the balcony with coffee and croissants.

"Yes, Captain?"

"Our ship is beautiful, isn't she?" Potter said.

"Very beautiful. I can't wait until the cruise begins. She reminds me of the time I was with Xavier Cugat on a show at the dock in Havana. I think it was New Year's Even of 1954, maybe '55. Meyer Lansky brought the two bands together."

"Fernando, focus here, huh? The coffee."

"Sorry, Captain." Fernando Orlando poured hot milk into the large mug and handed it to his boss. Monty Potter continued to admire the cruise ship that lay at anchor near the harbor entrance.

It was his latest in a long line of scams. Monty Potter had arrived in Boomtown with a bang. He had run aground on a submerged rock near the entrance to the harbor that now bore his latest name. He had swum ashore from the sinking boat and walked into the Polar Bar and bought drinks for the house. "I guess this is where the Lord meant me to land," he had said.

The boat, of course, had settled to the bottom of the harbor and became an encrusted haven for the reef fish, but Monty Potter sprouted a new life on the rocky shores of the Sleeping Beauties.

He had told those interested enough to ask that he had been raised in South Africa, the son of missionary parents, but had been deported for his own missionary work and his stance against apartheid. This greatly increased his stature in the black community on the island, particularly impressing Gaston La Rue.

After La Rue's boating accident, Monty Potter handled the memorial services, relocated La Rue's black mistress into a town house in Guadeloupe, and settled in to become, as the French say, *le grand fromage*, "the big cheese."

Monty Potter had seen Colonel Cairo play the role with the despots and tyrants in Africa and always thought he could do a much better job. Now he ran Boomtown. He owned the shipyard, the ferry, Air Reality, a rum factory in Haiti, and the booming alien trade.

The idea for the "Cruise to Nowhere" came to him one afternoon while he was watching "Love Boat" reruns on the Superstation. His illustrious "Love Boat"—style cruise on the *La Brisa* was the perfect front for his alien-smuggling operation.

"And what are the spirits reporting today, La Bamba?" Monty Potter asked.

"Desdemona says she's picking up some very strange signals."

"Well then, perhaps you should schedule a second reading with the lovely lady this week," Potter said.

"I'll be seeing her tomorrow morning."

"Splendid. I would think Tuesday would be a fine day. Perhaps she would like a tour of the ship afterward? Mention it to her, would you?"

"Most certainly, Captain. Most certainly."

47

Time to Come Home, Cowboy

After Rudy Breno fired Darryl Lemma, he ran into some unexpected trouble on his way to Haiti. The Bahamians had a long history of suspicion of Haitians as voodoo worshippers, and they consequently maintained no real ties to their island neighbors. There were no flights to Port-au-Prince from Nassau.

Rudy caught a shuttle back to Miami, but when he went to board his Air France flight, he was told by the ticket agent that there had been reports of another coup d'état, and the airport in Port-au-Prince was temporarily closed. Rudy called his father but was told he was on the golf course, so he checked into the Miami Airport Hotel and watched CNN all day. There was a short sound bite about a tourist who had gone crazy and had seized a rental car agency at the airport in Port-au-Prince, but that didn't deter Rudy. He left the following morning on the early flight.

On the plane, he read a very brief description of Cap Haitien and a paragraph on the history of Henri Christophe and his Citadel in Fodor's *Travel Guide to the Caribbean*. Rudy was not a stickler for detail. To him, history happened too long ago to matter. The travel book gave him an idea for a story. He could link Michael Jackson and his weirdness to being the reincarnated black king of Haiti who awarded such titles to his nobles as the Duke of Marmalade and the Duchess of Lemonade.

In Port-au-Prince, Rudy changed into a new Banana Republic outfit in the airport men's room and boarded the Air Haiti Islander, which raised him above the jungle skies and deposited him in Cap Haitien just after noon.

He was attacked at the airport by a band of teenage boys offering to sell him everything from pearls to pussy, until two soldiers came over and the boys disappeared into the banana trees by the runway.

The ride to town was an indoctrination. Rudy peered out the window and wiped his forehead as the cab driver tried to make conversation in broken English. "You from da States, huh? I got lotsa cousins in Lawdadale. Dey woik fo da Yankees sellin' hot dogs to da stadium. I went to a game once, caught myself a foul ball, too. I tink to myself I come all da way from Haiti to America to catch a ball dat's made in Haiti. Some luck. You know all da bazeballs in da woild is made here in Haiti?"

"No, I didn't know that," Rudy answered. The man's driving was astonishing. He could not figure out why they hadn't hit anyone in the crowded streets, but the people seemed to have an instinct to avoid trouble when it came too close, and they continued to slide out of the path of the oncoming car.

Rudy clutched the ragged armrest in the back of the beat-up Mercedes taxi. The radio blasted muffled bass tones through blownout speakers, spouting incomprehensible lyrics and a loud horn section. The driver sang every word and mimicked the trumpet lines in time with the music, which left him out of control of the car for most of the song.

"Think you could turn the volume down a little?" Rudy asked.

"No can do, sir. Dis here boxed be only able to play at one level. I tink da rain leak in and fuck it up good. Been to Cap Haitien befo'?"

"No, this is my first trip."

The cab driver swerved to miss a mule-drawn wagon filled with flour sacks. The wagon driver waved with a smile, and the cab driver shouted and blew his horn. "A very nice place, not like da city life in Port-au-Prince. You needs anyting, jus' give me a call. My name is Christophe, like da king."

"I'm Rudy."

Christophe took his hands off the wheel and turned completely, extending his hand to be shaken. He spun back around and got control of the car in the nick of time, putting on the brakes to keep from running into the police van that was stopped in the middle of the street.

A crowd had gathered around the charred remains of a body that lay on the curb. The police were standing around routinely. A smoldering tire hung around the neck of the victim, and a foul stench filled the cab. Rudy held his bandanna over his mouth. This was not a tourist-trap mecca like Nassau. This was third-world squalor, where life was cheap. The driver cursed in patois at the body, and Rudy picked up on the word *macoute*. Nothing else needed to be said.

Christophe looked up into his mirror. "You don' look so good, mistuh."

Rudy gained control of his weak knees when he got out of the cab in front of the Brise de Mer and paid Christophe, who bubbled with excitement at the size of the tip. Rudy had given him an extra twenty to make sure he didn't go home and stick a pin in some white passenger doll.

Rudy entered the bar and bathed in the cool air-conditioning. He made his way to the bar and ordered a beer. He thought again of the movies and then delivered his line. "Fast Eddie around?" he asked in what he thought was his best Bogart delivery. Nobody reacted, but everybody stared.

The bartender slid a bottle of beer down the bar, and it came to a stop directly in front of Rudy. "Merci," he croaked.

It was then that Rudy realized he was the only white person in the joint. Recollections of Wes Craven's voodoo film suddenly flooded his memory.

"What you want?"

The voice was behind him, and when Rudy turned around he was face-to-face with a pair of piercing brown eyes atop the small frame of a mulatto with long black rasta curls.

"Fast Eddie?" Rudy inquired.

"Maybe," the man said.

Rudy pulled a picture out of his safari shirt and handed it to Fast Eddie, who gazed at the fading photo. "I was told you might be able to help me find this man."

"Maybe, but it will cost you. Wait here. Enjoy the view. I'll be right back."

Rudy walked to the patio and watched the lighter boats moving passengers back and forth to the ship in the harbor. The beer had relaxed him, and he tried to tap his foot to the rhythm of the music coming from the blaster behind the bar, but he could never quite find the beat.

An hour later, Fast Eddie returned with a well-built man wearing leather chaps and a jacket. He looked like Eddie Murphy. "This is Mister P.," Fast Eddie said. "He can help you, I think."

Rudy extended his hand. "Rudy Breno, *National Lighthouse.*" Rudy leaned over to the big man and whispered, "I'm down here working on a story about—"

"I know who you afta." Mister P. looked down at Fast Eddie and asked a question.

"With guns or without?" Eddie asked Rudy.

"Oh with, with," Rudy replied, nodding his head up and down in affirmation.

"It will cost you two thousand dollars cash. Half now, half before you climb the hill," Fast Eddie told him.

"Great, great. But I'll have to get some traveler's checks cashed," Rudy said.

"I can do that in town, but it'll take me thirty minutes or so. You hungry?" Eddie asked.

"Starving."

"Try the turtle. It's fresh today."

"Turtle. Right," Rudy said.

Fast Eddie and Mister P. left through the back door, and Rudy ordered another drink and some grouper fingers to be safe. He was glad he had asked for his goon with guns. It sounded like ordering at the Taco Bell drive-through. He didn't want things to get out of hand in the jungle if Blanton got crazy. He had no intention of capturing the killer; he just wanted a sighting. He would let his imagination do the rest. This is what being a reporter was all about—sitting in a dingy waterfront bar in a mysterious country with the sound of voodoo drums echoing in the distant hills, not waiting for the morning paper on the courthouse steps to see if any judges or politicos had been nabbed for a DUI over the weekend.

• • •

Rudy had been up all night waiting for Fast Eddie to return with his cash. To make matters worse, his late-night snack had him worshipping the porcelain goddess. He had just fallen asleep when he was awakened by a loud knock on the hotel door. It was not Mister P. The small woman spoke no English, but made charadelike signs indicating a telephone call. Rudy stumbled to the lobby worried that something had gone wrong with the planned climb up the mountain. He put the receiver to his ear.

The connection was horrible and sounded like a lawn mower was stuck in the receiver, which only irritated his headache.

"Rudy, is that you?"

"Who is this?" Rudy asked.

"It's your father, numb nuts."

"Dad, is that you?"

"No, it's Elvis Presley. Rudy, what the hell are you doing in Haiti, and what's this about the boat captain?"

"I fired him."

"What?"

"I fired him. He was trying to fuck everything that moved in Nassau."

"I know. He's suing us for breach of contract."

The tiny black woman who had answered the door appeared from the hallway with a small glass of mango juice.

"Pardon me, ma'am."

"Ne parle pas anglais, monsieur," the woman replied.

"Rudy, you got a woman in your room? Son, don't you know that Haiti is where AIDS comes from? They fuck pigs down there. Don't you read the paper? Rudy, I'm pulling the plug on the Jet Ski Killer Expedition. It's time to come home, cowboy."

Rudy felt his heart drop into the ends of his toes. "What?"

"It's not the lawsuit by that dimwit captain of yours. Hell, Son, we eat, sleep, and breathe lawsuits at the *National Lighthouse*. It's that the Jet Ski Killer isn't a hot item anymore."

"Not a hot item? There's a fruitcake on the loose blowing up people, and you don't call that a hot item? For your information, Dad, I have an armed posse here, and I'm going after him later this morning."

"Son, it's last week's headlines. Things have changed since you've been out gallivanting around the Caribbean for clues."

"What do you mean?" Rudy asked.

"I mean that pervert director who Blanton Meyercord used for a human Roman candle just left town owing about fifty thousand dollars in hotel and bar bills, and the good merchants of Key West are not happy. That's the good news. The bad news is he took the sixteen-year-old daughter of the state's attorney general with him, and he was making her pose for nude home videos. People in Key West want to give that lunatic fishing guide a medal for blowing him up—they don't want to kill him. I have Candace tracking down the director. She's located him in Rosarito Beach, Mexico. She'll keep an eye on him until you get to the West Coast. Son, I'm sending you to dig up some dirt about him in Hollywood."

"You asshole. I don't want to go to Hollywood. I want to go to the Citadel and interview the Jet Ski Killer. It is my mission."

"Mission smishin. You write something and write something fast. Wind up this fucking story and get your scrawny ass out of Haiti unless you want to try and support yourself on your writing. And never call me an asshole again."

The phone went dead.

48

Revenge Is a Volatile Fuel

RePete Preacher had not fully recovered from the attack by Charlie Fabian. He still had a bullet hole in his leg and nightmares about the sharks feeding on Thorn Marshall. The dinghy ride across a hundred miles of open water to Boomtown had not been what one would call a pleasure cruise, either.

"You're sure about the tattoos?" Monty Potter asked.

"I will never forget them as long as I live. At first I thought it was Sledge or Little Elmo, and they'd found out we'd been double crossing them."

"The four-eyed bastard killed Little Elmo." Monty Potter laughed nervously. "Saved me the trouble."

"I thought they just wanted to take us out for treason, but he asked about that scepter thing."

"What scepter thing?" Potter asked.

"The one I sent to you with the Napoleonic coins. Thorn brought it in a box with some cannonballs."

"What would he want with that piece of junk?"

"He wasn't answering questions."

Monty Potter walked to the window and sighed. "So they've found me."

"Who?" RePete asked.

"Oh hell, it doesn't matter."

Monty Potter knew revenge was the fuel that drove Cairo's insanity. By now the Colonel surely must know that it was Monty Potter who had set up the ambush that had cost him his arm.

"RePete, you need some rest. I want you to take a suite on the *La Brisa* and lay low for a couple of days. Get some girls, get laid, prop your feet up, take a Jacuzzi. You deserve it."

"Whatever you say, Captain, but don't send me back to look for the wreck. Ain't enough money on God's earth for me to have to run into him again."

Monty Potter walked to the door with RePete and patted him on the back. He took a hundred-dollar bill from his pocket. "Stop by the bar and have a few drinks on me."

"Thanks, sir," RePete replied gratefully.

"That's what friends are for. Tell Fernando to come up, will you?"

Monty Potter walked back out onto the balcony and gazed down at the foot traffic. It was almost midnight, and Boomtown was rocking. Air Reality had flown in a fresh load of tourists today on the *Vomit Comet,* but Potter's world was now threatened. He looked out at the distant horizon and saw the glowing lights of a passing ship. Somewhere out there his old boss was steaming closer to him, no doubt looking for revenge. But what the hell did the Colonel want with that scepter?

Potter heard the beat of drums coming from the Polar Bar below, and the sound took him back to Africa. A distant memory slowly bubbled up like a thick red blob in a lava lamp.

In the name of Darwinism and survival of the fittest, he had betrayed Colonel Cairo. He remembered laughing aloud at the absurdity of the crazy old man taking on the helicopter. He had stopped laughing when Cairo shot it out of the sky.

The Colonel's remains were not included in the body count after the battle. Monty Potter had accompanied the raiding party into the village, and only now he remembered the old man in the cave. He had interrogated him about Cairo at gunpoint, but the old man had just stood there foolishly, clutching a wand, as if that could save him.

The memory hit Potter like a coconut dropping from a tree. "Jesus fucking Christ. It's the same scepter. He wants that goddamn scepter."

Quietly
Making Noise

49

That Time-Bomb Look

I didn't know what to say to Trevor, so I didn't say anything. Instead I focused on flying my plane and trying to figure out where we should go from here.

"Okay, fine. Don't answer me. Don't even think about answering me. I don't even *want* to know. I don't *care* why you didn't make it to Rudderville."

Her voice sounded strangled, and I did my best to block it out. Besides, I was angry, too. I'd just rescued this impossible woman against all odds, and instead of being grateful to me for saving her life, she was mad. Again. As usual, I thought. Well, at least I hadn't lost my plane.

We had made it out of the waves but had paid a price. Besides losing the left float, I had taken a load of water through the exhaust trumpet of the left engine, and it had settled in the lower cylinders. This was causing the engine to misfire. We were basically limping through the sky, fighting a head wind, and unable to land in the water because of the missing float.

I didn't really want to go to Boomtown. God knew what lay ahead for us there—Colonel Cairo, the four-eyed assassin,

Rudy Breno, Interpol, or some other screwball who might be waiting to hijack us, kill us, or arrest us. But these were the least of my problems. I had to deal with Trevor at some point, and I wasn't looking forward to it.

She sat in the back of the plane wrapped in a blanket, and her arm was around Hoagy. He still had her battered shoe in his mouth. There weren't a whole lot of options, but my idea of the Sleeping Beauties seemed like the best one.

You always remember the places you've had to land in a hurry; I had discovered Little Lorraine and the other small sister islands when I lost power in an old crop duster I was ferrying from Miami to Tobago and had to make an engine-out landing. I'd been welcomed like a wounded bird by the local Indians, who had taken me to their fishing village on the lagoon. I'd spent two incredible days there, living on coconuts and lobster, catching bonefish on the shallow flats, and just winding down. It had taken a lot of motivation to finally go on to Boomtown to get the parts I needed to fix the engine.

The more I thought about it, the better I felt about landing on Little Lorraine Island. Boomtown was only a hop, skip, and jump away, so it would be relatively easy for Trevor to track down Desdemona, but Little Lorraine was just secluded enough that we'd be hard to find—at least for now.

•   •   •

The pink beach was as beautiful as I remembered it. A veil of salt spray hung along the shore in front of the stand of Australian pines that grew wild on the bluff.

I made a low approach over a large plain of sand that ended abruptly in a sizable heap of old coral heads. Because of the damage done to the float, I would have to land on the beach. It had been packed hard by the receding tide, and the trick was to stay on it and away from the soft, fluffy sand that extended to the bluff. I checked the wind lines on the water and then turned my base leg.

As I passed over the north shore on final, I searched for the fishing village. Only the remnants of houses remained, like skeletons of sea creatures washed up on the shore after a hurricane. Things had changed since I had been here last. A new dock ran along the inside of Frenchman's Lagoon, and a peculiar cigar-shaped boat was tied up there. Blanton called out the final landing checklist as I banked over the beach.

The tires squeaked, and the pink sand beach of Little Lorraine Island seemed to be holding firm under the weight of the plane. I taxied back to the far end of the beach by the pines and figured we could hide the plane in a nearby clearing for the time being. I took off my headset and watched the propeller blade slowly take form out the window.

The silence was uncomfortable. The noise of the engines and the task of flying the damaged plane had taken precedence over everything else, but now I was going to have to face the music.

Trevor was sitting up in the back of the plane dressed in a pair of my jeans, a T-shirt, and a pair of Blanton's Nikes, which were much too big. She looked like a beautiful paradise rose that had been pounded by a summer squall. Her hair had dried into a collection of golden ringlets, and her eyes were now clear and focused. Tiny conch pearls were fastened to her earlobes.

When I passed her on my way to open the door, my eyes caught hers again, and once again I saw that time-bomb look that tells you that despite the calm exterior, this person could explode any second. I didn't have to think twice about who the target was going to be.

"Terra firma," I announced.

I swung the hatch open and went back to help her, but she ignored my assistance and climbed out by herself. Hoagy followed.

"After you," Blanton said. He knew my history with Trevor, and his eyes twinkled.

"Thanks," I replied dryly. "We need to get the *Dancer* covered up. Grab some of those palm fronds over there, okay? I'll help you in a minute, but I want to take a look at the wing."

"Aye, aye."

I climbed down the steps to check the damage on the wing where the float had ripped off. I ran my hand along the rivet lines where the struts had been connected. Fortunately, the shear bolts had torn away cleanly and had not damaged the wing panel. That was the good news. The bad news would be finding a spare float in these parts. It's not like changing a tire.

I was so deeply involved with checking the damage that I was caught off guard by Trevor.

"Is it going to be okay?" she asked.

"I've seen worse. I don't think we'll be flying this afternoon."

"Good," she said. Even though she had been soaked to the bone with saltwater, she still had a slight scent of Tahitian coconut oil on her skin.

I was relieved by the tone of her voice and the fact that she had actually come to ask me about the plane. This was as good a time as any to talk to her.

"Trevor, I know I owe you an explanation." I was crawling out from under the wing and couldn't see her for a moment. When I finally stood straight up, a tennis shoe caught me square on the end of my nose.

I was knocked back and lay in the brown pine straw feeling the sharp small cones puncturing my back. My nose was numb, and I could taste blood running down my throat. Trevor stood over me, like Muhammad Ali challenging Sonny Liston to get up. She waved the tennis shoe at me as if it were a billy club.

"You son of a bitch! I should have known better than to ever imagine that you could think of anybody but yourself. What took you so long to get here? Why didn't you tell me you were planning to take a vacation on the way?"

"Pardon the fuck out of me. If you haven't forgotten, I just yanked your ass out of a not-too-pleasant situation—at the risk of losing my plane."

"The plane, the plane! It's always the fucking plane. But what about me? What about your promise to meet me in Rudderville? What about your promise to take me to find Desdemona? I guess something came up that was way more important than doing what you said you were going to do."

"You're damn right something came up. And if I hadn't made a move when I did today, your ass would still be in the water."

"You put me there!"

"You're crazy."

"You're *making* me crazy!"

"I did not put you there. I didn't even know you were going to be there. And if I hadn't come and gotten you, you'd still be there."

"Frank, if you'd met me in Rudderville like you promised, I wouldn't have *been* there. I did what we agreed I would do. I went to Miami and got the money and waited for you in Rudderville. I waited and waited and waited some more. And there I was, stranded, waiting for you to fit me into your busy schedule."

"I was hijacked, for Christsakes," I said.

"That's still no excuse!" she screamed. "This has been going on for years! You have absolutely no idea what I've had to go through. And I wouldn't have had to go through any of it if it weren't for you. You are the most selfish person I have ever met in my life. I've had it. Thanks for nothing. I'm outta here."

"What are you going to do?"

"What I came here to do. Desdemona was right. Joe isn't dead. He was last spotted in Cuba—just like Rudy said he was. He's *alive*. By God, I came here to find some answers. And I'm going to look under every bush and tree until I find Desdemona."

"Trevor, try to stay calm for a minute. Regardless of what a loser you think I am, try to remember you've been in a very traumatic situation. You should rest first. Then decide what to do. Boomtown is only about half an hour's boat ride from here. You can find Desdemona tomorrow."

"My whole life is a trauma; I don't need rest. I need coffee and answers. Your concern is too little and too late. I don't give a shit what you think. Go fix your precious fucking airplane so you can fly away and avoid any responsibility."

Trevor turned and started walking down the path. "Desdemona!" she called out in a loud voice. "Desdemona!"

I pinched the end of my nose and bent my head back to stop the bleeding.

Blanton came up, dragging two large palm fronds. "She let you have it, huh?"

"She's nuts," I said. "She's mad at me for everything bad I've ever done."

Trevor was just about to the line of trees, and she was still calling out to the mythical Desdemona. I was afraid she'd gone over the edge. It seemed to run in her family.

All of a sudden a voice called from behind a strand of sea grapes. A large woman dressed in a bright orange-and-pink muumuu stepped into the clearing.

"You rang?"

50

No Ticky, No Laundry, No Mechanics

Barely two hours had passed since Trevor Kane had announced she was walking out of my life. Blanton had offered to help me work on the plane, but I knew we'd only end up talking about Trevor, and I felt lousy enough as it was. He elected to take a swim instead of watching me mope around. He was hungry and was going to look for lobsters, and he disappeared beneath the gentle turquoise waters inside the reef with my Hawaiian sling. I dug out my toolbox, hoping to lose myself in the repair work so I could get my mind off the mess I was in. I decided to start with the engine problem first.

• • •

"She be very pretty, your airplane, Cap'n. You need help?"

The sound of the voice rattled me, and I dropped the screw I was removing. I looked up, and a leathery old man stood at the edge of the mangos. When he saw me drop the screw, he spotted it immediately. He picked it up and handed it to me.

"I am called Toosay. I am chief engineer on da *Cosmic Muffin,* and am at your service."

"What's a cosmic muffin?"

"It is a ship dat Miss Desdemona is preparing for a trip to da stars."

"That would be the long, cigar-shaped boat at the dock?"

"Yes, yes."

"You work for Desdemona?"

"Yes, she is a very fine boss lady, and she send me to see if you need help."

"Well, Toosay, my name's Frank, and this here is the *Hemisphere Dancer.*"

"I take it you have some kinda trouble to be landing on dis island."

"You have no idea," I said, wiping beads of sweat from my eyebrows.

"I am da fixer of engines here, too."

"Well, I took some water through the exhaust trumpet of the left engine, and it settled in the lower cylinders."

"I don' know 'bout airplanes, but I know how to get da watah out of a sunk outboard."

"'Bout the same procedure, but that's not my biggest problem," I said, pointing to the missing float.

"Oh, I see," Toosay said. "If you want, I can run and get my tools."

I had dislodged the lower part of the cowling, and Toosay was under the wing before I had the chance to ask him to help. I placed the piece of aluminum in his outstretched hands, and he carried it over out of the sand and rested it in the pine straw against a cabbage palm. I removed the spark plugs from all the cylinders and handed them, one by one, to Toosay. He placed them in the doorway side by side.

"I need you to spin the propeller when I give you the word," I instructed. Toosay nodded his head, keeping his eyes on me. I stuck my finger in the vacant hole of the first spark plug socket. "Okay," I said.

Toosay turned the prop and continued until I felt the pressure in the cylinder build against my finger. I pulled my finger out, and a steady stream of water shot out of the hole.

"You a good mechanic, too, dere, Cap'n."

"No yellow pages out here," I said.

"What?" Toosay asked with a puzzled grin.

"Nothing," I said. I continued in the firing order and found water in only the number seven and number nine cylinders. Toosay cleaned the plugs, and an hour later, I fired up the old 985. She purred like a kitten.

We sat in the shade of the pines, resting, and I thanked Toosay. I tried to locate Blanton out along the edge of the reef, but I had no luck. Hoagy had run off after him, and he was nowhere in sight.

"So, Toosay, a friend of mine who came with us—"

He interrupted. "You mean da very beautiful lady?"

"Yes."

"She remind me of a goddess," he said.

I had never thought of Trevor in those terms. "Have you seen them?"

"Dey be gone over to Petite Place for a dip in da Healin' Hole."

"Where's that?"

"It be da last of da Sleeping Beauty Islands. Very powerful place," he said.

"Do you know anyone with a boat? I need to hire one to take me over to the airport in Boomtown."

"Oh, you don' need to hire nobody. I got a boat and will be glad to take you."

"Does a guy named Phil Clark still run the airport in Boomtown?" I asked.

"Oh no. He die in da boat crash with Mistah La Rue."

"Gaston La Rue is dead? When did this happen?"

"I not too sure of dates. You know Desdemona, she only use the Mayan calendar, but I guess she say maybe tree or fo' years ago. Maybe five. Monty Potter be in charge over dere now. Very strange man."

I looked out to the water for Blanton again, but I only saw his arms splash briefly before they disappeared below the surface. I scribbled a note on the small legal pad in my shirt pocket and stuck it in the door of the plane.

• • •

The trip across the narrow spit of water that separated the Boomtown airport from Little Lorraine Island took us only thirty minutes. Toosay steered us up a small inlet and raised the centerboard as we approached a small dock. He worked the big red mainsail like a brake, backwinding the boat; then he pointed it into the wind and nudged the boat right next to the dock, then dropped the sail.

He pointed and said, "Da Boomtown airport be over dere beyond da burned-up shrimp factory. Can't miss it. I be waitin' here for you."

I walked past the burned-out building that had once housed

the operations of a shrimp farm, another monument to another secondhand American dream. I remembered that it had burned while I was working in San Juan. A major food conglomerate from America had decided it would be more cost-effective to grow their own shrimp—ones that could fit neatly into microwave bags—than to have to buy and pick shrimp from boats. They had chosen Boomtown because it was remote, but they hadn't figured that the shrimpers might feel threatened by a shrimp farm. The construction crews came and erected the plant in swift, efficient style, and then it burned to the ground the night before it was scheduled to open. Gaston La Rue had openly admitted to torching the place, and the Americans recoiled, setting off to find more pleasant surroundings.

* * *

Boomtown International simmered in the distance as heat waves rose from the asphalt runway. It was another reminder of the days in World War II when U.S. Seabees built runways on every piece of coral they could find. Air Reality operated a couple of old Grumman Mallards between Boomtown and Port-au-Prince, along with the notorious *Vomit Comet*, which made the daily run from Santo Domingo.

The fraternity of fliers seems to be even more tightly bound in the outposts of the world, and you can usually locate a very helpful hand in the oddest places. I figured I might find a congenial seaplane mechanic who would have the tools and parts I needed to fix the float. I was also curious to find out how Phil Clark and Gaston La Rue had died and who this Monty Potter was.

It didn't take long to get a sense of how the new regime operated. I heard the gunfire and instinctively hit the deck. Another burst of automatic weapon fire was followed by a chorus of laughs. I raised my head slowly and relaxed. I was not the target.

Two men were firing at beer bottles lined up on the runway. They drained the bottles they were holding and set them down, then walked back and fired another round. By this time, shattered glass littered the runway.

As soon as the sound of airplane engines filled the air, the men threw their guns down, picked up a pair of brooms, and quickly began to sweep up the broken glass. They finished just as the old DC-3 touched down. The men with the guns ambled back to the hangar and went inside the Air Reality office.

Meanwhile, the engines on the old plane had rattled to a stop. The rear door was lowered, releasing a wobbly-legged line of passengers in flowered shirts and muumuus who weaved over to a fat woman holding a big sign that read "Cruise to Nowhere." Several passengers stopped to throw up along the way, and then they all moved like a lost herd of cattle into the terminal building and out to the waiting bus.

A few minutes later, the pilot climbed out, let loose a huge belch, and lit a cigar. He was about fifty, with one epaulet and several buttons missing from his sweat-stained khaki shirt. He strolled over to the pool of oil that was steadily growing under the left engine and coughed.

"Good evening," I said.

The pilot looked at me suspiciously and didn't say anything.

"Do you know if there might be a mechanic around I could talk to about buying a few spare parts?"

The pilot squinted and chewed faster on his cigar. "This ain't K-Mart, bub. Check inside."

The Air Reality passenger waiting area consisted of an old church pew and a restaurant counter with four stools. A large black woman was seated behind the counter, sobbing heavily as she watched Jimmy Swaggart crying on television.

"Excuse me. Do you know who replaced Phil Clark? I'm trying to find a mechanic," I said.

She was locked on the TV. I moved closer to the counter. "Excuse me—"

"Can't you see dees woman is in pain, senor?" a voice from behind me said. I turned and saw that the sweepers had exchanged their brooms or AK-47s and were standing on either side of the door. "Air Reality ees closed for da rest of da day, senor. Buenos dias."

"I'm not interested in a ticket. I was trying to find—"

The largest of the men cut me off. "Phil Clark ees dead. Dee airline belong to Monty Potter now."

"I was trying to find a mechanic," I said.

He lowered his gun and casually aimed it in my direction.

"No ticky, no laundry, no mechanics. Closed. Cerrados. Vamos."

51

Changing Channels

"**I** can't believe I found you like this. It's the first positive thing that's happened to me since I left New Orleans," Trevor said as she and Desdemona walked through the mangroves toward Frenchman's Lagoon.

"You didn't find me, Trevor," Desdemona told her. "You were sent to me. You're a very pretty piece to a very large puzzle."

"And you have the answers to my questions about Joe."

Trevor's three hours in the water had left her more hungry than weak, and Desdemona was soon putting her culinary talents to work in the galley of the *Cosmic Muffin*. In no time, she was busy flipping a cheddar-cheese omelet in her well-seasoned copper pan.

"You're not talking to some expert shaman who was destined from birth to do this kind of stuff. You're talking to a woman who ran away from home and joined a rock band, and then wound up in an observatory being fucked by a Puerto Rican, which brought on voices from another world who told her to build a rocket ship to go up to the Pleiades."

Trevor's mouth dropped open in disbelief. She didn't know whether to laugh or cry.

"I have these visions, you know. Visions, voices, whatever, but they speak to me. Only thing is, they seem to always speak in riddles, as if figuring out the meaning of life on earth is some kind of game to them."

"Voices told you about Joe?"

"Voices. I know it's not much to go on, and I may have been a little premature in writing you. All this stuff is pretty new to me, and sometimes I go farther than I should."

"Who are the voices?" Trevor asked.

"I call them the Generators after the first place I heard them. They're the ones who started this idea about Joe being alive. I know it sounds crazy."

"Maybe your voices know more than they're letting on. Colonel Cairo told me Joe isn't dead."

"Really? When?" Desdemona asked.

"Right before he shoved me into the sea."

Desdemona slid the plate of hot food across the galley counter and pulled two large slices of toasted coconut bread from the oven. Trevor covered the hot bread with butter and honey and launched into her breakfast.

"We're going to take a little trip today to a place where we may find some answers. What are you so mad at that pilot for?"

Trevor was caught off base by the change of topic, and she continued to chew, concentrating on the spicy flavor of the warm, soft eggs and melted cheese. She gulped half the glass of cold milk in one swig.

"I couldn't help but overhear your little tête-à-tête back there on the beach," Desdemona said.

"He used to be my boyfriend."

"You were fighting like you knew each other."

"I'm sorry about that, but it's something I had to do." She told Desdemona the story of her mother, Frank, the journey, and Colonel Cairo.

"I know some people in Hollywood who would pay millions for a story like yours. Only trouble is, it's your story, and it's true."

Trevor finished wiping the egg from her plate with a slice of coconut bread and sat back on the stool.

Desdemona smiled at her. "You look like you could use a little rest. Why don't you lie down for a while. First cabin on the left is all made up. I've got some things to do, and then it'll be about half an hour over to Petite Place. I'll wake you when we get there."

"I'm glad I found you, Desdemona," Trevor said as she stood.

"I hope I can help you."

•   •   •

It was late afternoon before Trevor awoke to the roll of the ocean and the rumble of diesel engines. Now she sat next to Desdemona on the flying bridge of the *Cosmic Muffin* and felt a bit like Alice in Wonderland. They were on their way to the Healing Hole, where Desdemona had promised to tell her about Joe Merchant. It was a postcard day, and Trevor felt energized by the sea breeze and the sun.

"Toosay is usually with me, but I had him stay behind in case your boys needed some help."

Desdemona worked her way up a small channel that opened into a perfectly round lagoon. She adjusted the throttle and gear levers and slowed the boat to a halt at a spot she seemed to have picked out. "Come on, I need a hand with the anchor."

The made their way to the bow and secured the anchor. A ray of sunlight reflected off an object that was fastened to the bow. It sent a slight shock through Trevor's body.

"What is that?" she asked.

"That's a figurehead."

Trevor examined the object and almost laughed aloud when she saw the ruby nipples on the bare-breasted figurine. "This is a remarkable crystal. Where did you get it?"

"That's a secret," Desdemona told her.

"Do crystals power your ship?"

"Come on, I'll show you."

Desdemona led Trevor to the engine room and flicked on the light. Two GM 571 diesels and an Onan generator filled most of the space. Desdemona walked past the engines and unlocked a metal door marked Life Jackets. Trevor was dazzled by the collection of crystals held together by a maze of wires.

"Some engine, huh?"

"What does it do?"

"It's going to take me to the Pleiades. It's actually pretty simple. Think of it as a television remote control."

"I never could understand those things."

"Smaller objects controlling larger, distant objects. Exerting pressure on certain crystals and ceramics produces piezoelectricity, which connects all corners of the universe through the universal energy network. These crystals contain the memory of Atlantis, and when they're agitated by the right elements at the right time, everything connects. And *whammo*, we're changing channels."

"And the naked woman on the bow of the ship?"

"All the ships of the great adventurers adorned the bows of their vessels with bare-breasted women. Legend has it that a bare-breasted woman can calm a raging storm. This is a rocket ship, you know. One day it will fly through the air."

• • •

"It's just around the corner here." Desdemona pushed back the mangroves and held them for Trevor, who passed through the opening and looked out at the Healing Hole. "Come on, maybe the Generators will call."

Desdemona climbed into the tube and pushed off for the middle of the spring. Trevor took off her clothes and dove into the warm sulphur water. She began to dive and swim like an otter.

"It's sort of like a galactic phone booth," Desdemona said. "I'm the receiver."

The Healing Hole seemed to soothe Trevor's aches and pains from her hours in the ocean. She took a deep breath, then dove down to the bottom of the spring and swam along the bottom, feeling the stones. She was intrigued by Desdemona, but there was still no answer to her questions about what had happened to her brother. Where was he? She shot to the surface. "Anything yet?"

"Maybe. Last night I was walking along the beach, looking up at the clear sky, marveling at how visible the Milky Way is at these latitudes. The Pleiades were directly above my head, and I got a big goosebump rush. I was naming the sisters, and when I got to Merope, I saw these flashing lights. And I thought, Oh, my God, the Generators have landed. I had so many questions that weren't answered. Maybe the aliens were finally here to put the puzzle together.

"Well, as the spaceships got closer, I realized they were lightning bugs. When you're that focused on a vision, you can't tell the difference between a spacecraft and a lightning bug twenty feet above the water."

Trevor swam to the shore and felt for the bottom with her toes.

"I may have missed something in that story. What does it have to do with Joe?"

Desdemona didn't answer. She lay in the inner tube with her head tilted back and her eyes closed. Her body twisted several times and sent waves out toward the beach. Trevor swam back to her, thinking Desdemona was having a seizure of some kind.

"Desdemona, are you all right?"

Desdemona opened her eyes wide and reached for Trevor's hand. She looked down at her. "The Colonel has the answers to your questions," she said.

"How do you know?"

"Some things I am sure about."

"I don't think I'm going to be able to walk right back up to him and say, 'Oh, hi, Colonel. Sorry you didn't kill me the first time, but I wanted to ask you where I might find my brother'."

"I think you are going to have to confront him, if you're going to find out about Joe. I believe the answer to this mystery is closer than we think. I have a friend in town who might be able to help us. He and his band play at the Polar Bar. You and I should go out and have a night on the town. If any mortal knows anything about Joe Merchant or this Colonel Cairo, they'll be in Boomtown at the Polar Bar. The place is jammed every night."

Trevor rolled onto her back and paddled with her feet to the shore and climbed out of the water.

"Now what are you going to do about your boyfriend over on the beach?" Desdemona asked.

"He's not my problem anymore," Trevor said.

Desdemona let out a belly laugh. "Oh, but he is. And the sooner you admit that, the better you'll feel. You don't hate him. You hate his awkwardness."

"That is Frank exactly. I think you underestimate your power."

"Men are a hell of a lot easier to understand than rocket ships. They'd rather stare at their watches than tell you they love you, but that doesn't make them bad. It makes them mysterious. We women are perceived as the mysterious gender, catlike, intangible. To me, men are the mysterious ones. They fight all their lives to figure out why the physical superiority they possess isn't the key they need to unlock the treasure chest called happiness. Once they find out, that's when they'll really be hard for us to deal with.

"You're actually at the best stage of your relationship when you're past all that storybook-ending mumbo jumbo. Too many people waste too much time trying to make the reality of their lives conform to the unreality of the myth of romantic love. Happily ever after, now and then, is what you're looking for, and that takes work. You're right where you should be. Like I said before, it's all a balancing act, like trying to stand on one of those balls in the circus. Your Frank can't get a grip on his feelings. He's just being selfish and doesn't know it. That's what makes you crazy. Once he's able to come to grips with the truth and make room for you in his life, it'll be easier. You can't be that hard on him. After all, he did risk his life to pull you out of the ocean regardless of how you got there."

"Did he pay you to say all this?"

"No, not at all. It's what I feel." Desdemona wiggled her toes and started to hum the chorus of a Joe Merchant song. "Your brother was a prime example of someone falling off the ball. He was never able to see that in his journey to escape from who he was, his music actually made a lot of people feel better. Yet he was never able to feel the joy himself at all. He became another person. I must warn you that if he is alive and we do find him, you had better be prepared for what you might find. One thing is for certain. He won't be what you want him to be."

"I know that, but I still want to find him."

"Then let's go."

Trevor heard the sounds of something moving in the bushes, and she quickly covered herself.

"Don't worry," Desdemona said. "It's just an old nutria or raccoon rummaging for supper."

Trevor looked over at the bushes but went back to getting dressed, and a few minutes later, they walked off, down the path.

When they were out of sight, Colonel Cairo emerged from behind a giant gumbo-limbo tree. He was dressed in camouflage fatigues. He walked to the edge of the Healing Hole, took a deep breath, scanned the clearing with his eyes, and smiled.

"This is the place," he whispered. "This is the place."

52

Blame It on the Stones

"Things have certainly changed around here, Toosay," I said. We were running on a broad reach in his small sloop, heading across the channel on our way back from the Boomtown airport.

"Not really. Boomtown be Boomtown. Mistah La Rue die, Monty Potter take over. Most people don' notice. Dey be baked by da sun or pickled by da rum. Make no difference to dem, but I don't know much about da men wif da guns at da airport. Dat seem strange. Miss Desdemona might be able to help you betta dere. She now workin' for Monty Potter sometime."

"Desdemona works for Monty Potter?" I asked.

"She tells his fortune." Toosay gingerly maneuvered the little sailboat with a series of short tacks and nosed the bow up to the beach a few hundred yards form the plane, and I jumped out.

"Thanks for the lift, Toosay," I called out as he jibbed the mainsail around and was already heading home. "Tell Desdemona I'd like to talk to her, alone," I shouted.

"I fix it up, Cap'n. Any message for your lady friend?"

"No, no message."

• • •

The no-see-ums were starting to feast on my bare arms as I walked over to the plane. Blanton had a fire going and smudge pots smoking to ward off the mosquitoes. He was filleting a very nice strawberry grouper, and a pot of peas and rice hung over the fire. Hoagy jumped up to greet me, and I sat down and began pulling some of the burrs and knots out of his fur.

"Any luck?" he asked.

"Very cold reception. Lots of guns and no mechanics. I think I might have walked into the middle of a dope deal or something."

"What about your friend?"

"He's dead. Got killed in a boating accident with the old pirate who used to run Boomtown. There's a new guy in charge, Monty Potter. Toosay says Desdemona is his fortune teller. I'm going to try to see her in the morning."

"You hungry?" Blanton asked as he dropped the fillets into the skillet.

"Starving."

"Trevor and Desdemona came by."

"What did she say?" I asked.

"Her exact words were, 'Tell Frank we have to talk tomorrow.' I gave her her purse, and she told me to thank you. She seemed a lot calmer than when she clobbered you with the tennis shoe. I think there's still hope for the two of you." Blanton flipped the fish, and the steam rose from the pan, bringing a wonderful aroma with it.

"Squeeze that lime into the pepper, Frank. It's about ready." Blanton dipped up the peas and rice and handed me a plate, then made one for himself. I stabbed at the fish angrily with my fork.

"It's already dead, Frank."

Blanton ate slowly, tasting the fresh grouper. He dropped a small amount of lime juice onto each bite. "You're in a spin, Frank. That's all. Remember, lack of rudder control gets you into a spin, and control of the rudder gets you out."

"What the hell is that supposed to mean?" I asked.

Blanton got up, walked to the water's edge, and bent down to rinse off his plate. "What's that old Stones song you're always singin'?" he asked.

" 'You Can't Always Get What You Want.' "

"Why do you think it's your favorite song?"

'It's got a good beat, and you can dance to it."

"Hey, shithead, I ain't Dick Clark. You love it because it says what you can't. If you want her back, you're gonna to have to make some changes. I think you have a shot here, bud. I'd take it."

"Why do you say that?"

"I could tell by the way she acted when she came by. I got very telepathic when I was in jail."

"What the hell do I have to do? I thought breaking out of jail and pulling her out of the ocean was some indication of how I felt."

Blanton looked back at me. "True, but you didn't tell her. We're all getting older, Frank, and it's a brand-new flight plan, buddy. You got to talk to these women."

I finished my fish and peas and joined him near the water. "What if I find her brother for her? That should count for something."

"Depends on what you find. From what I hear, the guy was a wacko. I wouldn't be so hell-bent on that idea."

"Then what the fuck should I do?"

"Don't get pissed off. Give her time to cool down."

"Jesus, this is surely why men die earlier than women."

"Frank, all it takes is a little jail time to show you how fast life is really movin'. All I'm sayin' is the show is gonna be over before we know it, and we ought to make the best of our time. Trevor is a good woman for you, and believe me, there ain't many good ones out there, buddy." He tilted his head up at the crowded sky and sighed. "Jesus, this is the kind of night most people dream about, huh?"

A swirl of pastels filled the sky, smeared in an irregular fashion above the sea in an amalgamation of pinks, blues, and grays. Blanton strolled down the beach whistling the melody to the song, then sang in a full voice, "But if you try some time, you just might find—"

From under the wing of the *Hemisphere Dancer* I sang with him, "—you get what you need."

53

You're a Mayan

Desdemona sat stooped over the log book that lay on the table in front of her. She had run the *Cosmic Muffin* aground on a sandbar leaving Petite Place, and they were waiting for the tide to set them free. To pass the time, Desdemona had brought out notes from her conversations with the dolphin Albion, and now Trevor sat in a chaise longue, mesmerized by what Desdemona was reading to her.

When Desdemona finally finished, she looked up at Trevor and gave her a penetrating look. "There's a reason for us being here," Desdemona said.

"Yeah, you zigged when you should have zagged at the end of the channel," Trevor answered lightly.

"No, I'm talking about a bigger reason. Now I know why I couldn't even figure out the messages. It's because the messages were leading me to *you.* If you weren't supposed to be here, you wouldn't be. You're here because of the Generators. Albion said the messages come from the painters of the universe, and you're a painter. I'm not the Mayan; *you* are."

"What?"

"They are coming," Desdemona told her solemnly.

"Who?"

"The Generators. I feel a real big message coming on. Like nothing before."

Desdemona was sweating heavily, and the color had drained from her face. She got out of the chair and moved it under the shade of the deck awning.

"You don't look too good," Trevor said. "Here, lie down and get out of the sun."

"No time to dally. I'm okay. Quick, run to my cabin and get my Walkman and a fresh tape."

Trevor went below and returned quickly with the tape recorder and a glass of water. She sat on the side of Desdemona's chair and wet her bandanna in the cool water. Then she wiped Desdemona's forehead.

"This is what it's all about. Talk to them when they get here. This is it. Ask them about Joe."

Before Trevor could respond, Desdemona passed out. Her chin dropped to her neck, and she bowed her head. Trevor reached for her wrist to get a pulse but was knocked on her butt by a sudden electrical shock.

All afternoon the wind had been gusting, sending cattails across the bayou. Now it dropped to nothing, and all that could be heard was the cry of an osprey circling overhead.

Desdemona raised her head and looked around the ship as if it had become a strange environment. She spoke in a low, raspy voice. "I am one of those your friend has called the Generators, and I now speak in your earth language. I know your questions. I know your life."

Trevor pressed the red record button on the Walkman.

"Desdemona, you aren't bullshitting me, are you?"

"The person you call Desdemona is not here. I occupy her now, and I do not bullshit. I can only tell you what I know."

Trevor's hands were shaking as she moved the tape recorder closer to Desdemona.

"I want to know about my brother, Joe Merchant," she blurted out. "He was a famous singer, and I thought he committed suicide, and now I think he might be alive. Desdemona says I've been brought here for a reason. Can you help me?"

Desdemona continued, her voice getting even deeper. "The stars in the sky are the holes in the floor of heaven. The artists of earth are not of earth but are the stars, the link to the Pleiades, the heart of the universe. They are the healers. That is why they are thought of as strange, or weird. You don't know you know, do you?"

Trevor was speechless and tried to control her fear.

"Hah, I am sorry. Sometimes I go ahead of where I am. It is difficult to revert to earthlike comprehension. I forget that you do not yet know your Mayan soul. I am unclear as to your brother's incarnation. His mystery is not present on this side. Perhaps he is simply the means to a more cosmic end. It must be a mortal question."

Tears welled up in Trevor's eyes. She checked the tape recorder to make sure it was running properly and cleared her throat.

"There's a very evil man I've come in contact with. He's the one who says my brother is still alive."

"The thoroughly vicious and ruthless man is like a black hole in the pattern of the universe. It is the opposite of healing, and it is this power that he revels in. It is a power far beyond the reach of ordinary mortals. Yet goodness in the hands of evil cannot be corrupted into evil. There is really nothing to fear."

"I'm sorry, I don't understand," Trevor said.

"The universe in twenty-five words or less—I will try. The sun rotates around the Pleiades every twenty-six thousand years. The Mayan cycles are twenty-six thousand years long. The central sun of this part of the galaxy is located in the Pleiades and is called Lacunae. The next star over from Lacunae is Maya," the Generator explained.

"You know the mystery of the Mayans?" Trevor asked.

"Not the Mayans of Mexico, but the Mayans of the Pleiades. The Mayans were the galactic scouts of the Pleiades, and their mission was to make sure planets and star systems were synchronized. The Mayans were sent to earth to mop up the mess the Atlantians created. Atlantians settled on your planet, and they eventually went a little crazy. Needless to say, the Atlantians did not come from the Pleiades.

"Their colony, Atlantis, was underwater," the Generator continued. "Big crystal domes beneath the Atlantic Ocean. They got into trouble. They started to live in disregard of cosmic law. That spelled doom. The last king of Atlantis was a man named Marcus Morpheus. He was another of your spiritual black holes. During his reign, he used drugs to keep people disempowered, and he used crystal devices like Walkman headsets to keep people under control. The negative power began to suck the planet under. So Atlantis blew up big time.

"The Atlantians created havoc on the planet about the time Homo sapiens was developing. As their punishment, the Atlantians had to stay on earth. From that point forward, they could not be physical Atlantians anymore, but their souls remained on earth, and they were still very much hooked into their collective dark dream. During the Ice Age and the years that followed, they continued to dream their Atlantian dream. All around the planet, little tribes and clans of humans were being sucked into the Atlantian network, dreaming the old dream of Atlantis. Remnants of Atlantis are scattered across the earth, and when gathered, they have enormous power.

"Around the time of the end of Atlantis, Mayan scouts were sent on a surveillance mission from the Pleiades to see if the earth could be salvaged as part of the cosmic scheme of things or if the planet was just another write-off. So the Mayans came down and checked out the scene, and they reported back that chances of salvage were fair, as long as there was Mayan intervention. They also strongly recommended that a generic-type Mayan soul should be left on the planet. And these Mayan souls would be the healers, the ones who would reverse the power of the black holes over time."

"You mean there are still Mayan souls on earth?" Trevor asked.

"I'm talking to one," the Generator responded.

Trevor dropped the tape recorder. "But how can I have a Mayan soul and not know it?"

"Relax," the Generator said. "It's not as bad as P.M.S. You are a Star Dweller."

Trevor picked up the tape recorder and made sure she hadn't damaged it. "This is too much. I'm not sure I can believe what's happening here. Pardon me, but I'm overwhelmed."

"Okay, okay. Let me help you. Having a Mayan soul, you remember not only who you are right now, but also who and where you have been in the past, and who you might become in the future. You have a memory hot line connected to your ancestry. In your case, it just hasn't been active in, say, three thousand years. Now try to put yourself between one time and another."

"I don't understand."

"Like when you take a siesta. During a siesta you do not

really sleep. You hang between dimensions, between the physical plane and the dream world. Just be patient. Mayan souls are patient. They are also masters of time. Now try to connect to your Mayan side. Just concentrate on that side of you that paints what you see. Your art is your soul. And your soul is a natural healer."

Trevor closed her eyes and went to that place that was the source of her visions.

"Tell me the cosmic laws," the Generator said.

Without hesitating, Trevor answered, "One: Honor intelligence. Two: I cannot interfere with the evolutionary destiny of others; everyone has natural wisdom. Three: I am another myself."

"Which means?" the Generator asked.

"That when a planet is infiltrated, the ones who come from space do not add to the planet's karma," Trevor replied.

"See? Life is not like instant pudding. Your planet has accelerated quite rapidly, yet you forget where you came from. You must find your Mayan soul. You must complete your mission. Then you will understand."

The click of the end of the tape in the machine made Trevor open her eyes. "Fucking amazing," she said.

"What?" Desdemona asked, shaking her head.

"It's you, right?"

"Yes, it's me. He's gone. Pretty wild, huh?"

They listened to the tape over and over again until dusk when the hull of the *Cosmic Muffin* floated free from the sandbar and Desdemona steered the familiar course for Frenchman's Lagoon. Trevor sat next to her as she steered.

"I've been so stupid," Desdemona said. "It all makes perfect sense now. The messages were never meant for me. I was just the transmitter. You are the receiver."

"I'm a Mayan," Trevor said softly.

"You're a Mayan," Desdemona repeated with a laugh.

"This morning I was minutes away from being a shark snack, and this evening I'm talking to a voice from the Pleiades who tells me I live in the past, present, and future."

"Maybe that's *why* you weren't a shark snack. You know, it is a miracle you weren't, in those waters. So let's add this all up," Desdemona said. "We got you and Frank showing up here. This Jet Ski Killer fella. Cairo, the black hole, is lurking in the water somewhere. And Joe Merchant out there, who knows where? Something is drawing all of this here. Holy shit! It's the eclipse."

"What?"

"Steer for a minute."

Desdemona dashed to her cabin and came back with her *Star Guide,* a thick old book with a weathered leather binding. "There's a total solar eclipse tomorrow. Here. Listen to this: 'By the end of April, the Pleiades have slipped to the west and put in their last evening appearances before disappearing with the sun.' Cairo is looking for something that's here in Boomtown. If we can find out what it is, we can use it to make a deal."

"He's not Monty Hall."

"No, silly. We trade it to him for what he knows about Joe."

"He could have been lying, you know."

"No, I don't think so. He's a madman, this Cairo. And he'd take sheer delight in telling you that your brother's alive right before he killed you. I think he's on a quest for something. You and your brother are a means to his end. We've both listened to this tape enough times to see that Cairo is one of those black holes—this is serious. Cinderella, let's get a move on. We are going to the cosmic ball."

"What's that?"

"You tell me. You're the Mayan."

54

Fly-Boy in the Ointment

I was taking an after-dinner nap when a rap on the hull of the plane woke me, and I peeked out the window to see who it was. Blanton and Hoagy were nowhere to be found, but a note said Blanton was going to town and would catch up with me later. The smell of fresh-baked bread permeated the interior of the plane, and I put on my shorts and opened the hatch. The evening air was cool, and the breeze made me shiver slightly.

"So you're the fly-boy in the ointment of love. Nice to meet you, Frank Bama. I'm Desdemona, the woman you came looking for. Here—I brought you a peace offering from the other side of paradise." She stood in the darkness and held out a paper bag.

I ran my fingers through my hair. "I just woke up, and I'm a little too sleepy to be thinking."

"Will coffee help?"

Desdemona pointed her flashlight at Blanton's makeshift dining area, and we walked over and sat on the coconut-tree stumps. She put the flashlight down, poured me a cup of coffee from her thermos, and I opened the bag and pulled out a piping-hot *pain au chocolat* and took a bite.

"Much better. Thank you."

"What do you want to talk about first, Frank? Your plane or your girl?"

"You don't waste any time, do you?"

"I just feel the hourglass is emptying pretty fast here, and we got to get a few things worked out."

Hoagy appeared out of nowhere with a long wet stick in his mouth. As soon as he smelled the bread he dropped it, and Desdemona threw him a croissant, which he caught in midair and gulped down.

"How's Trevor?" I asked.

"Now, that's a great start. It's a good sign that your first question is about her. I like that. I have plans for you two. Do you dance?"

"Yeah, I love to dance. Why?"

"We're going to town later tonight to see my friend's band. Why don't you meet us at the Polar Bar around midnight." Desdemona patted Hoagy and looked at the plane and laughed. "You actually landed this in the ocean to save your girlfriend?"

"Yes."

"You're not bad, Frank Bama." She threw another croissant to Hoagy. "Well, I've got to run,' she said. "I guess you could call this a secret mission." Desdemona picked up her flashlight and pointed it into the trees. "See you later." Then she disappeared into the thicket.

As soon as she left, Hoagy went charging off down the beach after something, and I slid out of my shorts and headed for the ocean. The water was cold at first, but I swam long, hard strokes with my eyes closed. I switched to the butterfly stroke, bobbing up and down in the darkness like a porpoise, wondering what the night would bring.

So many discoveries were made by accident: a ship that was swept past its destination on the Asian mainland by typhoons in 1542 made the first sightings of Japan; "Wrong Way" Corrigan had set out in 1932 from New York to California, and when his compass malfunctioned, he crossed the Atlantic. The older I got, the more I felt that life was not one continuous movement. It bounced, swerved, and gyrated like a Mexican jumping bean. Today I had felt as if my world were caving in, but tonight I had the feeling that things were getting better. I sensed that some strange, accidental discovery lay ahead, and I wondered if my world would seem as complicated when I got back on dry land again.

Cabbages
and Kings

55

Mambo on the Wind

Charlie quickly packed a duffel bag and left the *Nomad* after overhearing the Colonel on the phone Saturday afternoon. He made sure no one was following him and went straight to the Rudderville hospital. Gunshot wounds were as common in these parts as a strawberry on the knee, and the doctor cleaned the wound, bandaged it up, and gave him a new prescription for Percodan, all for ten dollars. Charlie bought a quart of guava juice at the market and swallowed a handful of the pain pills; then he walked out of town in the direction of the deserted brown hills in the distance.

Charlie spent the rest of the day sitting in the shade of a tamarind tree, looking out at the ocean in the cool, circulating air. The trade winds brushed the side of the hill, and the scent of tea olive hung in the air, reminding Charlie of Africa. On his way to the hills, he had come across a small herd of skinny cows and had followed the trail of cow shit until he came across a pile that nurtured a small bunch of magic mushrooms. He dined that evening on a ham sandwich and more Percodan, and then he brewed up some mushroom tea to help him sleep.

The chemicals in his body painted the night. The soundtrack of animal calls and bird cries was better than the soundtrack of any movie. He decided to camp out in the hills over the weekend, and on Monday, at dawn, the roar of a low-flying seaplane awakened him as it skimmed the tree line. He didn't know if he was tripping or not, for the plane looked exactly like the one he had hijacked. He fell back into a deep, mystical sleep and decided to stay in the hills another day.

• • •

When Charlie showed up at the Rudderville airport on Tuesday, the concentration of armed policemen made him nervous. He stopped at a nearby domino table to pick up the news from the old men gathered round sipping rum and coffee. There had been a jailbreak the day before, and the Jet Ski Killer had escaped in a seaplane. This made Charlie eager to get out of Rudderville as soon as possible.

His psychedelic weekend had sharpened his focus, and his mind felt as dilated as his pupils. If the Colonel saw him in this state, Charlie knew it wouldn't be long before Cairo would figure out that he wasn't ready to die yet. Besides, Charlie knew where the scepter was, and the Colonel didn't.

• • •

The vibrations of the big radial engines shook Charlie Fabian. His face was carved into a huge grin that made his cheeks hurt. He stared out the window at the big propellers whipping the moisture from the air. The water appeared in a circular pattern that expanded into a rainbow of colors. The mushrooms had him humming.

He watched the tires leave the runway and retract into the wheel wells, and he felt the plane lift into the air. He was headed to Boomtown and was going to find the scepter before the Colonel did. It was all becoming clear now. He flipped the tape over in the Walkman he had bought in the duty-free shop, readjusted his headphones, and turned the volume up.

Charlie did not even notice that there was anybody else on the plane until the stewardess brushed the gunshot wound on his shoulder. His eyes sprang open immediately as the pain registered. He turned to the passenger seat on his right and saw the back of a man's head. The man's face was concealed by the white sickbag. As the man heaved forward, something fell out of his lap and into the aisle. Charlie reached down and picked it up. It was a cassette box, and there on the cover was the young and innocent stare of Joe Merchant.

The stewardess came by and offered her brightest smile to the barfing passenger.

"Just relax, Mr. Breno, the takeoff is the worst part."

• • •

There was quite a commotion upon their arrival in Boomtown as the *Vomit Comet* was greeted by an ambulance, which took the sick reporter away. Charlie slipped through the crowd and caught a cab to the most remote beach on the island, where he spent the day watching the windsurfers race back and forth across a shallow lagoon protected from the ocean swells. Several young women were sunbathing naked at the far end of the beach, and Charlie walked by them, admiring their perfectly shaped bronze buttocks.

He stayed on the beach until sunset and then made his way to the cemetery, passing a very long line of people standing in front of a French phone booth under a coconut tree. "Popular spot," he said to a pretty tanned girl standing in line. She was eating a croissant.

"It's broken," she said.

"Why are you in line if the phone's broken?" he asked.

"I don't mean like broken. I mean like the phone works, and you don't have to pay. It's been like this all week. Great, huh? Screwing the phone company just once in your life. I come every day after the beach. Call all my friends. Last night I talked to my sister in Bali. You should try it. It's great. Call all your friends."

"All my friends," Charlie repeated as he walked away. He had none.

• • •

Charlie Fabian sat on top of the old mildewed crypt in a peaceful little graveyard on the edge of the Caribbean Sea where he could hear the sound of the waves slapping gently on the sand beach. He watched the thin crescent moon disappear behind a drifting cloud.

He undressed completely and stood naked in the night. He felt the fresh scar from the gunshot wound near his shoulder, then traced the old scars that documented his history as a mercenary. Some still hurt; some were numb. He could hear the land crabs scurrying around his feet. To them, this was not a cemetery. It was a picnic. The moon reappeared, and a big fiddler crab with one giant claw stared at him from the next crypt.

Across the path from where he sat, a fresh mound of earth was piled next to a deep, dark hole. Charlie began tossing the contents of his duffel bag into the hole: boots, fatigues, compass, field jacket, camo hat. He pointed at the crab. "You bastards are the lucky ones. You all live by one rule: eat or be eaten. It's that simple." He pointed at his head. "It's the brain that complicates it for us humans."

• • •

Charlie thought how ironic it was that he had escaped death only to wind up in a cemetery. He reached into his pocket and popped the last mushroom into his mouth. The lights of Boomtown glowed in the distance at the end of the narrow road that followed the shoreline to the harbor. He could hear the sound of drums and the faint refrains of a mambo on the wind. He tried to keep time, but the drummer had no rhythm. He recognized the song—a bad rendition of Carlos Santana's "Black Magic Woman."

Charlie stood up and took out the Joe Merchant tape that he had lifted from the sick reporter and put it into his Walkman. He listened for a while and then got lost in the music. He started to sing along with Joe Merchant and danced through the cemetery, first very slowly and then faster and faster, spinning and turning to the music and singing at the top of his lungs. Suddenly he was six feet below the ground, flat on his back in the freshly dug grave.

He closed his eyes, but he could still see. His tattooed eyes were fixed on the heavens, and Charlie could see that the seven sisters of the Pleiades were directly over him, highlighted by the blackness of outer space. He groped for his flashlight and shone it up from the hole, and the beam caught the tiny red eyes of the big crab, which was peeking down at Charlie.

"Not yet, you motherfuckers."

56

At Arm's Length

Monty Potter loved his food, and even the threat of Adrian Cairo did not deter him from stuffing his face. He was a true believer in the French paradox, a phenomenon that allows the French to eat reams of pâté de foie gras, butter, and cheeses, all washed down with a couple of glasses of red wine a day, and still be at minimum risk for heart disease.

Potter was extremely horny. Danger had always made him horny. He had spent a playful evening welcoming the new girls at the whorehouse to town. He'd fed them lobster in his big, four-poster bed and then sent them home around four.

He had a plan to get the scepter back. He might need a little insurance policy, along with his newly hired security force, to make a deal with the Colonel. He had been able to wiggle his way out of tighter spots than this before.

Potter pulled a whole mango from the icebox next to his bed and began slicing pieces from it. He walked to the balcony. He had hired the three Ramos brothers, ruthless bodyguards from Santo Domingo, to protect him from the Colonel's revenge. He knew that was why the Colonel was coming, but Potter had a plan. He waved to Flavio Ramos, who stood on the roof of the old marketplace across the street, then put on his Kevlar bathrobe and sat in the old planter's chair, waiting for the morning.

He studied the horizon through his spyglass, looking for signs of strange vessels that might be carrying his adversary toward him. Monty Potter had decided to do the proper dictatorial thing and flee his empire for safer ground and negotiate with Cairo. Money mattered even more to the old man than revenge. That was where he had always been able to deal with the Colonel. Potter always had a plan.

• • •

Fernando Orlando had just fallen asleep on top of the baby grand piano when he heard Potter bellowing his name from above like God on Judgment Day. It had been a long night at the Polar Bar. A convention of Wackenhut airport security guards from Miami had taken over the place, and the drums chained to the walls had been held hostage for the evening by an army of Cuban grandmothers who thought Fernando Orlando was God's gift to Latin America. They had taught Brigette, the barmaid, how to make *mojitos,* and they spent the night yelling "Fuck Castro!" and singing patriotic songs.

It was truly as close as Fernando had ever come to being Ricky Ricardo. But the evening had turned sour when one of the grandmothers confronted Fernando. "Ricky Ricardo never wore gold chains," she complained.

"It's a new look."

She had grabbed the biggest chain and had tried to snatch it from his neck, but the clasp wouldn't open. Fernando thought he was going to be choked to death until Rafael Ramos, one of Potter's new highly paid bodyguards, gave the grandmother an elbow to the midsection.

Fernando Orlando was still in his show clothes. His hands hurt as much as his head, and the raw red circle around his neck stung. He straightened his gold chains, crawled off the top of the piano, and marched up the stairs to Potter's apartment. Carlos Ramos stood at the top of the stairs, shouldering an M-16. He looked at Fernando with a demeaning frown.

"I'm here to see Mr. Potter," Fernando said.

The guard burped, scratched his belly, and knocked on the door.

"Come in," Potter called out. The guard took his hand from the gun and swung the door open.

Potter was pacing back and forth across the room in his pajamas. "That wand I gave Desdemona—I want it back," Potter said.

Fernando's mouth dropped open. "Boss, that's Indian giving, and the gods look very unfavorably on a person who takes back gifts. She has powerful friends in high places."

"Fernando, I don't give a fuck about the gods. They don't run this town. I do, and I want that scepter back here by sundown. You go tell her I want another reading and to please bring the scepter with her. Bring her to the Café Auberge at one o'clock. I'll be waiting."

"What if I can't find her?" Fernando asked.

"Then I would suggest that you start looking for another job, Fernando, because you will be the one with the bad luck. Tú comprendes?"

"Si."

• • •

Monty Potter was escorted by his bodyguards to the Café Auberge on the far side of the island for his lunch date with Desdemona. He waited for an hour, watching the Ramos brothers pick their teeth, and then he realized he'd been stood up. The wait only made him more hungry, and he ordered two grilled salmon streaks, fried potatoes, Creole boudin sausage, a bottle of Chablis, and a tourte aux cerises with crème fraîche for dessert.

After lunch, he stopped by the airport to check the plane he would be taking, and then he sent one of his bodyguards to find Desdemona. Potter set off for his small bungalow in the hills to take a nap.

He would need his rest for the flight. At midnight, he would take one of the Air Reality seaplanes and head for Buzios, a small seaside village north of Rio, where he would wait until he made contact with the Colonel. He would inform Cairo that he would alert certain friends in Paris of the Colonel's presence in the Caribbean. Cairo knew too much embarrassing information, and a lot of governments would be only too happy to remove the Colonel from the big picture, once and for all. But if the Colonel was willing to forgive the past, Monty Potter would make him a peace offering of the scepter along with half a million dollars in treasure.

The Ramos brothers were now stationed in back and in front of the property with their guns locked and loaded while Potter prepared to snooze. He dropped his frame into the rope hammock, which sank six inches but still had enough ground clearance for the servant to gently swing it. Monty Potter fell asleep, confident of his bargaining position.

It was the lack of motion and the still blades of the ceiling fan above his head that made him open his eyes. The folds of fat that encircled his neck like a collection of dog collars were soaked with sweat.

"Maria," he called, but no one answered. There was only the sound of parrots squawking in the hills.

Something was wrong. He had been sleeping on his side, and his legs and arms were numb and tucked behind his back. As he tried to uncurl himself from the awkward position, he realized he was tied up. He struggled briefly and spilled out of the hammock and onto the floor with a thud.

"Rafael . . . Carlos . . . Where the fuck are you?"

"They all went home, Monty. Have a nice nap?" a voice asked from the veranda. Monty Potter felt his heart racing and thought he was going to throw up.

"Who the fuck is there?" Potter screamed.

"An old friend, Monty."

"Charlie Fabian, is that you? I know it's you. Let's talk, Charlie."

The late evening sun hung low above a distant hill, and shone blindingly onto the floor where Potter lay. He squinted to get a look at the figure who now stood in the door, casting a long shadow into the room.

"Charlie, what's going on here? Don't do anything rash. I need to talk to the Colonel. I've got a deal for him."

"Africa," the voice called out from the door. "Remember Africa? A little village near Timbuktu. I remember the laughter in the bushes as I was scrambling for my life. The old witch doctor in the cave. You killed him and took something that is mine."

Potter saw the green head first as the long snake slithered across the floor.

"Nooooo," Potter wailed from the floor as tears ran down his cheeks. He started to heave and then vomited.

Colonel Cairo stood in the doorway with a long machete in his hand. He pushed the snake to one side of the room with the backside of the long blade. "Hello, Monty. Long time no see."

Potter's eyes glazed over, and he shook his head back and forth, mumbling something incoherent. Colonel Cairo leaned down and wiped the vomit from Potter's mouth with a hand-kerchief, then dropped it to the floor.

"There now, that's better isn't it?"

"Colonel, don't kill me. We can work it out. I know where the scepter is. I was going to get in touch with you and see if we could make a deal. I have a lot to lose here."

"I'm a reasonable man, Monty. You have the scepter? My, my. It's my lucky day."

"Colonel, I don't have the scepter, but I know where it is. I can take you there if you won't kill me."

"Tell me, Monty," the Colonel said.

"You'll kill me if I tell you."

"Always the smart guy, always playing the angle. Okay."

The Colonel reached down with the machete and snipped the plastic ties that were wrapped around Potter's thick wrists. Potter rolled over and got up on his knees, rubbing his hands together. He reached for the hammock, to pull himself up, but instead he fell heavily back to the floor.

It took a few seconds for the pain to register. Potter screamed like a wounded animal in a trap. He was numb and in shock, and then he felt something wet on his face.

He looked up. The Colonel was holding Potter's severed arm. Potter was paralyzed with horror. Cairo spun the bloody arm above his head—again and again. Blood splattered everywhere, and when he let it go, the appendage went flying across the room.

Monty Potter reached for his wounded shoulder. Colonel Cairo towered over him and placed the machete in Potter's crotch.

"Now we're even, Monty," he said. "Unless you want me to continue separating you into tiny pieces, I suggest you tell me where the scepter is."

57

Jalapeno Hollywood

Rudy Breno was feeling a lot better, and he stared at himself naked in the mirror, admiring what the loss of seven pounds had done to reduce the size of his love handles.

He had been brought to his knees by a case of diarrhea that had kept him locked in his hotel room for a day. The flight to Boomtown hadn't helped, but the stewardess had nursed him back to health with a combination of fresh air, Hershey bars, Evian water, and an ambulance. Whatever it was, the idea of being treated for any ailment at the Boomtown hospital had been enough incentive for a speedy recovery.

A local cab driver had dropped him off at the Tropical Banana Hotel, where he had checked in and had gotten directions to the Shipwreck, the local whorehouse. He showered; shaved; covered his arms, face, and dick with Brut; and put on his favorite paisley shirt.

"Reporter, heal thyself," Rudy said into the mirror and then made an entry in his notebook. "Possible story for the *Lighthouse:* Lose Seven Pounds Overnight with Miracle Third-World Diet."

Rudy was furious at his father for taking him off the story, but he knew he couldn't find a job anywhere else. Maybe he had chased Joe Merchant for too long. Maybe this Val Vincennes director thing was his chance to get to Hollywood and be discovered. Maybe his father was right. But no matter what his next career move might be, it would have to wait until he spent a night in the last great pirate town in the Caribbean. He was going to get drunk and laid in Boomtown.

The Shipwreck opened at six o'clock, and Rudy was the first customer of the night. He picked out a pair of twins from the sad-looking faces in the parlor. The girls got on their knees, mumbling prayers in Spanish, and then walked upstairs with Rudy.

A bottle of white rum and a blow job later, Rudy Breno was in love with anything that moved. He could not remember the girls' names and called them Curly and Shirley. They had snorted sufficient quantities of bad cocaine to make Rudy more tolerable. Rudy took them to dinner at a small restaurant on the harbor, where they played with him under the table and kept repeating the words "You take us to Amayreeka, Rudy stud, si?"

Rudy promised to take them to America, to Disney World, to meet George and Barbara Bush, and to Hollywood. The girls did not know many words in English, but now *Hollywood* was one of them. The catchphrase for the evening suddenly changed.

After dinner, the girls told Rudy they were taking him out on the town. They skipped down Rue Christophe shouting their favorite new English word over and over: "Hollywood, Hollywood, Hollywood!"

58

Is There Anybody out There?

I left a note for Blanton and told him I was going to Boom-town in case he got back to the plane before I did. I was hoping he would meet me at the Polar Bar later.

The low tide had exposed the flats between the islands, and I carefully made my way across the dark and found a little Chinese seafood restaurant where I asked about finding a pay phone. I wanted to call Billy Cruiser before heading to town to meet Desdemona and Trevor. The owner told me there was one down at the beach that was broken and didn't cost anything, and it didn't take me long to find it.

There was an hour-long wait, so I killed time playing dominoes with a couple of hippies. When it was finally my turn, I dialed the pay phone at the Lone Palm Airport but got no answer, then tried Billy Cruiser's house and got an unfamiliar voice on the answering machine that gave me another number to try. I dialed the other number, and the operator answered "Florida Keys Memorial Hospital."

"Ah, I am trying to get in touch with a Mr. Billy Cruiser."

"Is he a patient here?"

320

"I really don't know." I was put on hold, and then the starched voice came back on.

"One moment, please. It's late, but I will ring the room." The connection was not the best in the world, but I was relieved to hear the raspy voice of Billy Cruiser.

"What the hell are you doing in the Key West Hospital? Don't you know people die in there?"

"Brillo, that you? Why, son, it's good to hear your voice." Billy sounded weak but as feisty as ever.

"What's goin' on?" I asked.

"They was filmin' one of those rock videos down here, and a bunch of them tall, skinny models was dressed up—well let's say undressed—playin' like they was mermaids, and I don't know if that's what caused my heart to go fuckin' haywire, but I hope it was. So they put me in the hospital for observation. Sounds like I'm a goddamn balloon or something."

"Just do what they tell you."

"I figured no news was good news. You okay?" he asked.

"It's been one hell of an adventure so far."

"Well, you kids kicked up quite a bit of dust around here, but things have started to quiet down."

I was dying to ask what was going on with the bank and the hunt for Blanton, but I had no idea who might be listening on the line. From the tone of his voice, I picked up that things had returned to the usual lethargic pace of the Keys. I asked him about my problem with the missing float, and without hesitation he gave me a temporary remedy right off the top of his head. It was perfect.

"Did Trevor ever catch up with you?" Billy asked.

"That she did."

"Well, you two take care and don't worry about me."

"Be good, Billy." I hung up the phone and laughed to myself when I thought about telling Billy what had gone on. I felt guilty that I wasn't in Key West, but I knew there really wasn't that much I could do anyway. The real world seemed like another planet. I hadn't read a magazine, watched the news, or talked to anyone in Key West about what had happened since I'd flown out of town.

I checked my watch and walked in the direction of town, stopping at the old windmill on the edge of the salt pond to take a leak. I could hear music down the road, and as I unzipped, a distant drum beat had me practicing dance steps in the dark.

"Trevor, I want to tell you that I know I've been an asshole. No, that's not it. Trevor, if you can try to be understanding just one more time . . . Shit."

"Just tell her you love her," a voice said behind me.

I jumped about three feet in the air and pissed down the front of my pants. I heard Blanton's unmistakable laugh and turned around. "Jesus Christ, look what you made me do."

"Excellent approach. I'm proud of you for facing the music here with Trevor." I zipped up, and we started walking.

"Ray Ban, I'm not good at this shit."

"Once you let it go, it'll get easier. Are we goin' dancin'?"

"Desdemona came by. She wants me to be at the Polar Bar around midnight. Where the hell have you been?"

"You know us criminals—I was practicin' a little criminology."

"Hey, I called Billy about the missing float. He's in the hospital—had another heart attack."

"He all right?"

"He sounded okay when I talked to him, a little weak."

"He's a tough old oyster."

We jumped clear of the road when a tiny, beat-up car came barreling around the curve, tires screeching and music blaring. It disappeared into the hot night. "You hear anything about us in town?" I asked.

"No. Seems to be more concern about the disappearance of Monty Potter."

"Somethin's going on down here. No doubt about that," I said.

"Wanna bet it has somethin' to do with the one-armed man or the four-eyed maniac?"

"My sentiments exactly."

Blanton laughed. "You know, you can sure pick some strange company to hang with, Frank."

"Startin' with you." We both grinned.

"Buddy, I got the feelin' this might be our last night on the town for a while. It's time for the Jet Ski Killer to be movin' on down the line. I think we'd all better get outta here. This Joe Merchant thing is a dead-end street. Those guys on the boat who kidnapped Trevor are into somethin' that's way too heavy for any of us. Desdemona obviously ain't dealin' with a full deck. I think you two should head home and think more about tryin' to patch things up between you than runnin' around chasin' ghosts. I want you to promise me that you'll talk to Trevor."

"I will. I promise. What are you gonna do?"

"Me? I'm as big a ghost as Joe Merchant. I can't go home—fuck, I don't *want* to go home. I got some ideas. I'm goin' south."

Blanton told me his plan as we walked, and I told him I'd help him. This fugitive business was changing him. It wasn't that he enjoyed being on the run, but he had an air of humor and contentment I hadn't seen in a long time.

At the edge of town we came upon an old stone church. The windows were all open, and the light from inside revealed a small congregation at a midweek service. The night air was filled with the fragrance of jasmine, blown across the island by the steady offshore breeze. Through the windows I could see a guitar player and drummer behind the pulpit, keeping a steady beat while the congregation swayed and moved to the music.

"Think they might have a prayer for us sinners?" Blanton asked.

"They say God watches over fools, drunks, and children."

"That's a comforting thought, old buddy. Let's be all three."

59

Matador in the Broken Mirror

Fernando Orlando stared into the broken mirror. He was sitting behind the bar in the liquor closet, which doubled as a dressing room. The Polar Bar was jammed, but he took a few minutes to ponder the strange events of the day.

When Desdemona hadn't shown up for their lunch, Monty Potter had ordered Fernando to lure her into a trap. But Fernando had finally decided the time had come. First of all, he was a man of principle, and he couldn't betray his friend—not to mention the fear of curses and spells that might hang over such a deed. His first instinct had been to run, but then he'd made a courageous decision. He was going to confront Monty Potter and tell him that he was quitting.

He had started for Monty's apartment about half a dozen times, but each time he turned back at the last instant. Finally he'd made it all the way up the stairs to the apartment, but Monty was gone. So were the bodyguards. He'd made the trip all the way out to Monty's cottage in the hills and found the same story—nobody home. There was no sign of Monty anywhere. Something strange was going on.

Fernando returned to the Polar Bar, relieved that at least

his problem was solved for the time being. Now he was ready
for his big move. He had a plan so secret that not even Desdemona knew about it. He would play the midnight show
with the Cane Thrashers and then board the *La Brisa* for the
Eclipse Cruise. He'd stay on board until they reached Florida.

Next week he was due in Miami for his change of life. The
night of the invasion by the Cuban grandmothers had given
him the idea. If he couldn't contact the ghost of Ricky
Ricardo in the spiritual sense, then he would have to use the
tools of modern medicine to achieve his purpose. He had
scheduled a week of plastic surgery: tummy tuck, pec im-
plants, and a hair weave. It would cost him his life savings,
but it was time to take a risk. He knew it was worth it. A
dozen cruise ships in Miami attracted thousands of Cuban
grandmothers who would pay big bucks for a Ricky Ricardo
imitator. Of course he hadn't told Monty Potter of his plan.

Fernando did a turn in front of the mirror, checking out the
costume he'd assembled for his final performance at the Polar
Bar. If this was going to be the last show, then he'd make it
one hell of a night. He wore a pair of tight black tuxedo
pants, a red cummerbund, and a hot-pink polyester shirt with
huge pink-and-white puffed sleeves, unbuttoned nearly to his
navel. He checked the lock on the door, and when he was
sure it was bolted, he removed the stuffed sock from his bag
and carefully shoved it down the front of his pants and adjusted the bulge until he was satisfied with the look. In the
mirror Fernando saw a matador, brave and confident—new
qualities that reflected the courage it took to make such an
important career decision.

He jumped when he heard a knock at the door. Sweat began to steam his armpits. Maybe Potter had found out about
his plans. He was relieved when he heard Desdemona's
voice. Fernando tiptoed across the tiny dressing room and
opened the door.

"Get a load of you," Desdemona said.

"Get a load of *you*," Fernando replied.

Red, orange, and yellow swatches swirled around Desdemona's tie-dyed muumuu like different flavors of cotton
candy. On her head she wore a purple turban.

The day in the sun had baked away the bleached-out pallor
of Trevor's nightmare hours in the ocean. She had assembled
a variety of Desdemona's scarves, and they were gathered on
her left hip to reveal her smooth brown thigh. A white scarf

painted with large frangipani blossoms was now a halter that covered her breasts and was tied around her neck. Her hair was loosely pulled up on top of her head, and the conch-pearl earrings were radiant in the dim light of the room. Fernando's eyes fixed on Trevor.

"And who is this lovely creature? Buenos noches, senorita."

"Trevor Kane, Fernando Orlando," Desdemona said.

"Now, darling," Fernando began, "I am so glad you came. I need to talk to you about something, but it will have to wait until the break."

"We'll be here," Desdemona told him, and Fernando swashed off to the stage.

60

Feeding Frenzy

Rudy Breno was having the time of his life. Curly and Shirley had taken him to a strip joint at the end of Rue Christophe called the Mermaid Lounge. They worked the Mermaid as topless dancers when things were slow at the whorehouse, and tonight the place was packed with a fresh load of tourists who were waiting to board the *La Brisa* for the Eclipse Cruise.

Tuesday night was Land Shark Night. Curly and Shirley happily stripped down to their G-strings, and now they were part of a group of a dozen girls who swam provocatively in a see-through hot tub. Above them, a waterfall cascaded down from a fifty-gallon oil drum hanging from the roof.

Rudy sported a large gray plastic fin strapped to his back. He had rented a mask, a snorkel, and an underwater camera, and he sat at the bar with the rest of the land sharks and waited for the cue from the emcee.

"Feeding frenzy!" a fat man shrieked into a microphone, and Rudy dove into the pool. He landed in a pile with the rest of the spawners, splashing and snapping away at the naked mermaids in the waterfall. Curly and Shirley found him and made what they called a shark sandwich out of him.

The feeding frenzy sobered Rudy up a bit, and when he ran out of film, he tried to use it as an excuse to go back to his hotel room for a quickie. But Curly and Shirley were just getting wound up. Though he protested vehemently, they led him dripping wet to the Polar Bar.

It was almost midnight. The Polar Bar was crammed with people and had taken on the disposition of a defective nuclear reactor. By the time Rudy walked in, the place was on the verge of a meltdown. Bodies were packed together like cordwood, and the temperature was well over a hundred. The rows of ceiling fans only managed to stir the mushroom cloud of smoke into long, visible swirls.

A naked woman with a pair of handcuffs dangling from her wrists was being escorted out. She was screaming all kinds of obscenities back at somebody in the crowd. Rudy, Curly, and Shirley were guided through the metal detector, where Rudy paid the cover charge and Curly checked a small handgun.

"Geet a drum, Rudy. Geet a drum!" Shirley yelled.

"That's fifty francs more, pal," the doorman barked and took the bill from the change Rudy held in his hand. Three large black men in the middle of the Wall of Drums were laying down the rhythm line. Their eyes were closed, and their hands moved in perfect time as they pounded out the primal cadence. The rest of the drummers were playing to the pace of the black men, and the beat fueled the already excited crowd.

A fight broke out over by the pool tables in the corner. Bodies moved left and right to avoid the bouncers, but the rhythm of the drums held steady. Curly and Shirley were on the beat, bumping Rudy from each side and grinding him at pelvic level. Rudy just hopped up and down like a giant rabbit with no idea that the point was to move your body to the beat.

One of the drummers near the end of the line passed out and fell into the shallow puddle of beer that covered the floor. The bouncer pointed at Rudy. "Number ten."

"Play for us, Rudy! Come play for us. Make us hot for you," Curly said. She put her arms around Rudy's neck and then violently ripped his rayon shirt open to the waist, exposing his hairless fish-white chest. The buttons exploded like popcorn, and Rudy got a boner, which made the girls laugh hysterically. They rattled on to each other in Spanish, pointing at the protrusion in his pants. Rudy Breno ordered tequila for them all.

"Viva Las Vegas!" Rudy snorted.

"Viva Los Wages," the girls repeated.

They downed their shots, and Rudy mounted the stool and began to beat wildly out of time on the drum. His eyes bulged, and his tongue hung from his mouth, giving him the look of a dog that had chased deer all day. Curly and Shirley writhed like snakes in front of him, rubbing their exposed breasts over his head and shoulders as he leaned over the drum. Beads of sweat pelted his face when they shook their hair. Rudy Breno was so lost in the beat he didn't see Frank Bama and the Jet Ski Killer brush by the girls and weave their way toward the stage.

61

Save the Last Dance for Me

"**A**re you sure?" I asked and then turned to look.

"See?" Blanton said. "What the fuck is he doing here? He's supposed to be lost in the jungles of Haiti."

"Maybe he's smarter than we think," I said.

Blanton was pissed. "Not a fuckin' chance, Brillo."

"Well, he's too interested in those titties flopping around his face right now to be thinking about the Jet Ski Killer."

"It still makes me nervous."

"Yeah, now you know how I feel." I pointed to the dance floor where Trevor was doing the cha-cha-cha with an older man in a sweat-stained suit.

We managed to squeeze in at the end of the bar and yelled for boat drinks. The bartender slid them over to us, and Blanton kept a watchful eye on Rudy Breno. The room was like a steam bath, and I was already dripping wet. My eyes stung from the smoke that hung over us like a thermal inversion.

"I guess you could call this a miniature greenhouse effect," I muttered.

"I've seen some shitholes before, but this one takes the

cake. Well, Brillo, here's to cuttin' in and cuttin' out," Blanton said. "This is your chance."

"I don't know. Look at this place. This isn't the right atmosphere. I want it to be quiet, where we can talk and maybe take a walk on the beach."

"This ain't a fuckin' movie. When the target presents itself, you fire. It's as simple as that."

"Ray Ban, this ain't the Vietcong. This is the woman I love."

"That's why you have to make the first move. Remember, all she can say is no."

I gulped down my drink and started for the dance floor. I took two steps, then turned around. "By the way," I shouted back at him, "what makes you such an expert on how to talk to women?"

"I've been in jail!" Blanton yelled. "There's no better place to fantasize about what to say to a woman. If I ever get the chance, I'll try some of my own advice. But right now you're the hamster on the treadmill, and you better get movin'!"

I crept through the bodies to the edge of the crowded dance floor. Fernando and the Cane Thrashers concluded their version of Sam Cooke's "Everybody Loves to Cha-Cha-Cha," and the drummers fell silent, waiting to pick up the beat of the next tune.

The room must have been a hundred and twenty degrees, but my feet were as cold as ice. I was more nervous than the day of my first communion, more nervous than the first time I soloed, more nervous than the day the mortars in the hills above Da Nang rained down on our planes in the harbor.

The band started into the Jimmy Cliff song "Many Rivers to Cross," and couples started to pair off for a slow dance. I saw Desdemona out of the corner of my eye, and she nodded her head. Trevor's back was two feet from me. I could smell the coconut oil, and I watched the muscles in her lovely shoulders expand and contract as she swayed to the music. The drums were getting louder again, amplifying the beat of the Cane Thrashers. The man in the blue suit spun Trevor sideways.

I thought about what Blanton had said and gently tapped the gentleman on the shoulder. He courteously smiled and held out Trevor's hand as he moved to the side.

I was standing face-to-face with Trevor, looking directly into her lovely green eyes. "Please don't leave," I said. It

took all the courage I had in the world to say it. "I want to
work this out. I don't want to be a lonely old pilot who only
talks to his dog."

We stood there for a moment, suspended in time.

"That wouldn't be fair to Hoagy," she said and placed her
hand on my shoulder. I smiled and felt a rush of warmth
come over me. I put my arm around her waist, and she rested
her head next to mine. We danced in a small circle. The tendons and muscles in my arms were rigid.

"Relax," Trevor whispered. "You're doing fine."

I closed my eyes and let out a deep breath and just enjoyed
the moment. Trevor pulled her head back and moved my chin
with her finger until our eyes met. "Do you know that's the
first time you've ever looked me straight in the eye and said
anything the least bit personal?"

"I was afraid," I said. I shifted uncomfortably.

"You? Afraid?"

"Yeah, me."

"What are you so afraid of?"

"I don't know," I said and looked away. Once again she
drew my eyes to hers.

"Well, it's what makes the difference. If you hadn't looked
me in the eye, I would have felt like walking away." Trevor
shook her head in disbelief and began to laugh lightly. "After
all we've both been through, this is a strange place to be talking like this. I feel like I'm in *Casablanca*. And I still don't
know what I'm doing here."

I started to laugh.

"What's so funny?" she asked.

"You reminded me of something Blanton said."

"Where is he?"

"He's lying low. Guess who else is here?"

"Who?"

"Rudy Breno."

"No."

"He's over on the drums."

Trevor leaned closer as she stretched up on tiptoe to look,
and I felt the softness of her breasts press against my chest.
I hoped she would take a long time to find him.

"Good Lord, there he is. I've been so lost in my own fog, I
don't know what's going on back in the real world."

"That makes two of us. You know, that director didn't die

after all, but Blanton's still a wanted man. You want to get some air?"

"God, yes," she said. "We can go out the back entrance by the bandstand."

Trevor held onto my hand, and we pushed our way through the crowd, pausing only to have our hands stamped as we walked out the door. The cool salt air felt wonderful. We walked across the alley to the dinghy dock where a fleet of small fishing sloops like Toosay's sat tied like horses to a giant iron loop. We leaned side by side against the rusty cannon and looked out over the water.

The faintest hint of a moon emerged from behind a veil of clouds that hung high in the heavens. It gave the sky an eerie feeling, and a pale halo encircled the harbor above us. Behind us, the music from the Polar Bar was muffled, and I listened to the crackling hulls of the boats at anchor in the calm water.

"Some people say that crackling is the language of the boats talking," I said softly.

"Do you know what they're saying?" Trevor asked.

"They're saying, 'Frank Bama, you fool, you better not let her get away. Change your ways before it's too late.' "

Trevor took my hand, and I looked into her eyes again— without having to be asked. "All I'm asking you to do," she said gently, "is to put as much time and effort into us and our relationship as you do into your airplane. If we can survive the craziness that seems to keep falling on us like some kind of test, then I'm willing to try."

"Trevor, I love you." I leaned closer and kissed her. She responded with a slow caress of her lips on mine, and I wrapped my arms around her. I brushed her ear with my mouth and slowly ran my fingers through her curls. "You feel a lot better than my airplane."

• • •

"So tell me what else the boats are saying, Captain," Trevor said, looking up at the drifting clouds.

"They're saying that life is a series of voyages—some good and some bad—and you can't make more than one at a time. All the past voyages are just that, and new voyages are mysterious and exciting."

"Frank," she said slowly, "this whole escapade of looking for Joe has left me even more confused about him. Desdemona is wonderful, but I think she might have a few loose screws. The weirdest things have been happening, and I don't know whether to believe them or not. She says Colonel Cairo has the answer. What answer? I don't even know the question anymore. I'm tired. I tried my best. I'm ready to call it quits. I don't want to be dropped in the ocean again. I want to go with you."

"It's very cold where I'm headed," I said.

"I'm ready to see the changing seasons. I've been in the sun too long."

Trevor rested her head back on my shoulder. We danced along the edge of the harbor under the crescent moon to the offbeat echo of the drums and a strange but familiar-sounding guitar. Then the drums stopped, and there was only the guitar music.

I heard Trevor sigh. "My God," she said, "I haven't heard that song in ages. It sounds so much like Joe." As the wail of the guitar sailed out over the water, Trevor took my hand, and we kissed again. I could feel her tears, and I wiped them away.

"It's going to be okay," I said softly. Slowly we walked back to the music.

We showed our hand stamps to the bouncer at the door and felt the wave of heat as we went back into the Polar Bar, following the strains of the guitar.

I stopped in my tracks at the edge of the stage.

"Frank, what's wrong?"

My hands were by my side, and my fists were clenched. I couldn't believe what I was seeing.

"Frank?" Trevor looked at me and then turned to the stage. There stood Joe Merchant, with a Stratocaster guitar hanging from his shoulder, playing an electrifying rendition of the classical instrumental break of his signature song, "Little Boy Gone."

"That's my brother!" Trevor screamed. "That's my brother!" She clutched my arm and gasped. "What's wrong with his *eyes?*"

It was Joe Merchant all right, but on his closed eyelids I saw the frightening tattoos—the same tattooed eyeballs that belonged to the man who had hijacked my plane. Joe Merchant was Charlie Fabian.

Commander's Moon

62

Qué Pasa?

Rudy Breno had stopped drumming when the first chords of "Little Boy Gone" had rung out from the stage. He could not believe what he was seeing. At first he figured it was the worm in the bottom of the mescal bottle that Curly had fed him in the waterfall, but no—there on the stage of the Polar Bar stood the man he had been hunting all these years. He had come looking for the Jet Ski Killer, and instead he had stumbled upon the Hope diamond of yellow journalism.

"He's fucking alive! I'm famous!" he screamed as he fought his way through the crowd.

"Qué pasa?" Curly shouted and ran after him. She grabbed for his pants but lost her balance and fell forward, sending Rudy catapulting over a table, which collapsed under his weight.

Blanton Meyercord wrangled his way out from under the table and grabbed the man who had fallen on top of him by the shirt. "You stupid son of a bitch!" Blanton had his left hand full of rayon and his right fist cocked and ready to smack the guy when he suddenly let go.

"Wait! I know that voice," Rudy yelped. He had landed in

337

a bowl of guacamole, and when he wiped the avocado off, he saw that he was inches away from the Jet Ski Killer. Rudy's eyes locked on the fighter-plane tattoo on the back of the killer's hand, and he groaned.

From the stage came the sound of a huge crash. The crowd was going wild. Joe Merchant had launched the guitar, the amplifier, and himself through the window behind the stage.

"It's Joe Killer! It's the Jet Ski Merchant! It's Joe Merchant!" Rudy screamed.

Blanton finally freed himself from the weight of the table and crawled across the floor until he could stand up. He saw Trevor and Frank and bolted for them. Trevor stood there in shock, staring at the broken window.

63

Propeller Talk

"**T**hat fuckin' Rudy knows I'm here—I gotta move *now*, Frank!" Blanton yelled.

"I'll meet you at the airport!" I yelled back. Blanton melted into the crowd.

Rudy Breno appeared from nowhere and began yanking on Trevor's arm. "That's your brother, isn't it? Joe Merchant is alive, isn't he? What do you think?" He was two inches from Trevor's face, and she looked as if she were going to leap out of her skin.

"Hey, what's going on?" Rudy hollered. I had a good grip on his ear and was hauling him away from Trevor, and as soon as I found enough room to stretch my arm, I wound up and drove a blow to the side of his head that sent him flying back into the arms of the two girls who'd been hanging all over him. They caught Rudy as if he were a foul ball.

"Let's get out of here," I said and grabbed Trevor's arm.

"That was Joe, Frank. I saw him."

We pushed our way through the crowd over to the rear entrance, and as soon as we were out in the alley, a familiar voice called out, "Trevor! Frank!"

339

It was Desdemona. Trevor rushed to her arms like a scared child. "Did you see him? Tell me you saw him," Trevor pleaded.

"I saw him, honey."

"Frank," Trevor cried. "Don't leave!" But I was already on my way down the alley.

"I've gotta help Blanton get out of here," I called back to her. "I'll meet you guys back at the *Cosmic Muffin*. I promise. Wait for me."

• • •

I jumped into one of the local fishing boats and gave the starter rope a yank. The engine came alive, and I sped out of the harbor and steered by the faint light of the moon up the bayou to the airport dock. I kept my eyes peeled for signs of trouble, trying to make some sense of it all.

Joe Merchant and the four-eyed man were the same person, which meant that my girlfriend's brother was not only alive but had tried to kill me. What kind of nut case would behave like that and hijack a plane? And what was Colonel Cairo's role in all this? It was like having a multiple-system failure on a plane: engine out, instruments out, storm approaching. My ears were still ringing from the drums, and I thought about the three words that apply to an emergency in a plane: aviate, navigate, communicate.

Trevor was safe for now with Desdemona, but Blanton was in big trouble. It wouldn't take Rudy long to get the story out on the wire that Joe Merchant and the Jet Ski Killer had been spotted in Boomtown, and every goddamn newspaper and television station in the world would have a reporter here in hours.

I ran from the dock to the airport but stopped about half a mile from the hangar so I could slow my breathing by the time I got to the building. I carefully made my way to the fuel truck that was parked about a hundred yards from the Air Reality office. Suddenly I realized that I didn't have a weapon of any kind. I quickly searched the truck for something I could use, but the only thing I found was a half-empty case of oil.

The spotlights above the Air Reality office lit the night like flares, and I could see the two guards moving back and forth in front of the hangar. I could make out the silhouette of one of the Mallards sitting in the hangar with the nose pointed out toward the tarmac. A solitary figure darted from the fuel tanks to the side of the Air Reality office. Blanton's escape plan was a dangerous one, but with luck we could pull it off. I grabbed two cans of oil and set off in that direction.

Blanton was sitting down behind a trash can when I caught up with him. "Just two of them. Potter's plane is inside."

We watched the guards turn around and amble back in the direction of the office. They were the same guards who'd given me such a hard time when I'd come to the airport looking for a mechanic.

"You get to the Mallard and get going. I'll stay here and take care of these guys," I said.

"Here they come. Let's do it," Blanton whispered and took off down the side of the building and disappeared.

The two men were coming my way. I could see the glow of the cigarette in the taller man's mouth. They were talking quietly and laughing.

I peeled off my T-shirt and tied one of the oil cans inside it, leaving the tail of the shirt for a handle. I measured the distance from the door to where I was hiding behind the trash can and figured it was two steps to the doorway. The shorter man pulled a key from his pocket and opened the door and went inside. The taller man popped his head in the door and called to his friend. "Blanco," he said and muttered something in Spanish before he came back outside. Then he walked to the far side of the office and took a seat on the long pine bench.

My heart jumped as the radio came on and a barrage of horns and Spanish lyrics shattered the quiet night. In the distance I heard a propeller spin and watched the man on the bench. He was unaware of the noise, but it wouldn't be long. I had about two seconds until the Mallard's engine would begin to roar and would drown out the radio.

I clenched the knot on my shirt and wrapped the tail around my hand and took a deep breath. My eyes never left the man on the bench. As I took the first step out into the open, the engine in the hangar came to life in a series of coughs. The man was up and lifting his gun as my right foot hit the ground, and just as he turned to the office door, I saw his eyes open wide and his mouth drop open. Several broken teeth shone brightly under the airport lights.

The oil can hit the side of his head with a thud, and he dropped like a big bowling pin. I scooped up his AK-47 and sprinted to the side of the office. I glanced to the left and saw the plane taxiing out of the hangar, then heard the office door open.

"Juliano, que pasa?" The short man called Blanco stumbled as he came out the door and stopped in his tracks when he saw his friend lying on the pavement.

"This is what the fuck is happening, pal," I said and jammed the barrel of the AK-47 into his side. "Drop it." His rifle tumbled to the ground. I motioned for him to put his hands on top of his head, and I nudged him along to the hangar with the AK-47 pressed against the back of his neck.

When we got to the hangar, Blanton had started the second engine and had pulled Potter's plane out.

"Habla inglés?" I said to the guard, but he stood there with a defiant look on his face. "Habla inglés?" I repeated. Still no answer.

I dropped the rifle from his neck and shoved the butt into the soft roll of his belly, and he bent in two, gasping for breath. I slung the rifle on my shoulder and grabbed his arm and twisted it behind his back. "Okay, motherfucker, here's the program. You tell me who you work for and what's going on, or I'm gonna ram your ass headfirst into that propeller." I jerked on his arm until he screamed, and then I pushed him forward. I signaled for Blanton to rev the engine.

"No, no! Dios mío!"

"English!" I yelled above the prop noise.

"We are working for Colonel Cairo. He killed Monty Potter. He is leaving tonight when he has the scepter."

"What scepter?"

"The one on the crazy woman's boat."

64

Quail Talk

I didn't tell Blanton what the guard had told me about Colonel Cairo. He wouldn't have gone. He would have stayed to help and probably would have gotten caught or killed.

"I gotta get out to the island," I shouted. "Desdemona and Trevor are waiting there."

"Get out of here, Brillo. This place is too dangerous," Blanton yelled from the window. "I guess this is good-bye."

"I know where to find you." I swallowed hard.

We shook hands through the window, and Blanton saluted. Then he reached above his head for the throttles. I returned the salute and put my hands over my ears to deflect the engine noise and watched the Mallard move slowly toward the taxiway. The engines revved, and as it lifted off and turned south, the plane was lit by the pale reflection of the crescent moon.

It had all happened so fast it was hard to believe, and yet there went Blanton, flying off to sanctuary in the Venezuelan jungle. As I watched the plane disappear, for a moment I wished I were going with him—back to Father Ignacio, back to the cowboys, back to the monkeys and iguanas.

The guard called Blanco still lay on the hangar floor like a scared dog.

"I got things to do. Let's go," I told him.

"Senor, I sheet my pants," the guard whimpered.

"No problem. Over there." I pointed the rifle at the portable toilet just beyond the hangar door, and Blanco waddled over to it like a pregnant duck with his hands still on his head. I followed with the gun and stuffed his mouth with a rag. Then I sat him on the commode and tied his arms behind the water pipe. That would hold him until morning.

I closed the toilet door. One down. Blanton was safely on his way. Now I had to haul ass to Frenchman's Lagoon, find Trevor and Desdemona, and get the hell out of here. Cairo had killed Monty Potter, and Desdemona had some scepter he was after. I rounded the corner of the hangar and took off for the dock.

"Freeze, motherfucker. Drop the gun."

Blocking my path was the guard I had walloped with the oil can. Now he stood with a sawed-off shotgun aimed at my chest. "I am going to shoot you in the balls first just to watch you die."

The blood from the nasty gash in his head flowed into his left eye, and he wiped it with his sleeve. I could hear Blanco's muted screams of joy. I had almost made it. I thought about how Rudy Breno would describe my death.

"Before I shoot you in the balls, I will let you make your peace with God."

I couldn't remember all the words of the act of contrition, so I just made a fist, struck my heart, and whispered "Mea culpa, mea culpa." Before I could finish, I heard the roar of gunfire. I waited for the buckshot to make mincemeat of my privates.

I was on the deck, waiting for the pain to come. I grabbed my crotch. My balls were still there. So was my dick. When I looked up, the guard was falling forward. He hit the concrete with a thud. Then I saw the bullet holes in the walls of the toilet.

Joe Merchant appeared from around the corner of the building with a Beretta in his right hand. "Relax, Captain, we're on the same side now."

He cautiously walked to the toilet and kicked open the door. Blanco was slumped over on the commode. Joe lifted the dead man's head and examined the bullet hole in the middle of his forehead. He let Blanco's head drop back down, then put the pistol in his pants.

"If I were quail hunting, that would be called a double."

65

An Appointment with the Moon

They heard the drone of airplane engines in the night sk
"There goes the Jet Ski Killer," Desdemona said. She studie
the halo around the thin slice of moon. "There's some strang
magic at work here tonight. We'd best be careful."

Trevor sat in silence in the front of the dinghy for a lor
time, and then she finally spoke. "Where did he get tho
eyes?"

Desdemona steered the dinghy close to the shelter
Frenchman's Lagoon, and not a minute too soon. Clou
rolled in from behind the hills, and the wind started to blc
from the southwest. Whitecaps materialized on the usual
tranquil harbor, and lightning flashes shimmered on the
horizon. By the time Desdemona and Trevor reached the
goon, they were both soaked to the bone. They nestled t
dinghy alongside the *Cosmic Muffin* and then made their w
up the slippery ladder to the dock. Rain started to fall, slow
at first and then in sheets.

They walked along the dock toward the gangway with t
rain stinging their eyes, following Desdemona's big spotli;
to the wheelhouse.

"The figurehead is gone," Trevor said.

Desdemona moved the circular beam across the bow. The light illuminated only large raindrops blowing across the desk; the crystal scepter was indeed gone.

"Right you are," a voice answered from behind them. The lights went on in the main wheelhouse, and there stood Colonel Cairo with the scepter in his hand. Carlos and Flavio Ramos flanked their new employer, carefully aiming their machine guns at Trevor and Desdemona.

"Well, Miss Kane. It seems tenacity runs deep in your family. I hear you finally ran into your brother. Not a nice picture, was it? Those eyes—hideous, aren't they? I molded him into quite a killer, didn't I?"

"If he's so loyal to you, what are you doing with these bozos?"

The mocking tone of Cairo's voice turned to pure hate. "He is a dangerous man now, but not as dangerous as I am. You're right, Miss Kane. Your brother deserted me. Desertion is such a sickening word. Would you like to see what happens to traitors, Miss Kane? Show them, Carlos."

"Catch!" Carlos yelled, and he hurled something. Trevor screamed. At her feet lay the severed arm of Monty Potter.

"Monty Potter was my most trusted aide in Africa before he stole my secret and cost me my arm." Cairo laughed. "And now I have it back."

Cairo poked the chilly white flesh of the arm with the scepter. Then he pointed the scepter at Trevor. "It was your brother who took Monty's place after my accident. They all think they are smarter than I am, and this is their big mistake. It cost Potter his life, the same way it will cost your brother his life when I find him." Colonel Cairo checked his watch.

Trevor didn't dare say a word. She stood beside Desdemona in horrified silence.

"Your brother turned into an amazing soldier, better than the usual scum of the earth who show up for hunting season to do a little killing for money. Joe had a passion for the business, but I couldn't very well have some silly rock star running around the bush shooting people, could I? And besides, there was all that money." A hideous smile lit the Colonel's face. "I must say, you Kanes certainly are hard people to kill."

The Colonel twirled the scepter in his hand and paced back

and forth. A flash of lightning nearby made the lights of the wheelhouse flicker for a moment.

"He's mad," Desdemona whispered.

The Colonel gave her a wicked smile. "So you are the magic woman Monty told me about. Apparently you never saw me in your cards, did you?" The Colonel reached out and touched Desdemona with the scepter. "He must have really wanted to fuck you to give you such a valuable piece of merchandise. You'll never know how close you really were to making this ship fly."

• • •

Colone Cairo leaned against the chart table and chewed with his eyes closed. "Mmmmmmm, this is the best raisin bread I've ever tasted."

The Ramos brothers were busy knotting the loose ends of the Dacron rope that now tied Trevor and Desdemona back-to-back in a tight bundle.

"Forgive the inexperience of my friends. They're new on the job. Monty Potter got word to certain authorities that I was in the area, and some of my regular crew decided to take a vacation. Good help is hard to find these days." Trevor's face was red and puffy. Fear and anger raged in her green eyes.

Cairo finished the raisin bread, licked his fingers, and again looked at his watch. "Now I thought I would tell you girls a little bedtime story, and then I must be going. In a few hours, there will be a total solar eclipse, and with this scepter and the light of the eclipse, I will begin my new life. You see, your Healing Hole is not some mere Indian superstition. Many civilizations, separated widely by history and geography, came to understand that the earth's natural magnetic and electrical energy flows closer to the surface at certain places than at others. These are the places where past civilizations built their pyramids, temples, and altars. These are the places where ancient space travelers aimed their explorations."

The Colonel held the scepter up to the light. "This scepter is connected to the secret of the universe. I felt its power once in Africa when it save my life. That scepter disappeared when Monty Potter betrayed me. Isn't it fitting that he should be the one who led me to the sister scepter on this side of the world? Yes, there were two. It took years to discover its existence, and now I have it. I will use the energy of the crystal to cook up a new arm for myself—and my new life. With your brother's money, Miss Kane, I will finally have the wealth and power a man of my importance deserves. Sorry ladies, but it's time to go. Have a lovely cruise."

Cairo glanced at his watch once more and nodded to Flavio Ramos, who started the engine.

"I must leave you now, for I have an appointment with the moon."

66

Who Are You?

"No hard feelings, huh?" Joe Merchant said. He was wrapped in a yellow foul-weather jacket and stood holding on to the lines that secured the fuel bladders in place. We were plowing through five-foot seas in the pouring rain, loaded with three hundred gallons of avgas—not exactly what I would call pleasure boating. "So what's my sister doing down here?"

"Looking for you."

A smile came across his face. "Sweet Trevor. She always did worry about me. I'm afraid I must be a disappointment to her. I don't want her to see me like this."

"Well, I'm going to let you tell her that," I said.

He turned and glared at me. "No, you don't understand. I mean it—I don't want her to see me like this."

It occurred to me that Joe Merchant might be able to switch back into the four-eyed maniac at any time, so I decided not to push him about Trevor.

I could barely make out the shoreline of Little Lorraine Island when lightning flashed and revealed a line of coconut palms twisting and swaying in the distance.

"Can you tell me something?" I asked.

"I can tell you as much as I can remember." The tone of his response was clear and honest. Again, his calm seemed strange, coming from a man who had left a trail of corpses through the Caribbean and had tried to send me tumbling out of the sky to my death.

"Am I talking to Joe Merchant or the other guy?" I asked.

He pulled something from his pocket and handed it to me, covering it with the sleeve of his jacket so it wouldn't get wet. It was an old photograph of a young military cadet standing under a gazebo with a beautiful young girl beside him. When I looked closer, I recognized Trevor.

"Give that to my sister when you see her," he said and pushed it into my pocket.

"What about you? She's come a long way to find you."

"I wish she hadn't," he said. A rogue wave crashed over the boat and covered us both with water. I tried to steer the out-of-balance skiff, and Joe held on to the fuel bladders. "Charlie Fabian is the other guy. Hey, I was sick of being who I was. A change didn't seem wrong to me. I had friends who found Jesus or were walking around airports draped in bed linens begging for quarters. Becoming a mercenary was no different to me."

"Yeah, but Hare Krishnas don't get paid to kill people."

"There's no right to life on this planet. It's survival of the fittest, pure and simple. Spend a little time in Africa, and you'll understand. I don't make any excuses. I'm the one who followed Cairo. But I was more loyal to Colonel Cairo than Monty Potter was. It's sort of strange that his fixation for revenge against Potter is what drove the wedge between us."

"What do you mean?"

"He was going to try to kill me. I could tell. And then the other day, I heard the music again. It came out of nowhere. A tape on the floor of an airplane. But I could *feel* it again. I guess it woke up Joe Merchant. Who knows? I'm not God."

"But can you become Charlie Fabian again?"

He was silent for a moment and tapped his fingers on the fuel cell. "I don't know. I buried my past in the cemetery, but I don't know if I can just be Joe." He turned and looked out over the water. "I can't see my sister. I want her to think of me as the boy in that photo."

"Do you have any ideas about what we should do if we run into Cairo again?" I asked.

"Don't worry about the Colonel," Joe said flatly.

"From what I've heard and seen, I think we ought to worry a lot about the Colonel."

"I have plans for him. Wait and see. You just get Trevor safely out of here."

Thunder rumbled above my head, and a lightning flash revealed the entrance to the lagoon. The boat was being pushed sideways by the following sea, and I grabbed the engine with both hands to hold my course. The rain started to fall even more heavily, and when I turned to look at the height of the waves, I heard a splash.

"I'll be leaving now," Joe called to me. I could barely make out a splotch of yellow off the stern of the boat.

"Come back!" I yelled. "What do I tell Trevor?"

"Tell her it was all a dream."

• • •

I stood there for a moment, hoping he would change his mind and come back, but of course he didn't.

Joe Merchant was a showman. He had the moves of a veteran thespian with a knack for the grandest entrances and exits. Yet from what I could tell, he seemed more comfortable watching from the wings. Now—lacking a proper backstage door for this performance—he faded into the obscurity of the stormy night.

I knew it would be futile to try to find him again; he was going after Cairo in his own way. Where he would appear again was anybody's guess.

I was brought back to the work at hand by another thunderclap and the sound of water breaking against nearby rocks. I had to get the tipsy boat through the cut and into the safety of the lagoon. The swells began to subside, and I eased the power on the outboard. Another flash of lightning illuminated the dock, and a sick feeling came over me. The *Cosmic Muffin* was gone.

67

Out of the Picture

Flavio, the youngest of the Ramos brothers, had not bargained for such a rough ride. He tried to steer the ship but could not keep the bow into the wind. Trying to stabilize the spinning compass had completely disoriented him.

"Foking Carlos," he said aloud. The Colonel had given him the distance and bearing to the spot where he wanted the *Cosmic Muffin* scuttled. It had all sounded so easy. His instructions were to shoot the women, open the seacocks, and return to Boomtown in the rubber Avon that now bounced behind the *Cosmic Muffin* as she twisted, rolled, and turned in the stormy sea like a giant bottle. The storm had intensified with almost no warning, and the lumpy seas had turned him greener than an Irish bar on St. Patrick's Day.

Flavio was no kamikaze sworn to fulfill the destiny of Colonel Cairo. He was a mediocre shortstop who had gotten stopped by Miami customs with twelve rubbers full of cocaine shoved up his ass and had gone to jail, where they moved him to outfield on the prison softball team. The highlight of his life up to this point had been the night he hit a home run, and the Dominican prisoners beat the Cuban prisoners nine to eight and caused the worst prison riot in Florida history.

He was technically an "island boy," having grown up on the shores of the Caribbean Sea in a ghetto of Santo Domingo, but Flavio was terrified of the ocean. Carlos hadn't mentioned Flavio's phobia to the Colonel when Cairo had asked if he could handle the job. "Flavio ees an expert sailor, Colonel."

Flavio had said nothing, fearing the wrath of his older brother, who had bullied him with physical abuse as far back as he could remember. Carlos had told him it was time to get over his silly fears. Now Flavio could give a shit about his overbearing brother, the one-armed Colonel, or the fucking scepter. He cursed them all as he sprayed a puke slick across the deck.

Trevor and Desdemona were still tied back-to-back, wedged into the corner of the cabin. Flavio had removed their gags, hoping they could help him in his hour of need. "Keep the bow pointed into the wind, or she won't make it," Desdemona called to him.

"Did you hear that?" Trevor asked Desdemona.

"Hear what?"

"The Generators," she whispered.

"I don't hear anything. Are you sure?"

"Positive," Trevor said. "Can't you hear them?"

"No," Desdemona said, "but do what they say."

Trevor watched as the macho man was reduced to a frightened child, and she listened to the voices. They told her to create a mental image of a small screen in front of her eyes. Her thoughts were suddenly filled with a vision of the scene in *Twenty Thousand Leagues under the Sea* when Kirk Douglas was caught in the terrible storm, fighting the giant squid. She traded Flavio for Kirk Douglas in her vision, and she traded the giant squid for the steering wheel.

Trevor watched Flavio's eyes. They provided a window into the panic that wracked his mind. Trevor turned up the amperage of her vision.

As soon as she did, the first big wave knocked the *Cosmic Muffin* sideways, shattering the portholes on the starboard side. Water poured in through the openings. Trevor and Desdemona were soaked, but they couldn't move.

Flavio was knocked against the bulkhead, and the gun he was supposed to use to execute his two prisoners slid across the floor. He scrambled to his feet and reached above his head for the radio. "Dees is Flavio, dees is Flavio. We are sinking, we are sinking. Where are da foking life jackets?"

"Below the chart drawer," Desdemona shouted.

"What is a foking sharp wore? I don' understand."

Flavio Ramos began tearing open every locker in the cabin, screaming curses.

"Untie me, you asshole, and I'll get one for you," Desdemona yelled.

Flavio loosened the ties, and another huge wave hit.

"Oh my God, we're flying! We're flying!" Desdemona screamed. She felt the boat lift. It tilted forward and hung in the dark, suspended in a freeze-frame of bliss. Then all hell broke loose.

The flight of the *Cosmic Muffin* lasted approximately three seconds, and then she pitched almost end over end into the trough of the gigantic wave. Flavio still had the microphone in his hand when he was launched like a clay pigeon through the windshield. The roar of the wind and water were indistinguishable. Trevor and Desdemona were thrown around the cabin like electrons circling the nucleus of an atom. Trevor was flung into the base of the captain's chair and managed to get a grip around the shaft.

Desdemona was washed to the open door, but she somehow grabbed hold of Trevor's leg. Water poured into the wheelhouse, and the whole boat shook like Jell-O as the *Cosmic Muffin* rammed into the jagged rocks.

Trevor's head hit the bulkhead, but she found the deck with her feet. The water was up to her waist. The voices of the Generators had been replaced by a steady ringing in her ears. She felt her shoulders, arms, and feet to see if anything was missing. She was numb all over but came to the conclusion she was okay.

"You alright?" she yelled to Desdemona.

Desdemona's tarot cards were floating in the debris. She swam through them and gathered two life jackets, a first aid kit, and a flare gun. The storm had transformed her home into a trash compactor. Her life floated before her in a stew: tarot cards, cookbooks, clothing, her log book. The engine room was flooded, and the crystal engine would never see the sky; it was now all history. She was just hanging on for dear life.

"I think I've got all my parts. Here, put this on. Jesus

Christ, what did the voices tell you to do?" She tossed a life preserver to Trevor.

"I thought Flavio out of the picture."

"Well, you did a hell of a job."

The boat lurched again and was driven farther up on the rocks. The *Cosmic Muffin* had split in two and was coming apart at the seams. There was nothing aft of the wheelhouse. Trevor heard the continuous crunch as the reef ate away at the rocket ship. The bulkheads expanded and contracted like the rib cage of a wounded animal gasping for breath.

"Oh, Desdemona!" Trevor cried. "Your rocket ship!"

She swam to the passageway and looked out into the storm. The sun was beginning to rise, and there was no horizon, just a gray gloom of air and sea that had been fused together by the storm. Everything seemed enveloped in a thick smoke.

The boat lurched again, and Trevor lost her grip on the rail.

"She's not going to hold together much longer," she called to Desdemona.

68

Mermaids in the Night

The *Cosmic Muffin* was gone, and the dock was deserted. The first parallel rays of light appeared in the east and revealed a stormy panorama that spread out over the ocean. The wind made a pennant of my shirt, and I guessed the gusts across the beach to be about thirty knots. It had the Australian pines swaying like a boxer staggering in the ring.

I was hoping that Toosay would be able to tell me where Trevor and Desdemona had gone. I was about to go look for him when I heard him yelling to me as he ran down the path to the plane.

"Cap'n, Cap'n, da boat is gone, da boat is gone."

"I saw, Toosay. Where did they go?"

"I don' know, Cap'n. Deed she go to space wifout me?"

"Toosay, if you don't know where they went, we're in big trouble. If the Colonel's out there, we don't have much time."

I knew I was probably wanted in Boomtown, and to fly now was foolish, but I didn't have any choice. First we would have to deal with the missing float. Luckily, when I'd called Billy Cruiser, he'd given me a solution so simple I'd had to laugh.

Toosay knew these waters like the back of his hand, and that would make things easier. I could search the ocean by the book, but Toosay would know the pages. The ocean is not one big flat piece of water. It is a moving puzzle with hiding places above and below the crests of the waves. Channels and eddies spread like arteries, carrying currents near and far—always concealed from the casual glance of someone on shore.

"I never been in a aeroplane befo', Cap'n. You a good pilot?"

"I'm a good pilot, yes, but I've got a serious problem with my plane. We have a repair to do before we can go anywhere."

"I can help you, Cap'n. Jus' tell me what to do."

Billy Cruiser had told me that the trick was to fill the good float with water to counterbalance the missing weight on the left side where the other float had been. Toosay and I took this a step further and rigged a cork in the drain hole in the bottom of the float. Working quickly, we attached the cork to a piece of monofilament fishing line that could be pulled out once we were airborne. This would empty the float.

When we were finished, Toosay tossed the end of the line through the canopy window on the copilot's side, and I helped him up the steps. "You're the copilot and navigator. Now where would you take a boat that big to blow it up or sink it—a place where no one would find it?"

"Da Troat," he said without hesitation. "But in dis wedder—" He scratched his head. "I would not take da *Muffin* out in dis wedder. She no oceangoing boat, she a spaceship."

I hauled Toosay in, whistled for Hoagy, and then pulled my seat belt tight. This was going to be an interesting takeoff.

I showed the chart to Toosay. He picked out a spot that looked to be about fifteen miles from Little Lorraine, where a deep trench in the ocean floor seemed to stretch like a tongue in the direction of the reefs and shallows of the Haitian coast.

"Dis be Bone in da Troat," he said, pointing at the chart. "She be da shy little sister of da Sleeping Beauties, same as the shy sister in da sky. She hide just beneaf da waves except when da storms call her to da surface. She may be dere, and den again, she may not. She be a most dangerous little girl and has scattered many a bone on deez beaches."

"Hold on Toosay." I put the headphones on him and talked through the intercom, and he was slightly startled when he heard my amplified voice. "Can you hear me?"

"I hear you fine," Toosay said, awestruck.

The wind blasted the pink sand into a blur across the beach. The shore break had eroded a good portion of the strip I'd originally landed on, and the grade of what was left was too steep for the float to clear the ground. There was only one way to the air. I had about a thousand feet of choppy water between me and the reef. With the wind blowing as hard as it was, I figured I could get airborne by then. If it stopped blowing, or the right engine faltered, my ass was grass, but there was no other way.

"Toosay, when I yell 'gear,' you turn that crank between the seats as fast as you fuckin' can. We have to get the landing gear up quickly. Comprende?"

"Si."

I did my run-up and let the number two engine stay at high RPMs about twice as long as was normal. I checked the mags, lowered the flaps, made sure my controls were freed, and moved her toward the beach. The *Hemisphere Dancer* rolled down the beach and splashed into the water like a two-year-old.

A wave came over the windshield and dropped a sheet of foam and sand on top of us. "Gear!" I yelled, and Toosay went to work on the handle. I felt the hull move with the water, and I put the throttles to the firewall and yanked back on the yoke.

The *Hemisphere Dancer* seemed to know this was it. She came up on the step, and I could see the brown blur of the reef below the clear water as we skimmed over it. I pulled back on the yoke even further. Normally I would have just let her fly off the water by herself, but today, in the eerie gray light of dawn, I jerked her into the air and hoped she would stay there. We were airborne for a moment, and suddenly the stall horn sounded.

I lowered the nose to try to pick up some speed, but the weight of the water in the float forced me back to the surface.

"Pull the line," I said.

Toosay gave the fishing line several yanks, and the cork finally popped free. The water poured out the drain hole.

"Stay with me girl," I said, patting the yoke. We hit and bounced once a hundred feet from the razor-sharp protrusions of the reef, and I pulled her up, trying to keep the unbalanced wings level. The airspeed held firm, and the vertical speed indicator showed a climb of two hundred feet per minute. We rose steadily.

"Alright!" I yelled.

"Alright!" Toosay echoed.

When the float finally emptied completely, I let go of the yoke and stretched my fingers. A low layer of scud hung out over the water about a thousand feet. Visibility was squat. The ocean had been whipped into a fury, and a salt haze added to the already bad visibility. I flew through the rain cloud directly in front of me, and raindrops rattled against the skin of the plane, washing the saltwater off and rinsing my windshield. We popped out on the other side, and I pulled the throttles and prop levers back. Toosay was staring out his window at the end of the wing.

"It worked," he said with a big grin on his face. I looked again at the chart and plotted a course to the Throat.

"Now, let's go find those mermaids, Toosay."

69

Bones on the Beach

The sea behaved like a mad child. Waves swirled and foamed and gathered into heaps. The air through which we flew participated happily in the mischief, and the wind came at us from every direction. The airspeed indicator fluctuated like an oil-pressure gauge as it felt the head winds and tail winds come and go. The only thing that distinguished the sea from the sky was the whitecaps, and I used them as my reference.

The sky had already taken on a peculiar shape and feel with the approaching eclipse, and visibility would be even further reduced when the moon crossed the path of the sun. We were running out of time. We worked our way through the small cays and sand spits that peppered the shallow waters between the islands, heading for Petite Place and the Healing Hole where Toosay would be able to get his bearings. He pointed with his finger, and I turned in that direction, picking up a heading from the compass.

"Where are we going?" I asked.

Toosay pointed his finger back to the north. "Da Troat be le mos' wicked place, Cap'n," he began. Then he suddenly

stopped talking and looked straight ahead. "I'll be damn—
dere she lay."

I gazed through the windshield but could see nothing, then
caught a flash of spray where the sea slapped at something in
the distance.

"Jesus, Mary, and Joseph," Toosay said and sighed.

I looked out his side of the plane just in time to see the
stern of the *Cosmic Muffin*. It looked like the heel of a loaf
of bread. The hull was facing skyward, revealing the naked
blades of the propeller and broken rudder stem. I followed the
line of wreckage toward Bone in the Throat and slowed to
minimum control speed. I circled the jagged peak of rock that
looked like a rusty old hubcap filled with dents and tried to
pick up the wreckage again.

"All ironstone," Toosay said. "Will cut you to pieces in a
second."

A flock of sea gulls had gathered on the peak. They exchanged puzzled glances as if trying to communicate to each
other their surprise at finding an island that hadn't been there
the day before. My heart sank. The outstretched arms and
legs of a body bobbed like a cork in the angry sea below.

Don't
Touch
That Dial

70

The Snakes Are Talking

The green mamba was coiled up in the corner of the glass cage. It lifted its head slightly and methodically worked its forked tongue in and out of its lethal mouth, responding to the thump of Colonel Cairo's finger against the glass.

"Today is your big day, Afro." Colonel Cairo drew heavily on the Monte Cristo and slowly blew the smoke out. The cigar smoke was the color of the sky.

The *Nomad* was tucked back into a false channel that led to the heart of the Sleeping Beauties and was out of the teeth of the storm. Cairo watched the tops of the trees being whipped by the wind. He looked at his watch and calculated the time until the solar eclipse would begin. It seemed that all the scattered paths of his life were finally converging. On Cairo's desk lay the scepter, the urn, the old book with Vickman's notes, and all of his own observations, theories, and geometric calculations. It seemed so simple now. He was waiting for the moon to cross the sun, which would begin the cycle to the serpent.

Cairo thought for a moment of the old witch doctor who had told him of his vision—a vision of a black king far to the

west who also had the power. After years of searching, the
Colonel had stumbled upon the book in Léopoldville that had
unlocked the secret and had led him to Vickman. Vickman, in
turn, had led him to Little Elmo and Monty Potter.

The Joe Merchant fortune was almost his. Hackney had
forged new documents to prove that Joe had signed away all
his rights to the money in Africa, and his sister was now at
the bottom of the sea, once and for all. Joe Merchant was
locked away in the unstable creation known as Charlie Fabian, and Cairo intended to track him down, just for sport,
once he had his arm back. The way Monty Potter had died
would be a nun's prayer compared to what he had in mind for
Joe Merchant.

The thought of being whole again brought tears to his eyes.
He picked up the scepter, closed his eyes, and took himself
back to the source of this moment, back to the day in the jungle.

He had been hired to lead a revolt against the government
of the kingdom of Kali. He saw the Cobra helicopter that had
his men pinned down tight while the government troops were
steadily coming at them. Monty Potter was supposed to rein-
force him, but he never showed up. The guns from the aerial
artillery platform were tearing his men to shreds. That is
when it happened.

Cairo saw himself stride out of the jungle and stand in the
clearing, taunting the pilot of the Cobra. The gunship turned
in the sky and came for him. The side-mounted machine guns
were blazing and kicking up the dirt all around him as the pilot focused on the range. He flinched, remembering when the
two bullets pierced his left leg, but he had balanced himself
and had stayed focused, waiting until the chopper came into
range. He opened up his automatic pistol and watched the
windscreen shatter and the blood fly. The pilot slumped over
the controls. Then came the horrible realization that the crip-
pled chopper was going to fall on him.

Cairo felt the explosion and saw the tail rotor come spinning out of the flames like a giant boomerang. He had never
forgotten the dull thud of impact that knocked him into the
trees. He was on fire and rolled around in the dirt like a
wounded animal trying to put out the flames. Death hovered
over him. Then the cave came into view.

A small man in a strange mask bent over him, and he
could see the scepter and the moon eclipsing the sun. The old

man held a large snake, which he passed above Cairo, and the energy from the crystal entered the Colonel's body. His muscles quivered. Patterns of light reflected on his torn shoulder. The witch doctor put his hands into each of the reflections and prayed to the stars in the heavens. The reflections were those of the Pleiades. Then, with just the edge of his hand, the witch doctor had cut away the mush that was his arm and had molded the shoulder like clay.

There was a knock at the door.

"Yes?"

"Colonel, the boat is ready to take you ashore."

"Very well."

The Colonel opened the door where Rolf stood at attention. He handed Rolf a piece of paper. "Plot this course, will you? We'll be leaving for Panama City as soon as our work here is finished. Mr. Primstone made arrangements for us there."

"But this storm, Colonel—," Rolf protested.

"Storm? I don't see any storm. It's a beautiful day. Now help me with my jacket."

As Rolf maneuvered the jacket around the Colonel's shoulders and stuffed the empty sleeve into the pocket, Cairo smiled at the thought of seeing the sleeve filled when he returned. Rolf would react with astonishment when he saw the Colonel's new arm.

"God, how I love surprises," Cairo said.

"Yes, sir."

71

Back to the Drawing Board

A huge object tumbled in Trevor's direction, and she could not get out of the way as it crashed down on her. She expected to feel her flesh tear and was shocked when the giant object bounced off her without leaving a scratch. It was the rubber dinghy.

She grabbed the line that lay alongside the dinghy and swam for the rubber boat. She pulled herself in, grabbed the life rail, and pushed the bow around so she could work her way back to where Desdemona stood in the companionway.

When Desdemona jumped for the dinghy, she landed on the pontoon and almost capsized it. At that moment the *Cosmic Muffin* began to turn on her side. Desdemona found some kind of support under her and pushed herself the rest of the way into the dinghy. Trevor lowered the motor and gave it a yank, but it wouldn't start. She pulled again, but no dice. The wind was pushing them perilously close to the jagged ironstone rocks of Bone in the Throat.

"There's only one thing to do," Trevor said and fought her way on hands and knees to the bow of the dinghy. She untied her flowered halter top, arched her back, and pointed her breasts at the rocks. Cold rain hit her nipples, and she could hear crashing waters dead ahead. Desdemona watched in amazement as Trevor closed her eyes and turned herself into a human figurehead. She shouted at the rocks:

> *"Sirens rule the stormy seas,*
> *And Triton's madness holds no slaves—*
> *Steer now for the Pleiades,*
> *And bare your bosom to the waves."*

Instantly the wind fell to a whisper around Bone in the Throat, as if it had been sucked away. Trevor opened her eyes and saw a bright light above her head.

"What the hell is that?" Desdemona cried out.

At first Trevor thought it was a star, but it moved along with them, staying directly overhead. Bone in the Throat had disappeared below the surface, and the dinghy floated over the spot that had threatened them like an armed bandit seconds before.

Desdemona was laughing uncontrollably. "I think you just flashed a spaceship." Trevor started to laugh, too.

"Show us your tits, show us your tits," Desdemona said mockingly, and Trevor pointed her breasts to the sky and shook them like a topless dancer. "Wait—did you hear that? I think somebody's out there. I heard a splash."

Trevor quickly pulled the halter top back up. "Who's there?" she called out.

"I'll be damned," Desdemona said. "Albion, is that you?"

"Who are you talking to?" Trevor asked, looking but finding nothing but the waves.

"It's the talking dolphin I told you about. Look—over there."

"I don't see anything. Desdemona, are you feeling okay?"

"I'm fine. But what the hell is that?" Desdemona pointed to a glowing light above the dinghy.

"It's a star car," the dolphin told her.

"What's that?"

"It's a single-person craft generally used by tourists and explorers for traveling between planets. That's your Generator."

"Desdemona, who are you speaking to?" Trevor asked impatiently. "I don't see any talking fish."

"Dolphin," Desdemona and Albion said at the same time.

A high-pitched wave of feedback cut through the night, and a deep, mechanical voice bellowed from the star car, "Is this thing on?"

"Oh my God," Trevor said. "Did you hear that?"

"I guess we're not in Kansas anymore, Toto."

The voice made a rumbling sound, and then it said, "Causes and effects will soon be in their proper universal sequence again. You have fulfilled your Mayan destiny, but you Earth people are very unpredictable. It's been fun. Time to run."

The ship vanished.

The women sat in silence for a moment. There was no way in heaven or on earth for Trevor to express the disbelief she was feeling. After a while, she caught her breath and spoke. "That was a goddamn real live UFO. I can't believe it. Desdemona, why are you acting so calm? That's life from another planet up there. We're witnesses."

"It's no big deal."

"You consider a UFO no big deal?"

"It makes life exciting, doesn't it?" Desdemona patted Trevor on the knee and chuckled. "Anyway, it's better left alone. If you try to tell somebody about what just happened, they'll lock you up, or you'll wind up on the cover of the *National Lighthouse.*"

Trevor stared up at the empty sky. She was quiet for a long time, and then she spoke softly. "But what do you think it means?"

"Let's ask Albion." As soon as the words left her mouth, Desdemona knew that Albion was gone, too. The ocean was silent.

"He's gone, isn't he? And now I'll never get to see him," Trevor said, disappointed.

"Come on, fair maiden who calmed the raging seas with your breasts. We aren't out of this yet."

A single ray of light fought its way through the darkness and hit the surface of the water. Low clouds hung above the ocean, and slivers of lightning scattered through the sky as the storm moved on toward the Healing Hole.

On the horizon, the unmistakable red and green running lights of a ship were clearly in view. Desdemona lit one of the flares and sent the orange streak skyward. They looked back at the twisted and torn remains of the rocket ship.

"Well, she flew," Desdemona said, sighing.

"She flew," Trevor repeated.

"I guess it's back to the drawing board."

Half an hour later, the sky was clearing, and Trevor and Desdemona climbed the gangway of the *La Brisa*. They were welcomed aboard by the worst rendition ever of "Let the Sunshine In," played by Fernando Orlando and the Cane Thrashers to the applause of three hundred blue-haired ladies all wearing silver reflector eclipse-proof sunglasses.

"I guess they got more than they bargained for," Desdemona said as she climbed the ladder that led to the promenade deck.

Trevor looked up a the three hundred pairs of sunglasses looking down at her. "Yeah, and who are the *real* aliens?"

72

So You Want to Play Pirate?

"There is a magician in the sky this morning, gentlemen, playing tricks on the inhabitants of planet earth. But the real magic is about to happen here."

Colonel Cairo waited until the bow of the boat was grounded on the pink sand before he stepped out. He felt like an early conquistador stepping onto the beach of a new world for the first time. When he returned from this jungle, he would be perfect again, and he would be rich, very rich. Hackney Primstone III was waiting in Panama with the papers that would clear the way for Cairo to get his hands on all of Joe Merchant's money. Even the Colonel was astonished at the amount. According to Hackney, more than fifteen million dollars was locked away in Switzerland, ready to be transferred to the phony hospital corporation in Africa. Once it was there, the Colonel could do whatever he wanted with it.

Hackney had brought up his cut again. The colonel thought it was nice to have money, but it would be awful to think about it 365 days a year. Hackney would never have enough. The Colonel was doing him a favor. Hackney Primstone was already an accident looking for a place to happen, and Pan-

ama was a dangerous country for a gringo. The Colonel had
seen to that.

The morning storm had passed, and the day was now equa-
torially hot and humid, with the usual pandemonium caused
by the menagerie of crickets, tree frogs, and birds mixed with
the sound of the wind whistling through the palm trees. The
Colonel was already covered in sweat. He glanced at the sun.
It was amazingly bright and burned its way through the
clouds overhead that were unsuccessfully trying to hide it. He
had trekked thousands of miles in jungles in sweltering heat,
but he had never felt an energy like that he felt today. The
Colonel marched rapidly through the jungle, slicing away at
the mangroves and prickly Spanish bayonets with a machete.
Carlos and Rolf wrestled with the mahogany chest and followed behind.

They came to the Healing Hole and rested for a few minutes.
Carlos circled the pond, poking his rifle into the mangroves and
checking the trees overhead. Then he squatted down to scoop
up a drink.

"Do not touch that water!" the Colonel ordered.

Cairo instructed them to carry the chest to the stone slab
on the ledge above the Healing Hole. It was a difficult as-
cent up the narrow face of the cliff, but the men made it, and
now they lay exhausted at the edge of the water. Cairo
walked slowly up the steps and stood over the slab and
called down to them.

"Your work is through here. Wait for me at the boat. Do
not look directly at the sun unless you want to go blind. If
anything goes wrong, I will fire one shot. Other than that,
stay at the boat. Is that clear?"

"Yes, sir," Rolf snapped.

"Si, Colonel," Carlos chimed in.

Cairo waited for the men to disappear into the jungle, and
then he opened the chest. The snake lay in a canvas sack atop
his necessary accoutrements. He opened his notes and studied
them until he noticed a definite change in the level of sunlight. He placed an ancient goatskin on the slab and peered at
the hieroglyphics painted on the hide, then rested the urn of
ashes on top of it. He removed a long, shiny knife with a
carved rhino-horn handle from its sheath and placed it on the
stone. Last, he picked up the scepter and laid it perpendicular
to the knife blade—this formed a cross. He picked up the

book and turned to his notes of that day. "This is the way it happened, Afro."

The Colonel began to read aloud from his journal:

After the accident, everything went black. I woke up some time later in a hut, and the old man was there. He thanked me for trying to rid his country of the evil men in power, and told me the legend that had been handed down through generations from the first witch doctor, his great-grandfather Kalalui Kali.

They knew somebody had come from the Pleiades a long time ago and had given them the power of the heavens. The crystal was a powerful fragment left from an ancient underwater civilization, he told me, and when it was bathed in the light of a solar eclipse, it could heal the sick, mend broken bones, and make flesh out of mud. He showed me a small jar and said it was my present. I opened it and saw only an urn half filled with black ash. He told me it was the remains of my old arm, and he would use it to make me a new one—"when the sun ran from the moon and hid in its shadow and the serpent ruled the dark." The serpent must die, he said, for the transformation to take place. It was death creating life.

The next day, government soldiers attacked the village, and I was hidden in the elephant grass. Fire ants covered my body, biting me savagely, but I did not make a sound. I bit through my tongue trying to conceal my pain for fear of discovery. When the screams and gunfire stopped, I dug myself out. The village had been burned, and all the people had been massacred for helping us. I followed a trail of blood that led to the cave and found the old witch doctor's body. In his stiff hand, he still held the urn with the ashes. I searched the cave for the crystal, but it was gone. Then I found the old mahogany box hidden behind a rock in the far corner of the cave. There were holes in it like one would see on a cribbage board. I opened it, and a green mamba sprang at me—barely missing.

The Colonel tapped the canvas sack. "That was you, Afro."

Also inside the box was a weathered goatskin. I knew the hieroglyphics had to be very powerful and secret if they were guarded by the most deadly snake in the world. I carefully gathered up the snake and placed it back in the box

"I searched for years, Afro, all over Africa, for clues to the meaning of the goatskin. The wars, the campaigns were all orchestrated around rumors of the crystal. I wanted my arm back, and now I am going to have it."

Cairo closed the journal as darkness began to descend. Nothing flew in the ecliptical sky. Giant frigate birds reacted as if night were once again suddenly upon them, and they came in to roost and folded themselves into large black balls.

"It was not so difficult a riddle to solve, Afro. The answers to so many complicated questions are simple if you know where to look." He took a flask from his jacket pocket and unscrewed the cap. "To the tormented land of Africa, cradle of civilization that molded me into what I am and what I will become. To the black king Henri Christophe who discovered the magic of this place—held this very scepter—but was unable to unlock the mystery. To the space men who seem to leave us on this earth as pawns in a universal chess game. To Colonel Cairo, who today holds his destiny in check."

He gulped the contents of the flask and then carefully removed his shirt and stood in front of the slab like a priest about to say Mass.

The moon covered the sun, and the Colonel raised his head to the heavens. The sun had become a crescent as the moon crawled in front of it and now gave off a pink glow for a second. Cairo studied his notes.

He lifted the top from the urn and poured the ashes into a large ivory chalice. Opening the canvas bag, he dropped Afro onto the slab, grabbing the green mamba quickly behind the neck while it was still disoriented. He lopped a thin rope around Afro's neck and tightened it, then hung the snake from a nearby tree branch.

The Colonel began to chant in Swahili and jabbed the knife into his shoulder. Blood spilled down his ribs. In a split second, he slit the green mamba open from its head to its tail and let the blood of the writhing snake drip into the ivory cup. Holding the cup to the wound in his shoulder, he mixed his blood with that of the snake.

Cairo returned to the slab and turned the pages of his book. "It was written long ago that the serpent in the sky is the life-giving Caterpillar Jaguar—who climbs higher and higher into the heavens."

He reached for the scepter and held it up, focusing the light of the eclipse through the crystal and onto his arm. "It is a time of immortality, and I call upon the Sisters to show themselves, for they are the magicians of the sky. It is the passage of life from death and back again; it is loss of innocence, evaporation of youth, transformation, order, and renewal. I have solved the mystery. I have found the pieces of the puzzle. Now make me an arm!"

Cairo drank the mixture in the cup and walked to the tree where the limp snake now hung with its entrails touching the ground. Cairo cut the snake down and wrapped it around his shoulders like a mink. The corona of sunlight shimmered around the shadow of the moon as the total eclipse neared. It shone a pearly white, bounced off the sharp peaks of a distant lunar valley, and created a diamond ring surrounded by a chain of brilliant points. He waved the scepter at the sun, and the rays passed through the crystal and bathed him in white light. Cairo stood like a statue.

· · ·

"Colonel, you are a mess—just look at you."

The Colonel's eyes popped open with rage as he sought the sound of the voice in the near darkness. He stared down at the pitiful carcass of the snake still hanging on his shoulders, covered in blood. The taste in his mouth was of the deepest, foulest bile.

"That's the thing about antiques—you don't know if you have the real thing, or if somebody might have tricked you into buying a fake," Joe Merchant said. He stood at the foot of the bluff with a scepter exactly like the one the Colonel held in his hand.

"I found out about the scepter a long time before you carved up poor old Monty. That baby you're holding was custom-made at the flea market in Boomtown. Cost a hundred francs. I figured I'd better hang on to the real one in case you had some trick up your sleeve. And you did. Only thing is, you didn't plan on ever talking to Joe Merchant again, did you? You figured I'd be lost in Charlie Fabian forever, or at least long enough for you to kill my family and get all my money. Well, asshole, here I am. Surprise, surprise. I'm not your killer anymore. But I'm going to give you back the monster you created."

Colonel Cairo let out a roar that echoed off the bluffs that surrounded the Healing Hole and sent shock waves across the water. "You give me nothing, fiend! I take what I want!"

Cairo flung the phony scepter at Joe, and it splashed into the water. He drew the gun from his pants and began to fire.

The first several bullets kicked up the sand, but one found its mark and knocked Joe into the bushes. He felt around the wet spot on his shirt and put his finger in the hole in his chest. He grabbed a tree branch and pulled himself up with one hand. In the other he held the scepter.

Cairo stumbled as he climbed down and searched the jungle. "You are history, you bastard. I am going to tear you limb from limb. I want that scepter—now."

"I got nothing to lose, Colonel. How about you? Let's see if it works."

The sun was now completely covered, and the corona surrounded the moon. The sky seemed to dance. Joe Merchant closed his eyes, and through the tattoos on his eyelids he beheld a strange vision. There, in front of him, was the face of Steed Bonnet, along with Little Elmo, the divers from the treasure ship, and countless other victims he had killed for the Colonel. They were all looking at him with tattooed eyes and were singing a variation of the words he'd said to Little Elmo:

> *Pray then, ye learned ghost, do show*
> *Where can this brute Colonel Cairo go*
> *Whose life is one continuous evil*
> *Striving to cheat God, Man, and Devil.*

I'll be damned, Joe said to himself. Then he shouted at Colonel Cairo, "I give you back your evil, and I give you back your creation!"

Joe held the scepter against the totally eclipsed sun, and it lit up as if someone had thrown a transformer switch. A blue beam of light stretched in a laser from the sun to the crystal and then split. It hit both men directly in the face. Joe was knocked back to the ground and heard the splash when Cairo hit the water.

"Help me! I can't swim! Help me!"

Joe heard the old man's cries for help, but he couldn't have done anything if he wanted to. The last things he saw were the ghastly tattoos floating away from his eyelids, and then the lights went out. He felt the heat of the scepter in his hand, and it lifted him, sightless, to his feet and pulled him into the jungle and toward the sea.

Carlos and Rolf came rushing into the clearing. They dove into the water and pulled the Colonel to the shore. Rolf turned him on his stomach and began artificial respiration. After a few minutes, the Colonel belched a mouthful of sulphur water, and his chest heaved as air filled his lungs. The remains of the green mamba were still wrapped around him, and the Colonel tore at the snake and hurled it into the Healing Hole.

"I am alive; I have cheated death once more. I have the power." He gasped for breath and then fell facedown in the mud. Rolf helped the Colonel to sit up. "I want that scepter. Find Joe Merchant. I want that scepter. I can try again. I, alone, know the secret."

"Colonel, try to relax for a minute."

Carlos came with a wet rag. Rolf started to wipe the mud from the Colonel's face but dropped the rag in the mud. "My God," Rolf gasped. "Oh my God."

"What is it? What is it?" The Colonel grabbed Rolf by the shirt and pulled himself up, then let go when he saw the look of revulsion on Rolf's face.

"Colonel, how did you get those tattoos on your eyelids?"

• • •

Joe Merchant stumbled onto the beach. He blindly probed the darkness with his hand and found nothing, but he allowed himself to be pulled by the scepter that seemed to be taking him to a better place.

The wind swept his footprints from the pink beach as if someone were covering his tracks, and he felt cool water on his feet. Slowly he walked into the roaring surf. He held the scepter the way he'd once held his guitar and sang the words to his favorite song:

> *Little Boy's thinking of the things he's seen,*
> *Scary as the werewolf on a matinee screen.*
> *Little Boy's shrinking like a leprechaun.*
> *Good-bye cruel world, Little Boy's gone.*

Waiting
for the
Sails to Fill

73

Happily Ever After, Now and Then

The banging and bouncing of my kamikaze takeoff that morning from the beach had rendered my radio panel useless. I had no communications with the outside world. The good news was this: the body I had seen floating was neither Trevor nor Desdemona. I had made a low pass over it and saw for myself that it was a man.

The sharks had already laid out their claim, and clearly I could do nothing for the dead man. We continued to comb the stormy waters around Bone in the Throat, hoping to spot the orange life raft Toosay knew had been on board the *Cosmic Muffin,* but the big storm moved into the Sleeping Beauties and forced us to seek shelter.

Trevor and Desdemona were nowhere to be found. My optimistic side was telling me that they had been shielded from our rescue attempt by the recent storm and had ridden out the tempest. I tried not to listen to what my pessimistic side was saying.

"Dey be okay, Cap'n. I feel it in my bones. Dey be alright." Toosay was convinced that both women were alive, but I needed more than Toosay's reassurances.

The *Hemisphere Dancer* was the only bird in the sky as the day seemed to become night, and we made our way back to Little Lorraine Island in the semidarkness of the eclipse. Hoagy had been watching us intently from the back of the plane, sensing that something was up. In the sudden darkness, he barked, and Toosay leaned back and calmed him.

By the time I made my approach to the lagoon, the eclipse was over, the sun was shining brightly, and the moon had faded into the light of day. Birds had returned to the air, and as I watched them circle, I wondered what I should do next. I could not go back to Boomtown for fear of landing in jail again. It had been dangerous enough flying around Bone in the Throat just now.

We loaded the rest of the fuel onto the plane, and then I sat Toosay down on the beach. "Toosay, I'm between a rock and a hard place here, but I'm going to look for Trevor and Desdemona as long as I have fuel. I can't go back to Boomtown since I helped a friend of mine steal a plane, and things aren't much better back in Key West, where I came from. I broke out of jail in Rudderville, so that's out of the question." I was making myself more and more depressed as I talked, and thank God Toosay interrupted me.

"Cap'n Frank, Desdemona saved my life. I have no home here without her and da ship. I will go wif you. I will search dese waters wid my eyes until dey fall out of my head."

"I have no idea where we might wind up," I told Toosay.

"Den we will be like old Columbus, no?"

"No. I mean, yes."

"We will find dem, Cap'n. It is not der time yet."

We filled the right float with water again and repeated th takeoff maneuvers we'd come up with early that morning Then we set off in the direction of the Hispaniola coast, look ing for the raft. The storm had moved through the islands an was now lashing the tops of the Haitian hills. Still no sign c Desdemona and Trevor. We flew until the fuel gauges behin my head were half-full, and then we slipped into a cove o the north coast of Haiti for the night. I still had no radio, an the idea of landing at a port of entry was the furthest thoug from my mind. For all I knew, I was the newest face on th Wanted poster at customs.

That night, I lay outside in my sleeping bag with Hoag beside me, and I watched the clouds sail off beyond th moon. I counted the falling stars and sent a prayer heaver ward, asking for Trevor and Desdemona to still be alive. When I fell asleep, I dreamed about a dolphin that could talk. He was swimming and chatting with Root Boy and Trevor. I yelled to them, but they couldn't hear me. I woke up with the first hint of light, and Toosay already had the coffee ready.

"You slept good?" he asked.

"On and off."

I climbed out of my sweaty khakis and dove into the water. Hoagy came charging in after me, wanting to have some fun. The exercise would clear my mind and sharpen my senses for the search ahead. I threw a stick for Hoagy and then swam in a straight line for about half a mile before I turned and headed back to the plane. I thought about the dream and wondered if it might be a sign or something.

I was still in the water, checking the left wing of my plane, when I heard Toosay shout out, "We got visitors." I looked around in fear of what I might see, thinking first of Colonel Cairo, then of soldiers. But what I saw were dolphins. They surrounded the plane, rolling and frolicking as they circled us. I laughed and shouted and splashed among them.

"You okay?" Toosay called out from above.

"I know where to find them," I called back.

• • •

By noon we were sixty miles south of Rudderville, flying the wavetops on our way to the place where I had a hunch both women would be. Suddenly, out of the blue, my VHF marine radio came back on, and we could just make out what the two ships were saying. "Yeah, we got two female-type persons on board, picked up near the Sleeping Beauties. One is a looker; the other is your type, Cap."

"I guess some people have all the luck, rescuing mermaids out of a storm. Maybe one day it'll happen to me. So how you doin' with them eclipse tourists, pal?"

Toosay heard the message and began clapping his hands. "I knew it was not da time. I told you, Cap'n."

• • •

The sun danced on the waters of the inlet at No Man's Cay. A flock of pelicans reacted to the sound of my engines and took flight to a small sand spit on the opposite side of the harbor. I eased the *Hemisphere Dancer* down and felt that wonderful rush of contact with the sea. I retracted the throttles, and the *Dancer* came off the step; her nose settled gently on the water.

My heart rate jumped a notch when I saw Trevor Kane standing at the dock. She was barefoot and wore a white linen dress and had a shocking pink hibiscus blossom perched behind her ear. I lowered the gear and came up out of the water onto the old boat ramp, shut the *Dancer* down, and quickly jumped out the forward hatch, bumping my head. Trevor stopped the slowly rotating prop with her hand.

"I hope you're not a mirage," I said.

"No, it's the real me," she said softly. "Hello, Toosay. What brings you this far north?"

"You and Miss Desdemona."

"They're all up at the bar. I know she's dying to see you. I want to spend a minute alone with this man, if you don't mind." Toosay grinned and took off up the hill to the bar.

I held out my arms, and Trevor walked right into them and put her arms around me. "Boy, am I glad to see you," I said.

"You can copy me on that one, Captain."

We kissed, and I smelled the familiar scent of coconut oil that always made me think of her. I shook my head and snickered. "I'm sort of in a state of shock. I had the craziest dream. There was a fish talking to you."

"Dolphin," she said.

"How did you know?"

"Just a wild guess," she answered with a smile.

"What happened to the ship? How did you ever get away from Cairo?"

"Wow." She threw her head back and laughed up at the sky. "Oh, it's all pretty simple. We were rescued by aliens, and then we were picked up by the *La Brisa* on the Eclipse Cruise. Fernando and the Cane Thrashers welcomed us aboard while three hundred blue-haired ladies applauded. They were all wearing eclipse-proof sunglasses. Fernando dropped us off in Rudderville, and Percy brought us here. We tried, but there wasn't any way to get in touch with you. But I knew you'd eventually come this way."

"How?"

"A fish told me," she said and giggled.

"So is Desdemona okay?"

"She's fine. She's up at the bar with Root Boy. They all wanted to welcome you here, but I wanted you for myself for a minute. Did you see Joe again?"

I took her hand and led her down the beach to a stand of coconut trees, and we sat down in the sand. I pulled the old photograph that Joe Merchant had given me from my shirt and handed it to Trevor. She stared at it, and first she laughed in puzzled disbelief. Then she shook her head.

"He wanted you to have it."

"You did see him," she said.

I put my arm around her shoulder, and she moved closer to me.

"He told me he was going after the Colonel. That's all I know, other than the fact that he saved my life when I was helping Blanton steal a plane at the airport. And he told me he wanted you to remember him as the boy in the photo."

Trevor smiled. "So Blanton got out okay?"

I nodded, and she looked again at the picture.

"I remember this day as if it were yesterday," she said. "Joe was too shy to find a date for his graduation, and I told him I would come to Charleston for the dance. It was a bore, so we bought a six-pack and went to the Battery. He wanted to show me the monument to Steed Bonnet.

"Joe hated my father for sending him to military school. He did his damnedest not to adhere to the rules and regulations. He was fascinated with pirates, not war heroes, and right after graduation he rented a beach shack on Sullivan's Island and joined an acid-rock band. Did I ever tell you this?" she asked, wiping away the tears with the back of her hand.

"No. Tell me now."

She leaned back, looked up into the trees, and sighed. "Joe was really something. Back then he took to wearing a baseball cap with a note pinned to it that said 'I have been hit in the head with a brick and can't talk.' Nobody paid much attention to him. I went to see him one weekend, and I overheard an old shrimper say, 'He's just that way.' Beach bums and hippies were a dime a dozen on Sullivan's Island in those days, remember?"

I nodded, and Trevor placed her hand on mine. "Frank, you know I never had any idea that coming here would be this kind of a mess." She leaned her chin on my shoulder. "But I found Joe Merchant, didn't I?"

Trevor's eyes filled with tears again, and she stood up, lifted the hem of her dress, and wiped them away. We stood for a moment, side by side, and watched the bubbles and sprigs of turtle grass ride the current that connected the Atlantic Ocean with the Caribbean Sea. The swiftly falling water had already exposed the roots of the mangroves, and tiny snappers fanned out along the bottom, instinctively knowing where to look for the next meal.

"I've cried enough for all of them—for Joe, my mother, my father. I love them, and I'll always miss them, but I need to have a life of my own."

She tossed the old photograph into the water, and we watched it move out to sea.

"The tide is changing," I said.

Trevor looked at me and smiled and squeezed my hand. "For both of us.'

I held on to her tightly as we walked back to the dock, knowing I did not ever want to let her go again.

74

The World Is My Oyster

THE WORLD IS MY OYSTER

If you look hard enough, you will find what you're looking for, and sometimes even more. Ask Don Quixote, ask Don King, ask Rudy Breno.

As I look back on the incredible Jet Ski Expedition, I see it as a large aquarium where the lives of strange and innocent people move along the clear glass like catfish. What a lucky guy I am to be able to find the stories that really move my readers. Your children may have MTV and "Downtown Julie Brown," but Rudy is here for *you,* the parents in search of adventure. That is my job. To find the right stories.

It is both a happy and a sad moment for me now as I write my last editorial for the *National Lighthouse.* I am leaving the paper and moving to Hollywood, California, where this fall I will be the host of my own syndicated television show.

I'll be using the conclusive documentation of videotape to bring my stories to you. As always, I will keep my ear to the pavement, my pedal to the metal, and I will continue to keep you in touch with the likes of Joe Merchant, Elvis Presley, Bigfoot, elusive time travelers, aliens, movie stars, and presidential candidates—all for you to enjoy in the comfort of your own bed or behind your favorite TV snack tray.

The world is my oyster, and you never know what is inside until you pry the sucker open. See you on TV.

75

Changes in Latitudes

The little man in the grease-covered brown overalls pulled a small notebook from his pocket and scratched some numbers hurriedly, then ticked away at his calculator. I closed and tightened the caps on the wing tanks and rubbed my hands together to ward off the cold.

"Comes to three-hundred-forty-four dollars and sixty-seven cents. That'll be all you be needin?" he called from the truck.

"A tail wind would be nice," I said. The old man closed the fuel truck door and walked to the wing, admiring the plane. "Never seen a Goose with a totem pole on it," he said and chuckled. "That bring you luck?"

"Always has," I said.

"Ain't too many of these babies left around, is there?"

"Not too many," I said, watching my breath frost over as the words came out. I climbed down and handed him four hundred-dollar bills.

"I remember right after the war I caught one of these out to Catalina Island and damn near broke the casino. I was up twenty-five thousand bucks at the crap table and had my future planned. Airplanes, whiskey, women. Then a goddamn

389

earthquake shook the whole casino on my roll. The entire table moved two feet to the left, and the dice came up craps."

"That close, huh?"

"That close. You hang on to this airplane, sonny. She's your ticket out of a dull fuckin' life. Oh, pardon me, ma'am."

Trevor walked up behind the old man and handed him the key to the ladies' room.

"It's nothing I haven't heard before."

"I'll be right back with your change."

"Look at this," Trevor said, pushing a copy of the *National Lighthouse* at me. Rudy's face was on the cover.

"Rudy on television," I said.

"The thought of it nauseates me."

Hoagy came bounding across the tarmac from the snow patch on the other side of the picket fence next to the line shack.

"Come on, Hoagy," I called out. The old man shuffled like Walter Brennan toward the plane and handed me the change and a receipt.

"Where you folks headin'?"

"Alaska," I beamed.

• • •

It was a happy pilot who rolled down that tiny runway in Grand Isle, Nebraska, cranked the gear up, and climbed into the sky. Hoagy had squeezed himself between Trevor and me in the cockpit, and he surveyed the panorama. It was a sublime morning. We were in the heart of the Central Flyway, and the birds had just started to migrate. The warm air from the heater felt good on my toes.

We climbed to a thousand feet. Trevor read to me from a brochure: " 'Approximately eighty percent of the sandhill cranes in North America stop along the Platte River each spring en route to their breeding grounds in Canada, Alaska, and the Soviet Union.' "

"They call this spring?"

"Hey, you're the one who wanted to go to Alaska."

"Damn right," I said with a smile. "Jesus Christ, look at that." Out the right side of the plane, below us, an enormous flock of sandhill cranes was amassed in an ice-free bend in the river. They overflowed onto the sandbars and into the cornfields in the distance.

"It says here that the size of the population ranges from three hundred thousand to five hundred thousand."

"Fucking amazing," I said and pulled the throttles back.

The orange light of the rising sun reflected on the frozen river and became an optical illusion, a winding, silver highway leading into the clouds to the west. I rubbed Hoagy behind his ears with my right hand and smiled when I saw the ecstatic look on his face. Then his ears shot forward. A huge flock of Canada geese were fanned out like a squadron. They seemed to sense us behind them and cleared a path for us. A Goose among geese, a man and his dog and his girl. I was watching the bird life around me and did not see Trevor take out her sketch pad and pencils.

"I've never seen anything like this," she said as she scribbled. A lone eagle circled above us, studying the mallards skimming the surface of the river.

"This is the only place where you can really feel the Earth, you know," I said.

Trevor sketched the silver river. "Keep talking," she said. "You're inspiring me."

"Roads are built in the easiest places we can put them. Standing on the ground is like being an ant on a hill. The world is a different place from the sky. You feel it as a living thing, not just a street running through the middle of a town full of houses." I rubbed my hands together and placed them back on the wheel. "I think I'm going to like this change in latitude."

Trevor put her pad down, leaned across Hoagy, and kissed me on the cheek. "I love it when you talk to me." My hand was on the throttles, and she put her hand on top of mine. "Tell me again where we're going."

I mustered up my best Gabby Hayes imitation and pointed north. "We're headin' for Kodiak Island, Alaska, where nighttime comes down like a curtain on the shale cliffs overlookin' Deadman's Bay, and the cottonwood shadows dance in the moonlight that comes down Horse Marine Canyon like a laser beam. We're goin' where the bears run to the sounds of gunfire lookin' for a quick easy meal, where the king salmon in the Karluk River are as thick as mosquitoes, and the steelhead are as big around as your calf. We're goin' to seaplane country. Care to join us, ma'am?"

Trevor looked pensive and then said, "Well, I was planning to go to the mall this afternoon, and then I was going to play a little tennis with the girls, and then maybe stop by the frozen yogurt stand."

"Little girl, the mountains are made of frozen yogurt where we're going."

"Buy me a cone?" she asked.

"You bet."

76

Store in a Cool, Safe Place

Dear Desdemona,

Well hello from Kodiak. Don't even ask if it is cold. That would be a cruel joke. We are very much looking forward to our trip south. I can't believe it's been a year since it all happened. Needless to say we were thrilled to hear about Blanton, and the pictures of the new rocket ship look great. Frank has been in touch with Curtiss and hopes to talk to Blanton soon. This would be a perfect place for him to get away for a while. Hey, it worked for us.

I think the idea of a family reunion at Root Boy's is a great idea, especially for all us wackos who aren't related. There is an acquired love of Alaska that grows on you like moss, but there are times when I do miss the Caribbean. With any luck at all we will have things worked out by next year where we can spend the summers here and winters in the islands.

Last week, I flew down to Anchorage. There is a saying up here that the best thing about Anchorage is that it is only ten minutes away from Alaska. I hadn't been to the big city in a while and there was a Russian exhibit at the art museum I wanted to see. Well wouldn't you know it, I am walking by the Woolworth's store on my way to the computer shop, and there he was—Rudy Breno on the demo television in the window, talking to Geraldo. They looked like a set of living bookends. It seems Rudy is my albatross.

I was on a mission to buy a laptop computer. I have finally broken down and become a propeller head. It is a far cry from paint brushes, turpentine, and sketch pads, but I am helping Frank get all of his flying journals on disk before they are eaten by the neighbors. The other day a family of raccoons got into his old flight bag full of yellow legal pads with the story of his flying misadventures and started chewing. They ate up half a story about the first time he got laid in New Orleans and was knocked down the stairs of this hooker's apartment by her "other" boyfriend and rolled right into the middle of a movie set where the director yelled "Cut" and Natalie Wood bent down and wiped the blood from his nose. I was jealous, but I promised Frank I would get a computer if he would learn how to use it with me. He said he could not afford to have his life story eaten by raccoons so we are on our way to computer hell.

Frank has gone off for a few days to Talkeetna, a little town north of Anchorage near Mt. McKinley. He is learning to fly the mountains and land on glaciers. He says it is just frozen water. I am going up this weekend and we are spending a few days at an isolated cabin overlooking the Ruth Amphitheatre. It was built by Don Sheldon, the famous bush pilot from Talketna who pioneered mountain flying around Mt. McKinley or Danali as the locals call it. Frank brought back some Polaroids of the view from the little cabin. It is wondrous. It sits on the Ruth Glacier, and the summit of Mt. McKinley is only ten miles away.

The mountains have hooked me and I am learning to climb. It is a unique new way to look at the world. I am working on a series of oil paintings called "Bird's Eye View" based on my photos taken from the sides of mountains. It is a different kind of painting altogether, and I think I've finally figured out what the Generators were talking about. I am doing what I'm supposed to be doing, I can just feel it. It is so beautiful here, you just want to share that. I had hoped to join an expedition to climb Mt. McKinley this summer, but we are going to Africa to check on the foundation's work. Frank says it will still be there next year. I guess he's right.

Well, there is a very big storm brewing outside now. Nighttime is pulling the curtain down on the shale cliffs overlooking Deadman's Bay. It's that time of the year when you can't tell whether it's raining or just damp. I call it the soggy season because I always feel like a wet sponge. I have figured out my word processor enough to be able to save, delete, cut and paste. I am stored in a cool, safe place, hibernating like the bears and happy to be here. But some nights when I can see the faint ribbons of the aurora borealis in the northern sky, I can't help but wonder where Joe is. It would get me depressed, but Frank talks to me about it and helps me through. That's the big difference now. Frank is talking and that makes me happy. Give my love to everyone and we will see you in the spring.

Love, Trevor

EPILOGUE

Further Adventures in Restless Behavior

Frank Bama and Trevor Kane made it to Kodiak, Alaska, where Frank went to work for Penninsula Airways flying fishermen and freight up and down the Aleutian Islands in the *Hemisphere Dancer.* One August evening in the Russell River basin, he caught the world's record steelhead using a fly rod.

Trevor was named sole heiress to Joe Merchant's estate and her mother's hemorrhoid ointment fortune after the long and highly publicized trial of Hackney Primstone III. She set up a trust in Joe Merchant's name for children's hospitals throughout the countries of West Africa. As well, she has become an international force in the movement to preserve the wilderness. She took up rock climbing, and her most recent series of oil paintings, *Bird's Eye View,* opened in San Francisco to significant critical acclaim. She and Frank spend their summers in Alaska and their winters in the Bahamas.

• • •

Colonel Cairo was convicted of the murder of Monty Potter and was sent to the prison in Pointe-à-Pitre, Guadeloupe. While awaiting extradition back to the Bahamas to stand trial for the murders of Thorn Marshall and Pete Moss, he escaped and hijacked a British West Indies Airways flight from Antigua to Port-of-Spain and flew to Havana. He is now in the custody of the Cuban government in the maximum security complex on the Isle of Pines, which is currently run by Luis Mercedes.

• • •

Root Boy discovered the location of the wreck of Henri Christophe's treasure ship and became a millionaire overnight. He bought a huge piece of property on Dafuskie Island that was targeted for development and turned it into a playground for young pirates. He took up flying and bought a new Cessna 206 as well as the bar on No Man's Cay where he had worked. He put in a runway and renamed the place the Space Station. It is a very popular stop for pilots.

• • •

Hackney Primstone III disappeared from Miami but was later arrested in Panama City for conspiracy to commit murder. He is presently in the state penitentiary in Raiford, Florida.

• • •

Desdemona returned to Little Lorraine Island for a short time. When she and Toosay excavated the engine of the *Cosmic Muffin,* she found that the accident had jolted the crystals, shifting them into their proper placement. She has only to find a few missing pieces. An approaching hurricane sent her to No Man's Cay. She and Toosay gathered all her remaining books, plans, blueprints, and research material and caught the last plane north. The morning of their departure, Desdemona went for one last walk on the pink beach of Petite Place and stubbed her toe on something buried in the sand. It was the scepter. She is building a new rocket ship on No Man's Cay with her insurance money from the *Cosmic Muffin* and additional funds provided by Trevor's estate. Toosay built her a small bakery near the Space Station where she still makes the best coconut macaroons in the Caribbean. Desdemona has what she calls the "Scepter of the Seven" well hidden.

• • •

Blanton Meyercord made it to Venezuela and hid out with Father Ignacio at the mission. Six months later, he showed up at the Monroe County courthouse to face charges for destroying the Jet Skis. By that time, many people in the Florida Keys had grown sick of the obnoxious inventions, and a grass roots movement, led by Blanton's brother, Curtiss, sprang up. Using Blanton as a symbol, they lobbied for a ban on Jet Skis within a one-mile border on either side of U.S. 1. It passed the Florida legislature, and all charges and civil lawsuits against Blanton were dropped, setting him free. Blanton settled a libel suit against the *National Lighthouse* for an undisclosed amount of money, which was enough for him to purchase a turbine-converted DeHavilland Beaver, which he flew back to Venezuela. With the help of Father Ignacio, he established an air ambulance for people in the remote parts of the rain forest where Jet Skis are not known—yet.

• • •

To this day, Rudy Breno continues to investigate sightings of Joe Merchant, which still occur as often as sightings of Elvis. Rudy's trek through the Caribbean caught the attention of an executive at the Fox network, and Rudy was made host on his own TV show, "The World Is My Oyster." The program is a hit and can be seen on Thursday nights just after "Beverly Hills 90210" and "Tales of Plastic Surgery."

• • •

Billy Cruiser recovered from his third heart attack and is now equipped with a pacemaker that doesn't flutter when pretty girls walk by. He is writing a book about his experiences in the Black Cats during World War II and is still giving flying lessons and air tours from the Lone Palm Airport.

• • •

Fernando Orlando's surgery was successful, and his cruiseship scheme worked perfectly. He put together a group of elderly women investors and bought the *La Brisa* from the bankrupt estate of Monty Potter. He renamed it the *Havana Daydreamer,* and it leaves every other day at sunset from Mallory Square in Key West and crosses the Gulf Stream to Cuban territorial waters. There, on clear days, the blue-haired ladies can see the distant old highrises of downtown Havana as they manipulate the one-armed bandits that line the promenade deck.

• • •

Val Vincennes was hunted down by Rudy Breno on his television show and was caught on tape exposing himself to the St. Theresa All Girls Drum and Bugle Corps during the Rose Parade in Pasadena. After he served his time, he changed his name and is now in the frozen yogurt business in Southern California.

• • •

Curly and Shirley made it to America with the help of the pictures they had secretly taken of Rudy Breno in Boomtown. They live in Laurel Canyon and are currently being considered for a centerfold in *Hog Tie* magazine.

• • •

Captain Darryl Lemma retired from the sea and is now in the home-security-and-poodle-grooming business on Stock Island.

• • •

Fidel Castro is still in the ballgame in Havana, but the home field advantage is not what it used to be.

• • •

Jimmy Buffett has finished his book and has gone fishing.

• • •

Where is Joe Merchant?

Some people never find it
Some only pretend
But I just want to live
Happily ever after, now and then